"I'm thrilled to have found Lisa Alber and *Kilmoon*. She's first and foremost, a wonderful teller of stories. I was drawn into the mystery within the first pages. Her richly drawn characters move about in a setting painted for us with lovely detail and that offer us the opportunity to travel with her. Though this is primarily a mystery, it is also a complex and fascinating journey to a place and people that will stay with you long after you close the book."

—Kathleen Cosgrove, bestselling
author of *Engulfed and Entangled*

"In this successful debut of a new mystery series, Lisa Alber has set into motion a unique cast of characters, and readers are certainly going to want to know what else she has in store for them."

—BOLO Books

"In the captivating *Kilmoon*, Lisa Alber serves up a haunting tale of Merrit Chase, a woman who travels to Ireland to sift through her family's dark past in search of a future seemingly fated to elude her. With exquisite craft and a striking sense of place, Alber serves up a rich cast of unforgettable characters and an intricate, pull-no-punches plot. Raw with grief and painful honesty, *Kilmoon* is a soulful and beautifully told tale that never lets up, and never lets go."

—Bill Cameron, author of the
Spotted Owl Award–winning *County Line*

PATH

INTO

DARKNESS

OTHER BOOKS BY LISA ALBER

Kilmoon

Whispers in the Mist

PATH

INTO

DARKNESS

A COUNTY CLARE MYSTERY

LISA ALBER

MIDNIGHT INK
WOODBURY, MINNESOTA

FIRST EDITION
First Printing, 2017

Book format by Cassie Kanzenbach
Cover design by Ellen Lawson
Editing by Nicole Nugent

Midnight Ink, an imprint of Llewellyn Worldwide Ltd.

Library of Congress Cataloging-in-Publication Data
Names: Alber, Lisa, author.
Title: Path into darkness / Lisa Alber.
Description: First edition. | Midnight Ink : Woodbury, Minnesota, [2017] |
    Series: A County Clare mystery ; 3
Identifiers: LCCN 2017004418 (print) | LCCN 2017010863 (ebook) | ISBN
    9780738750576 (softcover) | ISBN 9780738751801
Subjects: LCSH: Murder—Investigation—Fiction. | Family secrets—Fiction. |
    Ireland—Fiction. | Psychological fiction. | GSAFD: Suspense fiction. |
    Mystery fiction.
Classification: LCC PS3601.L3342 P38 2017 (print) | LCC PS3601.L3342 (ebook)
    | DDC 813/.6—dc23
LC record available at https://lccn.loc.gov/2017004418

Midnight Ink
Llewellyn Worldwide Ltd.
2143 Wooddale Drive
Woodbury, MN 55125-2989
www.midnightinkbooks.com

Printed in the United States of America

From "the creative one" to
"the numbers one" and "the computer one,"
my sisters Nicole Sidlauskas and Kara Alber.

ACKNOWLEDGMENTS

So many people to thank—seems like the list grows with each book! The Irish are so helpful and so easy to talk to. I'd like to thank former Detective Sergeant David Sheedy and Detective Sergeant Brian Howard for their excellent counsel; Hazel Gaynor for introducing me to the Quays Pub; my first Irish friend, Teresa Donnellan; fantastic hosts Ireen and Kris of Slieve Elva B&B; Eilish Neylon, A.D. of Nursing; Enda Elynn and Michael Healey, Lahinch historians; Mary Lucas, who helped solve a mystery; Lou of Ginger Lou's for being hilarious and letting me hang out writing for hours; and last but definitely not least, Willie Daly, matchmaker and all-around raconteur.

All mistakes are mine, that's for sure, especially when I decide to use creative license for the sake of the story—this is especially true for the liberties I took with all things psychiatric and medical, and for naming an obstacle at Lahinch Golf Course "Devil's Pit."

And how could I not thank my writer pals who provide feedback, sympathetic ears, endless support, and bright ideas? I hope I haven't forgotten anyone: Cindy Brown, Debbie Dodds, Warren Easley, Holly Frank, Alison Jakel, Kassandra Kelly, Janice Maxson, LeeAnn McLennan, Angela Sanders, and Kate Scott. Plus a special crew of "eight mystery writers you should be reading now": Michael Guillebeau, Kathleen Cosgrove, Chris Knopf, Jessie Bishop Powell, Larissa Reinhart, Jaden Terrell, and Lisa Wysocky.

Special shout-outs to Jennifer Goodrick for her crème brûlée French toast; Crystal Elverud of Oak & Olive Ristorante for her good cheer and endless glasses of red wine while I wrote like a fiend; and Nancy Boutin for her medical expertise.

And thanks to the people who make good books happen in the real world, not just inside my computer: Terri Bischoff, Sharon Eldridge, Jill Marsal, Katie Mickschl, and Nicole Nugent.

There are resurrection themes in every society
that has ever been studied, and it is because
not just only do we fantasize about the possibility of
resurrection and recovery, but it actually happens.
And it happens a lot.

Sherwin B. Nuland

Presumably what happened to Jesus was what happens
to all of us when we die. We decompose.
Accounts of Jesus's resurrection and ascension
are about as well-documented as
Jack and the Beanstalk.

Richard Dawkins

ONE

Saturday, early morning, 13-Mar-2010
22 days before Easter

NATHAN TATE'S RECURRING DREAMS were so vivid, so frequent, and so familiar they'd become memories, as real to him as his wedding day to Susannah, as the pot he'd lifted out of the kiln yesterday, as the dead fly on the windowsill.

He flicked the fly away and pressed his forehead against the cool window pane. Moonlight filtered into his bedroom, highlighting sweat-soaked sheets and the water glass he'd knocked over. He couldn't get the goldfinches out of his head, always memories of goldfinches.

No, they were dream figments. Weren't they?

Memory was a slippery mistress, indeed.

At least he hadn't screamed this time. He knew this because Zoe wasn't in the room with him, hovering, comforting, insisting that it was just a dream.

He backed away from the window and its peaceful view of the pastures beyond his cluttered backyard, taking care not to step on the floorboard that liked to squeal underfoot. He pulled off his damp t-shirt and knelt to sop up the water. The water glass hadn't broken, and he set it back on the night table.

Behind him, the door creaked as it swung open. Nathan kept wiping, holding his hand steady.

"Dad? Are you all right?" Zoe hurried to his side and knelt. "Here, let me help you."

"I'm fine. Woke up thirsty, that's all."

She plucked the shirt from his hand and swiped at the floorboards he'd already dried. He climbed back into bed and closed his eyes, forcing himself to breathe evenly. He congratulated himself for not tensing when Zoe kissed him on the forehead as if she were the adult and he the child returned to the nest. Child, no. She was twenty now, but still young in so many ways. She didn't realize, or maybe she didn't care, that she'd brought the memories back with her when she'd shown up on his doorstep two weeks previously.

I'll be fine, he reassured himself as Zoe padded across the room and clicked the bedroom door shut behind her.

TWO

DANNY AHERN HESITATED AT the threshold of a farmhouse with faded red gingerbread trim and an overgrown hedge border, remembering the last time he'd stepped into a house with a collapsed body inside it. His own home. As ever, his thoughts returned to Ellen in the hospital, still in a comatose state six months later.

This house, unlike his own, stood outside Lisfenora, on the other side of Kilmoon parish near Corkscrew Hill with its panoramic view of limestone hills and coastline. Clouds in every color of grey whipped by on their way to the Atlantic. Hopefully they'd let loose their rain over the ocean, but Danny already felt a drop or two. He knocked on the front door and Detective Officer Simon O'Neil met him at the door to sign him in to the crime scene. As usual, his overlong hair flopped across his forehead and he'd forgotten to button up his collar over an entwined leather braid he wore as a man necklace.

O'Neil called back into the house, "Detective Sergeant on premises, wipe your arses!"

A few groans and greetings followed.

"What have we got?" Danny said as he suited up in coverall, booties, and gloves.

O'Neil stepped ahead of Danny from area rug to area rug like colorful stepping stones. A giant sectional couch in brown leather faced a flat-screen television mounted on the wall. Lots of primary-colored pillows and prints of Irish wildflowers rounded out the decor.

"Prepare yourself," O'Neil said.

"You've never worried about my sensitive feelings before."

Danny stepped around O'Neil toward a pair of feet peeping out from behind the sectional. The victim wore house slippers that looked oddly threadbare against the jaunty yellow and green rugs. Danny steeled himself against what he was about to see, thrusting aside an image of Ellen crumpled on the kitchen floor.

"—and nothing appears to have been stolen," O'Neil was saying.

Danny didn't catch what he'd said, his attention riveted on purple dots dappling the victim's signature little blue bow tie where blood had soaked into the fabric.

"Ah Christ, Elder Joe?" he said. "Who hates an old fella like him that much?"

Everyone knew Elder Joe, one of Danny's fellow regulars at the Plough and Trough Pub. Unlike Ellen, his injuries didn't appear to be head trauma, but it didn't matter; the sight of pooled blood caused Danny to step back involuntarily.

O'Neil pointed at spatter arcing across the walls. An abstract painting in blood. "Quite the goring, I'd say."

Elder Joe's undershirt was weighty with the red stuff. The material sagged over his flaccid chest and stomach, and light from the windows caught the blood in a cheery crimson hue. Danny counted six holes in the shirt—six spots where a sharp implement had jabbed through tender tissue and organs.

5

"His name was Joseph Macy," Danny said. "He goes by Elder Joe, or EJ."

"Oh, I know his name, all right." O'Neil's voice turned sour. "An ex-girlfriend's father."

Now this was interesting. Danny redirected his gaze from the blood-soaked holes in Elder Joe's undershirt to O'Neil, who always appeared too nonchalant and easygoing for life's complications.

"Benjy the Bagger's supposed to be here within an hour," O'Neil said. "I've got it handled if you want to get on."

"And why would I do that?"

O'Neil paused. "Today's Saturday."

Right. And Saturdays were reserved for visiting Ellen with their children, Mandy and Petey. Danny checked his watch. He might still have time later this afternoon.

"Tell me what you know about EJ in two sentences," he said.

"He has one daughter, Róisín, who detested him. No clue why, only that they fell out and she moved away. She said he was nothing but a sniffer dog after the money."

Danny gazed at the giant flat-screen television and tried—and failed—to reconcile this picture of the man with the one who liked to buy rounds at the pub. But then, crime tended to occur because of or within people's hidden worlds. Half the battle of investigating crimes was cracking the mirrors that reflected back people's polite façades.

"Tell me about his daughter, your ex-girlfriend."

"She owns a tourist shop in Galway now. I met her when she worked at the Grand Arms as a concierge. I wandered in one day to ask her if she knew the name of a local seamstress."

"Seamstress?"

"Bloody hell, man, even a bloke like me needs bedroom curtains." O'Neil grinned. "I'm no heathen."

"As long as they weren't lace curtains."

"Feckin' hell, no. A nice sage green linen, I'll have you know. Róisín owned a sewing machine, so one thing led to another. Guess you'll be wanting me to travel up to Galway to talk to her? Wouldn't put a bother on me."

"I'll bet." Danny stepped out of the way of the scenes of crime photographer. "Who found EJ?"

"Ah." A disturbed expression flitted across O'Neil's face. He pointed toward an open doorway. In the corner of the kitchen a uniformed officer stood with a petite woman encoiled by a scarf the size of a boa constrictor. She patted her chest in a way that Danny recognized.

"Bloody hell," he muttered.

Merrit Chase, Lisfenora's leading Californian-in-residence. Danny habitually looked for "tells," and her chest patting signaled that she was struggling to remain calm. Other than that, she looked like her usual self as she turned to face him: hazel-eyed, enigmatic, just this side of neurotic. Today she wore one of her flippy summer skirts over black leggings. A leaking carton of eggs sat at her feet.

"Have her wait outside," Danny said. "She's not to leave yet."

His mobile rang. He accepted the call from Marcus, his father-in-law, who now lived with Danny and acted as child-minder while Danny worked.

"On your way then?" Marcus said. "The children are ready to visit Ellen."

"There's been a death," Danny said. "I'll be here for a while." He continued when Marcus didn't respond. "It'll have to be tomorrow instead."

"What about during this evening's visiting hours?" Marcus said.

Danny's chronic sense of guilt lived as a congealed mass lodged at the base of his throat, sometimes softening, sometimes hardening.

7

Right now it was hard as a golf ball. "This is a bad one. You'll be putting the kids to bed tonight, I expect."

"Ay, right. I understand." Marcus's tone said he didn't quite, though. "Tomorrow, then."

He rang off without asking Danny who'd died, which wasn't his usual behavior, that's for bloody sure.

"Okay?" O'Neil said.

"I'll manage."

A uniformed officer named Clark approached. "Excuse me, sir, we've got something else. Back there."

He led the way down a gloomy hallway with disintegrating fleur-de-lis wallpaper and water stains. A gust of wind flung raindrops against the roof, a sound the children called goblin footsteps. Sounded like pricks of remorse to Danny.

Several doors hung ajar, revealing bare mattresses and shabby dressers.

"His own B and B," O'Neil said. "Let the rooms during the Matchmaker's Festival, eh?"

Possibly, but to Danny the place felt haunted by people who were more for the grave than a boisterous festival. A moment later, Danny's instinct started to resemble reality when Officer Clark pointed into the last room along the corridor. "Overhead light is burned out," he said.

Danny grabbed O'Neil's torch as he pushed through the men and into the room. The light beam bounced off another old dresser and landed on a crucifix. The place reeked of decrepitude and loneliness, of an unwashed human enclosed for too long.

From the corner of the room, a rustle of fabric and a groan caused Danny to swing the torch around. A wash of urine and feces greeted him when he approached the bed. An elderly man blinked against the torch light. "About time," he rasped.

Danny passed Clark an empty glass from the many that sat on a side table. "Call for an ambulance. Get blankets and water. Not cold, the water. Tepid, you hear me?"

"Yes, sir. Ambulance already called."

"You gave us a fright." Danny sat on the edge of the bed. "You have a name?"

The man's words got caught around his swollen tongue, making it hard to understand him. "Of course I bloody well have a name."

Clark returned and passed along a thick woolen blanket that Danny tucked around the poor man. Next, Danny held a glass of water toward his mouth. "Sip. See how it goes down first."

The man swallowed twice and let his head drop back onto the pillow.

"Do you remember your name?" Danny said.

The man frowned. "I may be half into the ground, but I'm no halfwit. Cecil Wallace."

"How are you related to Joseph Macy, Cecil?"

"This is his place, innit?"

"That's the point," Danny said. "You. Here."

"Where else would I be?" Despite his feisty responses, Cecil's eyes darted around the room as if he wasn't sure about it anymore. "Where's Joe?"

"Ay, there's the rub. Was Joe caring for you?"

A nod.

"Joe is paid to care for you?"

Another nod.

One of the men called out that the ambulance had arrived, and a moment later a fresh batch of voices echoed through the house. The paramedics shooed Danny and O'Neil away as they entered the room. Upon seeing them, Cecil raised his arms like a toddler begging to be held, reminding Danny of his children, Mandy and Petey, at home, waiting for him. And of Ellen, his wife, not at home waiting for him. Not that she had been in the months before the attack, but marital difficulties didn't lessen his remorse.

This life. It was like to squash him flat as roadkill. "Right, let's see about Merrit," he said.

THREE

MERRIT HUDDLED ON ELDER Joe's front stoop, out of the path of the scenes of crimes men who bustled in and out of the house. She re-wrapped her scarf around her neck and head and tried not to think about Danny's reaction to her presence at the crime scene. It may have been her imagination, but the way his head had sagged on his neck stank of the most profound resignation and annoyance.

Doesn't matter, she told herself, and shifted her gaze away from the doorway through which Danny would soon appear. Beyond the ambulance, Garda cars, and other vehicles crowded in front of Elder Joe's house, there stood an abandoned gravel quarry. The earth's interior excavated and reshaped into rock hills like sand dunes. The decimated grey wasteland had to be one of the loneliest views Merrit had ever seen.

Footsteps approached. Detective O'Neil smiled, friendly enough, as he assessed her with blue eyes shaded with what Merrit thought of as Irish police, or Garda, skepticism. At least when it came to her. Inside the house, Danny's voice rumbled low among a medley of male voices. He'd arrive soon enough to question her.

She scooted over on the bench to provide space for O'Neil. He sat and leaned back against the house with an expansive sigh and flattened his accent until it resembled a stoned John Wayne. "And how does a pretty wee lass like you find yourself within spitting distance of a corpse?"

Merrit couldn't help smiling. "That's inappropriate, isn't it?"

"Ay." He waggled his eyebrows, unrepentant. "My mom used to say I had such a mouth on me, I'd land tits up in a peat bog someday."

"Making you the comic relief to Danny's straight man."

"Worked, didn't it?"

"For a second." She lapsed into silence, once again caught up in her own thoughts. What was today? It had to be close to the Ides of March, a day of prophetic misfortune. She leaned against the house alongside O'Neil, her heart heavy with more than Elder Joe's death. "It's Liam. He's sick again."

"Oh Jesus. The lung cancer returned?"

"After nine months of remission, I thought we were in the clear. You can tell Danny, but please don't go broadcasting it all over the county. I haven't had a chance to process the news myself."

"What a thing you must be feeling," he said. "I'm sorry to hear it."

Merrit nodded her thanks, realizing that O'Neil was the first person in a long while to acknowledge her feelings about her father's illness. "I've been told that I'm only here for what I can get out of him."

"People say that to your face?"

"You know they do. It's a common pastime around here."

Liam, her father, was first and foremost a matchmaker who presided over an annual matchmaking festival. Such an arcane and unusual profession—in this modern era, who would have thought?—yet the Lisfenorans loved to point out to her that the local economy depended on the tourist income from the festival each September. And more importantly, they insisted that tradition must be followed, integrity maintained, history respected. In other words, the festival, the village, the entire county was doomed without Liam's particular skill.

"You don't sound keen to be the next matchmaker," O'Neil said.

Merrit swiped at the shiny egg goo that had splattered her boots. "As life trajectories go, it wasn't what I expected when I arrived. Now I've lived here for eighteen months. *Eighteen* months. I can't believe it. What have I been doing?"

"Being a daughter, I expect."

"Difficult at times, that. Liam's been acting the maggot." She paused. "Did I use that phrase correctly—'acting the maggot'?"

"If you mean he's acting a right jerk, then yeah, spot on."

"That's not quite what I meant, but he's grouchy—"

"Narky."

"What?"

"For 'grouchy.' As in, he's a right narky old bastard."

"Hah." Merrit had never spoken to O'Neil at length before; he had a nice way about him, for a Garda officer. "Yes, Liam's on the road to becoming a right narky old bastard."

"There you go." He stood. "And here we go."

Danny appeared and sat down beside Merrit. For the first time, she noticed a smattering of grey near his temples. He was a tall, lanky man who had grown too thin. He'd lost his usual facial contours and now his nose appeared beaky, his eyes too big, his cheekbones sharp. He slouched with elbows on knees for a moment, scrubbing at his face, and then straightened.

Elder Joe and Danny had known each other for years—this Merrit knew. And she also knew Danny well enough not to express condolences. Instead, she preempted his first question. She knew the drill by now.

"I arrived around ten a.m. to pick up eggs. I heard the television so I knew he was at home." She waved toward a battered van. "Van's here, too. When he didn't answer my knock, I tried the door—"

"To confirm, the television was on when you arrived?" Danny said.

"Yes. I turned it off before I called the guards." Some of Danny's coiled tension transferred itself to her. She shoved her hands into her jacket pockets. "The door was unlocked, so I went inside to fetch the carton of eggs. Organic. From Elder Joe's hens. The carton was waiting for me on the stand near the front door."

"Do you usually walk in unannounced?" Danny said.

Merrit clenched her hands together. He knew her well enough to know the answer to that question. "As need be. Drop off the money, take the eggs. It's a weekly routine. He doesn't always greet me at the door."

"Right. Go on."

"I grabbed the eggs, but once I got inside, I could … sense, I guess, that something was off. The air was thicker." Her lungs tightened in reaction to the smell memory. She pulled an inhaler out of her purse and pumped two shots of spray into her lungs.

Danny didn't comment. He didn't need to. He knew the drill with her anxiety just as she knew the drill with his questioning technique. She glanced at him. Expression still neutral. She supposed that was a good sign. "The smell before there's a recognizable smell. You know what I mean."

"The smell of death, yes," he said. "It's the blood."

She swallowed, thinking back to her arrival in Ireland and how she'd first met Danny. Another body. Another bloody death. Danny didn't need to remind her that she would once again be the talk of the town, reinforcing her status as unwelcome guest and interloper.

"That's pretty much it," she said. "I stepped into the living room, checked that he was deceased—"

"Obvious, I'd say," O'Neil said.

"Oh yes." She exhaled sharply to rid herself of the remembered smell, of the image of desperately bright area rugs that had led her straight to Elder Joe. "That's when I turned off the television."

"Did you hear anything?" Danny said.

She thought back. "The opposite. Even the hens were quiet. It was eerie. I thought I saw someone, though. When I retreated to the kitchen to call you—the guards—I swear something moved out there, almost blending into the gravel from the quarry."

"A fox?" O'Neil said.

She shook her head. "A person. The movement startled me and I dropped the eggs I was still carrying. When I looked out the window again, I didn't see anyone."

"How sure are you that you saw someone?" Danny said.

"Pretty sure."

In front of them, the jagged gravel expanse sucked up what little light penetrated the cloud cover. Without turning her head, Merrit tried to observe Danny. He fiddled with a pair of used latex gloves, stretching and rolling them around in his hands. She didn't consider him the agitated type.

"Did Elder Joe say or do anything in the last few weeks that struck you as unusual?" he said. "Did he mention visitors, arguments, problems?"

"God, no. We weren't friends like that. He didn't talk much." The words *right narky old bastard* popped into her head. "I bought eggs, that's all."

Danny slapped the gloves against his thighs. "We'll contact you if we have any follow-up questions."

"Except," she said.

"Except what?"

"Except last Saturday he asked me in for tea."

"Not all that surprising, I'd think," Danny said.

"That's exactly what it was—surprising. Elder Joe could take me or leave me as far as I could tell. His invitation didn't make sense. Maybe he was that desperate with loneliness."

He squinted at her, seeing her rather too well, she thought.

From inside the house, a flurry of voices and footsteps approached. The paramedics carried a gurney out of the house. The sight of an elderly man who was not Elder Joe and very much alive jolted Merrit to her feet. "Who is that? He was inside the house?"

Danny patted the bench beside him. "Sit, please."

She sat back down. "But who was that?"

"What happened with tea?" Danny said.

The paramedics loaded the man into the back of the ambulance and, within a minute, sped away. "Tea? Nothing. I made my excuses. Elder Joe reacted as if I'd offended him."

"Maybe you did," Danny said. "Knowing him, I wager he'd finally felt comfortable enough with you to extend a friendly gesture only to be rebuffed."

"I didn't 'rebuff' him." Merrit stood. "Are we done now?"

"For now. We have your fingerprints on file. We'll use them for elimination purposes."

Here we go, she thought, getting his parting shot in. He wasn't all that neutral when it came to her; he simply hid it better than most of the locals. After arranging a time with O'Neil to give her official statement, Merrit trotted to her car, eager to get out from under the looming gravel dunes.

She started the engine and turned up the heat. Elder Joe had caught her off-guard with his invitation, and the sorry truth was that she hadn't wanted to drink tea with him anyhow. She couldn't recall how she'd begged off, but she remembered his last words to her well enough: *Ay, well, you're that way, I suppose. But mark me, you might as well be hung for a sheep as a lamb.*

Which made no sense at all. She could swear the locals enjoyed confusing her with their most obscure sayings. As Merrit drove past the quarry, she felt a pang of regret for sidestepping his gesture of friendship—or whatever it was. Perhaps he had something on his mind, something related to his death. There could be a lesson here.

FOUR

Sunday, 14-Mar

I woke up this morning to the chill of an overnight frost that silvers the hawthorn along the hedgerows. Their branches on the verge of green appeared petrified until sunshine thawed them out, and now it's a gorgeous day with yellow gorse lending its vanilla and coconut scent to the breeze.

This won't do. Munge-ing on about what the breeze smells like is all very fine, but not what I'm supposed to be addressing. I can hear you loud and clear in your most unprofessional manner: "Annie, cut the shite."

Right. I'm supposed to be "processing" and "healing."

The problem is that I'm not a reliable narrator anymore, even of my own life. I doubt what I had always taken for granted about myself, my objectivity, my insights into people—everything my training enhanced feels like a lie now.

Fact: News has circulated about a "suspicious death."

Fact: Today I'm going to the wake even though I don't know the victim.

Fact: Something niggles at me—yes, a fact buried within the sorry news, but it eludes me at the moment.

There. Objectivity. Not so difficult, after all. You now have a summation of my day with no undue effort from me. I'd rather forgo undue effort, if you don't mind, not to mention forgo my usual cycle of self-recrimination and regret. This is a difficult time as it is, and soon to be April, the month of resurrection, the earth nodding its way toward summer, a pretty pagan season. But I've always found the notion of resurrection creepy because I envision undead beings scuttling under cover of night.

I'm not sure what I mean by that, so never mind. The only thing that scares me these days is him, out there somewhere. I helped resurrect him in a way, didn't I?

God, I'm a sick person. Given my life choices, especially moving here to County Clare, I expect I deserve whatever comes.

FIVE

NATHAN'S HEAD SAGGED TOWARD his chest, and before he realized that he'd fallen asleep, he jerked awake again. Dazed, he depressed the power button with his foot, and the potter's wheel decelerated, circling ever more slowly. His eyelids drooped again.

The vase he'd just thrown listed to the right and then caved in on itself. Irritated with himself, he grabbed the cutting wire and, with a practiced movement, sliced the lump of clay from the wheel and dropped it in the plastic tub he used for his slip. His right hand ached. He'd opened up the scabs on his knuckles again.

"Dad," Zoe said from behind him. "You'd better hurry now. For the party?"

He turned and caught his breath as he always did when it came to Zoe. He still couldn't believe she was his daughter, this creature. A sun break through the clouds turned her blond curls into a halo shimmer around her head.

"Not a party, a wake," he said. "EJ helped me when I first moved here last year."

"I'm sorry." Her somber expression didn't last long. She tucked her arm through his and swung along with him as he made his way into the kitchen. "I'll be your date. If we were back in the age of Jane Austen, I'd proclaim the wake my coming-out to society." She raised his hand and twirled under it. "I'm glad to be here."

After a pause Nathan wasn't quick enough to fill, Zoe squeezed his hand. "It will be like before. You'll see."

He squeezed back, and she seemed content with that. "I'll get dressed."

He closed his bedroom door and dropped onto the bed, staring at a hole in the wall. He wasn't sure which *before* time Zoe had meant. Did she mean before Susannah's death? Or after Susannah's death when it was the two of them for a short while? Probably the latter.

The problem was that with Zoe back in his life, he felt as slick as the sludge he cleaned off his potter's wheel at the end of each day. There wasn't enough of him left for her to mold into anything. She'd be disappointed when she realized this.

Without glancing at the mirror he began to undress. He opened his closet to find all his shirts ironed and hanging on wooden hangers. He ran his fingers along the hangers until they clacked together. So now he owned wooden hangers, and Zoe considered this afternoon's wake in the Plough and Trough Pub her coming-out to his friends. She appeared to be bedding down for a long stay. Making up for six years without him.

Nathan pulled a clean jersey-style shirt over his head, the one Zoe said made his eyes sparkle.

"There you are, and don't you look nice," Zoe said when he reappeared.

"And so do you," Nathan said.

An understatement if ever there was one. She wore a simple cobalt blue dress that brought out the color of her eyes. She'd grown into a tall and svelte thing, similar to Susannah, the two of them a different species of human from Nathan, who often felt as ill-formed as a lump of clay.

She bumped him along with her toward the front door and handed him a jacket. She leaned her head again his shoulder. "Do you like the hangers? Just like we used to have, right? I'll tidy you up. It will be nice."

He nodded rather than fake enthusiasm. Best to go along with her mood. There was nothing wrong with a daughter happy to be home with her father, right? In fact, most single fathers would welcome a daughter to take care of them and the house.

A few days ago she'd bounced in waving a black box. "You couldn't slice butter with your knives, so I've had them sharpened. You can store them in this knife block now."

Zoe had laughed when he tossed a towel over the knife block with its troop of sharpened knives. The shiny black handles preyed on his imagination, taunting him with their razor edges.

"You look knackered," she said now. "I'll chauffeur you tonight."

Nathan lived in a rental house that was neither picturesque nor rustic. Suburban-style enclaves had cropped up along the main roads between villages. His housing estate, located between Lisfenora and Corofin, was more bland than mash with peas, but the anonymity suited him. The attached town home with its minuscule front patch of grass was a place to live. No more, no less. As long as the neighbors left him alone and he had space for throwing and firing, he was fine.

Nathan gripped the armrest as Zoe barreled down the road toward Lisfenora. Outside the passenger window, a fifteenth-century tower house coasted by, its walls dwarfing the farmhouse that huddled within its shadow. How oppressive to live with a piece of history outside your kitchen window, forever reminding you that the past casts a long shadow.

SIX

DANNY POKED HIS HEAD into Ellen's hospital room before entering. He didn't normally arrive this late in the day on a Sunday, and he had a fleeting thought that he'd catch Ellen at something. If a coma patient's fingers twitched while no one was watching, did they really twitch?

Ellen lay on her hospital bed the same as always, with her tubes and wires and monitors for company. The head bandages had come off long ago and three inches of hair growth shone a brighter red than her previous hair color. She'd never been partial to bangs, but now they lent her an otherworldly androgynous air, as if at any moment she'd wake up as an enlightened being.

Danny dragged a chair to the bed and rearranged the stuffed flamingo and stuffed Persian cat the kids had brought their mother for her "long sleep." He had no idea how Mandy and Petey had arrived at this phrase, but it seemed to comfort them. He often eavesdropped on their conversations as they drifted to sleep. The nightlight threw a faint blue shimmer into the hallway, and most nights Danny sat on the floor outside the room they shared with his back against the wall, elbows on raised knees, hoping to glean insight into their emotional health.

"Easter is coming up," he said to Ellen's still form. "I'm not sure how to celebrate it this year. Mandy and Petey have whipped themselves into a frenzy of belief that on Easter Sunday you will rise like Jesus. Except in your case, you'll come back to life here on Earth rather than in Heaven." He scooted his chair closer to the bed. "Ay, I know, they've muddled the point of the Bible story. I'm not sure what to say to them."

He picked up Ellen's hand, light as butterfly wings, and massaged it. Her skin felt warm. He leaned closer to peer at her flushed cheeks. "Ellen?" he whispered. "Are you surfacing?"

Every day, all day, a moral tug ate away at him. The chances of her waking were slim, yet he couldn't, absolutely would not, let her body die while her brain still had a chance to reignite itself. Disengaging Ellen from the life-support equipment would be the same as killing her. Or would it? If she woke up, she'd exist in a living purgatory, a nothingness. A vegetable. He couldn't decide which was worse: death or a living death.

If he were a better Catholic, he'd have faith that her soul still resided inside her, that even a breath of life meant the soul was intact. That her life, however curtailed, was more sacrosanct than his concerns about the quality of the life.

"Detective Ahern." One of Ellen's regular nurses bustled into the room. "There are you. No kids today?"

"Not today. I'm here for work. Thought I'd grab my chance to visit Ellen for a few minutes."

The nurse patted his arm as she scooted around him to check Ellen's equipment. "A few minutes with her is better than nothing."

Faint praise, indeed. While the nurse emptied the drainage bag, Danny flicked open the novel he was reading to Ellen. A classic that she'd sworn he would love: *The Count of Monte Cristo.*

One of the machines that tracked Ellen's vitals dinged. With a frown, the nurse squinted at the monitor and exited the room with Danny following close behind. "What was that?" he said.

She ordered him to wait a moment; she needed to check with a doctor. Danny paced the corridor outside Ellen's room. He no longer noticed the scuff marks on the hospital walls, and the sterile smell of the place had become second nature, like the smell of the Garda station. But this? An ominous ding from a cycloptic machine? Not normal.

The nurse reappeared. "Don't be alarmed. Your wife has spiked a low fever."

"Fevers and comas don't mix," he said. "Even I know that."

She moved to the machinery and turned a knob. After a few more moments of what appeared to be random fiddling, she stepped back. "This is why we have antibiotics. A mild fever, no more. Didn't you say you're here for work? You'd best be about it before visiting hours end."

She ushered Danny out of Ward 2B, his wife's home away from home. The nurse's parting words—"If we're not worried, there's no need for you to be worried"—grated on him as he wound down the stairs to the first floor.

Ward 1A, unlike Ward 2B, was a closed ward. Danny waited at the entrance for a nurse to escort him to Cecil Wallace's room. In an effort to drag his thoughts back to the investigation, he pulled out a pad and jotted notes. Cecil Wallace. Cecil Wallace. He was in the house when EJ died, with six empty water glasses next to his bed.

The ward door opened to him at last. "A hardy old soul, that one," this nurse said. "Rallied as soon as we got the fluids and food into him. He'll need physical therapy, though."

Danny entered Cecil's room to find the patient slurping what smelled like homemade chicken soup. A young nurse with freckles and a braid hanging down her back tipped spoonfuls of broth into his mouth.

"Hello, Mr. Wallace, do you remember me from yesterday?" Danny said.

Cecil rolled his eyes toward the nurse. "Get him." Then back toward Danny. "Of course I bloody well remember you."

The nurse snorted. "All aggro, this one."

"I'd like to speak to Cecil in private, if possible," Danny said.

"Ay, have at him." She held out the soup bowl. "You can feed him while you're at it, but don't tell anyone I brought the soup."

Cecil winked at the nurse. "Ta, and give us a wiggle."

"Bad, you are." But she gifted Cecil an arse shimmy before turning into the corridor.

Cecil transferred his grin to Danny. "Eh, and what's after you, clamp got your balls? What did you say your name was?"

"Detective Sergeant Ahern. I need to ask you some questions about Joseph Macy."

"Downed like an old goat to slaughter, was he?"

Danny pulled a recorder out of his pocket. He held it up and Cecil nodded assent. After introducing the two of them, the location, date, and time, Danny began with the basics. Three months ago Cecil Wallace fell and broke his hip, and EJ was supposed to help him with physical therapy.

"He didn't help you?" Danny said.

"If you call dragging me to the living room to watch the telly with him 'physical therapy.' He'd step me through my moves during the commercials. I suppose that's something. I did the exercises on my own most days."

"Do you have family?"

"Not so you'd notice. My wife died a few years ago. And the kids. Three of them." He grimaced as he swallowed the spoonful of soup that Danny held in front of his mouth. "Two of them live the high life in Dublin now. They'll waltz in to cry fake tears and ensure I haven't signed my money away to a stranger. They have no use for the likes of me, and I refuse to see the oldest, the one who might have cared."

He huffed, but Danny caught fear beneath his bravado. "When do you last recall seeing Joe?" he said.

Cecil bunched up his bushy eyebrows in thought. "The day before your lot appeared, in the morning. I'd had a bad few days. Couldn't get out of bed on my own. He helped me that morning, but after that, he didn't come when I rang the bell."

"Did you hear anything?" Danny said.

"Well—" He hesitated. "The telly was always on in the background. Sometimes all night when he couldn't sleep. But I thought I heard footsteps, sneaky like."

"Sneaky like?"

"Not Joe, in other words. Someone prowling around, checking on things."

Danny tapped the spoon against the bowl. Cecil was mentally spry, true, but he'd been bedridden in the back of the house. Danny doubted his hearing was perfect, and besides, homicides were often quiet affairs. Surprisingly quiet. According to Merrit, the television was on when she arrived. With the sound blaring, Cecil wouldn't have heard odd noises from the living room.

"You heard the prowler outside your room?" Danny said.

Cecil nodded.

"Okay. How often did Elder Joe leave you alone?"

Cecil swallowed more soup. "All the time."

But of course he must have, because EJ frequented the Plough almost every night.

"Did EJ have visitors? Anyone you heard arguing with him in the weeks leading up to his death?"

Cecil waved away the bowl. "Ay, but I can't recall when this was, mind you." He burped with fingers over his mouth. "There used to be more of us there. The last one to go had the room next to mine."

"Do you recall his name?"

"Her name. She was a she, but I never knew her name. I didn't know she'd died until the day I heard yelling."

"Did you recognize the voice?"

"Voices. EJ's and the other's. Whoever he was, he cared mightily." Cecil's wrinkles deepened as he shook his head. "Poor woman. No one to take care of her to the end."

On that dismal note, Danny's thoughts veered back toward Ellen alone in her room. He'd take care of her to the end. The question was what kind of end that should be.

SEVEN

In the Plough and Trough Pub, wall lanterns cast a warm glow over shabby wingback chairs and the mourners who had gathered to toast Elder Joe's life and early death. Merrit stooped to pet the pub's mascot, Bijou, a drooling French mastiff with the personality of a lap dog. Next to them sat a pile of antique farm implements and faded photos of dour farmers from County Clare's real plough and trough days. Normally they hung on the wall above Bijou's dog pillow, but Alan Bressard, the pub owner, was sprucing up the place with a new coat of paint.

Merrit shuddered as she shifted a mean-looking pitchfork so its tines faced toward the floor. She hadn't slept well the previous night, what with images of Elder Joe's injuries beating against her inner eyelids.

"You found EJ, did you?" Alan said.

Merrit nodded and scratched under Bijou's jowly chin while Alan observed her in his usual laconic way. French-born, he said much with his expressions, and right now his highly Gallic frown of distaste irked her.

"I didn't find him on purpose," she said. "And you can wipe that look off your face."

With a shrug, he returned to the bar where the crowd congregated around the taps, growing larger by the second. Liam had educated Merrit about what to expect: enough singing and cheering to bring down the rafters. The Irish had a beautiful array of "drunk" phrases to choose from. Liam had used a new one to Merrit: "off their bins."

Off their bins or not, Merrit didn't feel comfortable within the crowd. Even from her stooped position against the back wall of the pub, she could see the curious glances that flicked in her direction.

She'd often seen Elder Joe here in the pub, in the center of it at the bar. One of those garrulous, red-faced men with a quick tongue and not a care in the world. His soulless view of a gravel quarry told a different story, though, and his invitation to tea still didn't make sense unless his loneliness had overcome his reticence toward Merrit. It might be that simple.

With a final pat on Bijou's head, Merrit stood. Across the pub, Nathan Tate, another relative newcomer to the village, entered and paused to prop the door open. A young blond woman bounced in after him and clapped her hands as she looked around the room. She wrapped her arm around Nathan in a quick side hug before stepping ahead of him toward the thick of it near the taps.

"Oh, that would be the daughter," Mrs. O'Brien, local matriarch, said. She spoke to one of her church lady friends and hadn't noticed Merrit come up behind her. She had an ample figure and enough money to buy shiny black dresses custom-made to fit her amplitude. "Zoe. Looks a lovely thing, no thanks to that deadbeat father of hers."

Merrit imagined Mrs. O'Brien eyeing Nathan with the same curl of lip she bestowed on Merrit on a regular basis. The resemblance between Nathan and the woman, Zoe, was evident now that Merrit knew to look for it: both slight of build—Nathan compact, Zoe willowy—and with the same wide-set eyes and small noses. Nathan was small-boned for a man. On his daughter the same features had resulted in a woman of exceptional beauty.

Merrit tended to discount obvious beauty as a sign of superficiality, but that wasn't fair. She scrutinized Zoe in an attempt to read her as Liam, the showman, had taught her when it came to his chosen profession, matchmaking. He called it "absorbing." She was supposed to allow her instincts to take over, to let the essence of a person sink into her. Try as she might, she couldn't get a feel for what he meant.

All she saw in Zoe were the romance-novel clichés: blond hair bouncing against her shoulders in soft waves, full lips, wondrous skin, crazy good figure. Her beauty drowned out everything else about her. So much for Merrit's instincts. Liam insisted she had the makings for a good matchmaker, but Merrit had her doubts.

Mrs. O'Brien's next comment caught Merrit's attention again. "You watch, that Nathan Tate is hiding something. I've heard the rumors about him, anyhow."

More like he's guarding something, Merrit thought. His bloody privacy.

"Would you look at Zoe?" Mrs. O'Brien didn't bother to lower her voice. "She could charm the hiss out of a snake. I've never seen anyone pull off a white coat like that, and at this time of year, too. Why, she could be Our Lady of the Spring leading us toward summer. I'm sure she would like to help with Liam. I shall ask her to join Team Liam."

What the hell? "Excuse me." Merrit stepped forward to stand beside Mrs. O'Brien. "I couldn't help but overhear you. What are you talking about?"

Mrs. O'Brien rolled her eyes toward the ceiling. "What else? Liam's illness. Caretaking shifts."

As ever, the way news spread through town caught Merrit off-guard, as if it travelled with the breezes that brushed over drystone walls and wended their way toward Lisfenora, gathering strength to blow the latest gossip into everyone's minds at the same time.

"We don't need help yet," she said. "It's premature. You should have consulted me."

"Liam didn't mind the idea when I talked to him." Mrs. O'Brien smoothed down the front of her dress and turned toward her friend. "What was I saying? Oh, Nathan. He abandoned Zoe as a child, that he did. And his wife dead, too. An accident. Now he must face up to his paternal obligations at long last."

Merrit stood there, feeling an unaccustomed sense of helplessness, as if she banged on glass walls, the community around her visible yet beyond reach at the same time.

Time for her to go. She'd round up Liam or arrange a lift for him, then she was out of here. She scooted past Mrs. O'Brien's unyielding form and weaved her way through the crowd, catching a toast: "Cheers to EJ's endless supply of ugly bow ties!"

"*Sláinte!*"

With a grumble, one of the regulars edged sideways so Merrit could squeeze in between him and Liam at the bar. Another Joe, nicknamed Joe Junior to differentiate him from Elder Joe. He was in his forties with weathered skin and white squint lines that radiated from the corners of his eyes.

"You found Elder Joe, eh?" he said.

"Sure did. Do you have something to say about it?"

He rocked back on his stool. "There's plenty I could say, but never you mind."

"Fantastic, thanks. If you really want to know, I was picking up eggs, that's all. Organic eggs."

"You're a lippy one today. I don't give a rat's arse that you were the one to find him. Someone would have eventually." He started to say something else but clamped his mouth shut and stared into his beer.

"Time for a distraction," Liam said. "Meet Zoe, Nathan's daughter."

Hearing her name, Zoe excused herself from another conversation. Merrit turned and leaned back against the bar. Liam did likewise. Zoe held out her hand, the pressure of her palm against Merrit's firm—a quick squeeze—and fleeting.

"Lovely to meet you," Zoe said. "I was just after telling your father that I'd heard about him about two seconds after I arrived in Lisfenora. And you, too, of course. The local celebrities."

A few snorts greeted the last statement, and Zoe blinked in confusion. She didn't need eye makeup, Merrit noticed, what with her thick fringe of eyelashes and violet blue eyes.

"I'm sorry," Zoe said, "did I hear it wrong?"

"I'm not a celebrity," Merrit said. "Far from it."

"You will be." Liam jabbed a finger at each of the snorters. "You mark me. And sooner rather than later, too."

Silence settled around the group.

"Oh dear." Zoe tossed a swath of hair over her shoulder and held up her wineglass. "Enough of this. I'm new to town, and I'm here to meet my father's friends. To new friendships. *Sláinte!*"

"And old friendships!" someone called out. "May Elder Joe rate a mansion in Heaven!"

"Have you moved here?" Merrit said to Zoe over the noise of the crowd.

A few feet away, Nathan leaned with elbows against the counter. He tilted his head in their direction with gaze fixed on the whiskey bottles that adorned the wall in front of him.

"Could be." Zoe grinned. "I'm keeping my father in suspense, aren't I, Dad?" She reached past Liam and hooked Nathan's arm. She pulled him into their circle with a good-natured tut. "He moves around so much it took me ages to track him down. So I should at least give that decision some thought, right?"

A circle of welcoming nods met her question, but Merrit was struck by the tension around Nathan's eyes, their black circles and veiny reddened irises.

"Dad, how could you not tell me how nice your friends are? You gentlemen will have to share him with me, you know that, don't you?"

Joe Junior piped up. "Easy enough if you join us at the pub. You can fill in for Elder Joe, God rest him."

"I accept your invitation," Zoe said. "With pleasure."

"What, nothing out of you?" Joe Junior said to Nathan.

Nathan's smile didn't quite reach his eyes. "Zoe is the life of the party, not me."

"Aw, you weren't so bad back in the day," Zoe said. "When Mum was alive."

Nathan slid out of the group. "Bladder the size of a pea, excuse me."

"Stupid me. He's a sensitive one, my dad." Zoe stepped closer to Merrit, creating a small circle just for the two of them. "My mother died when I was thirteen, and then Dad … pfft"—she flicked her fingers—"gone by the time I was fourteen."

"That sounds rough, but Nathan was friends with Elder Joe, right? Maybe that's why he's sensitive today."

Zoe considered Merrit's statement. "You're right, of course. I only met Elder Joe once, when he grabbed up Dad for a jaunt to Galway and left me alone all day." Her gaze clouded. "Anyhow, I was going to say—about my mother—that it was a terrifically difficult transition after she died. She was English. We lived in England at the time."

"That must have been hard," Merrit said.

Zoe adjusted her shoulders and swung her hair about in an exaggerated shake. "Don't mind me. Everything's grand. It's nice that Elder Joe had so many friends, don't you think?"

Merrit's mind wandered back to the abandoned quarry in front of Elder Joe's house. No neighbors or sheep or picturesque drystone walls or even the bright green of new growth. Instead, yellowish grass lumps under a grey sky and limestone terrain marred by gravel dunes. She hadn't told Danny and O'Neil that she'd picked up eggs from him every week because, despite not wanting to share tea, she'd felt an odd kinship with him. And now she didn't comment to Zoe that drinking buddies weren't the same as true friends.

EIGHT

Tuesday, 16-Mar

The night before last, I forced myself out of this old house of mine. Fancy that, the shut-in emerges—kidding. I've mentioned the local murder. (And, remember the "niggle" I also mentioned? I still haven't figured that out.) At the pub where the mourners gathered, I made myself comfortable near the fireplace, glass of wine in hand, and people-watched. Too vigilant, you say? Ay, but I'm glad I went. I saw a few people I know. I felt safe enough.

As an aside, I met a man named Nathan. He escaped the crowd and dropped into the empty armchair next to mine with a soul-unburdening sigh. We chatted a bit, as one does. He, reluctant; me, socially desperate.

Fact: PatientZ was your garden-variety antisocial personality, well-hidden beneath his charm.

Fact: Nathan is so far on the other end of the spectrum that I'd label him neurotic.

Fact: I'm a sucker for a nice, transparent neurotic.

At first glance, Nathan appears to be the calm type, but upon closer inspection you can tell his stillness isn't relaxed at all. Oh no. He's a prey animal on alert for predators. I empathized. I suppose that's why I asked to visit his studio when he mentioned his pottery. The poor man didn't know what to do with my request. At best, I'd say he acquiesced. We exchanged phone numbers.

It occurs to me that it may be harder to decipher a neurotic's truth than a charming nutter's. Not that I'm about to pursue anything with him, but the notion has to come up, correct? I must overcome my tendency to fall for the most awful man in the vicinity, because falling for PatientZ is why I'm here on the page "processing," after all.

Unfortunately, since Nathan intrigues me, he must be the most awful man in the vicinity. Is this a fact? No, I suppose not, but it feels like a fact. (I'm sure we'll dig into this in our next session.)

NINE

FOR THE FIRST TIME in two days, Merrit had a few hours in the house without visitors. Starting on Sunday, a constant stream of well-wishers had arrived, all of them bearing food for Liam. Desserts mainly. Creams made with last year's blackberries and cookies and crumbles and pies and cakes made with alcohol. Enough to last through the summer, so with Liam's help, she'd banished the sweets that Liam pronounced inedible and now hauled a heaping bag to the rubbish bin.

Merrit paused when she reached the bin, taking a moment to enjoy the vista as a newcomer ready to be awed. About a half mile away, a limestone hill called Mullaghamore spiraled out of the earth like a conch shell. Sometimes at twilight it caught the light and glowed, a bright gold thing, and sometimes the cloud-scapes created a moving light show as sunshine waxed and waned.

Other times, like right now, Mullaghamore resembled the earth's grey thumb print pressed against a sky bloated with gloomy cloud blobs. The vista didn't move her the way it had when she first arrived. Varied and beautiful, yes, but it didn't inspire the same awe.

Once the novelty wore off, you returned to your previous normal, baggage and all.

Merrit packed the rubbish into the bin and started back toward Liam's tidy ranch-style bungalow. Further along the track, his previous home—Fox Cottage—stood empty. Kevin, Liam's adopted son, had lived there before running away to parts unknown, then Danny for a while after his separation from Ellen, and now no one.

Fox Cottage sat as forsaken and lonesome as the famine cottages that dotted the hillsides. Flaking white-washed walls and disintegrating thatched roof. Maybe she could smarten it up for Kevin's possible return. Why not? She wasn't out to steal their father from Kevin or usurp his place in the community, despite what some locals might think. She couldn't care less about money. She had her own that came from the family business she'd sold off back in California, plus one of the trusts her mom's wealthy parents had set up for their grandchildren.

She wasn't sure about Liam's financial situation—he never discussed it—just as she wasn't sure about anything at the moment, least of all how she would cope with Liam's death. Early on she'd promised herself she would care for Liam through his cancer, and here she was again, facing her promise for the second time. But now the promise hurt.

Merrit understood that she was the child of Liam's loins. Unfortunately, somewhere along the way, he'd become her real dad. Not just biologically but emotionally as well. She hadn't mentioned this to him. He continued to pine for Kevin's return, Kevin being the child of his heart. The son might return, but it probably wouldn't be any time soon. He didn't know Liam was sick.

The sound of the house telephone jarred Merrit from her reverie. She sprinted the rest of the way to the house and grabbed the landline before it went to voicemail. At first, she didn't recognize the man's voice even though he addressed her by name. "Hi, Merrit, has Zoe arrived? She should be there by now."

"Nathan?" she said. "Hi, sorry, I don't understand. She's supposed to visit? Why?"

"To help with caretaking shifts"—Merrit suppressed a groan of frustration—"and I could have sworn I rang. I didn't? I meant to."

"I told Mrs. O'Brien to leave off with the caretaking schedule, but Liam welcomes visitors. Hold on a sec."

Merrit covered the mouthpiece and entered Liam's bedroom. Bijou lay on the bed beside him with her giant head on his lap. Alan had dropped her off to play therapy dog for Liam. Merrit sat on the edge of the bed and scratched Bijou's belly. The dog responded with a slobbery sigh.

"Are you okay with a visit from Zoe, Nathan's daughter?"

Liam set aside his novel. He grunted. Merrit decided to interpret this as a yes.

"How did Nathan get your number?" she said.

"Pfft, my number's everywhere. Had the same one for decades."

"It's fine," Merrit said into the phone.

Nathan sighed with evident relief. "Sorry for the confusion. I thought today might be a good time for her to visit. Zoe is keen all on her own anyhow."

Merrit recalled her bedazzling presence in Alan's pub. She appeared to be a keen kind of person.

"She's partially through her nursing training." Merrit caught quiet desperation as Nathan continued. "It would help if she had something to do."

Ah. Now Merrit understood. Get the daughter out from underfoot. She sometimes wondered if Liam thought the same thing about her.

"What was that?" Liam said when she rang off.

"You met Zoe. What did you think of her?"

"You mean aside from the obvious?"

She rolled her eyes. "Yes, please."

"Any man she marries had better watch out."

"Femme fatale in the making?" Merrit rose. "Too bad we won't have any eligible bachelors on Team Liam."

Liam grunted again. "Don't 'team' me."

"Mrs. O'Brien's words, not mine. I wish you'd put a stop to her."

The doorbell rang, and Bijou sprang off the bed with a deep-throated woof. She trotted ahead of Merrit to the door. "Hold on," Merrit called. "Don't mind Bijou. She's friendly."

"Bijou and I are old pals," came Zoe's voice. "From Alan's pub."

Merrit opened the door to see Zoe stooped and holding her arms out to the dog. If anything, she looked more exquisite than she had when Merrit met her at the pub. She wore a slim-fitting dress in an immaculate ivory under a tailored raincoat. She slipped the coat off with a dainty shrug and rearranged a cobalt blue scarf around her neck. Once again, she'd left her face unadorned except for a touch of light lipstick and the bounteous head of blond curls.

"What a beautiful scarf," Merrit said.

"Thanks! This shade of blue is my signature color. I wear it all the time. I love butterflies, too." She held up an end of the scarf so that Merrit could see the butterflies woven into the cloth in a darker shade of violet blue.

"If you like butterflies, then you'll love the Burren in the summer. If you're here, that is."

"The big *if*. I'm in negotiations with my dad about that."

"Negotiations?"

"I'm joking, of course, but I mean, really, my dad is incorrigible. He's a wanderer, and I'm more the staying-put type. So"—she clasped her hands together—"what can I do to help?"

"Nothing at the moment. Liam doesn't need round-the-clock care yet. I'm not sure why Mrs. O'Brien is moving ahead with her plans."

Zoe placed a warm hand on Merrit's arm. "I've heard the gossip, so I know that you came here to be with your father, too. It's hard, isn't it?"

Merrit nodded, caught off-guard by Zoe's sympathy. "I don't know what your situation is with Nathan, but I hope it works out."

Zoe's smile remained, but subdued. "My dad wasn't the same after my mother died. To be honest, her death left me clinging to him harder than ever, which helped drive him away, I think. I couldn't see how troubled he was. Still is. He has the funniest notions sometimes." She clapped her hands. "But we're not here for me. Can I say hi to Liam now?"

Merrit called out "knock, knock" before they entered his bedroom. "You're grand," he said by way of permission.

"Hello, Mr. Donellan," Zoe said. "Do you remember me? Zoe? We met at Elder Joe's wake."

Liam braced himself as if Zoe were an overexuberant puppy. Which, in a way, she was. Merrit had never heard anyone call Liam "Mr. Donellan."

"Of course you remember me," Zoe said. "What a dolt I am. You look very dapper."

He'd pulled on his bed jacket and tied it with a jaunty bow at his side.

"Bijou needs to be let out," he said.

"I'll take her. Glad to help." Zoe whistled for Bijou, and the dog barreled after her toward the front door. A moment later her voice called to Bijou, ordering her to fetch.

"I don't have the energy for her today, after all," Liam said. "She's the high-maintenance sort, you mark me."

"Because she might charm you out of your bad mood?"

"Bugger that. I'll be in a bad mood if I want." Bijou yelped. "What was that?"

Merrit ran to the living room and arrived at the window in time to see Zoe stooped in front of Bijou, holding her front paw. Bijou appeared to be fine. Merrit sagged with relief, imagining Alan's reaction if his dog got hurt on their watch.

Zoe opened her hand and Bijou dropped her paw, lifted it, and then settled her weight on it. Zoe's mouth formed what looked to be the words "good dog." She patted Bijou's head and returned to the house with Bijou trotting ahead of her.

Zoe waved and smiled at Merrit. She was already talking when Merrit met her at the front door, saying she'd be happy to walk Bijou if they needed help. Liam had arrived by then also. He leaned on his cane, his breath raspy. "What happened?" He eyed Bijou and then Zoe. "What's that on your hand?"

"Just a little blood. Poor Bijou stepped on this." She unfurled her fingers to show them a shard of glass. "I'll throw it away so she doesn't cut herself again."

"Maybe we should take her to the vet," Merrit said.

She called Bijou to her and stooped to check her paw. Whatever ailed the dog had passed. She wagged her tail and laid a gooey dog greeting on Merrit's cheek. A close inspection of Bijou's paw yielded a smudge of blood and a thin, pink scar on one of her pads.

"She's good as gold, that one," Zoe said. "I fixed her right up."

"Be clear, lassie," Liam snapped. "What are you after doing?"

"A little trick of mine. I'd appreciate it if you'd keep it to yourselves though. I know it's odd, but"—she looked away—"what can we do sometimes, right? Life is an odd thing."

Liam threw a *see, told you, high-maintenance* glance at Merrit.

"Wonderful to meet you again, Liam," Zoe said. "I hope I can help you and Merrit. I'm a fantastic cook. It's one of my hobbies. I'm trying to fatten up my dad. You could do with a little fattening up yourself." She wrote her name and number on a pad next to the phone. "There."

She picked up her raincoat and purse. "I have some errands to run for Dad. The basics. I swear I don't know how he's gotten by. He was using paper towels as toilet paper, if you can believe that."

"Hold on, missy," Liam said. "What the bloody hell happened with Bijou?"

Zoe paused at the front door. She raised her hands with palms toward them. "I healed her cut paw. Cheers, then."

She closed the front door before they had a chance to react to her statement.

Liam's exasperated expression eased. "Well, well, the girl fancies herself a healer. Intriguing. I'd like to know more about that, and by association about Nathan. I think I could use some extra help around here, after all."

"No way—" Merrit said.

"No arguments. I must be humored because I'm sick. You can contact Zoe, and I'll let Mrs. O'Brien know that we don't need a sodding Team Liam."

That was good anyhow, but Merrit wasn't sure which bothered her more: Zoe's absurd claim or Liam's interest in Zoe's absurd claim.

TEN

Nathan splashed cold water on his face and scrubbed his skin dry with a fragrant towel that Zoe had left next to the sink in his studio. The fresh spring scent smelled like a sham. He tossed the towel aside.

On second thought… He retrieved it from the floor where he would have left it if a guest weren't about to arrive. The studio was a bloody disaster, as usual. Glaze drips enlivening the flagstones, a half-thrown vase drying out on the wheel. This was his space, and he'd put his foot down with Zoe about tidying up. He'd told her—no, *told her* wasn't correct. He'd *suggested* she leave his studio alone. Yet Zoe couldn't resist adding her stamp to the room.

He draped the towel over the tap. To his chagrin, he'd gone along with the idea when Annie Belden requested a studio visit. "Pottery has fascinated me ever since I took a class and failed miserably." She'd laughed, a sound like chimes. "I think I have uneven hands. At least that was my excuse. My right hand knew what to do, but my left hand always cocked it up."

Nathan watched himself as if from a distance, saw that he smiled as Annie confirmed the day—today. She appeared happy with the prospect, but as soon as the words, "Brilliant, I'll see you then," were out of his mouth, he'd longed to suck them back up.

Now here he was, squirming with uneasiness but also looking forward to seeing her.

The wall clock said 1:10. Ten minutes late. He'd hoped she was the punctual type. Zoe wasn't due back for a few hours, but since EJ's wake, she'd been hovering more than usual, asking him questions, wanting to know more about EJ than Nathan felt like answering. Finally, he asked her why she cared, to which she'd answered that all of his friends interested her.

Nathan had put many things out of his mind in the years since returning to Ireland. By necessity—for his mental health, one might say—these things included Zoe. He refused to think about the many ramifications of her reappearance, one of which had already become apparent: Her need to involve herself in all aspects of his life.

"Hello? Nathan?" Annie's voice called out. "The door's open. I hope you don't mind that I came inside."

Nathan checked the clock again. 1:16. Time slipping away from him, as usual. "I'm in here. Come through."

He turned the taps on and let water play over his hands. The coolness against his sweaty palms helped ground him. Something about Annie had penetrated the dead zone that surrounded him. Maybe it was her perfect salt-and-pepper hair that formed a messy fringe around her face. He liked that she didn't bother to camouflage the early grey. Maybe it was her careful smile, neither friendly nor fake friendly. Or her sharp jaw and long neck—

"Sorry for the state of me," Annie said as she entered the room. "You live in a bloody maze. How many Meadowlarks can there be? I must have driven a street, a lane, a court, *and* a place before I landed on the correct one."

Nathan turned off the taps and dried his hands. "Crest," he said. "Meadowlark Crest."

Annie laughed. Dimples appeared in her cheeks. "The only thing crested about it is its sense of self-importance."

"True. Well, here's my studio."

Annie's smile dimmed but her gaze didn't waver. "Right. Of course. Daft of me. You'll be needing to get on with your work." She stepped past him toward the connecting door that he indicated. "I don't have a creative fiber in my body. Maybe that's why I'm fascinated by people who pursue art. I get to wondering if they have special insights that allow them to capture life in their art. Does that make sense?"

"Not really. I make pretty things. There's nothing deep about my job."

"The creative process is one of the deepest endeavors of all." Annie stood on the edge of the enclosed patio that Nathan called his studio. "Now this is more like it. I love the glorious disarray of the place."

She'd turned to look at him again, assessing him but not in a judgmental way. He couldn't tell what kind of response she expected, and in any case, he didn't have the energy to try to anticipate her. Zoe had used that bit of him up for today.

He glanced down at his mobile and showed her around the studio. The potter's wheel, boxes of clay, canisters of chemicals for the glazes, shelves of vases in various stages of completion, a giant worktable, the discards pile, and trays filled with every tool imaginable. Glazing tongs and trimming tools and wooden ribs.

Annie wandered toward the far corner of the room, where an old desk covered in dust hunched in the shadow of the shelves. Her fingers brushed over a black painted birdcage. One of Susannah's antiquing finds. She'd called it Chinoiserie in design, and it reminded Nathan of a miniature pagoda. It wasn't big enough for a songbird to flit around in, yet many a bird had no doubt languished trapped and singing their poor hearts out.

Annie's voice floated back to him: "*But a caged bird stands on the grave of dreams, his shadow shouts on a nightmare scream.*

"Do you know that poem?" she said. "By Maya Angelou."

Yes, he knew the poem. He knew it well. Sometimes it haunted his dreams.

Annie pointed to the ceramic figurine of a goldfinch with its red and black markings positioned inside the cage. "You sculpt, too?"

Nathan spouted words, the first that entered his head. "Did you know that people used to poke out their eyes with red-hot needles to force them to sing better? They sang in memory for what they'd lost."

Annie's hand dropped limp to her side. "That's a distressing image."

"It's blinded memory," he said, "and memory is a slippery mistress." He pivoted away to lead her to the pretty things. The finished vases. "This way, please."

Annie's footsteps followed. They sounded deflated. Nathan picked up a tall, slim vase with a tuliped lip. He'd used the last of his lichen glaze to imbue the vase with its rich green hue. Like spring, that color. Which reminded him that he'd forgotten to buy magnesium carbonate to make more glaze. "Please, take it. I insist. Please."

Annie's reaction surprised him. "Shame on you, devaluing yourself that way."

Money. He hadn't thought about it in a serious fashion since Susannah died. "Take it or leave it, either way."

"If I were a dog owner, I'd say you weren't well socialized when you were young." Annie smiled as she picked up the vase and cradled it in her arms. "Thank you. It's beautiful. Don't mind my mouth. It's hard to let go of old patterns."

Nathan understood about old patterns. The mobile gripped in his hand slipped. He wiped his hands on his jeans and swiped a glance at the time again. After a few more minutes of chat, he steered them outside. The air helped ease the queasiness that had settled over him. This was the first time he'd forgotten to cover the birdcage before a guest arrived.

"Most people are interested in the firing process," he said. "I can show you that now if you'd like."

"I'd like, indeed."

The firing shed took up most of the space in the minuscule yard that backed up to a gentle hillside undulating into the next gentle hillside. Zoe had carved out a spot for herself in a corner. One stool, but its presence oppressed him. He didn't like her out here when the kiln was going. He needed focus to transfer the molten pots to aluminum rubbish bins for the last stage of firing.

Nathan had given the raku firing talk so often he could spout it without thinking. Today he spoke faster than usual. Annie interrupted with pertinent questions along the way. She wasn't going to let him hurry her along. In her own way she was as strong-willed as Zoe.

"Why is raku a low-fire technique?" she said. "What does that mean?"

Nathan nodded toward the giant silver-colored gas kiln in the corner of the shed. "It refers to the temperature up to which I fire the clay. The key to raku is removing the pots from the kiln when they reach their maximum temperature. You don't wait for them to cool."

"That must be dangerous."

"I wear protective gear and pull the pots out with tongs." He lifted the lid off one of the bins to reveal a brick pedestal and lots of soot and ash. "I transfer the pots into these bins and cover them. They are so hot they ignite the combustible items—like leaves—I've put in the bins. I'm forcing the pots to cool rapidly, which stresses the glaze, causing it to crackle. The smoke from the burning leaves soaks into the cracks."

"Craquelure," Annie said, sounding proud of herself.

"Yes." Nathan tapped the lid back down on the rubbish bin. "The smoke also has an interesting effect on the glazes, which is why raku is known for its metallic sheen."

"Your pieces are lovely."

"That's all they are. Their only function is beauty."

Annie held out the vase that Nathan had gifted her, admiring it. "Isn't that enough?"

"I'm not sure."

She cocked her head at him, looking interested. He supposed it did sound odd. Here he was, a potter who created vases that leaked, that existed only to be praised, and that he wasn't convinced deserved a place in the world.

On the other side of the house, the front door slammed, startling Nathan. He stepped away from Annie. "My daughter is home."

"Dad?" came Zoe's voice. "'Allo? Oh! Why, hello."

The air crackled like his glazes when Zoe stepped into the yard. Nathan rubbed at his side. It had begun aching a few weeks ago.

"This is brilliant." Zoe wrapped an arm around him and squeezed. "Glad to meet one of your lady friends for a change."

"A studio visit, that's all," Nathan said. "Giving the tour."

Zoe beamed; she positively radiated good cheer. Nathan grabbed the vase from Annie, murmuring that he should package it up.

"Oh, you bought it, wonderful," Zoe said.

Nathan sneaked another peek at his watch. "You're back early. I thought you'd be at Liam's for hours."

"He was in fine form today," Zoe said. "Besides, I need to change. See here, I got blood on my dress."

Nathan winced against a softening around the edges of his vision. The cotton batting that surrounded Nathan most of the time began buzzing, all around him a loud buzz that radiated from the base of his skull. He touched his fingertips to the tabletop to steady himself.

Annie opened her mouth to comment, but Zoe barreled on. "Not to worry. It's not my blood. Bijou stepped on a shard of glass." She pulled it out of her jacket pocket. "But she's as good as new now."

She dropped the shard on the table near Nathan's hand. He jerked away, his stomach rising, and made it to the sink in the nick of time to throw up.

"Blimey, Dad, I didn't know you had issues with the sight of blood," Zoe said.

"That surprises you?" he retorted and immediately regretted it. "Not always," he amended.

He sank onto the stool that Zoe set down beside him. Annie picked up the unpackaged vase, reassuring him that she'd be careful and that she'd enjoyed the studio tour.

"I'll walk out with you, shall I?" Zoe kissed Nathan's cheek. "I'll change fast and be off again, too. We need more coffee. You be good."

It took all of Nathan's effort to nod. Yes, be gone. When her voice had faded into the house along with Annie's, he stood, set the stool back in its spot in the corner of the shed, and sank down onto the floor instead.

ELEVEN

DANNY HAD PICKED THE wrong time to chat with Elder Joe's cohorts at the Plough. The din of a pounding hammer disrupted their afternoon pints, and they shifted and squirmed on their bar stools, calling out to Alan to quit with his bloody renovations already. Even Bijou had abandoned her pillow in favor of blocking the front door.

Alan stood on a ladder in front of a newly painted wall. Gemma, his girlfriend, motioned Alan to shift a nail a few inches to the left. At her nod, he pounded it in, raising his voice above the clamor to ask Gemma where the *sleán*—or turf cutter—had gotten to; did they send it to the restorer?

Alan waved his hammer at Danny. "Don't be leaving before I ask you a question."

Joe Junior and a couple of other regulars—Mackey and Mickey— grumbled their hellos when Danny sat down.

"You here official-like," Joe Junior yelled over the hammer thuds, "or unofficial-like?"

"Sorry to say, official."

Danny knew how to play the game. As long as he didn't lord his position over them, they'd see fit to talk to him. One whiff of superiority and they'd tell him to feck off.

They waited in silence while Danny ordered his pint. As soon as the junior barman set it down, the men raised their pints. "God rest him, a saint among drinkers," said Mackey.

"*Sláinte.*"

Danny sipped his Guinness and set the pint down. He waited for the pause between hammer blows. "What have you heard?"

"Someone killed Elder Joe in his own home," Mickey said. "Gutted, I am."

"Pure madness," Mackey added. "Blood everywhere. A *sea* of blood."

They were off then, the three of them bellowing over each other when Alan's pounding started up again. Lamenting the demise of Irish culture and declaring that this was what came of letting go of the old language and letting in the violence from the States through television and movies.

"And the Internet, don't ye be forgetting that!" shouted Mackey.

Alan glanced at them from his position mounting a pitchfork onto the wall. Its sharp prongs could do some damage, but nothing like EJ experienced.

"Tell me about Elder Joe," Danny said.

Mackey's red nose twitched. "How do you mean?"

"You've sat here with him for the last two decades. Tell me about him."

Mackey shook his head with a puzzled expression, as if Danny had asked the question in Latin.

"He's just Elder Joe," Mickey said.

"You mean to tell me that in all these years he hasn't talked about his family or his work or his pet cat?"

"He has a cat? First I've heard of that," Mickey said. "Didn't strike me as a cat person."

Danny swallowed down a hefty mouthful of the black stuff. "Right, let's put it this way. Why do you think someone would kill Elder Joe? I'm taking ideas."

Mackey gurgled into his pint and came up guffawing. "That'd be easier than a Saturday night tart. He was a right old bastard, that one."

"Can you be more specific?" Danny said. "What about his business?"

Again, the puzzled look. "You mean the lodgers?" Mackey said.

Lodgers. Is that what he called them?

"EJ rented rooms out of his house," Mackey said. "He has a huge house for one old codger. The family home." He shook his head. "One of the big families around here until a few generations back—before you were born, anyhow. Three generations of Macys lived in that house. Full of children and baking wives."

"I know his daughter is up in Galway," Danny said. "The next of kin, but she refuses to travel down here to see to his affairs. Any idea why?"

"You'd have to ask her," Joe Junior said. "She gave up on him years ago."

"We haven't found any other family members. No one else you've heard of?"

"Dunno, quite." Mackey stared into a middle distance with bleary eyes. "Yet another family with too many girl daughters and unmarried sons."

"I find it hard to believe that you know nothing personal about Elder Joe," Danny said. "If he was as much of a bastard as you say, he'd have had enemies, full stop."

Joe Junior snorted.

"Did he mention anything unusual of late? New lodgers?" That question earned Danny three head shakes. "How about this—when did you last see him?"

Joe Junior spoke up. "Last Friday night. He went fishing that afternoon with Nathan. You know Nathan."

"I do." Nathan Tate, the potter with a damaged way about him that attracted women.

"Nathan, now," Mackey said, "he might be the one knowing more about EJ, seeing as how he lodged with EJ for a while. I'd say the two of them were decent friends, all in all. At least, here in the pub, they'd chat."

"That's helpful. What about Elder Joe's other lodgers?"

"What about them?" Mackey said. "Just something he did. He didn't pay it no mind."

Which was too obvious, given Cecil's state. Danny swallowed another mouthful of beer. "So, what you're saying is that you're bloody useless when it comes to helping me find Elder Joe's killer."

Head wags all around. "About the size of it," Joe Junior said, "but if we think of anything we'll ask Alan to ring you."

"Helpful of you."

As Danny stepped away, Mackey took ownership of the half-full pint he'd left behind on the bar. Alan intercepted Danny halfway toward the door. He rubbed his bad shoulder, a holdover from his hurling days. "What do you know about a lass named Zoe, daughter to Nathan?"

"Nathan, eh? What about him?"

"More to do with the daughter," Alan said. "An hour ago I picked up Bijou from Liam's house and received an earful about his daughter fixing a cut on Bijou's paw. There's a scar on her paw, all right, but I'd never noticed it before. We got to wondering—"

"We?" Danny didn't like the sound of that. "You're not turning into a meddler, are you? Merrit's a bad influence."

"Cool your ever-mighty jets." Alan lowered his voice. "It's only this—Zoe will be helping out with Liam's care. You heard his cancer is back?"

Danny nodded, curt, not wanting to delve into it.

"There's something off about Zoe," Alan said. "That's my interpretation, anyhow."

Danny considered Alan. Except for his sometimes fiery half-French temperament, Alan was a hard one to read. That said, he had one tell: the way he rubbed his shoulder when he was bothered by more than a muscle ache.

"Go on then," Danny said.

The junior barman called out a clogged toilet. Alan swore under his breath. "*Merde*. In a nutshell, Zoe fancies herself a healer. Liam, and by association Merrit, has taken an interest. You might want to check in on Liam, see how he fares."

Alan strode away after dropping that oversized hint about Danny's fractured relationship with Liam. Danny had considered Liam a father figure until the events that followed Merrit's arrival estranged Danny from him, all but ended Danny's marriage, and caused Liam's son Kevin to take off for Christ only knew where. A bloody mess all around. After that murder investigation, Danny had preferred to keep his distance, especially after Merrit moved in with Liam.

It seemed he was about to venture over the threshold of Liam's house for the first time in a year and a half. However, he had a funny feeling it wasn't Liam who needed the talking to.

TWELVE

Wednesday, 17-Mar

Yesterday I visited Nathan in his studio.

Fact: Nathan almost jumped out of his skin when his front door slammed. A deer in the headlights, wanting to flee but caught tight.

Fact: Nathan didn't appear capable of returning his daughter's affection.

Fact: Nathan gets sick at the sight of a few drops of dried blood.

My theory: PTSD. He exhibits many of the common traits: disconnected, vigilant, jumpy. When I quoted a poem about caged birds, I caught a pained expression flaring from deep within his soul. He has what I'd call a shrine tucked into the corner of his studio. A cage with a ceramic bird inside it—a talisman perhaps.

Also odd, Nathan gave me a vase, and then he let his daughter Zoe assume that I'd paid for it. He doesn't value his art. It struck me that, likewise, he doesn't place value on his daughter either. Or, more precisely, on his relationship with his daughter. She, on the other hand, knows her worth.

He may not know it, but he's lucky his daughter lives with him. Sometimes PTSD sufferers don't realize how difficult they are to deal with on a daily basis. His daughter has adapted well. She responded to him appropriately: attentive but not smothering, accepting but not submissive.

Fact: I now own a gorgeous, "useless" vase, an empty vessel. Seems fitting somehow.

THIRTEEN

ALONG QUAY STREET, GALWAY City, strands of green pennant flags flapped in the breeze above jaunty tulip and daffodil baskets. Celtic music floated through the air from buskers who had set up outside the Druid Lane wine bar. They played for a healthy crowd that sauntered along the pedestrian thoroughfare. Some of the Americans were already drunk.

Danny and O'Neil sidestepped a sandwich board announcing live music that evening and paused to get their bearings. Róisín Macy's gift shop was located on this block somewhere. Further along, a few tourists braved the chill in the seating area outside The Quays pub. The pub's vibrant blue façade reminded Danny of Nathan's daughter Zoe. Eye-catching but a bit of a spectacle after all that.

Funny that Zoe lived with and doted on her father whereas Róisín disliked her father enough to refuse to drive down from Galway to formally identify his body. Danny hoped his daughter Mandy survived childhood healthy enough to land in the middle between these two extremes.

Beside him, O'Neil pushed back on a drunk who veered into him. "Jumped-up gobshites. St. Patrick's Day brings them all out." He led the way toward another cheerful shop front, this one cherry red, that announced GALWAY GIFTS. A bell jingled when they entered the shop. A display table featured gear perfect for St. Patrick's Day festivities. Two teenage girls jammed giant green Leprechaun hats on their heads and burst into laughter.

A woman with classic ginger coloring sat behind the cash register. A smile lit up her face when she recognized O'Neil. "Look at the sight of you!" She trotted toward them down an aisle jammed with novelty foodstuffs, mugs, and socks—dozens of socks, more socks than Danny thought possible—and grabbed O'Neil in a bear hug. "You bloody wanker."

O'Neil grinned at Danny from over Róisín's shoulder. "You see my boss there, full of censure. Hugs unbecoming an officer."

Róisín stepped away from O'Neil and saluted Danny with an irreverent finger flick. She appeared younger than her years, with ponytail, dimples, and a spray of freckles over her nose and cheeks. Danny could see why O'Neil had liked her once upon a time.

"Moira, the shop's yours for a few minutes," she called.

"Right," someone called back from behind one of the aisles.

A door led to the back of the shop, where a sagging plaid couch stood next to a half-fridge with a coffeemaker on top of it. Róisín waved them toward the couch and dragged a chair to sit in front of them. "You'll be wanting me on the firing line, I suppose. Have at me, then."

A giant tortoiseshell cat wandered into the room and settled between Danny and O'Neil. Its purrs rumbled over the hum of the refrigerator.

Róisín raised her eyebrows. "And so?"

"You're not what the boss expected," O'Neil said. "Give him a moment to figure out what to make of you."

"Ay," she said. "I can't be helping my cheerfulness. It's a curse. Find myself in the worst predicaments when I'm supposed to be serious. Not that I don't have my blue moments, but, yeah, you boot me out into the rain and I'll see rainbows."

"What kind of rainbows are you seeing with your dad's death?" Danny said.

"I'm sick that he died in pain, and I hope you find who killed him." She no longer smiled, but her open expression didn't exude sadness either. "I grieved for him years ago when I decided to abandon my role as his daughter."

The cat's tail flicked against Danny's thigh. He scratched under the cat's ear and earned a toothy yawn. "Why did you do that?"

Róisín glanced at O'Neil.

"Don't be looking at me," he said. "You never talked about old EJ."

"Didn't I? How odd. You must have figured it out by now—his 'alternative' income?"

"Lodgers," Danny said.

"Lodgers, my sweet arse," she said. "My grand old da found his way into their hearts, earned their trust, and then took over their bank accounts. Not stupid enough to steal all their life savings, but, yeah, he earned a decent enough salary." She waved a hand. "At least he didn't take their last shillings. That's a bright spot."

"I suppose it is," Danny said. "When did he open up his house to lodgers?"

"While I was away at university. My mother had passed away when I was sixteen. Dad insisted I pursue an education and not worry about the expenses, which I considered grand of him. After graduation, I returned home and landed a job at a hotel. One day I was hunting around for my birth certificate in his office. I fancied a trip to the States with friends, so I needed a passport. I assumed the important papers were stored in his office somewhere." A wry smile flickered. "Of course, there was a locked drawer in his desk, and, of course, I thought nothing of unlocking it."

"With what key?" Danny said.

"I'd known where he hid the key since I was a girl. I had no reason to care about his office before I needed my birth certificate. I'm not the worrying type, fussing after what's none of my bloody business. I'm not convinced that knowing Dad was a thief was worth the pain it caused. Ignorance is bliss ... ay, well, I learned it that day."

"What did you find?"

"Checkbooks mostly. I think he forged their signatures." She sighed. "These people, they had no one else in their lives, so I suppose that's on the bright side, too. My dad was there for them."

"For a premium," O'Neil said. "How did he target them?"

Róisín flinched at the word *target*. "Jesus, you make it sound bad."

"It is bad, innit?"

"I'm not condoning his behavior." She stood and stretched. Walking around the room, she continued talking while touching the refrigerator, the coffeepot, and other random things. "I think he found most of them by putting the word out, unofficial-like, that he had rooms that were available and so he was less expensive than a proper continuing care home. We fought over it when I confronted him. He didn't understand the problem." She grimaced, which only made her dimples look more cheerful. "He fancied himself a companion rather than a caretaker. He insisted that he provided a service, and how else did I imagine he'd paid my annual student fees and most of my living expenses?"

She picked up the cat and, nuzzling him, returned to her seat. "I told him I wanted nothing more to do with him and moved away. It's awful knowing that my education came out of their pockets."

"Why didn't you turn him in?" Danny said.

"Couldn't do. He was still my dad, and I held out hope for him." She pressed her cheek against the cat's head. "Someone else didn't, though."

"Did you talk to him in the weeks up to his death?"

She kissed the cat's head and let him settle on her lap with idling engine purrs. She raised her eyebrows at O'Neil again, causing him to say, "Out with it, then."

She smiled. "On with you, Mr. Garda Officer. Thing is, he still rang me. Left long messages about his latest news and like that. Lately, he'd rung more often. A few times a week for the last few weeks. I could tell by his tone that he was worried about something." She pressed her fingers into the cat's fur. "I feel horrible. I should have returned his calls."

Which might explain why EJ had reached out to Merrit, asking her in for tea. A daughter surrogate of sorts. EJ was old Ireland through and through. Not the sort to confide in the lads at the pub or call the guards. Hale and hardy, that was EJ.

"Do you still have the messages?" O'Neil said.

"The last one." She pointed to a coat that hung on the back of the door. "Mind the cat and fetch my mobile for me, Officer Man?"

"Saucy minx." But O'Neil looked happy enough to do her bidding.

Róisín tapped on her mobile and held it out so they could hear the message. Elder Joe's voice sounded softer than usual, none of the usual blaring and cawing that Danny heard in the pub.

"*Ro,*" he said, "*ring me back. I'd like to be knowing you're safe. This morning the hens were let out, and I had a time of it catching them again.*"

"Someone was harassing him," she said. "That's what he thought, anyhow. I still wasn't sure about it, thought he was creating drama to persuade me to visit."

"Where were you this past Friday night, into Saturday morning?" Danny said.

"Easy enough to answer. Pickled in Dublin. Hen party weekend."

O'Neil gathered the names of Róisín's mates to confirm her alibi. Danny plucked the mobile out of her hand and passed it to O'Neil to bag. "We'll keep your mobile safe for a few days."

"Away with you," she said. "What am I supposed to do without my mobile?"

"Live life?" O'Neil grinned. "You'll have to drive down to Lisfenora to pick it up. The pints will be on me."

Bloody O'Neil and his one-eyed willie. "We'll contact you if we need more information," Danny said. "Detective O'Neil?"

Danny stepped into the shop ahead of O'Neil. From behind them Róisín called, "You'll buy me more than pints, Officer Man! I demand dinner, too."

A refrigerator magnet caught Danny's attention. *Irish girls don't start fights, they finish them.* Could be Róisín was this type of Irish girl.

FOURTEEN

Too tired to stand, Nathan sat on the toilet to pee, blinking at a green towel still damp from Zoe's mid-afternoon shower. He stood, shook himself, and tucked his bits away. Strange to share a bathroom with a woman after so many years. He'd forgotten how good their conditioners and creams and bath oils smelled. How *clean* they were. Most days, Zoe showered twice.

And Annie yesterday. He hadn't let himself approach close enough to sniff her, but he imagined her skin smelled fresh like the outdoors.

A gloomy nostalgia overwhelmed him. His wife, Susannah, had always smelled good too. Scent memories wafted straight into the silent core of himself that he'd long ago locked away, the part of him that didn't want to remember sitting on the ground next to a giant clawfoot bathtub, trailing his fingertips back and forth in the bubbles while Susannah soaked. Sometimes he climbed in with her, sometimes he loitered like a voyeur. He'd talk about a new glaze recipe that had flunked the firing test. She'd ruminate about a painting that was up for auction that one of her clients might bid on.

Those were the most perfect moments in their marriage, and the memories came along with the scent that teased him now.

He splashed cold water on his face in an effort to shock himself back to his senses. This wasn't Susannah he smelled; this was Zoe. Citrus and vanilla rather than sandalwood and jasmine.

Downstairs, the doorbell rang. Nathan listened with towel pressed against his face. Zoe called, "Coming." She knocked as she passed the bathroom. "Hello in there."

A moment later, her voice carried back to him, a cheerful hello aimed at whoever had rung the doorbell.

"Dad, it's a Detective Sergeant Ahern," Zoe called.

Nathan hung the towel over the bath rod, taking his time, and left the aromatic shelter of the bathroom. Zoe had changed out of her street clothes and into fleecy pajama bottoms, ivory and slung low on her hips, and a cobalt turtleneck jumper. She was as effortless as Susannah had been, as if she'd skipped off the pages of a fashion magazine with her hair bundled in crazy curls on top of her head and butterfly earrings sparkling from her ears.

"Nathan, hello?" Danny said.

He'd missed something and now he stood at the bottom of the stairs with no memory of descending them.

"Don't mind Da," Zoe said. "He hardly sleeps."

Danny smiled at Zoe, keeping it professional, but Nathan noticed the pause as he took her in, his curiosity apparent, before stepping inside. Nathan led the way to the sofa in the living room.

"It's a pleasure to meet you, Detective Sergeant," Zoe said. "It must be pretty obvious that I'm Nathan's daughter."

"Yes," Danny said. "I'm aware of that."

Zoe laughed. "Fair play. I'll make coffee. Dad guzzles it by the gallon. Back in a wink."

Nathan dropped into the closest chair, forcing himself not to rub his side, and indicated the chair opposite him for Danny. Nathan followed Danny's gaze to his hands clutching the armrests. With a jerk, he dropped them to his lap. Somehow he'd opened the scabs on his knuckles again.

"You should get those seen to," Danny said.

"It's nothing. The work dries out my hands."

"I'm here about Elder Joe's death," Danny said.

Nathan rocked forward on his seat and settled his head in his hands. The familiar buzzing revved up at the base of his skull, a presage of one of his episodes. Perhaps the imagined scents in the bathroom had short-circuited his brain.

It was happening more often, these reactions. His body taking over. Older men sometimes asked Nathan where he'd fought, and he'd lie. Sometimes Afghanistan, sometimes the Balkans. They knew what to do: talk, distract, and listen. They knew how the outer battlefield could mutate into an even worse inner terrain.

He needed to survive this conversation with Danny and then escape the house for a while. Land himself in the Burren, walk off his agitation on that strange limestone pavement that didn't remind him of himself or his family or his former life in England.

"Right." Nathan straightened up. "What about Elder Joe?"

"This morning Detective O'Neil and I spoke to his daughter, Róisín. Up in Galway." He paused, waiting, but Nathan didn't know what to say. "Have you met her before," Danny continued, "perhaps while she visited Elder Joe?"

"Oh, no. She doesn't come around. Not that I know of, anyhow."

Zoe entered and circled around the back of the sofa to sit down beside Danny. She'd done the best she could with Nathan's collection of chipped coffee mugs. A small pudding bowl held sugar.

"What am I after missing?" she said. "You two look too tragic for words."

"I need to talk to your father in private," Danny said. "Would you excuse us?"

"Really?"

"Really."

"Dad?" She stood. "Never mind. That's grand." Halfway across the room she turned around. "You'll come find me when the detective leaves, right, Dad? No secrets, remember."

She left the room before Nathan could muster an answer, not that he had one.

Danny picked up a coffee mug and stirred in a teaspoon of sugar. He sipped and settled back, apparently waiting out Nathan again. Nathan liked Danny, thought of him as a Garda officer with an open mind, not likely to jump to conclusions. The problem was that Nathan himself was confused. Was he supposed to have done something?

He swiped at his clay-encrusted jeans, trying to rub away the trembles. The buzzing ratcheted up a notch. "Elder Joe was a friend," he said.

"That's why I'm here. Mackey at the Plough said you lodged at his house when you first moved to Lisfenora."

"Yes." On a deep fortifying breath Nathan managed to pour milk into his coffee without spilling.

"Were there any other lodgers at the time? This would be starting at the end of last summer, true?"

"Sometimes he had other guests. Older people. Sometimes I'd come in to watch the telly with them. I stayed in one of the outbuildings."

"Nothing struck you as odd with the other guests?"

Nathan thought back, trying to remember anything about his two-week stay. The buzzing onslaught continued unabated. "No. I was intent on finding my own place fast. I had my own problems."

Danny nodded, understanding. "How did you find out Elder Joe took in lodgers?"

"I don't understand what all of this has to do with Elder Joe's death. Unless—do you think one of the lodgers did it?"

"We have to check it out," Danny said. "We found one of his current lodgers in a bad way."

Nathan set aside his coffee. "That's bloody awful."

"You know nothing about this business of his with the lodgers?"

"No, and to answer your question, he told me himself that he took in lodgers. The Plough was the first pub I hit when I arrived in the village. I asked Alan if he knew of a place to let, and he pointed me to Elder Joe."

"Fair enough." Zoe's voice rose and fell from her bedroom, singing in a tuneless way. Danny smiled. "Nice to have our children nearby, isn't it?"

Danny studied Nathan with too much interest now, no doubt pondering his mental fitness. It was Zoe. In her reflection, Nathan appeared deficient.

"Was there anything else?" Nathan said. "About Elder Joe, I mean."

"When did you see him last?"

Nathan's mind went blank. "What day are we today?"

"Today is Wednesday."

"I haven't gone to the pub as much as usual because of Zoe, even though she threatens to go with me every night." His joke that wasn't a joke fell flat. Danny gestured for him to continue. "Last week sometime. Thursday or Friday."

"You were seen with EJ at the Plough on Friday night, the night he died."

"Oh right, we went fishing that day. Ended up at the pub afterwards."

"You knew EJ well, then."

"Uh—"

"A few minutes ago you said he was a friend."

Sweat coated Nathan's skin. The clammy moistness of it made him twitchy. What did that mean, *friend*? Nathan hadn't had a friend since Susannah died in 2003. "I knew him to fish with, but he didn't confide in me."

Which made him a safe friend. Confidences required reciprocity, and if Nathan didn't receive them, he wouldn't be held to the social contract of revealing his own either.

Danny sipped his coffee, never taking his eyes off Nathan. "He didn't mention any troubles or concerns in his life?"

"No. We went up to Galway to trout fish. I drove. Elder Joe could be garrulous or quiet depending on his mood. He was quiet that day. More so than usual." Nathan wasn't sure this was true, but he needed something to tell Danny that didn't contradict Nathan's memory of that day, which was faulty at best. "We stopped by the Plough when we returned. I left around ten."

"EJ found his own way home, then."

"He always manages a lift somehow."

"Where did you go after that?"

"Home. Zoe can corroborate."

Danny held his mug with both hands. He surveyed Nathan's meager belongings interspersed with a few fine antiques. The dusty ficus, a stained glass window pane mounted on the wall, the teetering pile of books next to his chair, the six-foot Rococo grandfather clock. "What secrets was Zoe referring to before she left the room?" he said.

"No bloody idea. She wishes I talked more, though."

Danny took his leave, and Nathan followed him out. He continued walking after Danny drove away, far out into the countryside where the wind swept back his hair and whistled in his ears. An hour later, Nathan's head finally cleared, but he kept going. He couldn't bear his house at the moment.

He pulled his mobile out of his pocket, hesitating, thinking about who his friends were and weren't. Without Susannah to ground him, his relationships were illusory at best. Go on then, he ordered himself, and pressed Annie's number.

FIFTEEN

Thursday, 18-Mar

Fact: Yesterday Nathan rang me.

At first I didn't clock his phone number. My first instinct was to ignore the call and try an Internet reverse search on the number. The red warning flags aflutter in my brain. Paranoia at full throttle. Thankfully, I got hold of myself, recognized the number, and answered.

I was surprised to hear from Nathan after the awkward (some might even say "disastrous") studio visit. The clinician in me tried to read his mental state. He sounded as if he didn't want to be ringing me, yet was anyhow. Sweet, actually, and without artifice. I accepted his invitation to take a walk and offered to pick him up at his house. He defused that idea straight away, and I ended up picking him up off the side of the road like a vagabond.

In the Burren, early purple orchids and rock roses waved on a wild-garlic-scented breeze, but Nathan didn't appear to notice spring all around us. He led an excruciating pace up to Mullaghamore's summit. I struggled along, and by the time we reached the top, the lines of exhaustion and tension around his eyes had smoothed out.

We sat for a while on the summit overlooking a mosaic of dry rock walls, pastures, and lanes. He refused to be drawn into conversation about himself. Instead, he invited me to talk about myself. So now he knows that I'm "between jobs" and "investigating opportunities."

At one point he leaned in and sniffed my neck. "You smell good," he said.

I wore my old anorak. He'd rung while I was in the garden. "I smell like mildew and potting soil."

"Perfection."

Then ... these facts, above all:

Fact: Nathan kissed me full on the lips.

Fact: I rather enjoyed it, even the tinge of desperation that came along with the kiss.

Fact: I might be doomed.

SIXTEEN

MERRIT SHUT THE FRONT door with her foot and paused, listening. From the kitchen, an animated girl's voice rose. "I want that one!" she called in a joyous tone. In echo, a boy laughed with what Merrit could only describe as glee.

Yes, actual childish glee in the house. She smiled, wondering who Liam had invited over. He'd been restless and increasingly, as she'd learned, "narky." A narky old git, in fact. She resettled the SuperValu grocery bags in her arms, but stopped at the sound of one man's voice. Deep and rumbly, Merrit couldn't hear what he said, but she knew the intonation.

Holy Jesus, Mary, and Joseph—or however the saying went. Danny. Here. At last he'd stepped foot over the threshold of Liam's house. News of Liam's health must have inspired him to do a very un-Irish thing: let go of the past. Forget Zoe's so-called healing, this was the miracle of the week.

Merrit retreated to open the front door and shut it again, louder this time. "Someone's here!" Danny's daughter Mandy called.

Merrit pushed her way into the kitchen to see an array of desserts covering the kitchen island and a small crowd sitting and standing with laden plates. First, Liam. She scanned him up and down, noting his easy grip on his cane and his not-too-labored breathing. His wink roused Merrit's suspicions. He was up to something.

"Danny called, so I decided to make an occasion of his visit. Afternoon tea to help us eat all these infernal desserts."

"Look, I have three desserts on my plate," Danny's son Petey said.

Merrit smiled at him. "You are one lucky boy."

"So am I, but a girl," Mandy said without looking at Merritt.

Danny leaned against the counter near the sink. Unlike the others, he didn't have a plate in hand. He gazed at Merrit with that neutrality that she had come to detest. To her surprise, the other adults in the room included Nathan Tate with a woman friend—no Zoe in sight—and—

"Marcus!"

Merrit dropped the grocery bags on the counter and wrapped her arms around Danny's father-in-law and her first, dear friend in Lisfenora. He'd helped her negotiate village life before he went to rehab, and now here he stood without the alcohol bloat and bleariness. His arms wrapped around her in a bear hug. He was strong enough to lift her onto her toes.

"I heard you were back." She managed not to glance at Danny when she continued, "I wasn't sure of the best way to contact you."

"Never you mind, lassie. Understandable given the circumstances."

Merrit made her way around the island to Nathan and the woman. In her forties, she had a plain elegance that attracted Merrit. The black slacks and abstract-designed scarf knotted around her neck in the way sophisticated European women had perfected told Merrit that she probably wasn't local either.

Liam's self-satisfied smile confirmed Merrit's suspicions. This impromptu dessert party had many purposes besides welcoming Danny to feel at home again. Reuniting her with Marcus being one. Curiosity about Nathan being another. And it didn't escape Merrit's notice that he'd timed the dessert party to ambush her. His way of having fun, the blighter.

"Too bad Zoe wasn't available," Liam said, "but Annie here more than makes up for her absence."

"I'm the tagalong," Annie said. "Nathan was kind enough to invite me."

"Where's Zoe?" Merrit said to Nathan.

"At what she called an informational interview. Something to do with nursing."

"Nursing?" Annie said.

"She started her college courses in that direction and wants to transfer her education from England to Ireland. Would like work experience."

He didn't sound thrilled about his daughter's aspirations.

Annie set aside her blackberry cream. "I can talk to her about the field in general terms."

"That's grand." Nathan's left eyelid twitched, and he picked at inflamed scabs on his knuckles. "But I don't think she's suited to nursing. Her mother and I thought she'd be good in business. Sales, customer relations, marketing, that sort of thing. Zoe's too fearless for nursing."

"Isn't that a good thing?" Merrit said.

"Maybe if you're a skydiver, or"—he nodded his head toward Danny—"a copper."

Danny turned an inquiring gaze toward them. "I'm wary of fearless Garda officers. They're liable to put themselves and others at risk."

Annie agreed. "Fear is a healthy response—a survival mechanism—especially in response to danger."

"Perceived danger or actual danger?" Nathan said.

"I'd be interested in knowing the answer to that, myself," Danny said. "From a Garda perspective, we have to treat perceived danger as actual danger."

Annie perked up with this turn in the conversation. "Ah, Detective Sergeant, your situation differs from the usual person. For most of us, perceived danger stems from irrational fears and long-standing anxieties. They are imaginary"—Nathan frowned—"but still real in the mind of the person with the fear."

"It could be the other way around." Nathan flexed his injured hand. "An actual danger that you refuse to believe is real, that you talk yourself out of believing to maintain your sanity. What's that called?"

Mandy and Petey's sugar-powered antics broke into their conversation. Danny circled away from them, saying as he went, "Self-delusion?" He grabbed for the children but they made a run for the back door and within seconds were outside yelling in the rain.

To Merrit's surprise, Danny tossed Mandy's rain slicker at her and requested her help wrangling the kids. She grabbed her coat on the way out. "Walk with me," he said as soon as the door closed behind them.

After outfitting the children in their coats, he took off down the track toward Fox Cottage while the kids cavorted ahead of them. Danny tilted his head toward the sky, closed his eyes, and walked along that way for a few strides with rain droplets sliding down his cheeks. He didn't look at her when he opened his eyes again.

"I might have an issue with you," he said, "and I'd prefer to avoid that complication if possible."

"Seriously? What have I done now?"

"It's not what you've done. It's what you might do, seeing as how, of all the people in our fair county, you were the one to find Elder Joe. There's also this business about Nathan and Zoe Tate. The healing."

"Who told you that? Oh, wait, Alan. Right." She stopped and pulled on his arm to halt him, too. "So you're not here to visit Liam, after all?"

Danny called to Petey not to wander too far away. "I think we've had this conversation before, but let me repeat that you can't meddle in a murder investigation. You've got Alan interested in Nathan, and Liam appears to be interested, too. Leave off with the amateur inquiries."

"Wait just a second." She continued walking. Danny kept pace on her right. "I love how you jump to conclusions. Liam is the ringleader, not me, and he's curious about Zoe more than Nathan. She says she's a healer, so of course he's interested. Nathan is a byproduct of that, and besides, what does all of that have to do with your investigation?"

Danny continued past her. Dang, the man was a stubborn sod. She considered the word *sod* but dismissed it as good enough for the moment. She caught up with him in front of Fox Cottage. Paint flaked off the shutters and moss covered the roof. The cottage needed help.

"Did Elder Joe ever mention Nathan to you?" Danny said.

"Is Nathan a suspect?" she said. "Do you think he's the person I saw outside EJ's house?"

"Answer the question, please."

So Nathan *had* landed in Danny's sight lines. "No, EJ never mentioned Nathan. He sold me organic eggs, and I obliged him by picking them up on Saturdays."

She was still looking at Fox Cottage, at all the many ways it displayed its neglect. She felt Danny observing her in his Garda detective way.

"Why did you oblige him?" he said. "He could have left the eggs for you at the pub."

"True." She pushed at an ancient garden gate until the hinges squealed. "I suppose I wanted to prove a point."

"What point?"

"Does it matter? Maybe it felt like the insider thing to do, to pick up eggs from his house."

She didn't want to elaborate on Elder Joe's cryptic last words to her about lambs and sheep, or that he'd thought of her as the snobbish type. The type of person who was "that way," he supposed, because she'd begged off his tea invitation.

Changing the topic, she said, "Who's taking care of his chickens?"

"That's sorted. No worries about the chickens."

"I'll buy eggs from whoever owns them now."

Danny grunted. "We'll see." He called the kids and turned back for the return walk to Liam's house.

"About Nathan," Merrit said. "He seems rattled, doesn't he? And distracted. Ever since Zoe arrived."

"Now who's making assumptions?"

"No, that's a theory. There's a difference." The rain had lightened to a fine mist. A mossy, verdant scent saturated the air. She let Danny's silence stand for a moment, then continued. "I had no idea you were interested in Nathan. Now that I know, I'll keep my ear out."

"No, you won't."

"Or how about this? A deal. I shall ignore everything about Nathan or anything else I think might be of interest to your investigation if you agree to continue visiting Liam. He misses you."

"Bloody hell, woman. You'll tell me what you happen to remember or see or overhear or learn, but leave Nathan be—and Zoe, too, for that matter. The man's confused enough without you muddying the waters."

"Fine." Merrit crossed her fingers behind her back. "Deal?"

He walked two steps ahead of her back to Liam's house. Before opening the back door into the kitchen, he paused long enough to say, "Deal. I'll visit Liam again soon."

"What about Elder Joe?"

"What about him?"

"Don't you have more questions for me?"

"We're square." He squinted at her. "You didn't forget to tell me something, did you?"

"Of course not."

"Hmm. Well then, you arrived for eggs and entered without invitation—which didn't surprise me—and found his corpse. Except for inviting you in for tea the week before, he didn't say anything unusual to you. You're not a person of interest."

"Good." But Merrit felt oddly let down.

SEVENTEEN

Two hours after talking to Merrit at Fox Cottage, Danny barricaded himself in his tiny office to stare out the window at the parking lot. The rainclouds had drifted away, leaving a sharp blue sky and a rainbow. He'd lifted his self-imposed ban on visiting Liam, and by association Merrit, and felt nothing but ambivalence as a result.

He tossed his pen toward the pen holder. Ambivalence would have to satisfy him because he had more pressing things to think about. Like Nathan. His comment about perceived and actual danger intrigued Danny. Some fact—or some perceived fact—scared him. The question was whether his fear was related to EJ's death.

A knock sounded on the door and O'Neil poked his head into the room. "We're ready for you."

The door clicked shut. Danny leaned back in his swivel chair and stretched out his legs. Think about it logically. Nathan lodged at Elder Joe's house for a short while, and they were decent friends as far as that went for loner types. Nathan had spent the afternoon with EJ fishing. Maybe they fought.

Nathan wasn't a likely candidate for murder, but then, he hadn't explained his injured hand either. Not to mention his twitchy, spacey behavior when Danny talked to him at his house. And Zoe's statement about his secretiveness.

He rocked the swivel chair backwards and forwards. What about Zoe? He had trouble reconciling the conventional young woman he'd met with her claims that she was a healer. The notion disturbed Danny, although he understood the temptation to believe in such things.

Another knock. To Danny's surprise, O'Neil entered and closed the door behind him. "A word before the meeting?"

"Have at it."

"It's like this, between us, man to man."

Danny straightened. "'Man to man,' for the love of Christ? This should be good."

"I don't know about that, but I'm after your opinion about Merrit. Since taking her statement I'm thinking she might be fun for an outing or two. Get the lay of it, so to speak."

Christ almighty. Only O'Neil would take Merrit's statement and come to the conclusion that she'd be good for a night out. Couldn't keep his prick to himself.

"Seeing as how you have a relationship with her—" O'Neil continued.

Danny held up a hand. "I have nothing to do with her social life."

"Brilliant. I wanted to satisfy myself, is all."

Danny heaved himself out of his chair. "What she does, what you do, is your own business, except that she's connected to the case. In other words, leave off with satisfying yourself for now."

O'Neil leaned against the door in a relaxed pose with his hands in his pockets. He jiggled loose change. "She's not all that connected. Found the body, wrong time, wrong place, that was all."

"Know that for a fact, do you?" Danny said.

"Don't you?"

"As your superior officer, I've told you what I think. Enough said. Whatever you do, don't talk about the case—and she'll ask you, believe me."

Danny had no illusions about Merrit's promise not to meddle. He followed O'Neil to the office where the DOs worked, trying not to think too hard about O'Neil's "man to man" reveal. Before Ellen's coma, Danny had been separated from her long enough that some eejits had assumed he was interested in acting the bachelor, satisfying his needs. He wasn't immune to the temptation, but with Merrit?

He adjusted his thoughts for the impromptu meeting, thankful that Superintendent Alan Clarkson was on extended Easter holidays into April. With luck, they would solve EJ's murder before Clarkson's return. He had a brilliant way of destabilizing their good working order when he decided to oversee a case himself.

"Where are we?" Danny said as he entered the office.

Detective Pinkney picked lint off his jacket as he spoke. "Plenty of people saw EJ at the Plough on Friday night, sunburned and waxing on about the trout he hadn't caught."

"Where did he fish? Did anyone see him with Nathan Tate? How did he get home from the pub?"

Pinkney wrote a note on his pad to follow up on these questions.

"Where's the list of people who were at the pub over the weekend?" Danny said. "Since the Plough was EJ's local, we can hope someone has an insight or two. His regular crew were useless."

Pinkney handed over a sheet of paper. Danny scanned past the names of the usual Guinness-drinking regulars, and stopped at one name in particular. He tapped it. "I've got this one."

He handed back the list and Pinkney made another note.

"On with the canvassing then and fun for all," Danny said to the sound of groans. "Have Cecil Wallace's kids deigned to appear yet?"

"As soon as they heard their dear da was out of danger," Pinkney said, "they decided to take their time."

"I have an update on Elder Joe's daughter," O'Neil said. "Róisín. Met up with her again today."

"I bet you did," Pinkney said, along with various snickers and catcalls. "Took a little ride up around Galway yourself, eh?"

"Sod off, youse-alls." O'Neil grinned and cracked his knuckles as if readying himself for a bare-knuckle knockout. "Lucky's the girl who ever called me her boyfriend."

"O'Neil?" Danny said.

O'Neil mock-glared around the room. "Where was I? Right. I showed Róisín the paperwork we found that detailed Elder Joe's wee side business. She recognized a few names but couldn't tell us anything. She didn't recall any troubles with the few she'd met. I confirmed her alibi, too. In Dublin partying with her hen friends."

"How far did EJ go to take over their finances?" Danny said. "Was he the beneficiary for any of them? Any suspicious deaths under his care?"

"Don't know yet. He was clever. Kept it small and transferred most of his lodgers to hospitals when their health worsened."

Pinkney tapped his pencil. "Maybe he accidentally on purpose let some of his lodgers die. Could be he was a—what's the bloody name—an angel of death?"

"Hey ho," O'Neil said. "Mention that outside this room and next we'll see it headlined in the *Irish Times*."

"I'm interested in whether he'd been made beneficiary," Danny said. "First priority would be those who died under his care."

"Speaking of which, I've left the best for last," O'Neil said. "Cecil had mentioned the adjacent lodger who died and hearing an argument after that death. The deceased's name was Frances Madden."

Danny raised his eyebrows expectantly.

"Get on with your fair self," Pinkney said.

"Frances Madden is none other than the other Joe's—Joe Junior's—beloved auntie."

EIGHTEEN

Friday, 19-Mar

Fact: Once again, I've been questioned about a murder.

Fact: Once again, I'm two degrees of separation from the victim.

You must be shaking your head at my expense, reflecting that we relive the same lessons until we catch a bloody clue. If we were in the same room together, I'd say "eff off" before you had a chance to say it aloud.

It wasn't a serious questioning, thankfully. The detectives are gathering statements from everyone who went to the pub over the weekend before and after Joseph Macy's death. Makes sense, I suppose, but I was surprised that DS Ahern (I'd met him before while he was off duty—he's a good father) chose to speak to me personally. He honed in on Nathan, wanting to know when I met him, how long I've known him, and what I knew about him.

From the DS's questions, it's obvious that Nathan knew the victim. What could I say? I don't know Nathan well enough to venture opinions to the Garda about his state of mind. Not like I did with PatientZ.

This time around I can't help or hinder the investigation.

Fact: Once again, the man I'm attracted to is my connection to death.

NINETEEN

NATHAN LIFTED THE BLOCK of magnesium carbonate, otherwise known as chalk, off the back of his truck, staggering even though it only weighed fifty pounds. A blustery wind bent the grass tussocks and yanked the breath out of him.

Zoe appeared on the minuscule porch, dancing from side to side on her toes. She still wore her pajamas. "There you are. You were up and out early today."

"I couldn't sleep, so I picked this up for the lichen glaze."

"I thought you'd bought that already."

"I could have sworn I had. I'd forgotten that I'd forgotten."

She dashed toward him, unheeding of the muddy ground that slathered itself all over her feet. The viscous moistness of it on her skin churned Nathan's stomach. He swallowed against the pressure on his chest that had woken him before dawn. Panting and aching and his hand throbbing all over again. Vague nightmarish images of broken goldfinches and a sensation of restraints. His neck muscles had ached as if he'd struggled to sit up against an unseen force.

Despite his protests, Zoe pulled the block of chalk out of his arms. Slouching under its weight, she carried it toward the house. She spoke loud over the wind. "I'm still bothered by the detective. I don't understand why he questioned you the other day."

Nathan followed her muddy footsteps through the house into his studio. Zoe heaved the box onto the old desk next to the birdcage.

"Danny was doing his job," Nathan said.

"Oh, you know him?" she said. "Outside his work, I mean."

"Pub. He's 'Danny' to me. No title."

He opened up a fresh package of clay and sliced off a chunk with the cutting wire. His right hand ached, his knuckles swollen and oozing, but that didn't stop him from slapping the clay down on a work surface and kneading the bubbles out of it. His body worked on autopilot while his mind drifted away. He enjoyed kneading clay.

"Dad?"

Zoe's voice startled him out of his reverie. The light in the room had shifted. Zoe now perched on a box of clay that sat in the corner of the room. She held a cup of tea.

"I heard the detective mention Elder Joe before he banished me from the room." Zoe spoke from the middle of a thought Nathan had missed. He shaped the clay into a squat round cylinder and centered it in the middle of the wheel.

"He wanted your alibi, didn't he?"

Nathan's hands froze within the plastic container of slip that stood beside the wheel. The clay slurry stung his raw knuckles. The burning sensation felt good, numbing him.

"You were in bed," Zoe said. "I saw you myself when I woke up to go to the loo."

He slept with his door closed, so to see him, she'd have had to check on him. He wasn't sure which was worse: his daughter checking on him or his inability to remember whether he was in bed or not the night Elder Joe died.

He turned on the wheel and dribbled slip water on the clay as the wheel head gained speed. He cupped his hands over the clay, feeling its satiny smoothness. Malleable to the lightest of pressures. He narrowed the circle of his hands, pulling up so that the mound of clay rose into a slender cylinder. The clay was his to manipulate into a vase, a mug, a bowl. Whatever would serve him best.

He shifted his hands to assert downward pressure. The column flattened into a disk. He inserted his thumbs into the center of the shape and felt the clay part under their pressure. Easy now, use less force.

"You checked on me?" he said.

"Of course, I always do, because half the time you're not asleep. Sometimes we talk. You really don't remember?"

"No, but I am asleep. Please don't talk to me when I'm in that state."

"Don't be silly. You hardly talk otherwise."

He steadied his hands and forced himself not to dwell on the words that slipped out of his mouth while he was asleep. The fact of it scared the shite out of him.

He widened the hole in the center of the clay and eased out the sides. Easy does it. If he wasn't careful he could stretch the clay too thin, too fast. Safer to use slow, consistent pressure.

"Danny was curious about something you said," Nathan said.

"What an odd thing, these murder investigations. Poking around everywhere."

Nathan lightened up on his thumbs. It wouldn't do to push too deep. He dribbled more slip water onto the emerging bowl. "You mentioned secrets. He wanted to know what you meant by that."

He placed one hand along the outside of the bowl and, using the thumb of his other hand, continued to hollow out the inside and raise the sides. Balanced pressure.

Zoe's footsteps padded toward him. She stood behind his shoulder, monitoring his progress but careful not to touch him. He was off limits while at the wheel. He glanced at his drying shelves, filled with pots ready for their bisque firing. He'd been at the wheel more often lately.

"I'm sorry," Zoe said. "It popped out. You're tired and distracted, and you lose track of time." She pointed to the magnesium carbonate. "And you're forgetful."

Nathan kept his hands in place, with no pressure. The sides of the bowl slid against his skin.

She sighed. "It would be best if we didn't have secrets, that's all."

Yet secrets were the basis of their relationship.

He applied the lightest of pressures against the side of the bowl. "I understand, but there's something else—about Bijou. The cut on her paw that you said was as good as new. You didn't—?"

His thumb broke through the clay. The bowl collapsed. Too hard. Shite.

Her silence stretched out behind him, as thin as the clay that had split open. Nathan busied himself scraping the wheel clean with the wire cutter.

"Dad," she said.

One word, but it was enough to convey her disappointment. She knew he was incapable of loving her as a father should. It was the secret that didn't need revealing.

TWENTY

DANNY MARKED TIME BY Saturdays' arrivals. The day marked the end of his week, a sabbath of sorts on which he took the children to visit Ellen. He led Mandy and Petey into the hospital as he would a church, hand-in-hand and with reverence. He waved at the grey-haired matron who manned the reception desk and let the children veer him toward the elevator for the one-floor ride up to Ward 2B.

He tried not to think about the investigation. He'd spent half his work week wrangling the health care system. After Ellen's fever retreated, he'd fought for a transfer to the bigger Limerick hospital for a full battery of tests. Going into battle mode hadn't dented the system. Her temperature had returned to normal, hence, all was well again.

"I get to push the button this time," Petey said.

Mandy elbowed him. "Then I get to step out of the elevator first."

Marcus followed them into the elevator. On the second floor, the elevator shuddered to a stop with a grind of pulley wheels. Danny held the door as Mandy pushed Petey out of the way so she could exit first. "You go on," he said to Marcus, "I'll be back straight away."

Danny backtracked toward Ward 1A, where Cecil Wallace sat up in bed. A tray with scrambled eggs, toast, and orange juice perched on his lap.

"You again?" He stabbed his fork into the eggs. "You'd better hurry. Two out of three of my demon seeds will be here soon, and they're none too happy." Cecil grinned. A bit wicked was old Cecil.

Danny pulled up a chair and straddled it with arms resting on the seat back. "We had a nice dose of them yesterday at the station."

"Ay, and yer nothing but fecking useless according to my youngest." He forked eggs into his mouth. "What's the craic?"

"Now that you're—"

"Fully functioning? You can say it. Got my bolts screwed in? All my brain cells aligned?" He chewed and swallowed. "Go on with you."

"Now that you're the full shilling again"—Cecil hooted—"I'm hoping you remember more about the voices you overheard in the room next to yours. You heard Joseph Macy talking with another man?"

Cecil nodded.

"Did you hear him mention the other man by name?"

"Can't say that I did, but they knew each other well, I could tell that much." He sipped juice, thinking. "Joe threw a proper wobbler, he did. The mouth on him like to make me blush if I were the blushing sort."

Danny understood. We saved our best worst behavior for those we knew well. "About what?" he said.

"Couldn't tell you that."

"About your kids—"

"Those saints, yeah?"

"What do you think of the idea of one of them killing Joe to protect you?"

Cecil cackled with his hand in front of his mouth. "Oh, that's brilliant. Right this second I wager they're fighting over who's to take me in until they dump me into a rat hole of a care home." Tears of merriment streamed out of his eyes. "The choicest bit is that they don't know that I've decided to use the rest of my money on a first-rate clinic. Fecking hell, yeah, no more of this pinching to provide the ungrateful little sods with an inheritance. I knew what Joe was about with my money, but that wasn't going to happen. He contented himself with overcharging me for meals and physical therapy. The price I was willing to pay to keep my independence like."

Danny grinned. "You old bastard."

"You know it. Papers are signed and a car will pick me up later today. What my children deserve for taking their sweet time and for never visiting."

"Last question." Danny stood. "Nothing to do with the investigation."

"Eh?"

"You were sedated when you first arrived in the hospital. Could you hear anything?"

Cecil bit into his toast. "I'm not following."

"Did you hear people talking while you were under?"

"Odd kind of question, but, no, I don't remember a thing."

Useless question anyhow. Cecil's sedation and Ellen's vegetative state were very different breeds of unconsciousness.

He wrote down the name of Cecil's new facility and left the room feeling lighter than when he arrived. Cecil was one of the lucky ones. There were few good moments within a murder investigation, and Danny would take them when they came.

He returned to Ward 2B, where Marcus met him in the corridor. Mandy and Petey hung onto Marcus's hands. Petey's chin quivered.

Danny's heart clutched hard, a fist of a heart punching his chest wall. "What happened?"

By way of answer, Marcus nodded toward Ellen's room. "Now you're here, I'll take the wee ones down to the grab-and-go."

Inside the room, a doctor and a nurse stood over Ellen. A new machine on a trolley sat next to the bed. The doctor raised a tube while the nurse injected something into one of Ellen's IVs.

Danny stepped up to the doctor and stayed his hand. Ellen's face was flushed and her breathing labored. "Stop."

"This is preventative. Her fever returned, and we think there's fluid in her lungs. Possibly a lung infection. We'll have to transfer her to Limerick."

"Now you agree to transfer her, that's bloody magnanimous of you." Danny took a breath and switched to Garda mode. All business and authority. "Explain, please."

"I'm putting her on a ventilator to give her lungs a rest."

"Why? What are you preventing?"

A nurse crowded in on Danny in an attempt to usher him out of the room. "We'll stabilize her and transport her to Limerick within a few hours."

Danny stepped away from her. "Stabilize?"

"Nurse, escort him out," the doctor ordered. "Now."

The nurse directed Danny out the door ahead of her. Behind them, Ellen gagged as the doctor pushed the ventilator tube down her throat. All the Garda authority in the world meant nothing here.

TWENTY-ONE

In forlorn Fox Cottage, Merrit already had the living room furniture pushed against one side of the room and the paint supplies set up. For the last couple of days she'd obsessed about her conversation with Danny. She'd managed to get her way—Danny promised to visit Liam—but her persuasive tactics were less than desirable. She lied when she said she wouldn't meddle with Nathan. There was no help for it. Liam had his sights set on getting to know Zoe and Nathan better.

Oh, what did it matter anyhow? All the mental energy wasted.

This morning she'd jumped out of bed determined to think about something other than Danny and the nagging sense that she'd missed a point somewhere. Elder Joe and his barren view of a gravel quarry lurked at the edge of her thoughts.

Now, after a trip to the paint store, she was ready to begin her Fox Cottage beautification project. She pried the lid off a can of paint. After a vigorous stir, she painted a swath of soft orange-yellow called Afterglow over the hideous greenish-beige. It wouldn't do to be too bright or too feminine. She stood back. Nice. Warm but not obnoxiously cheerful.

"Merrit?" Nathan said from the open doorway. "Sorry I'm late."

Let the meddling begin, Merrit thought.

His appearance startled an "oh my god" out of her. A row of stitches decorated an angry bruise that covered the right side of Nathan's forehead. Merrit had noticed the circles under his eyes before, but now they rivaled the bruise in lividity.

He answered her unspoken question as he entered the room. "I'm not sure what happened. I can't remember—I was asleep, I think—and it doesn't matter. Things happen."

"Things happen?" Merrit said. "You were asleep? You think?"

"Maybe I banged my head against a wall. I don't know." He held up his bandaged hand. "For this one, I'm pretty sure I punched a wall. I know how it sounds, but until recently I've been doing well."

"But still, that's not good. Have you seen a sleep doctor?"

Nathan shook his head and picked up an unopened paint can. "Waterfall," he read.

"That's for the kitchen. You're okay with helping me? If you're not feeling well—"

"Won't knock a bother off me. Besides, you're paying me."

She painted more Afterglow on the wall. "I haven't been sleeping well, myself. I can't get the image of EJ out of my head."

Nathan coated his roller with paint and began on another wall.

"I found him," Merrit said. "Horrible."

Nathan continued layering on the Afterglow. She glanced at him but couldn't read his blank expression. He moved, therefore he had to be awake.

"Why do you suppose someone would kill EJ? It's all anyone's talking about. Nathan?"

"Hmm? Oh, I never put it together about his other lodgers. I lived on his property. I should have realized."

Lodgers? That was the first Merrit had heard about lodgers. "Realized what?"

"That they were sick and needed help. But I didn't want to know, I think. Other things on my mind when I first came here."

"It's too bad Zoe wasn't around to heal them."

Nathan shuddered in a slow convulsion of tremors that ended with him dropping the roller on the floor. "Bollocks."

Merrit tossed him a rag, and he wiped up the paint. "I shouldn't have brought it up, but, to be honest, Zoe perplexes me."

He froze at the sound of a mobile, then relaxed when Merrit grabbed hers out of her pocket. "Liam. I'd better check on him." She knelt down next to where Nathan still stooped on the floor, now staring at Afterglow-colored paint stains on the rag. "Are you okay, Nathan?"

He twitched back from wherever he'd sunk to inside his head. "Effect of the painkillers."

Maybe that was true, but maybe not. Merrit watched him, this gentle man who maybe wasn't so gentle—at least toward himself, at least while asleep. He'd lost weight. The tendons and muscles in his arms flexed all too visibly when he pried the lid off a second can of Afterglow. Nathan was losing whatever battle he fought while he slept.

She left him to continue painting on his own and trotted down the track to the house. She caught sight of Liam as she approached. The pale sweep of hand in front of the window in greeting. The sun had decided to make a hazy appearance today. Its light waxed and waned as clouds whipped past overhead. They appeared to be gathering along the horizon. More rain later, but for now, Liam enjoyed his sunny spot beside the front window. He'd agreed to let her move one of the recliners from the hearth. He lay under a mound of blankets, clutching a soggy handkerchief.

"Still short of breath?" Merrit said. "Maybe we should raise your chair?"

He shook his head. The movement caused him to cough in short bursts that looked painful. After catching his breath, he grumbled something that Merrit couldn't hear. She sat next to him, trying not to worry about the raised vein patterns visible in his temple.

"On a scale of one to ten, what's your pain level?" she said.

He snorted. "You keep asking that, and I keep telling you that the pain hasn't started yet. Minor achiness is all."

"We should see to your gimpy leg anyhow."

"Pfft, nothing to do with the lung cancer. It's improving on its own. I overdid it the last few days, is all."

Merrit would have liked to believe that. "You're a right narky old bastard today." She smiled as she said it, liking the way the Irish slang rolled off her tongue. "Or maybe you're an utter geebag. Or a poxbottle?"

Liam settled his head on a pillow, his breath easing. "Away with you. You could simply say 'stubborn old fart.'"

"Okay, you stubborn old fart, you rang?"

"What's that you're doing with Nathan at the cottage?"

"Fixing it up."

"Why?"

Because it's lonely. "I need a project," she said.

"Good timing," Liam said, "because I have a brilliant idea for you."

"That sounds ominous."

"But first, ring that Annie Belden. She's a good one. I could get fond of her." He widened his eyes in a bad imitation of innocence. "I need a shower, and she can help me better than you can."

He'd showered all by himself last night. "Mm-hmm, right."

"Then she can fix lunch." He handed her a slip of paper. "Here's her number."

"What, no Zoe today?"

"Not today. After my shower, you can invite Nathan over for more dessert."

"Oh, for crying out loud," she said. "They don't need a matchmaker. They're fine on their own."

His expression turned serious. "They need a push. Annie could help Nathan, but they need more time together for that to happen. Without Zoe to distract Nathan. Better yet, let Annie be the one to help him in the cottage. Grand idea, that."

"She may not want to help with the cottage."

"She will." He shifted in his chair. "I think I'll rest awhile before she arrives."

Taking the hint, Merrit walked back out of the house while dialing Annie's number. Halfway to the cottage, Annie agreed to visit and Merrit remembered that Liam had said he had a "brilliant idea" for her. Whatever it was, she had a feeling she'd rather not know.

TWENTY-TWO

O'NEIL WAITED FOR DANNY outside the hospital. He leaned against his car in the no-parking zone in front of the entrance and waved at drivers to go around him. Danny had sent Marcus home with the children hours ago, and after that, the waiting had resonated with the fizz of the overhead fluorescent lights, agitating him and sapping his energy at the same time. By the time the staff had bundled Ellen into an ambulance for transport to the hospital in Limerick, he'd felt bug-eyed and starved. Only, in his case, rather than nutrients he craved knowledge.

No joy there. Once the Limerick hospital got a hold of her, it could be a full day before he received news. It scared him that for a split second he'd stopped the doctor from inserting the oxygen tube. Relief had surged through him. Maybe he would no longer need to live a half life of waiting, of wondering. He could let her go and, best yet, do so without having made the tough choice.

A split second for this essential tawdry truth to reveal itself: He was a coward.

When Danny cornered the doctor again, he learned that, besides pneumonia, Ellen was at risk for congestive heart failure and something called acute respiratory distress syndrome.

"When can you pull the ventilator tube out of her?" he asked.

"As soon as the fluid in her lungs dissipates."

"When will that be?"

"It's hard to say. With luck, within a week."

With luck. With sodding luck? He longed to pound the word out of the doctor's skull. If they depended on luck then he could just as well wave sage sticks or ask Nathan's daughter, the so-called healer, to perform the laying on of hands.

The sound of Ellen's gagging reaction to the tube plagued him, the first sound he'd heard out of her since she'd fallen into the coma. A sound like a plea, begging the hospital and him to release her.

He forced his thoughts away from Ellen and back into the car as O'Neil sped them toward Lisfenora. After an initial questioning look, O'Neil drove as if he always picked Danny up from the hospital on Saturdays.

"We're contacting the family members of each person who died under Elder Joe's care," O'Neil said. "There are surprisingly few of them."

"He had a knack for picking lodgers with families like old Cecil's back there," Danny said. "Fancy that."

O'Neil clicked his tongue in disgust. "Cecil have anything new to add?"

"Elder Joe did most of the yelling after Frances Madden died, not the second man."

They had turned off the N87 from Ennis in the direction of the ocean rather than north toward Lisfenora. Ten minutes later, O'Neil pulled up in front of a low-slung brown and yellow building nestled on the edge of acres of meticulous rolling green lawns.

"Joe Junior could be anywhere," Danny said, "doing whatever it is groundskeepers do."

"Groundskeeper? That would be 'golf course superintendent' to you and me, matey."

Inside the Lahinch Golf Course clubhouse, Danny gazed out the wall of windows toward the Dough Castle tower ruins that sat in the middle of one of the two golf courses. It stuck up like a sentinel while white dots that were the Goats of Lahinch grazed nearby.

"What are you doing here?"

Mrs. O'Brien's proprietary voice called Danny's attention away from the goats. Along with her usual black dress she wore red lipstick that accentuated her thin lips. She eyed him like she'd caught out a poacher on the aristocrat's land.

"Routine work," he said. "Have you seen Joe Junior—Joe Madden—in the vicinity?"

She blanched. "Him? I know him, of course. He does a fine job here." She rubbed down her dress. "If you'll excuse me."

O'Neil returned from talking to the club manager. "What was that about?"

"Bloody hell if I know. We're about to sully the reputation of this fine club, I expect."

"Ay, then let's go about it. Joe's at the Devil's Pit. Hole 12."

O'Neil drove them along the Liscannor Road to a maintenance area and parked beside a pile of fresh sod. They walked into the green along an access path. A gentle curve revealed a view of the long fairway that ran alongside the Inagh River as it entered the Atlantic. Several goats popped their heads up from grazing and surveyed the men with inquisitive brown eyes. One of them ambled along with them, ears perking in their direction every now and then.

"You can take the lead with the questioning." Danny didn't want to admit how weary he felt. "You don't haunt Alan's pub the way I do."

"And I don't know Joe Junior personal-like, I get it."

They reached the lip of the trap called the Devil's Pit, a grass-covered divot in the earth that was deeper than it looked from afar. A golfer could lose a ball forever down there. Danny didn't play golf, so he couldn't imagine how the players lobbed balls back onto the green.

"Jesus, man!" Joe Junior shouted. "Stop right there."

Rather than his usual frowsy man-cardigan, Joe Junior wore heavy twill dungarees laden with pockets, a wind cheater over a fisherman's jumper, and a woolen skull cap. He hadn't noticed Danny and O'Neil yet. He half ran, half slid down the side of the pit to where several men stood around an overturned power lawn mower.

O'Neil waited until Joe Junior had helped right the mower before calling to him. "Mr. Madden, got a minute?"

Joe Junior squinted up at them. With a running start, he clambered up the steep slope using his hands.

"We won't take much of your time," O'Neil said.

"Hope not, laddie." He jerked a thumb toward one of the groundskeepers. "That waste of space thought he'd mow the grass inside the Devil's Pit. Now I'll be needing a hauler to drag the bloody thing out."

The goat that had followed Danny and O'Neil nudged Joe Junior's hand. Joe Junior dug into his pocket and produced a slice of carrot for her. "Molly here knows how to work it."

He led them to the end of the green where the grass petered out into a sandy slope down to a narrow beach. He hopped a shambling white picket fence. The wind gusted stray rain droplets against them. He looked from one to the other of them until Danny tilted his head toward O'Neil.

"That way, is it?" Joe Junior turned toward O'Neil. "Detective, what's it about then?"

"We have questions about your aunt, Frances Madden. We're interested in her time as EJ's lodger."

Joe Junior avoided looking at Danny. He dug into the sand with the toe of his boot and stooped to dig out a golf ball. "Right," he said. "That. God rest her. She raised me, she did."

"See," O'Neil said, "we know that she died at EJ's house and you weren't happy."

Careful there. Perhaps Danny should have taken on this conversation, after all. He knew Joe Junior well enough to converse with him fella to fella. He was starting to bridle at O'Neil's tone, his lips pursed like a little old lady's.

"No, I wasn't happy." Joe Junior continued wandering with eyes trained on the ground. "Would you be?"

Answer his question, fella to fella. Instead, O'Neil kept on track. "We're curious why you never mentioned an aunt who died."

One more mention of the word *die* and Joe Junior would fling the golf ball at O'Neil's head, full stop. Danny held up a hand. *Slow down.* O'Neil nodded.

"My favorite aunt passed away last month," O'Neil said. "It's a shock, even when you know it's coming."

Joe Junior long-armed the golf ball he held into the river, where it bobbed for a moment before sinking into the current. "That's the point, Detective. I didn't know it was coming."

"Oh?"

"Don't 'oh' me, for feck's sake. I know what you're fishing for, and you'd be right for guessing I no longer considered EJ a friend. But we landed on bygones and enough said."

"I hadn't noticed a difference between you two at the pub," Danny said.

"I'm after saying that. Made no bloody matter."

"It would be helpful to have the entire story," O'Neil said.

"Fine. EJ said he would help Aunt Franny recuperate from pneumonia. All she needed was another week or two of rest. We don't have money for proper continuing care, and EJ said he did caretaking on the side. I trusted the wanker."

Pneumonia. Danny watched a little egret skim the waves close to shore. "She was breathing okay when she arrived at EJ's? No fever?"

"I'm telling you she was past the worst. She needed a body to wait on her, that's all. I would have taken her myself but I work long hours." Joe Junior spat. "She was brought back to life by the miracle of modern medicine only to be dragged down again by that useless baggage."

Right, miracle. Danny stepped ahead of Joe Junior to pick up yet another stray golf ball.

"That doesn't sound like bygones to me," O'Neil said.

"What the bloody hell would you know?"

Danny tossed the golf ball from hand to hand. "Detective O'Neil has a point. You're still angry, so how did you reach a truce?"

"I persuaded EJ to refund my money for her care."

"What did your persuasion consist of?" O'Neil said.

"Nothing but words with a reminder that he wouldn't be welcome at the pubs if I happened to talk about my grief and the cause for my grief. Couldn't live without a pub, our Elder Joe, and who knows, maybe word would circle back to the guards. Maybe to you, Danny."

"You invoked my name?" Danny said.

"Indeed I did."

"He paid?" O'Neil said.

"Indeed he did, but he wasn't happy." Joe Junior smiled with lingering spite. "Bellowing like a demented banshee."

"Where were you Friday night?" O'Neil asked.

"I saw EJ at the pub, as usual, if that's what you want to know. I went home. Alone. Don't know what more I can say about that since I live alone."

"What time was that and was EJ still at the pub when you left?"

"I was home by eleven on the dot. When I left, EJ was hunkered over his pint talking his usual shite. On a roll he was, about his bloody chickens. The gobshite loved his chickens."

"How did EJ get home that night?"

"Like I said, I'd left by then. And I was alone after that. Alan probably rang a taxi man. Now if you'll excuse me."

Danny led the way back to the car with Molly the Goat trotting beside O'Neil. Rain patters landed on their faces and hands.

"Get the feeling he wasn't as alone as he said?"

"He doth protest too much," O'Neil mused.

"Must be good if he's willing to go un-alibied."

TWENTY-THREE

SEVERAL HOURS AFTER MERRIT left Nathan to get on with the house painting, he staggered out of one of Fox Cottage's bedrooms. He stopped midway across the living room, listening. Back in the bedroom, Annie snuffled in her sleep, the lightest of whimpering breaths. So, she had nightmares of her own. The thought comforted him. He almost turned back to wake her from her doze and ask her what she saw in her dreams. Instead, he made his way to the kitchen to drink water from the taps. The pipes gurgled and shot out a tepid orange stream of water. Nathan spat out the water and coughed against the metallic taste of it.

He returned to the living room, pausing again. Time had gotten away from him, and realizing that, his vision wavered around the edges. He caught hold of the fireplace mantel and stood still, reaching inward for the normal part of himself that didn't lose time. He closed his eyes, but it was too late. His hands shook and the buzzing began at the base of his skull.

"Stop it," he said, his voice sounding far away.

Nothing would happen to him here in Fox Cottage with a lovely naked woman in the next room. This was a safe place. Eyes still closed, he inched his hand along the mantel to the wall and let the wall lead him back to the bedroom. He jerked back at a sticky sensation—*blood*.

No, wet paint on newly painted walls, he reminded himself.

He opened an eye. Fingerprints in the paint, and paint on his hand. He squinted against the racket inside his head, his gaze still on the wall, but his focus on the rest of the room. An empty room. Nothing to fear here. He stood alone, and being alone, he was safe. He knew this.

Sunlight flared between passing clouds, brightening the room. With care, Nathan turned his head. He stood near inset shelves filled with dusty books. He continued swiveling his head. Nothing but a side chair, a pot without a plant, a plastic-shrouded couch. Paint fumes increased the pounding in his head.

Outside, the clouds shifted again. From the corner of the room, a metallic glint sprang out at him. Sharp in a beam of light, aiming itself at him. He ducked toward the bedroom, toward Annie, fingertips scrabbling against bare floorboards. The cotton batting that encased him squeezed, crushing his breath, squashing his reason.

A touch seared his back. He flattened himself onto the floor, but the tentacle grabbed tight enough to smother. More tentacles engulfed him until he couldn't breathe. No returning from the brink this time. He wilted, too exhausted to fight any longer.

After a while, he caught the strains of a melody. Below the blood thumping against his ear drums, a tune with no beginning and no end. He latched onto it and climbed up its notes like a lifeline.

"There now," Annie said. "Deep breaths."

She lay next to him on the floor, wrapped in a sheet. After several minutes, the molten press of one of her arms and one of her legs softened to the warmth of her skin pressed against his. Nathan caught his breath as his senses returned to him. The cool wood floorboards, the rain percussion, the stink of fresh paint. Fox Cottage, that was all.

On shaking limbs, he rose onto all fours and then to his feet. His body felt stiff, misused, unreliable. He glanced down at himself as he walked into the bedroom with mud-colored walls. He still wore his t-shirt but nothing else.

Behind him, Annie's sheet dragged on the floor. He yanked on his underwear and jeans with bum facing her, the ultimate disrespect, before turning to her. Better to get it over with, but rather than disgust or judgment, Annie smiled at him.

"You're full of surprises," she said. "Are you feeling better now?"

The breath he'd been holding fell out of him. "That's never happened before."

She cocked her head as if puzzled. "No?"

"It's fine. I'm fine. I'm not sure what happened."

"And I'm not sure I believe you, but I won't pry any further. As for that"—Annie pointed toward the mussed bed—"I know exactly what happened. You pounced on me."

"I don't pounce."

"Nearabouts anyhow." She let the sheet drop and stood in the center of the room with hands on her hips as she surveyed the ground. Their shoes and her clothes were scattered about, along with the throw pillows from the bed. "No worries. Faster than I usually go, but I've been trying to live in the moment. It's all we have."

Christ in heaven, she was a mighty beauty. He saw her with a sculptor's eyes, the protrusion of her tummy, the rounded contour of her collarbones, the soft flesh of her inner thighs.

"Ah," she said and toed a pillow aside. With a mischievous grin, she twirled her underwear around an index finger. "Can't forget these, can I? Can you imagine?" She hooted with laughter. "Having it off in Liam the Matchmaker's cottage. Talk about wagging tongues."

She collapsed onto the bed, overcome with the hilarity of whatever she was picturing in her head. "Oh my." She wiped laughter tears off her cheeks. "Excuse me, that was most unbecoming of me." She pulled on her underwear and found her jumper. "So much for maintaining a feminine allure."

Nathan perched next to her on the bed, longing for some of her aliveness to rub off on him. Maybe he had pounced on her, but not for the reason she thought. It hadn't been about copulation. It was this, right here. Her vitality. Her resilience. A vampiric need to attach himself to her almost overcame him.

She popped her head out of her jumper. A peep of west-slanting light caught the silver in her hair before the sky closed down again. The rain continued unabated. He glanced out the window. Too much time had passed. He'd arrived before noon, and now it was— he wasn't sure. Well into the afternoon. Past three. "Where's my mobile?"

Annie stood on one foot, hopping around as she fitted her leg into her jeans and pulled them up. After a moment, she said, "On the bed stand."

Nathan grabbed for the mobile, his pulse up into his ears again, zero to one hundred in three seconds flat. Not unusual, he told himself. He was still charged up from whatever had happened—the daytime nightmare. Before today, his mind had only tortured him at night.

With a button push, he had the immediate answer he required to calm down again: Zoe hadn't rung.

"What about Zoe?" Annie said as she fastened her belt.

"I'm sorry?"

"You mumbled something about her."

He shoved his mobile into his jeans pocket. "When Zoe gets antsy about me, she leaves messages, but she hasn't, so I'm safe from having to explain my absence."

Annie slipped on comfy-looking clogs. "I'm not a parent, so I'm daft about these things, but wouldn't she assume you're helping Merrit all day?"

Yes, but that didn't lessen the urge to hurry home. He excused his way past Annie and went in search of his shoes in the living room. He winced as sunlight flared again. On the floor, a paint can lid caught and held the light, bright as a beacon. A startle of light. He jammed the lid back on the Afterglow paint can and tamped it down harder than necessary.

Afterglow; Jesus, no afterglow here. As far as he could bloody well get from afterglow. He'd gone mad in broad daylight, all because a glint of light reflected off a paint can lid had ignited the figments inside his head.

TWENTY-FOUR

Sunday, 21-Mar

Fact of sorts: I haven't been in my right mind for the last few days. Fear.

Another fact of sorts: I suppose that's why I slept with Nathan yesterday.

I could have stopped him, but I didn't. He's quite nice with his fingers and lips, nice enough I didn't want him to stop, didn't want me to stop, didn't want our interlude to stop. I was the one who pulled him into the bedroom.

Two hapless creatures falling on each other. Nothing romantic about it. Now I'm sitting here with my morning coffee, trying to fathom Nathan. Bruised and stitched and bandaged Nathan. At one point, something triggered him into a break, and I'll wager anyone he was trying to escape the demons that terrorize him. I suspect he's rarely in his right mind. He breaks my heart.

Fact: Tomorrow is the year anniversary of The Event, as you prefer to call it.

TWENTY-FIVE

HELLO, MORNING. MERRIT PLOWED fingers through her hair and shuffled to her bedroom window. A haze of rain obscured the view of Mullaghamore and the countryside. She always seemed to be looking out windows. Her new pastime, watching the world from afar.

"Fantastic," she mumbled.

A depressing realization first thing in the morning. She needed coffee.

She shuffled into the kitchen only to pull up at the sight of Zoe Tate whistling a ditty as she filled a carafe with fresh coffee. She wore her hair tied back with a blue scarf in a house frau look that managed to emphasize her bone structure and movie star violet eyes. A butterfly pin sparkled from an immaculate cashmere jumper.

If Zoe had a superpower, it wasn't healing—it was maintaining her collection of winter white and ivory clothes in pristine condition. Meanwhile, Merrit's tatty bathrobe was more grey than white and featured holes in the armpits.

"You're here," Merrit said instead of a proper greeting. "Bright and early."

"Liam rang last night. He said you could use a break." Zoe grinned. "I told him about my speciality breakfast—crème brûlée French toast—and he said he wouldn't mind a taste."

Oh, did he? The bugger.

Zoe opened the oven door. The tantalizing scent of brown sugar and vanilla caused Merrit's stomach to grumble. "You have to refrigerate it overnight so I brought it with me."

She poured a fresh cup of coffee and held it out to Merrit, who sighed after her first swallow. Zoe even made a great cup of coffee, blast her.

"I helped Liam get dressed, too. You relax."

Merrit refrained from snickering at the idea that Liam needed help dressing. He wasn't that far along yet, but apparently he wasn't above milking his condition for extra attention in the name of investigating Zoe and her mythical healing properties.

She grumbled. She was the narky one today and not because of Zoe, though her sunny presence didn't help. The night before, Liam had revealed his "brilliant idea" to Merrit. She had no choice but to accept that she was in for the utter bollocks, to use the Irish vernacular.

She cocked her head. No, that wasn't the expression. Never mind. All she knew was that she was going to make a proper bollocks of it.

Yes, that sounded better.

Zoe stood at the counter, gazing toward Fox Cottage, visible through sliding walls of rain. "The cottage doesn't look any different. My dad's helping you, right?"

"We're painting the inside. It'll be nice when we're done."

"I'm glad." Her tone brightened. "It's good for him to get out of the house. He's such a recluse."

The doorbell rang. Merrit waved Zoe back toward the oven and muttered her way out of the kitchen. There had to be a way to stop the incessant well-meaning-ness of the Lisfenorans. Might as well be inside Grand Central Station these days.

She swung open the front door and almost spilled her coffee in surprise.

"Looks like you didn't sleep much last night, either," Danny said.

"What are you doing here?"

"You wanted me to visit more often, didn't you? We had a deal." He frowned. "Or have you already forgotten?"

She crossed her fingers. "No meddling with Nathan. I got it."

He crowded through the door and unpeeled his raincoat, scattering raindrops in the process. Merrit grabbed a random scarf off the coat rack and handed it to him. Danny patted his face dry. He wore his fatigue like a well-worn cap, with brown eyes revealing more hidden depths than usual. "Thought I'd drop in on my way to Limerick."

Something had happened. "Ellen?" she said.

"Breakfast is ready," Zoe called.

Danny whipped his head toward the kitchen.

"Too much Pollyanna in the morning for my taste," Merrit said, "but her French toast smells delicious."

Zoe popped her head around the swing door. "'Allo? French toast!"

"Settle down," Liam called from the corridor that led to the bedrooms.

"DS Ahern, hello again," Zoe said at the same time that Liam's delight made itself known: "Danny boyo, you're a sight for the saints."

Danny stepped forward to escort Liam into the kitchen. Liam's cane tapped the hardwoods while Zoe propped the door open. Merrit hung back, longing for her bed and a novel, but letting her curiosity about Danny's visit prod her toward the kitchen and the scent of Zoe's indulgent breakfast. Would probably be perfect, too, blast her again.

Merrit hadn't realized she'd grumbled aloud until Danny glanced in her direction.

"Don't mind her," Liam mock-whispered, "she's fit to be tied this morning and it's all my fault."

"Bah humbug to us all then," Danny said.

Zoe clapped her hands. "No bah humbugs allowed in my kitchen. I get enough of that at home from my dad. Grouchy pants, he is."

"She's making herself at home," Danny said in the low voice.

"You can thank Liam for that," Merrit said.

Zoe had already set the kitchen island and filled their plates with the custardy French toast. Steam dripped down the windows along with the drenching rain. The coffee machine issued cozy percolating noises. She'd even gathered a jaunty bouquet of daffodils for the center of the island.

No wonder Nathan was a grouchy pants. Who'd want to wake up to the perfection that was Zoe every morning? Zoe joined them on a stool and ate with gusto, keeping up a jovial stream of conversation. Danny sat across from Zoe, eating and observing her. Gauging her. Merrit knew the look because she'd been on the receiving end of it herself.

Zoe pushed her empty plate aside and sat back with a contented pat to her flat tummy. "Now, tell me all about the bah humbugs. I think I've nattered on enough."

Danny frowned, but other than that, no one responded. Zoe hauled an armful of dishes to the sink. She puttered in the background, ignoring the dishwasher in favor of filling the sink with sudsy water.

Liam placed a hand on Danny's arm. "Now then, I know Merrit used her persuasive tactics to bamboozle you into visiting again so soon, but I don't care. I'm glad you're here. What brings you?"

"Persuasive, ay, that's a way to put it." Danny rubbed his forehead. "Perhaps it was time."

"Merrit notwithstanding?" Liam said.

"Merrit notwithstanding."

Merrit let them have the jab. Liam had been joking, of course; Danny, not so much. She realized she didn't care. Joking at her expense had to be good for their relationship.

"What's your mischief, old troll?" Danny said. "Merrit doesn't look happy this morning."

"You're deflecting the conversation." Liam sipped his coffee. "And we're not telling yet, anyhow. You'll have to come to the pub tonight for the grand announcement."

Zoe let a dish slide into the water. She turned around, clapping her hands. "I love surprises! I'll be there."

"Can we move on, please?" Merrit said.

"As you wish." Liam patted her hand. "You'll do fine." He addressed Danny. "How's Ellen?"

Danny glanced at Zoe. Liam nodded the okay. Merrit reserved judgment about whether or not Zoe should be privy to Danny's private business. As Danny explained Ellen's health scare and transfer to Limerick, Zoe's clattering slowed and stopped.

"Under control for the moment," Danny ended, "but the ordeal has brought up some issues I need to think about for the long term. I thought I'd hash them out with you, Liam, but not now, after all."

Merrit could tell by his rigid stance that Zoe's presence made him uncomfortable.

Zoe dried her hands and leaned toward Danny with elbows on the counter. "I'm sorry to hear this, Detective. I had no idea. If you ever need any help—with Ellen, I mean—please let me know. You'll do that?"

Zoe returned to the dishes and Danny set his coffee cup aside. He rose, announcing that he should be getting on, the hospital awaited. Merrit walked with him to the front door. Danny shook out his soggy coat harder than necessary.

"Did that girl," he said, "offer what I think she offered? To heal Ellen?"

"Sounded like it."

"God help me, slap me silly if I ever consider her shite."

"With pleasure."

He smiled, the warm embers of him still alive beneath his concerns and stress. "I'll wager that."

Zoe's laughter floated toward them from the kitchen and followed Danny's sprint to his car. The wind blew stinging drops against Merrit's skin. She could have sworn she'd seen hope on Danny's face. For a second, his desperation leapt toward Zoe before he vanquished it. Zoe was either madder than a box of frogs or the most foolishly kind-hearted girl on the planet. Or maybe both at the same time.

TWENTY-SIX

NATHAN STOOD UP AND placed his hands on his lower back for a stretch. He'd turned on all the lights, creating a cozy studio oasis against the damp and wind. He had the house to himself. Even better, he'd spoken with Annie. After an awkward start, she'd agreed to accompany him to Ennis after Zoe returned with the car.

"Let me pick you up," she said. "I like driving."

"You're grand. It's my errand. I'll pick you up and drop you off."

"Nathan—" She hesitated. "It's about Zoe, I'm guessing. You want to keep me secret."

"That obvious, eh?" He'd woken this morning feeling somewhat alive, as if he'd slept decently for a few hours. It was a miracle. She was a miracle. He rushed in, words overtaking him. "I want to see you. Yesterday was—"

"Yes?"

"Yesterday was pure madness. We both know I was odder than a one-eyed potato." Annie laughed, that sound like chimes. "I would like to know you better, without hassle or interference, that's all."

At some point, he'd explain about Zoe. If not everything then at least how complicated it was between them—complicated in a way that he avoided acknowledging to himself most of the time.

He sealed a plastic container filled with white crackle glaze and shifted it under his worktable. He had thirty-six pots glazed and ready for firing now. Zoe would be back by noon, which gave him plenty of time to pick up Annie at one o'clock.

After washing up in the kitchen, he wrapped his injured hand in a clean bandage while eyeing the countertop knife block that Zoe had gifted him. The knives pricked at him, inciting his imagination and kickstarting his terror. Zoe should have known displaying them like that would trouble him. The knives were best kept in a drawer, out of sight.

He hesitated, then pulled the knives out of the holder. He settled an old placemat in a drawer and laid the knives down side by side on top of it.

Now for the knife block itself. Zoe had bought a nice one. A lid-less wooden box filled with black sand so that the knives wouldn't dull as fast. He set it beside the phone and stuck a message pad and various pens into the sand. Nothing wrong with that.

By the time Zoe returned, he'd boxed up ten finished vases for the gallery in Ennis that managed to stay in business despite the crap economy. Her voice called out, followed by trotting footsteps. She arrived with hand pressed against her chest. "You're after scaring the skin off me. Don't do that."

"Here I am, same as most days."

She dipped her shoulders, one then the other, to slip her coat off. "No, that. In there." She pointed with her chin. "The knives. They're gone. Vanished. What was I supposed to think?"

Nathan taped a box closed. The stitches on his forehead itched. Now he wasn't sure why he'd hidden the knives away. His squeamishness wasn't related to what he might do. Or perhaps it was.

He shook his head and reached for the next box. No. Zoe couldn't have mislaid the facts of the matter. It should have been obvious enough to her.

"What are you doing there?" she asked.

"I've got to make a gallery run."

"Fun!" Zoe clapped her hands. "Give me three minutes to change."

A sensation like doom crawled up Nathan's spine. He couldn't force the *no* out of his mouth if he tried. "Go on then," he managed.

"Three minutes, tops," she called as she bounded up the stairs.

Detesting himself, Nathan pulled out his mobile and texted Annie. CAN'T MAKE IT. I'LL EXPLAIN LATER.

TWENTY-SEVEN

DANNY SAT IN ONE of the Plough's wingback chairs near the fireplace, trying to slough off the day before heading home. Joe Junior arrived and threw Danny a terse nod as he passed him by on the way to his usual spot at the bar, where Nathan already sat nursing a Guinness. He leaned in to Nathan. Whatever he said, Nathan responded with a head shake.

No, Danny could have told them, he wasn't on duty. After breakfast at Liam's, he'd spent the day in the hospital while monitoring the sagging investigation into EJ's death through text messages and phone calls. He swore he lost a day off his life for every hour he spent in the hospital. It didn't help that he'd alternated between guilt for letting work take a backseat to family and more guilt for yearning for the work.

Danny set aside his half-full pint. All he tasted was bitterness. Time for dinner with the kidlings and an early bed. He'd hear about Liam's grand announcement tomorrow in the midst of catching up with the investigation.

Zoe entered the pub from the rear, accompanied by Alan, who couldn't get a word in against Zoe's enthusiastic gesticulations. They stopped to admire Alan's reconstructed wall of Clare artifacts and photos. Danny caught the words "wall sconces." Perhaps she was positioning herself as a healer for interior decors, too.

Nathan swiveled on his stool to watch her, his expression inscrutable, and returned to slouching when Zoe took her leave of Alan.

Danny dropped money for his pint on a side table. A gust of chilly air just this side of spring entered the pub along with Liam and Merrit, with O'Neil catching the door to enter after them. He waved at Danny. "Thought you'd be here," he called.

Annoyed, Danny picked up his pint again. While he waited for O'Neil to join him, his gaze wandered back to Zoe. Now she stood with a couple of young bucks who hung on every word she said. To look at her, you wouldn't think she harbored fanciful notions about herself.

O'Neil arrived and relaxed into the chair next to Danny. Danny forestalled his questions about Ellen with a prompt for the latest information about the case. "What did I miss today?"

"Nothing of note," O'Neil said. "Less than nothing, a black hole of nothing. You were right about EJ. He preferred his lodgers to come from, let's call them 'non-loving' families." His eyes flickered toward the bar where Merrit and Liam sat along with the rest of the regulars. "We found the taxi man who drove him home. He dropped him off and went straight to another call."

From the other side of the pub, the discordant sound of a drumstick clanging a cowbell interrupted Danny's conversation with O'Neil. "Excuse me," Alan called. "Shut your maws. Liam has an announcement."

Liam stood. He coughed into a handkerchief that he carried with him these days, but his grin was still the one of old—a little mischievous, a little mysterious. "As most of you know, I've been spending a lot of time at home. Yes, yes"—he waved down the condolences—"my health isn't optimal. The point is that I have too much time on my hands. And I've had a thought."

Next to Liam, Merrit patted her chest and turned aside to root around in her purse. While Liam drew out the suspense with a funny matchmaking anecdote about a documentary film crew that had attempted to film him, Merrit found her inhaler, as Danny knew she would. She shot the spray into her lungs. Her chest expanded in a full breath. Her shoulders eased.

Witnessing her struggle for breath reminded Danny of Ellen gagging against the oxygen tube. If she were here now, she'd scoff at Merrit's distress. She could be a right catty wench, his wife. Danny longed to hear her mutters in his ear, then see the way she'd cast her eyes toward the ceiling with a whispered, *Sorry, I'll stop now*, as if God or Jesus, or both since she was a believer, floated out of sight but within earshot.

So much for her faith. She had nothing to show for it but her own personal purgatory.

"Right then, now for my announcement," Liam said. "For my last hoorah as matchmaker, I invite everyone to my house on Easter Sunday for a spring festival. I consider it my final bacchanalia, a nod to the pagan spring fertility gods. Even though I'm on the way out"—he waved a hand at the protesters again—"spring is a time of resurgence, of new beginnings, and rebirth. We'll celebrate with a few traditions, but the star of the show will be Merrit."

In the profound silence that followed Liam's announcement, Danny heard a toilet flushing at the other end of the pub. Merrit's shoulders inched up toward her ears, and even Liam seemed to be at a loss. Perhaps Merrit had protected him from the worst of the locals' dismissal of her.

"Jaysus," O'Neil said, "she looks like she's about to be pilloried."

Liam rapped his cane against the floor with three hard knocks. "Listen up, you bloody bastards. Even I can't cheat death. Change is change, and you're in for it. The least we can do is celebrate it and welcome Merrit into the fold." He glared around the room. "And I mean properly. Like it or not, the matchmaking festival will continue with Merrit at its helm."

"I'll welcome Merrit!" Zoe walked to the center of the room for all to see. Her skin glowed and her hair shone like spun gold in the subdued lighting. "Tell us more, Liam."

"Spread the word that, after church services, I'm hosting a spring festival that will include games for kids and a bar for the adults. And most importantly, Merrit as matchmaker. This will be Merrit's debut. Her practice run before this September's festival. I expect everyone there and having a good time."

"I'm first," Zoe called. "You can match me, Merrit!"

Several men eyed her up and down while everyone else returned to their drinks with a subdued air. Liam announcing his latest bowel movement would have garnered more enthusiasm than this.

"Bloody disaster," O'Neil said.

"Could be," Danny said, "but you watch, everyone in the county will be there to see how Merrit handles herself."

Danny stood and put on his coat. It was as hard to imagine Merrit as matchmaker as it was himself a single man seeking the services of a matchmaker. He might as well wrap his heart in plastic wrap and stick it in a drawer. "Anything else about EJ's investigation?"

"One interesting fact, anyhow. About Nathan Tate."

"Oh?"

"He's spent time in a psychiatric hospital."

TWENTY-EIGHT

MERRIT EXCUSED HERSELF FROM Liam and escaped down the corridor to the rear exit. She pushed open the door and inhaled until her lungs crackled. No signs of spring in the air at the moment. She zipped up her jacket and rubbed her hands together. Misty rain cooled her cheeks. Her knee joints felt slippery, as if coated with butter.

She was tempted to walk home. Right now. Stomp off the stress of Liam's illness and his expectations of her. At last, he'd seen for himself what she'd contended with all these months. She'd gone her own way while trying her best not to let the locals' attitudes affect her. They didn't matter. Only her relationship with Liam mattered.

Unfortunately, she did care about their responses to her. Their expressions after Liam's announcement had reminded her of Elder Joe's the day he'd said that thing about sheep and lambs, as if he'd decided to renounce her. He and many others judged her for reasons she didn't understand. In their eyes, she hadn't proved herself, and she'd bet that many of them were convinced she never would. She was a transgressor within the sanctity of their community.

"I'm not ready," Merrit had said when Liam revealed his oh-so-brilliant idea. "More precisely, I'm not you. They want someone like you—the bigger-than-life sort."

"You are ready. Besides, you won't know until you try." He'd paused. "And I must witness your start, of course."

And, of course, he had to play the ace up his sleeve. Merrit had known she couldn't refuse. And it was too late to retreat now. Now the pressure was on to prove herself.

She stepped outside. Behind her, rough wood floorboards creaked under approaching footsteps. Detective O'Neil shimmied through the door before it clicked closed without spilling the two pints he carried. Lights from the neighboring building lit his lopsided smile and thick fringe of hair as he passed her one of the pints.

"That was the bloody bollocks, wasn't it?" he said. "You'd think Liam was selling the antichrist as matchmaker."

Hah, spot-on. She swallowed a mouthful of Guinness. "You didn't know that I'm the antichrist?"

He stepped backwards with eyes rounded in horror and blessed himself with the wrong hand. "*En nomine espiritu sancto, exorcizo—*"

She slapped at him, laughing. "Okay, okay, Mr. Latin, I'm exorcised now."

"Exorcised, me arse. I don't know Latin from leprechaun gibberish."

"On that note," Merrit said, "what can I do for you, Detective?"

"Call me Simon." He shoveled hair off his forehead, his habitual insouciance in place. "Fancy you should ask. You could say yes to dinner."

She swallowed more Guinness to hide her surprise. This had to be a fishing expedition on behalf of Danny and the investigation. Simon as the spy against Merrit's meddling. "Let me see if I'm understanding you correctly. You want to buy us dinner and engage in non-investigative conversation?"

"You're thinking about it too hard, but, yes, that."

A spasm of doubt prevented her from replying. It didn't feel right, not with Liam sick. She almost asked Simon if he'd broached the topic with Danny. There had to be rules about extracurricular dating activities. Danny would disapprove.

"Don't be so bloody American about it," Simon said. "Drink, food, a cracking good time—what's the harm?"

Sod it. This was Simon's personal business. And hers.

"No harm." She swallowed another mouthful of beer. "I'll bite on the cracking good time, Simon O'Neil, not to be mistaken for the playwright Neil Simon."

Simon chinked his pint against hers. "Feisty. I like that."

He turned away to open the back door. Merrit felt her smile sag. A frisson of fear startled her, a vision of dating leading to a relationship leading to marriage. Married to an Irish bloke.

Married to Ireland.

The truth was that she lived with one foot pointing back to her California homeland, telling herself that she was free to leave if things didn't work out. She wasn't wedded to Ireland.

The issue wasn't dating so much as the eventuality of life, the way one event led to another that led to another until the day you woke up trapped in a life you'd never wanted. The issue, she realized, centered around life after Liam and her fear that being her father's daughter—inheriting the matchmaking mantle—would be her trap.

TWENTY-NINE

Monday, 22-Mar

Fact: I'm sitting here drinking midmorning tea with a shot of whiskey and with muscles tight enough to shatter.

I've taken to wandering the house late at night, peeking out the windows, carrying a fireplace poker. I had a man out to install motion sensor lights on every side of the house. Starkers I may be, but I insisted that all the lights be on the same circuit. If one triggers, then they all do, and the motion sensor alarm goes off on the keychain remote I carry on me at all times. I need to see PatientZ coming, you see.

Vanquishing my demon, yes. It must happen one way or another, but I can't bear to be alone today. Yesterday Nathan cancelled an outing with me, no explanation. As his punishment, I'm going to visit him at Fox Cottage. I don't care if this isn't a healthy coping mechanism.

You were right about one thing: I'm using Nathan as a distraction from my fear. But he's using me, too. Maybe he considers me a soul-healing balm he can rub all over him-self. Which is fine. You know I like to be needed.

Fact: If something's going to happen, it will be today—anniversary day.

THIRTY

In Fox Cottage, Nathan leaned his paint roller against the wall and surveyed the bedroom he was about to paint. Exhaustion tugged him toward the bed, where he pulled off the plastic sheeting and wilted onto the mattress. He brushed his hand over the well-washed and softened quilt cover constructed from fabrics left over from a simpler time. A triple Irish chain design, he knew. Susannah had loved vintage quilts. She'd searched everywhere for the perfect baby quilt for Zoe's crib. Susannah would have appreciated this one.

He kicked off his shoes. Nap for an hour, then paint. His muscles, tendons, and ligaments released with a silent groan as he relaxed. The blissful quietude of this cottage. Nothing but the rain on the roof to lull him into a sense of safety. His head sank deeper into the pillow. He lost track of time for a while, but then the rain returned. Warmth spread through him. He shifted back into it, wanted to burrow into the heat source.

A hand touched his cheek, the press of fingers, and he jerked away with hammering heart. He landed on the floor with a painful thump against his knees.

"Nathan, my God," Annie said. "It's only me."

"Not a bother. I startle when I'm asleep, anyone touching me, you know—"

But she didn't know; that was evident enough.

"I didn't mean to startle you," she said. "You looked peaceful and also chilly."

Nathan crawled back onto the bed and felt the mattress shift when Annie spooned him. She lay stiff behind him. He grabbed her arm and slung it over his body. "You're grand. Touch me all the way to Bombay and back."

"But not when you're asleep, is that it?"

"I'm a fragile lad."

"We're all fragile in our ways."

He rolled onto his back and she snuggled into him, her head a perfect fit under his chin. His body responded randy as a teenager, but he remained still, resisting yet relishing the urge to press himself all over and into Annie.

"You don't seem fragile to me," he said. "The opposite, in fact."

"Hah," she snorted. "If you only knew."

"I could know if you'd tell me."

She hugged herself against him. "Thank you for saying that. Maybe sometime. It's been a brutal few days. Today's an anniversary that's not the kind you celebrate."

"I have a few anniversaries like that, myself."

She petted his arm, playing with the fabric of his shirt, tracing his biceps. He had good arms, he knew that—a byproduct of working with clay—but he didn't think about them unless someone else noticed them.

Annie poked him. "And," she said.

"And?"

"And your terse text message yesterday didn't help. Why did you cancel our outing to the art gallery?"

"Okay, that's it." He grabbed her by the waist and swung her on top of him so that she straddled him.

She grinned when she felt him below her. "You. Nice way to avoid answering."

Every nerve ending in his body aimed itself at his groin, the signals overwhelming everything else, including coherent conversation. Annie quit laughing and struggled with his arms to yank his t-shirt off while he struggled with her belt to pull off her jeans. A haze of limbs. He obliged her by raising his arms, the press of cotton over his face, and then her hands landed on his chest.

"Look at you," she sighed.

She spread-eagled her fingers and inched them down toward his jeans. He shifted but restrained himself from forcing her to quicken the pace. He enjoyed the exquisite torture. Her hands tensed against his skin and went still.

Oh, shite. He'd kept his t-shirt on the first time they'd met up on this bed, but in his haze he'd forgotten today.

He rolled away from her, his erection forgotten, already disappearing.

"No," she said. "Let me see."

She grappled him onto his back again. Her eyes locked on the area between his hip bone and belly button. Her fingers traced the scar to where it disappeared into his jeans. The skin was numb—the nerve endings had never healed—but the pressure of her finger was enough to want to fling her off him.

He held his breath, his heart racing. To his surprise, she didn't ask him to explain the scar. She relaxed on top of him. Her spiky, short hair tickled under his chin. He inhaled her fragrance. She didn't have a strong scent, perhaps because she didn't use perfumed products, and he liked this.

The rain softened, allowing the real world to enter his sanctuary. Down the track near Liam's house, a car door slammed and Merrit called a greeting. Nathan scrambled out of bed and pulled on his t-shirt as he ran into the living room. The main window provided a perfect view toward Liam's house, where Zoe hugged Merrit hello and gestured toward Fox Cottage.

Nathan ran back into the bedroom. "You have to leave. Zoe's here."

Annie gazed at him in that frank way of hers. "You're overreacting?"

Perhaps, yes, but that didn't change the fact that he didn't want Zoe to find Annie here.

Annie obliged him by pulling on her jeans. "Zoe's a grown woman. She must know you have a life."

As gently as he could manage, he placed his hands on Annie's shoulders and steered her toward the kitchen and back door. "It's hard to explain."

She stopped. "I'm not running away and I'm not hiding. We're not doing anything wrong."

"Dad?" Zoe knocked on the door. "You there? Need some help?"

"Go. Please." Nathan's vision wobbled around the edges. He pushed at Annie. "Please."

Instead of exiting through the back door, she grabbed his chin and forced him to look at her. "What is this really about?"

"It's more complicated than you know."

The front door opened. "Dad? A friend dropped me off. Bored out of my mind at home."

Annie's gaze remained on his, studying him before stepping away and refastening her belt. "Hi, Zoe," she called in a jaunty voice. "I'm admiring the color in the kitchen. Cheerful, don't you think?"

Nathan leaned against the counter with shaking hands behind his bum. Thank Christ they stood in the kitchen rather than the bedroom. He felt faint with the "if"s. If the rain hadn't stopped so he could hear beyond the cottage. If Annie hadn't seen his scar and halted them right before having sex. The thought of Zoe interrupting their antics on the bed made his scar ache.

"I love the living room." Zoe bounced into the kitchen. Her warm smile included Annie in the conversation. "The kitchen looks nice, too. Merrit picked the colors, didn't she?" She leaned into Nathan to give him a quick kiss on the cheek before hooking her arm around Annie's in a companionable way. "Did you hear about Liam's Easter party? Merrit will be matchmaking for the first time. You want to be a guinea pig with me?"

Nathan expelled a long, slow breath.

THIRTY-ONE

DANNY PULLED UP IN front of Nathan's semidetached home, located at the end of a row of identical semidetached homes. The tidy and uniform house surprised him, but perhaps it provided camouflage—or comfort?—for a man who had been institutionalized. Nothing better than living in a housing estate to prove your normality.

A folder sat on the passenger seat. He opened it to peruse the minimal facts that O'Neil had collected about Nathan. It would take them a while to wrangle the details about his mental health out of the system, but this would do for a start.

A compact Nissan SUV that Danny recognized as Nathan's swung into the driveway as he walked to the front door. Nathan shot out of the car, followed by Zoe.

"Detective Sergeant!" Zoe said. "Good timing. We've been house painting at Liam's cottage."

Nathan passed Danny with barely a nod of acknowledgment. Zoe kept up a patter as they caught up with Nathan at the front door, where he attempted and failed to fit his house key into the lock. "You need to talk to me, I suppose," he said to Danny.

"Please, Dad." Zoe held out her hand for the keys. "Don't do this."

"Can you leave?" Nathan turned on her, not in anger, but in desperation. "Please. You mentioned going into Ennis."

Zoe smiled at Danny. "He'll get used to me yet, you'll see." She patted her dad's hand. Nathan flinched when she touched his bandage. "I did mean to go to Ennis, didn't I? There's a sale at this lovely little shop that Mrs. O'Brien told me about. I looked it up online last night. I'd like to buy an Easter outfit." She laughed. "Just like a girl, wanting a new Easter dress."

Nathan rested his forehead against the door.

"Remember Mum?" Zoe continued. "How she'd dress in her Easter finery before we woke up? She'd be waiting for us in the kitchen, dressed in a color she wouldn't be caught dead wearing except on Easter. She hated pastels, but she always looked perfect, didn't she? In pink or yellow with a ridiculous hat that made me laugh."

Nathan frowned with his eyes closed.

"I suppose that's why I want an Easter dress," she said.

She clattered down the steps in her immaculate heeled boots while burrowing in her purse. Nathan straightened and watched his daughter with frown still in place. Danny stepped backwards to give him some space. Nathan didn't move until the car turned the corner and disappeared. He exhaled long and slow.

"Shall we go inside?" Danny said.

Nathan unlocked the door and waved Danny into the house. "She changed the past."

"What?" Danny said.

"Not important. A thought that should have remained in my head."

Danny followed Nathan into the kitchen and took a seat at a rustic farm table. Two cups half-filled with cold coffee sat on the counter along with an empty knife block. Everything about Nathan felt more significant now that Danny knew he'd graduated from a psych ward.

"What did you mean by Zoe changing the past?" Danny said.

Nathan rummaged around the refrigerator and plonked two beers on the table as he sat down across from Danny. They left wet rings that he didn't bother to wipe up. "It doesn't matter."

"I prefer to decide that for myself."

For the first time since Danny had arrived, Nathan looked him in the eye. "I'm telling you, it has nothing to do with EJ's death. That's why you're here, right? More questions?"

"You avoid talking about Zoe. Why is that?"

"Hard to know what to say."

"She's a delightful young woman."

"And look at this place. It's immaculate. I should consider myself lucky."

"But you don't?"

Nathan didn't oblige him by filling in the silence about all the many ways he should feel lucky. Instead, he sipped his beer.

"You're an expert at silence. A trick learned inside the psychiatric hospital?" Danny took out the single sheet of paper stored inside the folder he'd brought inside with him. He tapped it. "It says here that you were in the Broadmoor Psychiatric Hospital in England for two years starting in 2004."

"That would be correct."

His voice had no affect, as if they discussed the common cold.

"You were committed about a year after your wife Susannah's death."

Nathan picked at the label on his beer.

"She came from money, your wife. She was educated, had a posh accent, I imagine, and an expensive home in Sussex." Danny sat back, crossed his legs, and entered into the spirit of the story. "The

Internet is wonderful, isn't it? I zoomed in on the property to get a feel for your life back then. Quite the life it was. Landscaped gardens and a country house ready-made for a movie set. Susannah dealt in fine art, but here she was married to a scruffy Irish potter. You can see how the police were interested in you after she died."

"She was a lovely person, my wife," Nathan said. "We had a wonderful life together."

"I'm sure you did. You, your wife, and your equally lovely daughter."

Nathan nodded.

"The police didn't find evidence of wrongdoing. Susannah's death was a tragedy. A fall down the stairs. Broken neck. Your recovery from the grief didn't go well, and a year later the white coats escorted you to Broadmoor. Zoe was fourteen at the time. She went off to live with your in-laws."

Nathan set his beer on the table so the bottle aligned with the wet ring. He gazed out the window without expression.

"Two years later, you were released, but instead of a joyous reunion with your lovely daughter, you returned to Ireland and got lost. You did everything legally possible not to be found again. Moving often, not using the Internet, keeping your pottery business local. Meanwhile, poor Zoe was abandoned by the one living parent she had."

"Crap father, yeah, but not for the story you think you understand."

"I'm interested in *your* story," Danny said.

Nathan swung his head toward Danny. The movement seemed to require an effort of will. Danny expected his vertebrae to creak under the strain. Nathan gripped the edge of the table and levered himself into a standing position. Danny forced himself to remain still and silent as Nathan undid the top button of his jeans. He let them sag low on his hips and pulled up his t-shirt. A monstrous red scar snaked its way out from under his jeans. The tissue appeared thick and inflamed, even though the scar was old.

Danny's gaze drifted back to the empty knife block. "Knife attack?"

"You could say that." Nathan sank back onto his chair without buttoning his jeans again. He returned to staring out the window.

Danny leaned forward. "Nathan, listen up. You look like warmed-over shite." He pointed at the stitches on Nathan's head and the bandage on his hand. "Are you on the way toward another stay at a hospital?"

Nathan snorted, a half smile rising and falling again. "Good question."

"For Christ's sake, man, talk."

"I showed Annie my scar today, too. The day of my unveiling." He grabbed Danny's untouched beer, opened it, and drank half of it down in three long swallows. "Why are you here? It can't be about my Father of the Year award."

"Did EJ ever talk to you about your stay at Broadmoor?"

Nathan's confusion appeared sincere. "Why would he?"

"Wondering if he knew about your past."

"You think I'd kill him for knowing that fact? He may have poked through my things, but if he discovered anything, he never let on." He stood. "Finished now?"

Back on the front stoop, Danny said, "Need a lift anywhere? Zoe might be hours buying an Easter dress. Fond memories of her mother and all."

Nathan shook his head. "Zoe forgot to mention that every year Susannah had matching dresses handmade for her and Zoe. Zoe hated those dresses."

"Memories have a way of softening over time, especially after a tragedy." Danny thought of Ellen as he said this, a fleeting acknowledgment that these days he didn't linger on their marital estrangement so much as their good times together.

"Yes," Nathan said, but he didn't sound certain. "Or memories slip away altogether."

"Do you remember your time at Broadmoor?"

"Not well. A haze of drugs. Why?"

"We don't have access to the gory details about your arrest and therapy yet, but the initial police record states that you were raving, delusional, and violent. What set you off?"

In answer, Nathan clicked the door shut. Danny lifted his collar against a prickle of unease. Nathan could be dangerous to himself or he could be dangerous to Zoe. He could be dangerous, full stop.

THIRTY-TWO

Tuesday, 23-Mar

Fact: Nathan has a scar, and not a tidy surgical or child-hood one either.

Fact: A fat snake of a scar with hard, lumpy scar tissue. The type of scar I've encountered once in my career, and that was a war wound that had gotten infected. In other words, major trauma, major neglect, major violence.

You keep warning me to not identify with Nathan. You used the dreaded "transference" word. God, I detest that part of our lexicon. So what if I transfer my trauma onto him? If I'm willing to be with him and accept him, I think you'd agree that I'm beginning to lean into that attitude toward myself, too.

Right?

There's guilt and then there's shame. I'm filled with guilt, as well I should be. Nathan, meanwhile, is filled with shame. It oozes out of him, especially when his daughter is in the vicinity. He's preoccupied with how she perceives him. It would be comical if it weren't so distressing to witness.

Oh, I don't know. All this self-work is tiresome. The fact that matters is this:

Fact: Nothing happened yesterday. All that anniversary fear for nothing.

Fact: Here I am this morning, drinking my coffee with a celebratory shot of Irish cream, overjoyed that I'm home with the doors locked, security system on, barricaded—and blissfully alone.

Do you think I can consider myself safe now?

THIRTY-THREE

MERRIT SLOGGED HER WAY toward Fox Cottage. She'd never owned galoshes—rather, wellies—until she moved to Ireland, and now she lived in them for half the year. Puddles squelched underfoot and a giant grey mass of rain hung overhead. She stomped a puddle hard enough to splash muddy brown goo on her leggings.

Life was complicated.

She still didn't know what to make of Detective O'Neil—no, Simon—asking her out. On a date. And then there was the Easter festival. She jumped with both feet into another puddle. The wind caught the resulting mud spray and blew it back at her. She spit and sputtered, and swiped her hands down the front of her raincoat.

Merrit's annoyance aside, the project had buoyed up Liam. He was resting in bed but in good spirits as he brainstormed ideas with Mrs. O'Brien. "You want something done in the village," Liam had said, "you put her on the committee."

And here Merrit thought she'd gotten rid of the woman for a while.

The wind blew off Merrit's silly plastic rain hat and she trotted after it. She caught the hat midair and jammed it back on her head. A moment later she entered the cottage. The golden hue on the living room walls made a huge difference on such a dreary day. The kitchen, ditto, with its cheerful mint green. A quick check of the main bedroom showed a rumpled bed cover and no new paint yet. Good for Nathan and Annie, having it off, as the Irish say, on the sly. Gave the place a lived-in feeling that it sorely needed.

She walked around the cottage, noting missing baseboards. The back door stuck, too. She pulled hard to open it. It needed to be re-hung, but in the meantime she would buy the Irish equivalent of WD-40 to lubricate the hinges. The two wooden steps down to the ground were as springy as fresh mown grass. Add replacing them to the task list.

A makeshift shelter leaned against the back wall. According to Liam, Kevin had rigged it up a year ago for the neighbor's sheep that jumped the drystone wall. She'd grown fond of the sheep since moving into Liam's house. In particular, the two wall-jumpers amused her with their decidedly un-sheeplike behavior. She peered into the shelter. There they were, chewing cud and looking pretty content.

The smell of soggy wool and lanolin comforted Merrit as she scratched their foreheads. She pulled out some sliced apple that she'd brought with her in case they were about. They lifted the slices off her palms with their precision lips. A plastic tarp that Merrit didn't recognize caught her attention. Slipping between the sheep, she stooped and peered under the tarp. Oh, but Nathan didn't need to store his supplies out here. That was ridiculous. She scooted aside a paint roller and paused.

With a quick wrist flick, she shifted the tarp aside. The plastic crackle startled the sheep into trotting outside, leaving Merrit alone with a strange implement caked with red stains. She didn't know what it was, but it looked suspiciously like a murder weapon.

THIRTY-FOUR

DANNY STOOPED FOR A closer look at a wooden stave, battered but smooth from years of use. At one end of the stave, a sharp metal blade resembling a garden spade formed a ninety-degree angle with a wing that jutted out like a spear, the purpose of which was to cut square corners. A camera flash lit up blood and rust almost indistinguishable from each other.

Danny silenced his ringing mobile and backed out of the lean-to to make room for the scenes of crime team, bumping into O'Neil as he did so. O'Neil peered over the photographer's shoulder. "What the bloody hell is that?"

"A *sleán*. Antique turf cutter," Danny said.

"I'll check on Merrit."

"You stay here," Danny said.

Danny passed two huddled sheep and ran against the sideways rain into the cottage. Merrit sat on a bed in one of the bedrooms, contemplating a section of painted wall. The musky chemical scent of fresh paint brought a welcome change from soggy sheep. "Did you know you can cut a large onion in half and leave it in a fresh-painted room overnight, and voilà, no paint smell when you throw the onion away the next day?" she said.

Danny sat down next to Merrit. "That's a nice color you've chosen."

She cocked her head at the dusky rose color. "It's called Raspberry Parfait, and it's too pink. It's utter crap, in fact. I hate it." She dunked the paintbrush she held into a bucket of clean water. "I'd just been thinking about how complicated life is, you know?"

He did, indeed.

"Then I find that thing out there." She waved her hand. "I'm sure Alan will be thrilled when he finds out."

"What do you mean?"

"You don't recognize it? I may be wrong, but I think it's supposed to be hanging on his wall of old farm tools, along with the photos."

She was right. He should have recognized it himself. "Good eye," he said.

"What about the Easter festival?" Merrit said. "Liam's looking forward to it. Can we still do it?"

"Yes, but fair warning that you'll attract a larger crowd once the news about the murder weapon—if it is the murder weapon—spreads."

"Yippee, but we both know it's the murder weapon. Someone decided the lean-to would be a good place to hide it. Why here? It doesn't make sense."

But things always made sense to the perpetrator. The problem was figuring out the perpetrator's perspective.

"You've had more people coming and going lately," Danny said. "Visiting Liam."

"Exactly," Merrit said. "Why not throw the weapon in a bog?"

"Unless you want it to be found."

"Lucky I'm the one who found it, then."

"Why's that?"

"Those are Nathan's painting supplies. He's the one painting the cottage."

"Fancy that," Danny muttered.

"He wouldn't incriminate himself."

Given Nathan's shaky history, maybe that was precisely what he'd do. Or maybe he thought no one would find the turf cutter in the shed. He didn't strike Danny as a criminal mastermind.

"Someone trying to throw the blame on Nathan?" Merrit said. "Or maybe on Annie?"

"Why Annie?"

"They've been meeting up here in the cottage."

There was a new wrinkle. Danny returned to the kitchen without saying goodbye to Merrit. A muted buzzing caught his attention. He answered his mobile, still lost in thought.

"Jaysus and Mary wept," Marcus said, "where have you been? I've been trying to ring you."

Danny snapped back to the present. "What's wrong?"

"It's Ellen. You need to come to the hospital. Now. Her heart stopped."

THIRTY-FIVE

A SHADOW SHIFTED ALONG Nathan's bedroom wall. It slithered just within taunting range at the edge of Nathan's peripheral vision. His lungs heaved on a silent gasp, and the space around him resolved into grey light seeping in around the edges of closed curtains. Something hung from the curtain rod. A coat. He didn't own a proper wool coat. Then he remembered. Zoe had bought it for him. On sale, she'd said.

He sank back onto his mattress. His hand throbbed. Blood dotted his bandage. He tried making a fist, but his fingers refused to close all the way.

A shush of breath froze him. A shift, a glint in the half light.

"Dad?" Zoe said.

"Jesus, what are you about?" he said with his voice higher, more tremulous, than he'd have liked. He pulled the blankets around himself.

"I wasn't sure whether to wake you or not. They say you're not supposed to." Zoe sat on a chair in the corner of the room. "You've slept the afternoon away. It's gone five already."

Earlier he'd decided to lie down for a while. She must have pulled the curtains shut. He couldn't shake the feeling that she'd been monitoring him while he slept. Or a dream figment had been watching him. He glanced at the coat that hung on the curtain rod.

It was all in his mind. He hoped it was. He wasn't sure anymore.

"I was asleep?"

"What else? If you can call that sleep." She rolled her eyes and made as if to pat his head. Something glinted again. A knife. Nathan jumped out of bed and stumbled as a wave of pain shot up his leg.

"Stay back," he said.

Zoe retreated from the bed. She held up a paring knife. "I didn't mean to spook you. Dinner is almost ready, that's all."

Nathan limped to the opposite side of the room from his daughter. He couldn't think straight when she was nearby. She hugged him, hung on his arm, patted him. Always touching him. Her touch made him want to shed his skin.

His voice shook as he said, "Remove that thing."

Her expression wilted, but he'd worry about her hurt feelings later. She knew the rules. No sharp objects in his bedroom, not even cuticle clippers. He'd have thought this was obvious.

Zoe tossed the knife into the hallway. It skidded on the floorboards and bumped up against the wall.

"You can't come in when I'm sleeping," he said. "You know that, too."

"You're being ridiculous. I'm not some silly girl testing boundaries anymore."

This was exactly what she did. All the time, with a new coat, with everything. Nathan unslung the coat from the curtain rod and slipped it over his arm. This was the last place he wanted it hanging, lurking over him like a headless fiend.

"Chicken Florentine for dinner," Zoe said as she closed the door. "Ten minutes."

Nathan limped back to his bed and fell onto it. He dragged the coat over himself. Zoe had good taste; the coat warmed him up. His big toe throbbed and after a few minutes he sat up to examine the swelling. Pain shot up his foot when he tried to bend the toe using his fingers.

He surveyed the room in search of a sign that he'd kicked the wall while fighting shadows in his sleep. He didn't see anything amiss and sank back onto the bed. The trouble with reality was that it felt too dreamlike, while his dreams seemed too real. And the past hovered somewhere in between.

THIRTY-SIX

Wednesday, 24-Mar

Last night—or rather, early this morning—Nathan scared the living bejesus out of me. The keychain remote dinged at me as it does when movement triggers the outside lights. And there he was, a figure silhouetted in the rain. I didn't recognize him at first. My heart about stopped until he hobbled closer. He wanted me to take a look at his toe. I joked, "What did you do, kick a wall?"

He considered it for a second, then said, "Fighting a coat."

Twitchy, disturbed. More so than usual, I should say. I gave him a leftover pain pill and ordered him to see a doctor. Then he was gone with a hope that he could sleep now. I invited him to stay, but he said he didn't want to ruin my chance for a good night's rest.

Fact: Nathan worries me and—

———

Up-to-the-second fact: A letter arrived in the post.

My fingers are shaking. I haven't opened the envelope, but I recognize the writing. And here I thought I was safe. Just like PatientZ to dash my hopes.

Fact: PatientZ is nearby, and he hasn't forgotten about me.

THIRTY-SEVEN

DANNY HELD ELLEN'S LIMP hand, watching her chest rise and fall in time with the rhythmic whoosh of the ventilator. She was back on the intensive care ward surrounded by a small cavalry of equipment. One of many poor souls in the large, depressing room. Beeping heart monitors and murmurs from the attending nurses and family members surrounded him but sounded muffled.

Danny found himself breathing in time with the ventilator's whoosh. The machine paused, and Danny held his breath. A moment of fear caused by the absence of noise, and then the ventilator returned to its normal rhythm. He beckoned a passing nurse, who grimaced in response.

"Is there something wrong with the machine?" he said. "It stopped for a few seconds."

Her expression cleared. "We're weaning your wife off the ventilator so that her lungs can start working for themselves again. The ventilator pauses and if she doesn't fill the gap on her own, the ventilator pressure increases again. It's perfectly normal."

There was nothing perfect about this. Or normal.

"Is it necessary to wean her off the ventilator now?" Danny said. "She's still recuperating from—"

"A cardiac incident, yes."

No, Danny wanted to yell. From death, you useless baggage. Her heart stopped and you brought her body back to life. To live like this. All hail the miracle of modern medicine. "Yesterday, she died," he said.

The nurse frowned at his bluntness. Maybe most civilians used pretty turns of phrase such as "pass on." Like taking a pass on the second helping of dinner. *I'll take a pass on this life, thanks.* As if the patient had a choice in the matter. The crux of it, that. Ellen should still have a choice. Somehow. What was it like locked inside her head? Was she screaming for him to let her go or to not give up?

"She's on the mend," the nurse said. "Her lungs are clearing up."

From a side table she picked up a small canister of salve and handed it to Danny. He covered his fingertip with a cool dollop, rubbing it with his thumb. She instructed him how to dab the salve onto Ellen's nostril where the feeding tube chafed the skin. The ventilator paused. Danny froze, hoping to see Ellen breathe on her own.

A few seconds later the machine whooshed more air into her lungs.

THIRTY-EIGHT

MERRIT RINSED OUT EMPTY teacups and placed them in the dishwasher. A fine coat of rain misted the windows. Without the wind, the countryside appeared sodden but soft. A riot of new vegetation had sprouted over the last week of spring weather. When the sun made an appearance, the land sparkled, the greens so vibrant they appeared artificially enhanced.

Unfortunately, all Merrit saw was Fox Cottage marring her view. Off limits now and with crime scene bunting across the door. No more painting, and no more secret rendezvous for Nathan and Annie either. This disheartened Merrit. They were good together.

Liam had sensed a connection between them that Merrit had missed. She wouldn't have paired them up, and once again, she had to wonder about her fitness for the role of matchmaker. Something eluded her, staring out windows, focusing on crime scene tape instead of the glorious vista beyond it. She shook her head against the image of the bloodied *sleán* and turned off the running faucet.

Voices rose from the living room. Mrs. O'Brien called out a final reminder about their meeting tomorrow—time was running out!—

to talk about the cake dance, Easter egg hunt, and a puppet show for the children. "And Merrit," she said as an afterthought.

Her cue. Merrit dried her hands and returned to the living room. Twenty women stood and sat around the room. Most of them already wore their rain gear and clutched their purses, eager to be gone, she suspected. Mrs. O'Brien got things done, sure, but in the most disagreeable and bossy manner possible.

"Merrit," Mrs. O'Brien said over the chatter, "we'll provide you with your own station near the center of the pavilion."

"God, no." The room went quiet. "I'd prefer to sit at one of the tables and people can come talk to me as they wish."

"That won't do. Whether we like it or not, you'll follow in Liam's footsteps. There's tradition to follow. You'll have a seating area—"

"But I'm not Liam. I don't need a dog-and-pony show."

As soon as the words were out of her mouth, Merrit longed to suck them back up.

"Dog-and-pony show?" Mrs. O'Brien said. "If you think so little of our customs you can always return to California."

At last, she'd spoken the words aloud. Merrit could handle words spoken aloud; it was the unspoken that wore her down. Maybe she did belong back in California, away from blood-streaked turf cutters and gravel dunes and cancer and expectations.

"I'll ask Liam what he thinks about a station," Merrit said, "but I refuse to make a speech. And no banners either."

Mrs. O'Brien's lip curled. Merrit held her ground for an extra beat, doing her best to smile, before retreating to the kitchen again. As soon as she left the room, the chatter rose. Merrit perched on a stool and waited them out. It didn't take long for the house to empty, a mass exodus of the scandalized.

Where was the juicy Irish slang when she needed it? "Crap," she said into the silence. "Shoot, bugger, dammit."

For Liam's sake, she'd have to apologize to Mrs. O'Brien, try to explain that she hadn't belittled the custom, only its showiness. The distinction would be lost on Mrs. O'Brien though. "Double crap."

A whoosh of cold air set the kitchen swing door to creaking, and a moment later Zoe's voice called out a hello. She bounced into the kitchen wearing her signature cobalts and winter whites and butterfly accessories. Merrit would have groaned, but she didn't feel up to reacting to the sparkling creature.

"I missed the festival meeting." She filled the teakettle and set it on the burner. "Since I'm here, I can help with Liam."

"Annie's been keeping him company," Merrit said.

The swing door opened again. "Is it safe to come out now?" Annie said. Merrit could swear her smile dimmed when she saw Zoe, but her tone remained friendly as she said, "You survived the meeting, too."

"I arrived too late to become ensnared," Zoe said.

"How's Nathan's toe this morning?"

Zoe looked at Annie with a quizzical expression.

"He popped around my place in the middle of the night for me to take a look at it."

Zoe's expression brightened. "I thought I heard him. I imagined him sneaking out like a naughty teenager to see his girlfriend. Looks like he was!"

"He's too accident-prone," Annie said. "I'm concerned."

Merrit studied them, the two women in Nathan's life. Zoe was quite tall, taller than either she or Annie. Whereas she shone bright and new, Annie had a mellowed and burnished solidity about her. A beauty that comes with age, like some antiques. A little worn, some scratches and dents, but all the better for them.

Zoe had found the tea bags. She poured tea and handed cups around. "I've never thought of him as accident-prone before. He's the world's worst sleeper, though, crashing around in the dark. I've told him it's okay to sleep with the lights on." She shrugged. "He does what he wants. I'm not going to change him after all this time."

Merrit knew better than anyone that no one was perfect. Not fathers, not daughters. Watching Zoe blow on her tea with her perfect lips on that perfect face, she realized that she and Zoe had more in common than moving to Lisfenora to find their lost fathers. Like Merrit, Zoe needed to adjust her expectations about her father. She didn't appear disillusioned the way Merrit had been when she realized Liam wasn't the paternal type. But still, she wondered if changing Nathan wasn't what drove Zoe. Change him into the perfect father.

"Would Liam like tea?" Zoe said.

Merrit led the way to his bedroom and knocked on his door. "Can we come in?"

A groggy mumble in response. Liam rolled over and struggled to sit up. He patted down the fluff of hair around his scalp. Merrit placed an extra pillow behind his back. His skin had a greyish tint and he huffed with short labored breaths.

"Are you in pain?" Merrit said.

"No. A slight cold, I think. What happened with Mrs. O'Brien?"

"I offended her. Don't worry, I'll set my ego aside and apologize."

Liam smiled. "She'll like that."

Zoe sat on the edge of the bed and handed Liam his tea. He cradled the cup in both hands.

"You," he said to Zoe. "I've been meaning to chat with you."

He set the tea aside and shuffled through a pile of papers near his elbow. "I managed to print this article out all on my own." He pointed to the laptop sitting at the end of his bed. "You made me curious, lassie, about healing."

Zoe sat up straighter, if that was possible. Liam handed the printed article to Zoe. "There's a long tradition of folk healing in Ireland."

"I didn't know that," Zoe said. "In England, it's associated with the crazy Bible thumpers—the faith healers."

"Healing?" Annie said.

"Oh," Zoe said. "I've an interest, that's all." She smiled but with a pout thrown in. "I wish you hadn't brought it up, Liam."

"How could I not be curious? My folk tradition, matchmaking, is of the same ilk." He glanced pointedly at Merrit. "A charmed talent."

"Let's not go that far," Merrit said. "It's a tradition, sure, but there's nothing charmed or mystical about it."

"You say that, you, who are charmed for it—"

"I'm not charmed for anything," Merrit said.

Liam raised his voice. "—and by the same token, why can't Zoe be charmed for healing?"

The cancer must have gone to his brain. Granted, Liam was uncanny with his matches, uncanny in a way that begged for a rational explanation, but matchmaking was one thing, healing quite another.

Annie peered over Zoe's shoulder. "I remember reading this article in the *Irish Times*. Only in Ireland would a reputable newspaper tout healing as a bona fide phenomenon. Despite the usual charlatans. May I?"

Zoe passed the sheet of paper back to Annie.

"Yes, yes," Annie said, scanning the text. "They call it 'the cure,' and it's all quite secret, and at least here in Ireland, it's a tradition from before the time of Christianity, handed down through families." She tapped the page. "It's taboo for healers to profit from helping others."

"Eh, lassie," Liam addressed Zoe, "what's your story? Are you a charlatan or are you a keeper of the cure?"

Zoe clasped her hands together and gazed down at her lap. "I learned a long time ago not to talk about it. My dad doesn't like it. The truth is, I've never tried to analyze it or learn about it."

Liam nodded. "Quite right. If something is, it just is. What more is there to know?"

"Just *is*?" Merrit said. "Even if we believe in charmed talents, there's a learning curve. Look at me trying to learn matchmaking. I wouldn't call me a natural."

"You haven't given matchmaking a chance, and you know it," Liam countered.

"That's not true."

"It is true." Liam directed more questions to Zoe. "Answer this, lassie, how did you learn to be a healer? What was your learning curve? When did you discover that you could heal?"

Zoe blinked rapidly. Wordless. That was a first. She wrapped and unwrapped a curl around her finger. "I never said I was a healer."

Liam snorted. "Your little display with Bijou? Of course you did. Unless you faked the blood on the glass and gave Bijou a pinch to make her yelp. But why would you do that?"

Zoe resettled her scarf around her neck. "I'm happy to be part of a tradition, but I prefer not to analyze it. It's not that big a deal."

Annie observed Zoe with an attentive eye. "In the article it says healers are seventh sons of seventh sons," she said. "That's the lore of it, anyhow."

"I don't know anything about that," Zoe said.

Annie excused herself with a comment that she must get on with her day. Taking her cue, Zoe stood and aimed an indulgent smile in Liam's direction. "You old pisser, you know you want me to lay my hands on you. All you have to do is ask."

She departed in a swirl of cobalt and white, calling to Annie to wait up for her. At the window, Merrit observed Annie pointing toward her hiking route across the pastures and along the Burren Way. Zoe opened the passenger-side door and Annie accepted the lift.

As soon as the taillights faded into the grey day, Merrit turned on Liam. "You truly believe Zoe is a healer?"

Liam settled himself under a blanket, contented as one of Elder Joe's roosting chickens. "The world would be a more interesting place if she were."

THIRTY-NINE

NATHAN SNAPPED AWAKE WITH the boom still ringing in his head. He lay there for a few moments, paralyzed except for his heart banging around in his chest. He'd left a lamp on, which allowed him to check the room without moving anything but his eyes. Smudged mirror hanging above a chest of drawers. Yesterday's clothes heaped near the closet, which he now left open at night. Bed covers crumpled at his feet. His restlessness had caused the fitted sheet to unhook itself from the corner of the bed and settle itself into cottony lumps beneath his back.

All normal, in other words.

Relaxing his vigilance, he pulled off the gloves that he now wore to protect his hands and listened to the night, the singularly boomless night. The only war zone was the one inside his head. Night after night after night.

He was dying; this he knew. Death like a lobster in a pot as the water temperature rose, slow enough you didn't realize it until it was too late. Perhaps he was already dead, a species of zombie living in an endless twilight. Perhaps he should be dead. Perhaps this was why Zoe had found him, moved in, and taken over his life. Yes, she was the one turning up the heat on him.

He knew this. He did. Or did he? Maybe he was still inside his dreams.

Nathan grabbed onto the night table and hoisted himself out of bed. Exhaustion penetrated his bones, causing him to stagger instead of stand, shuffle instead of walk. In the mirror he caught a movement. A quick jolt, a threat. His heart rate skyrocketed again before he caught his own eyes in the looking glass and ordered himself to calm the feck down.

He spread his hand over the scar near his hip to view himself without it. Its lumps were like the sheet lumps. They shouldn't be there, yet they were. It didn't matter what the doctors had said in the psychiatric hospital or the tricks his mind played on him now. The scar was his proof. It was proof. It was proof.

He wasn't crazy. He wasn't crazy. He wasn't crazy.

The thought repeated itself like a metronome, the beat to which he dressed himself. He'd showed up at Annie's house once before in the middle of the night. That had been an experiment, like sleeping with the light on. Now that he and Annie were out in the open, now that he'd risked Zoe's disappointment—which she'd hidden well, he'd grant her that—nothing would stop him from visiting Annie. Maybe then he'd be able to sleep.

Sometimes when he drifted off, he imagined himself sleeping in Annie's bed. He wouldn't mind her in the room with him when he woke in the middle of the night. He'd fall back asleep like a baby without first needing to quiet his heart, check his body for aches, listen for sounds in the house. He'd drift back to sleep and wake up refreshed.

He hopped toward the bureau on his good foot. He grabbed a pair of socks and shut the drawer. Zoe liked to ball the pairs together and lay them in neat rows. He found his shoes, trying not to think about all the ways that Zoe had taken on Susannah's role. The little habits like the socks and the little items like the wooden hangers. But they added up.

He leaned against the bedroom door with ear pressed against the wood. Beyond the white noise inside his skull, he thought he heard a shush, the slightest whisper of fabric, and then a knock burst through the wood.

"Dad?" Zoe knocked again. The knob jiggled but the door held. "Dad! I can't get in! Are you okay in there?"

Nathan willed the shiny new slider lock he'd installed the previous day to hold fast. "I'm fine. Go back to sleep."

"What are you on about now? But that's grand, since I'm awake, I'll fetch a snack. Would you like some cheese bread, too?"

"No, no thank you."

Nathan slid down the wall. Now he was locked into a boiling pot of his own design, waiting out his daughter. He'd have to leave the room sometime, but not until Zoe fell asleep again. *Please, Zoe, go back to bed, you who are forever refreshed and bouncy and full of energy. Please.*

He wept.

FORTY

Thursday, 25-Mar

Fact: Nathan's daughter fancies herself a healer.

Fact: Nathan is riddled with self-inflicted (during sleep, I think, I hope) injuries.

Fact: She's not healing her father.

I'm flummoxed at this point, because I don't understand what they're about. Nathan had me examine his toe. Why not consult his budding-nurse/healer daughter? If I were an academic I'd make a case study out of them.

I had a chance to talk to the daughter when she offered me a lift home. I let her know I was here for her and Nathan, that I hoped to get to know her better as well as Nathan. That's all I can do for the moment.

Notice that I'm thinking about the future. Does this rate as a breakthrough?

Another possible breakthrough: I know what the "niggle" is now. You remember, something bothered me when the news came out about Joseph Macy's death. I'm going to DS Ahern. At last, I see a way to redeem myself of my follies once and for all.

Fact: I want this done so I can get on with my future.

FORTY-ONE

THE SMELL OF RASHERS and coffee permeated Nathan's house even though it was just gone noon. Danny's stomach growled, but he staved it off with a sip of water from the glass that Zoe handed him.

"I didn't know who else to call," Zoe said. "I'm trying to entice him out of his room with good smells."

Upstairs, O'Neil held a one-sided conversation with Nathan through the locked bedroom door.

"What happened?" Danny said.

Zoe grabbed the sizzling rashers off the stove and set them in the sink. The pan hissed. "I wish I knew. He locked himself in his room sometime last night and hasn't come out."

"Jesus, man, the smell of that would entice the dead," O'Neil said as he entered the kitchen. "You mind?"

Zoe tossed him a fork. "Someone should eat it."

O'Neil managed to talk and eat without appearing rude. "I can hear him pacing back and forth."

"The question is whether he's a danger to himself," Danny said. "Zoe, stay here. Let's not agitate him any more than we have to."

Danny led O'Neil through Nathan's studio and out the back door. A firing shed occupied most of the backyard. Nathan's bedroom overlooked the yard from the second floor. Danny peered up to see Nathan fading back into the shadows.

O'Neil continued talking as they went on the hunt for a ladder. "I'm on to meet Merrit for dinner tomorrow tonight," he said. "So you know."

"She's a material witness now that she's found the murder weapon that killed Elder Joe. The *sleán*'s your priority, not Merrit."

They'd gotten the lab results back. Someone had stabbed EJ with the *sleán*, which meant that someone had nicked it from Alan's pub. Danny and the men would pass the next twenty-four hours talking to everyone who had entered the pub over the last few weeks.

A ladder leaned against the side of the house near the trash bins. O'Neil tilted and lowered one end while Danny picked up the other end. They maneuvered the ladder around the corner of the house and leaned it against the siding below Nathan's window.

O'Neil anchored the legs into the soggy soil. "You know Merrit better than I do..."

He let the sentence hang. Danny didn't oblige him by either confirming or denying the statement.

"It's this," O'Neil said. "Do you think she'd prefer Doolin for a night of good music or Ennis for a proper low-lit restaurant?"

"You're treading thin, you daft prick." Danny climbed the ladder while O'Neil braced it. "Have you thought about asking *her*?"

"No."

"There's your answer. She'll have no qualms telling you which she'd prefer. I don't want to hear any more about it. That's an order."

Danny peeked over the window trim. Nathan perched on the end of the bed, rocking in place. His blank expression spooked Danny. Also odd, Nathan's slackness reminded him of the children when they slept. The smooth terrain of sleep, yet Nathan's eyes were open.

Danny pried at the window but it didn't budge. He hesitated and then tapped the glass. Nathan pressed his hands against his ears, muttering to himself.

"Grab a brick," Danny said to O'Neil.

O'Neil picked one of the bricks piled up against the side of the firing shed and climbed partway up the ladder behind Danny to hand it to him. With a hard thrust, Danny shattered the window and reached in to unlock the latch, taking care not to cut his arm on the broken glass. The window opened easily once he unlocked it. Danny spilled his long body onto the floor.

Nathan gaped at Danny with slow-dawning awareness. "What are you about?"

"It's gone twelve. You've been locked in this room since Christ only knows when."

Nathan's eyes shone a bleary blue from within taut, bruised skin and gaunt face. His gaze darted around the room, pausing on the bedside clock and jumping to the lock on the door.

"Painkillers." He reached for the crutches propped next to his bed. "I'm not supposed to put weight on my toe."

Danny let that lie go for now. Or the half lie, at least. Nathan's toe may have been painful, but no way in bloody hell did a pain pill cause the fugue state that Danny had just witnessed.

Nathan crutched his way toward the door to unlock it. The smell of rashers rolled into the room along with Zoe, who wrapped her arms around Nathan. Nathan let her hug him.

"You frightened me silly," she said when she let him go.

"I'm fine. Didn't I say I was fine?"

"Not exactly." She ushered Nathan down the stairs ahead of her with Danny in the rear. "Breakfast. You need breakfast."

Nathan paused at the foot of the stairs while Zoe rushed ahead. "Did she call you to check up on me?"

"Yes," Danny said.

Nathan peered into the kitchen, where Zoe laid a fresh portion of rashers in a pan with O'Neil loitering nearby. Instead of the kitchen, Nathan settled himself in the living room. Danny followed, more perplexed than ever by Nathan's behavior.

"Zoe's a social creature," Nathan said. "Quite the chatter monkey, but she doesn't say anything of substance. All those words with nothing to show for them."

"I expect that's good for you," Danny said. "She keeps your secrets like a good daughter."

"Good daughter." Nathan pondered that for a moment with head tilted back and eyes on the ceiling. "*Dutiful* or *doting* are more precise, I think."

And that was it. No explanation about the interior lock, no apologies for worrying Zoe, not even annoyance at the broken window.

Danny pulled a photo of the *sleán* out of his pocket. "Do you recognize this implement?"

"It looks familiar. What is it?"

"An antique turf cutter."

"Right. Off Alan's wall."

"Look closer."

Nathan squinted at the photo. "Is that blood?"

"Yes. Do you know anything about it?"

Nathan's expression shuttered; that eerie slackness again. Danny almost shook him, but Nathan roused himself on his own. "Should I know something about it?"

"That's my question to you."

"I don't know. My memory's nothing but a sieve these days. Lack of sleep does that."

"Did lack of sleep have anything to do with your stay in the psychiatric hospital?"

"You could say that, but I don't see the point of your questions."

Danny thought it was obvious enough. "Someone used this weapon to kill EJ."

Nathan's expression remained glassy-eyed and blank. "I can't help you, I'm afraid."

"When was the last time you saw the *sleán*?" Danny said.

"I don't know. I remember it on Alan's wall, though."

Zoe arrived and arranged a breakfast tray on Nathan's lap. Scrambled eggs, more rashers, and coffee.

"Eat, please." Her attention caught on the photo that Nathan still held. She pulled it from his grasp and handed it back to Danny. "That's nothing to do with him. He's overtired from his antics last night. Let's rest, shall we?"

Nathan's gaze jumped around the room like it had in his bedroom. "Antics?"

Zoe returned to the kitchen.

"Did you go out last night?" Danny said.

"No." Nathan peered down at his jeans, his jumper, his socks and shoes. "At least, I don't think so. Zoe was referring to my usual restlessness at night."

"Tell me about your psychiatric stay. Involuntary, wasn't it?"

Nathan shoveled in a mouthful of eggs as if he hadn't eaten in a week. Danny waited while Nathan finished the meal. At last, he sat back with a spark of life entering his eyes. "I had a mental breakdown."

"Caused by?"

Nathan smiled. "They labeled me delusional and self-harming." His smile faded. "I never agreed with their diagnosis. Here's a tip: Best to go along with what the doctors say so that they'll deem you sane."

Out of the corner of his eye, Danny felt rather than saw Zoe hovering beyond the doorway. Nathan fell silent. A moment later, water gurgled from the kitchen taps.

"Would anyone like more coffee?" Zoe called.

"What did I tell you?" Nathan said. "Doting."

FORTY-TWO

MERRIT HAD LET SIMON O'Neil decide where to go on their Friday night date. She hadn't cared, to be honest, still nonplussed by the idea of an outing with him. She sat at a crowded communal table in McGann's Pub along with a pack of tourists and locals. In the corner, a trio made up of tin whistle, banjo, and accordion played a folk tune. Voices rose in song and in conversation while Merrit waited for Simon to return with their pints.

A few minutes later he pardoned his way through the crush of drinkers. He mouthed "help me," grinning all the while. Merrit liked his off-duty style. The jeans hanging low on his hips, the leather man-bracelet, the blue t-shirt layered under a casual v-neck sweater.

He edged his way into the empty chair next to Merrit. "That was the mighty gauntlet."

She didn't mind his arm pressed against hers or their knees knocking together. It wasn't purposeful. They had nowhere to maneuver once seated.

She lowered her voice. "You must know I'm going to ask—what's the latest with the case?"

"*Sláinte.*" He tapped his glass against hers. Someone jostled him. He held up his pint over the table to let the liquid settle down. "So that's why you agreed to go out with me. To get information."

Merrit played along. "Of course, why else? I'm sure Danny must have mentioned my tendency to meddle."

"He did, indeed, and I was told not to humor you." Simon lowered his voice. They leaned against each other in an attempt to privatize their conversation. "Between you and me? We've confirmed the turf cutter—the *sleán*—has EJ's blood on it."

"You're no fun. I already figured that out."

"Fish and chips!" One of the barmen arrived at the end of their table carrying two steaming plates. "On your way, then."

The plates traveled hand-to-hand down the length of the table to Merrit and Simon. The food smelled heavenly, the fish fresh, the batter light and crispy. Humming "yum-yum-yum" under his breath, Simon sprinkled on salt and malt vinegar, and forked up a piece of fish.

"Brilliant," he said with mouth full. "Should be its own food group. Go on, then, give it a go."

"Tell you a secret. I've never tried fish and chips."

"What?" Simon addressed the table at large. "Do you believe this one? She's never tried fish and chips."

"Hey," Merrit laughed, "I'm from California. You're more likely to find hummus on menus than fish and chips."

"Time to remedy that." He repeated his seasoning ritual atop her meal and held up a forkful of fish in front of her mouth. Merrit paused amidst the urgings from their tablemates. This felt too intimate somehow, as if she was supposed to make a sexy production out of sliding the fish off the fork. Without fussing over it, she accepted the bite. The fish fell apart in her mouth, moist and savory with the crispy batter. Around them the crowd clapped as the band switched to a jig.

"Delicious," she said by rote, but after swallowing amended herself. "That is good."

"Now, a question for you," Simon said. "You and matchmaking. Not your dream job, so why do it?"

Merrit sputtered on a sip of beer. He was the first person to come right out and ask her this question. "I'm not sure." She set her pint aside. "I've never been the ambitious type, you know? I studied journalism but didn't do much with it. Career-wise, nothing grabbed me, so I drifted along like an untethered kite. And then along comes the father I'd never met before, ready to make my mind up for me. Liam keeps saying I'm charmed for matchmaking. What do you do when you're being handed the family business?" She poked at a piece of fish with her finger. "I take that back. Not a family business. More like being handed a life, a community, a purpose. What do you do?"

"Tricky, yeah," Simon said. "That Liam, though. He intrigues me. The man's a romantic at heart, don't you think?"

"Romantic? Liam?"

"Think about it. You're a matchmaker, bringing people together who've never met before. How could you not believe in love at first sight?"

She stared at him. He couldn't be talking about them, on what might be their first and last date. "Is this how you interrogate suspects when you're not being the warm-up act for Danny? It's quite effective."

He laughed. "Calm your qualms. It was only a question."

Merrit washed down her chagrin with a mouthful of beer. "Let's listen to music now."

Simon kept up a light patter as one song led into another. Three songs later, Merrit offered to buy the next round and rose, feeling relaxed for the first time in—what, weeks? Months, even? It had been a while since she'd gone out "on the town," or, since she was in Ireland, out "on the razzle."

Simon rose along with her. "Sit back, relax, I've got them."

Merrit caught a movement like colored plumage near the door of the pub. She craned her head for a better view over Simon's shoulder.

His smile disappeared. "Something wrong?"

Between the layers of bodies, a flash of blue and blond. "Zoe's here. Looks like she might be with someone."

Simon relaxed. "I'm not surprised. Everyone shows up when the Sons of Erin play."

"I'll come along with you for the beer anyhow."

Merrit eased her way out from between the community tables into the bar area. Simon fetched up behind her, his hands touching her shoulders for a second to stop himself from knocking her forward.

Zoe waved. "Merrit! Hello, Detective O'Neil. I thought Dad might want the car tonight so I cadged a lift from Sid here. If you'll excuse me, I owe him a pint."

She pulled her wallet out of her purse and disappeared into the thick of it along the bar. Merrit waited, expecting a greeting from Zoe's friend, but he stood by, smiling in a low-key way. Next to Zoe, he was so bland he needed the sartorial equivalent of a dash of salt and pepper. He unbuttoned a jacket that strained around his tummy and tucked his hands into the pockets. The stance emphasized his slouchy shoulders.

Liam would love this pairing. He'd have much to say, Merrit was sure. A rumble sounded from her purse. Merrit excused herself and pulled out her mobile. She scanned a text from a phone number she didn't recognize.

Please come. Hurry.

FORTY-THREE

Danny strode through the death scene and out the front door, where he paused to let his eyes adjust to the glare of the security lights. They were bright enough to sizzle ants, transforming night into day around Annie Belden's house. On the porch steps, the scenes of crime techs had set up a perimeter around a ragtag bouquet of flowers bound with a purple ribbon. Danny recognized yellow carnations but not the purple flowers that matched the ribbon.

Benjy the Bagger appeared from around the side of the house with an unlit cigarette dangling from his lips and hands adjusting his belt. As ever, the irreverent pathologist made Danny smile, and he welcomed the chance to smile.

"Taking a break, you lazy bastard?" Danny said.

Benjy managed to keep the cigarette in his mouth while he spoke. "A man's gotta piss, a man's gotta piss."

"Have you been inside yet?" Danny said.

"Ay. A peaceful death." Benjy ducked away to light the cigarette with yellowed fingers. He inhaled long and sighed with pleasure on a slow exhale. "We've been here a few hours."

Which was his way of asking how Danny fared. "I'd switched off my mobile at the hospital today and forgot to turn it back on. Ellen's recovering from a lung infection."

Benjy shook his head. "Nothing anyone can do to prevent such things when the body's prone like hers. I'm sorry for it."

Danny's paper coverall crinkled as he shifted. "Tell me what you know."

Benjy squinted up at him from beneath shaggy eyebrows. "That way, eh? Right then, the deceased is in full rigor. What time are we at?" He checked his watch. "Oh-one-hundred-hours, Saturday morning. None of this is set in stone, mind you, but I can state that she died on the couch, wearing her pajamas, about twenty-four hours ago. Thursday night, early Friday morning. That's my prediction, but you'll have to wait for the report like everyone else."

"You said she died peacefully."

Benjy pinched his cigarette butt out and dropped it in his jacket pocket. "Ay, but peacefully doesn't mean naturally," he said as he walked away.

Danny glanced at the bouquet of dead flowers that someone had positioned in front of Annie Belden's house. Not thrown down, but propped up against one of the steps. With care. With the same care that saw her covered with a blanket. The scene didn't make sense. The shriveled flowers said "contempt" but the blanket pulled over Annie's face said "respect."

Beyond the bright circle cast by the lights, O'Neil waved Danny over from the edge of Annie's property. O'Neil sat on a drystone wall between Merrit and Nathan. Danny called O'Neil toward him. "What's Nathan doing here?"

"He received the same text message as Merrit. From Annie's mobile number. He was here when we arrived. In his car banging his head against the headrest."

"Bloody hell." Danny glanced over O'Neil's shoulder. He recognized Nathan's slack appearance. Awake, sort of, but lost somewhere inside his head.

"He got here fast because he recognized Annie's number," O'Neil continued. "Merrit didn't know who the text was from until I got her home. She wanted to check that the message wasn't about Liam. He recognized the number."

Danny nodded understanding, not interested in hearing how the text message had curtailed their date night. "Did you try calling Annie's mobile number?"

"Yes. Turned off. And so far no mobile found in her house."

"First thing tomorrow, put in the paperwork to track the phone. We can hope."

Danny surveyed Annie's house, a traditional stone-built farmhouse with a solarium addition on one end. Decorative red shutters on the second floor matched the door, and a stained glass fantail window above the door added a classic touch. Outdoor lanterns had probably infused the yard with a friendly yellow glow. Instead, they'd been disengaged in favor of the obnoxious security lights.

"She hasn't had the security lights for long," Danny said. "The lanterns are relatively new and in good shape. This is all wrong. Annie didn't send the text messages. According to Benjy, she died yesterday. We'll proceed as if this is a suspicious death."

"I'd say so, and look at Nathan. He's about to slip out of his skin he's that terrified."

Nathan braced himself on the wall with his hands gripping the stones. His jaw vibrated up and down. Danny called him over and sent O'Neil back to wait with Merrit. Nathan hobbled forward on his crutches.

"Tell me about Annie," Danny said.

Nathan rubbed at his side, looking pained. "She lived in the moment. That's why I liked being with her. I think she wanted to help me. I think that's what she does—helps people. Or what she did."

"She didn't work?"

"I got the impression she was between jobs or maybe on hiatus."

"How long has she lived in the area?"

"Not long—a year?"

"Where did she move here from?"

"I don't know."

"When was the last time you saw her?"

"I'm not sure. Wait, let me think." He continued rubbing his side. "Today is, what?"

"Early Saturday morning."

Nathan closed his eyes. "Thursday, then. Thursday night. Or Friday early. She took a look at my toe."

"You're sure about that?" Danny said.

"That's what I remember."

Which was the problem. Nathan's memory.

Danny softened his voice. "Friday morning, yesterday, after you had locked yourself in your room, Zoe mentioned your antics. Is that what Zoe meant? That she'd heard you go to Annie's house in the middle of the night?"

Nathan shook his head, but he couldn't hide his uncertainty. "I must have gone the night before, then. Wednesday night."

Benjy's voice rose. "Careful!" Two men approached the house carrying a stretcher. "Don't step on the bloody bouquet. There's meaning there."

Danny excused himself from Nathan. The men eased their way past the withered bouquet. Danny overheard one of them grumbling about Benjy the Bagger needing his bloody nicotine fix and Danny caught up with Benjy as he lit another cigarette near his car.

"What was that about the meaning of the bouquet?"

"The meaning of the flowers more like," Benjy said. "Red roses mean love and such like. That's one bloody strange-looking gathering of flowers over there. Find out what they mean. Symbolism, yeah?"

Benjy had a quirky, unscientific streak that never failed to surprise Danny.

"They're withered," Benjy called after Danny's retreating back. "Too withered. And I know what that means. Unfortunately."

"What then?"

"Rejected love, that's what."

FORTY-FOUR

Nathan overheard the pathologist calling out to Danny: rejected love. He rocked and concentrated on his throbbing toe, the way the pain radiated up his foot with the same pulse as his heartbeat, making his head ache and his teeth chatter. The last time he'd seen Annie, he'd stumbled in out of the rain, flinching against the glare of the outdoor lights. Annie had appeared in the doorway like a waxen effigy, her skin pale and tight over her face. "I'm glad it's you, but you gave me a startle like to scare the bejesus out of me. It might be good if you forewarned me next time."

She had beckoned him into the house without stepping backward. She let him brush against her and grabbed him in a fierce hello hug. "Frightful messes, the two of us," she'd said and let him go.

She took one look at his toe and pronounced him fit for a doctor. "You'll lose the nail. Do you sleepwalk?"

"I'm not sure. Zoe might know."

"But night terrors for sure."

It wasn't a question so Nathan didn't respond. Lately the terrors had worsened with a vengeance.

Annie helped him along the passage to her front room. Two sofas sat at right angles to each other in front of a fireplace. Wall shelves laden with books rose to the ceiling. The vase he'd given her sat on a side table in front of a picture window. "I'll tape the toe to its neighbor but that's not a long-term solution. Promise me you'll go to a doctor."

"I promise." He spied a spiral-bound notebook opened to a page filled with writing. "I interrupted you."

"Just my journal." She tucked the journal into an antique escritoire.

He'd never have guessed her for a scribbler in the dark of night. Scribbling his thoughts had always felt dangerous, as if consigning his nightmares to paper rendered them more real. At the behest of his therapist in the psychiatric hospital, he'd tried, only to feel more paranoia than relief.

He asked her when she returned with bandages, "Do you find journaling helpful?"

She cut a length of bandage. The security lights that he'd triggered were still on and they shone through the window. Their harsh light made the grey in her hair glow. "I do. Writing helps me process my thoughts."

She'd fixed him tea then, and they'd sat for a while in the dark when the security lights clicked off. Now, back in their glare, he thought about her journal. She'd probably processed a few thoughts about him. It would be odd if she hadn't, given his erratic behavior. A knot tightened in his stomach. He tried to tell himself that it made no bother what she'd written about him. It was none of his bloody business.

But it bothered him. He saw the way people reacted to him, with impatience, with wariness, with fear as if he were contagious. However, Annie had seen past his teetering surface to his core, a core that he knew could be as solid as one of his fired vases. He longed to feel that strength, to know what she saw in him. Annie's insights would reveal the truth about himself; reading her journal would be his own personal firing process. He wanted that journal.

Nathan forced himself to loosen his grip on the wall when Danny returned and sat down next to him. "How are you?" he said.

"I can't feel my feet."

"You're in shock, I expect. Can you show me the text message you received?"

That was easy enough. PLEASE COME. HURRY.

"Annie's in your contacts list, I see," Danny said. "You knew to come here when you read her text?"

"Seemed logical."

"When you arrived, what did you do?"

"The bouquet made me uneasy, and her indoor lights were off even though her car is here. I checked." He pointed to a detached garage with windows. "I rang the bell for five minutes straight. After that, I called the guards."

"You didn't go inside?"

"No." Nathan shifted, wincing. "Am I free to leave now?"

"Hold tight," Danny said. "Not long now."

He excused himself again, and Nathan hoped to Christ that would be the last of it. He didn't want to have to lie again. His vision was already blurred around the edges. He was in for a bad night made worse because, although he'd searched, he hadn't found Annie's journal in the escritoire. Or in the office desk. Or in the night table.

She lived alone. She wouldn't hide the journal under a floorboard. She'd store it someplace easy. All he wanted was a piece of

187

her to keep for himself, to help himself, but someone had gotten to the journal ahead of him.

Nathan averted his gaze from the desiccated bouquet. His teeth chattered. Yes, tonight was going to be horrific.

FORTY-FIVE

THE RECEPTIONIST AT CORNMARKET Psychotherapy ignored Danny in favor of beaming her smile at O'Neil. "Dr. Browne is with a patient at the moment, but she can see you after her session."

Danny wandered to the windows and gazed down at the *Clare People* newspaper office across the street. He pulled out his mobile, checking for a message from the hospital about Ellen's transfer back to Ennis. The roundtrips back and forth to the Limerick hospital were killing him. He tried to keep up with the paperwork for the investigation after the children went to bed but found himself nodding off at the kitchen table. This morning he'd studied the bags under his eyes in the mirror and for a moment entertained the idea that he was going mad like Nathan.

"Dr. Browne will see you now," the receptionist called.

She led them out of the reception area and down a corridor with in-session signs hanging on several doors. Eileen Browne met them in her antechamber. Soothing choral music played on a hidden sound system and a deck of playing cards sat on a side table, ready for nervous fingers.

Without word, the doctor beckoned them into her inner sanctum, where a couple of ergonomically correct chairs stood in front of her desk. She tucked stray hairs into the braids that encircled her head and considered them with a neutral expression.

"Thank you for seeing us on short notice," Danny said.

"You're fine. I keep Saturday mornings free for emergency appointments. This counts."

"As I mentioned on the phone, we found your weekly appointments listed in Annie Belden's calendar. Why was she seeing you?"

Browne's professional expression broke. She grabbed a tissue from a box on her desk and dabbed her nose. "You don't need me to answer that question."

"How do you figure that?" Danny said.

"Her journal. It's all there, I'm sure."

Danny glanced at O'Neil. He shook his head, his puzzlement evident.

"We didn't find a journal," Danny said.

Browne crumpled her tissue. "That's odd." She twirled her chair so she faced the window and blue sky that peeped through rainclouds. "Or maybe it isn't. Do you have a cause of death yet?"

"Not yet, but soon. She looked peaceful though."

"Indeed. As she would."

Danny leaned forward with waning patience. What was it with medical professionals? They spoke in half thoughts and left the most important bits of thought out of the equation altogether. "Come on, then," he said. "Say what you mean."

Browne tapped her fingers on the desk. "There's a confidentiality issue here, as you know."

Danny clamped his mouth shut and let O'Neil take over. Danny knew when to unleash O'Neil's natural lady charms.

"We encountered a couple of oddities when we arrived at Annie's house," O'Neil said. "And now there's the missing journal to consider. We're hoping you can help us sort through what might be happening. It seems that you were as much a friend as a therapist. We could use your insights."

Browne threw her tissue into a wastebasket. "I hate that Annie died. She wasn't meant to. She was meant to live. In many ways she was improving." She rose. "Please leave now. I'll meet you at Charlie Stewart's on along Parnell Street. Give me twenty minutes."

Out in reception, Dr. Browne shook their hands. "I'm sorry I can't help you. You'll need to go through the courts like everyone else."

Dr. Browne arrived at the pub on time to the minute. She sat down without removing her coat. "There's an unofficial truism in therapy circles: Don't trust depressives when they're past the worst. Why? Because that's when they're most vulnerable to suicidal ideation. They have the energy to follow through on it, you see?"

"Suicide," Danny said, testing the notion.

"Annie was diabetic," Browne said. "An overdose of insulin would look peaceful, indeed."

"Ah," O'Neil said. "I'd best let Benjy know to check for insulin." He pulled out his mobile and excused himself to make the call outside.

"We found syringes in the house, unused, but no medications," Danny said. "Was she on any other medications?"

"Antidepressants."

"Did Annie talk to you about what she wrote in her journal?" Danny said.

"Not always. I often recommend that patients write as if they're talking to me, which is self-serving. I find that if they've pretended to

191

talk to me in their journals, they're more apt to talk to me in reality."
She smiled, showing dimples that turned her face impish. The smile
fell as soon as it had risen. "Annie was too smart to fall for that trick."

"Why is that?" Danny said.

"She worked as a psychiatric nurse in Dublin before moving here.
Fleeing here, more like, to begin fresh."

"Why isn't it odd that her journal went missing?"

"She would have destroyed it. That I can say with certitude."

Danny thought about the missing journal, about what it contained that Annie might not want anyone to read, and likewise what
it contained that another person might want to read.

O'Neil slipped back into the pub and sat down. Outside, a laden
raincloud parked itself over Ennis and began emptying itself out.
The rain tap-tapped against the windows. Browne tapped her fingers in a similar rhythm.

"Annie worked in Dundrum," she said. "The big psych hospital
in Dublin. Harrowing work, to hear her tell it. Acute care, mind
you, for the mentally ill and criminally insane. She had one patient
on her watch, a man named Cedric Gibson. You've heard of him?"

"Vaguely," Danny said.

"The north-end kidnapping, on the quays," she said. "Cedric Gibson was found not guilty by reason of insanity. He played a pretty
game of it with his claims of diminished capacity. Fooled the lot of
them, and he was young, too. Nineteen at the time. A mad genius, really, landing himself in the psych hospital. Should have been life in
prison, full stop."

Danny remembered the case now. Gibson kidnapped the daughter of a Swiss diplomat after stalking her for months. She died while
tied to a chair in an abandoned warehouse. According to his defense,
he hadn't meant to hurt her. He'd only wanted to know her better.

He would have let her go. The usual shite. She'd died of heart failure, a fatal combination of terror and a congenital defect.

"You're saying that his insanity was a load of bollocks?"

"He knew what he was about. He was that sane he could have won a political election, or maybe that's a bad example. He knew how to play his game, anyhow. In Dundrum, he was a model patient, working through his anger-management issues and his mommy issues and his substance-abuse issues and taking his meds." She shook her head. "Along the way, he hooked poor Annie well and good. She became his number-one supporter for the review boards."

"Please don't tell me she fell in love with him."

"She did, unfortunately. He was assigned to her because she was the most senior psych nurse on staff. She saw him in session almost every day. I suppose it started there, the slow squirreling into her fond graces. But Jesus." She shook her head again. "Have you been?"

"To Dundrum? No."

"The place is grim, might as well be in the Middle Ages. We'll see what the coming mental health reform does." She sipped her beer. "Right, then. Annie. She advocated for Cedric Gibson to the review boards, swearing by all that was good and right that his years in the hospital had worked wonders on him. He was fit for the life outside, first at a residential outpatient home, and then another year later as a free man. She fought hard, and she believed his line all along."

Browne pulled off her coat and fanned her flushed face with a menu. "What's the first thing Mr. Cedric Gibson does as a free man?"

Danny shook his head.

"He abducted Annie," she said.

FORTY-SIX

When Merrit agreed to let the Earrach Festival be held in Liam's back field, she hadn't understood the magnitude of the event. First of all, she'd had to learn how to pronounce *Earrach*, Irish for "spring." *ARR-ack*, with trilling *r*s and an impossibly hard *k* from the back of the throat. She'd given up saying the word aloud—she sounded ridiculous—and reconciled herself to the Event, capital *E* intended, now a little over a week away.

Merrit had pictured a tent raised against the inevitable spring showers and portable heaters to lessen the chill. She hadn't given the logistics much thought until now.

She perused the showroom of Imperial Marquees, astounded by the diversity and extravagance of the available "tents" for hire. These weren't tents; these were temporary structures. She stooped to peer at a scale model of the Faery Light Marquee with a clear roof and strands of lights strewn throughout.

"Or we have the French Vintage Marquee," Louise, the event manager, said. "And then you must consider the liners and leg drapes and a platform."

"Platform?"

"The floor, dear. You can't have your guests stepping on sheep dung."

Feeling lightheaded, Merrit excused herself and wandered toward Liam and Zoe. They sat on chairs, perusing spec sheets and portfolios. Zoe held Liam's hand. She smiled and waved with the other hand.

"We found one that might be perfect," she said.

Liam slipped his hand out of Zoe's. He had insisted on coming along, that he was grand, and that Zoe should come, too, if Merrit was going to be such a bloody nuisance about his welfare.

"It's called the Chill Zone Marquee," Zoe said. "See? It has seating areas rather than formal table settings, and an area for the band."

"What band?" Merrit said.

Zoe peered at Liam. "Did I misunderstand?"

Liam shook his head. "Bank holiday on Monday, so why not let the festivities go long into the night? The Matchmaker's Festival includes traditional music."

"But this isn't the Matchmaker's Festival," Merrit said. "This was supposed to be—I don't know—a little party."

"Ay, a little party."

Merrit retreated back to the models, cursing the Irish tendency for understatement. "A wee bit of craic" could mean an all-night blowout. "Down the road" could mean five miles to the next village.

She found the model for the Chill Zone Marquee. It looked fine to her. Glancing up, she caught Zoe holding Liam's hand again. They spoke in a private manner, and Merrit suspected that if she approached, they'd go silent on her.

Liam had taken to Zoe, to be sure. Merrit understood the appeal. He needed variety and stimulation. But still, she didn't care for Zoe's overfamiliarity and didn't care for how she felt not liking it, as if she were missing out on something herself.

Merrit continued past more scale models toward the toilets. A long row of wall panels hid the toilets and offices from view of the showroom. Zoe and Liam sat on one side of the partition while Merrit hovered a few feet from them on the other side. Zoe's vanilla scent drifted on the air.

Zoe laughed. "Off with you, then. What more do you need?" Her voice turned serious. "I can't keep doing it, though. I worry about my dad. How he might leave me again."

Liam *hmm*ed like he did when people came to him to be matched. An open invitation. Merrit settled in, eager to know Zoe beyond her shimmering blue scarves and butterfly accessories.

"He could decide to have you match him someday," Zoe said. "He could meet a new Annie—God bless her—and leave me alone."

"Loneliness is a powerful emotion," Liam said.

Merrit let her head rest against the wall.

"Loneliness." Zoe didn't sound sure about this word. "No, abandonment. I used to have a lovely relationship with him."

Voices rose from inside the office behind Merrit.

"When did the loveliness end?" Liam said.

"Maybe it floundered the year before my mom died, when I was twelve."

The voices in the office approached the door. Merrit eased her way toward the toilets while still eavesdropping. She missed something Zoe said, but then her voice rose. "Liam, you did it again. I'm after trying to make a point, and you steer me in a different direction."

The office door cracked open. Merrit ran into the ladies' and then reopened the door as if exiting. Louise, the event manager, appeared with one of her colleagues.

"'Allo then, did you find your marquee?" she said.

Merrit let the bathroom door slam shut behind her. "The Cool Chill Marquee looks good."

"The Chill Zone, dear," Louise said. "Come along then, let's sort this out."

Liam released Zoe's hand when Merrit stepped around the partition.

FORTY-SEVEN

CEDRIC GIBSON ABDUCTED ANNIE Belden. Danny decided now would be a good time for pints all around. He signaled O'Neil to fetch them and then addressed Dr. Browne. "How did Gibson manage that?"

"Oh, easy enough, I'd say," she said. "He rented a car and followed her home when she got off her shift. Got right cozy living with her for a week."

O'Neil returned with their pints. Browne nodded her thanks and drank. Danny waited for the psychotherapist to continue. She remained quiet through several mouthfuls of beer, then said, "This may not make sense to you, but Annie would have healed faster if he'd molested her or beat her. Instead, he was a gentleman."

"Except for holding her captive," O'Neil said.

"Yes, yes." She waved that away. "They ate together and slept together in the same bed. He drugged her at night so that he could sleep, too. He went into the bathroom with her but turned his back to give her a semblance of privacy. He never saw her naked. He never touched her except when he secured her to a chair or bed. She said he conversed and invited her to converse with him. They listened to music, watched television, read. He wrote horrid short stories and read them aloud to her. Can you imagine discussing, I don't know, plot and character, all the while knowing that the writer was revealing his true disgusting self to you? It's enough to give me the sick if I weren't a professional." She blew out a long, slow breath. "Do you remember the movie—or maybe the book. Or maybe it was both? Anyhow, do you remember *The Stepford Wives*?"

Danny nodded.

"The wives were all the more terrifying because of their perfection. Annie described Cedric as the Stepford Kidnapper. By then, of course, she knew he was sane and far from rehabilitated, which made it worse. She couldn't forgive herself for being taken in by him, and she convinced herself that his future crimes would be her fault."

"The worst kind of torture," Danny said.

"Indeed. Then one day, he left. Just like that—*pfft*, gone. He loosened the ties while she slept and left a note. He'd enjoyed their 'retreat' together and thanked her for being the one person in the world who understood him. He looked forward to going on retreat with her every year and promised—promised, I ask you—to look her up a year from that date. He signed the note, *With love, your admirer*."

"That's diabolical," O'Neil said. "Did she report him?"

"She couldn't do. She wouldn't have, you see, because her professional conduct was already suspect on account of being so involved in Cedric's release. She was to be up before the Fitness to Practise Committee. She didn't want to give them more ammunition. Not that it mattered in the end. She was found not fit to practice anyway. She lost her license." Browne fingered her beer stein, rotating the glass this way and that. "She was planning to retrain as some brand of holistic healer."

At the word *healer*, Danny's thoughts jumped from Nathan's daughter to Ellen. He jerked off his coat and beckoned the barman to lay him down another pint. O'Neil raised his eyebrows but said nothing.

"Why didn't she report him after she lost her license?" Danny said, trying to regain his rhythm in the conversation.

"She had her own thoughts about how to heal herself. I didn't agree, but I couldn't stop her. She was waiting for the year anniversary, you see, waiting for him to find her again."

"Why? She didn't strike me as the passive sort."

"You're right, she's not. I urged her to be proactive, but he'd paralyzed her to the core. He'd eroded her sense of self. She had this idea that she had to face him again, one-on-one. She thought of his arrival as inevitable, but she was terrified all the same. I tried to talk her out of the fantasy of a miraculous redemption, especially because she'd met a man. I hoped this was a sign that she was on the mend."

"Yes, we're aware of him."

A spark of clinical interest sharpened Browne's gaze. "What's he about then? I'm curious."

Danny thought for a moment. "Damaged."

"*Tortured* would be the word," O'Neil said.

"She wanted to help him," Browne said, "but once again she forgot boundaries."

"Did Annie sleep with Cedric?" O'Neil asked.

"No, it wasn't that kind of relationship."

Danny's second pint arrived. He swallowed a mouthful. "Did he find her again a year later?"

"Oh, yes. Annie thought she'd made it through, that he might have let his obsession go, but then she received a letter two days *after* the anniversary date."

"Mind games again," O'Neil said.

"There was a point to Cedric's mind games: that she was his even when he wasn't there. He wrote that he was in the area and looking forward to their retreat this year. This idea that she had to confront him…" She shook her head. "It's one thing to imagine vanquishing a demon, another to actually face the demon again. You look for him. He's sure to still be nearby."

"What did she do with the letter he sent her?" O'Neil said.

"Burned to ashes."

Danny set his beer aside. "Would Cedric be the type to leave a symbolic bouquet of flowers, in this case meaning 'unrequited love'?"

"I'll tell you what type he is." Browne rose. "He's the type to graduate from stalking and kidnapping to killing. Now, if you'll excuse me. This conversation was more difficult than I thought it would be."

"I guess that was a yes," O'Neil said after she left.

FORTY-EIGHT

MERRIT SQUINTED THROUGH SUCCESSIVE rain curtains the sky saw
fit to unfurl on them. She turned on her headlights, catching sight of
flattened daffodils by the side of the road into Lisfenora. Liam dozed
in the seat beside her. In the back, Zoe contemplated the drenched
countryside. In repose, the loud attractiveness she emitted in all di-
rections went dormant. She appeared girlish, a solemn girl with solemn thoughts.

"Thanks for helping us choose a marquee for the party," Merrit
said. "Where did you want to be dropped off?"

Zoe perked up with an instant smile. "The Roadside Tavern. I'm
meeting Brian for a quick pint. He'll drop me off at home. You're
welcome to join us if you want." Merrit pulled up outside a pub with
a wagon wheel hanging on the front door. "Oh! There he is now."
Zoe rolled down her window. "Brian!"

A drenched fellow in a thick down jacket trotted over. "How's
the craic?"

Yet another suitor. Zoe needed matchmaking services like a leop-
ard needed spots. The man ducked to nod at Merrit with a quick,

penetrating squint. His smile revealed pointy canine teeth to go with boyish dimples. He opened Zoe's door for her and led the way into the pub at a sprint, Zoe laughing behind him.

Merrit continued to the plaza and found a parking spot near Alan's pub.

"I'm not in the mood," Liam said. "I could use a nap."

"We're not going in. I'm holding you hostage until you tell me the truth."

Liam coughed into a handkerchief. "What is it then?"

"What are you after with Zoe?"

"I'm experimenting, no more than that." He picked up an AdSense booklet tucked into the cup holder and flipped through it.

"Don't play the silence game with me, mister." She grabbed the booklet from him. "Spill it."

"Talk about the bloom going off the rose, disrespecting an elder like that. A question for you: how have I been for the last few days?"

Merrit hesitated. "Pretty good. And?"

"Improved, more energy, you'd say?"

"Stable." Realization dawned on her. "No, you're not."

"I am, and I swear I'm feeling better," he said. "Zoe might be a keeper of the cure, indeed."

Merrit digested Liam's statement, trying to look at it from all sides. Placebo effect. Delusion. Hope. Desperation. Whimsy.

Truth?

"You're feeling better than what?" she said. "Your doctor said right from the start that you'd have good days and bad." She couldn't keep the tension out of her voice. "I understand the temptation to believe in something, anything, but the cure?"

He smiled with a knowing look, one that hinted at the undercurrents of life that she was too American—or too ignorant—to understand. "Oh, ye of little faith, and here I'm telling you that I do feel better. I'm sure of it."

"Is that why you were holding her hand today?" Merrit said.

"Holding my hand, nothing wrong with that. Solace for the codger."

"What about the seventh son of the seventh son? Aren't they the ones who hold the cure? For that alone, I'd be skeptical of Zoe."

"True, but she's not full Irish, is she? Like you're not full Irish, and I've no doubts that you have the charm for matchmaking like I do. Why can't she be charmed for healing?"

The problem was that Merrit wasn't Irish enough to believe in such things. Every week she heard new tales that sane people accepted as part of their everyday reality. A standing stone in a sheep field that granted a wish if you climbed to the top of it. The faery tree that brought bad luck to the construction company owner who cut it down to make room for a road. The stories never ended.

Merrit said coincidence. Everyone else said, "Ay, maybe, but then maybe not."

She powered on her hybrid and turned on the lights. "Fine. You have every right to hold hands with Zoe. I have nothing to say about it unless she's hurting you, but I don't approve. Her behavior is odd— cruel, even. Maybe self-serving." Liam snorted. "She isn't charging you for the service, is she? True healers aren't supposed to profit from it, right?"

"So it's said," he said.

Merrit glanced at him as she eased onto the noncoastal road for the drive home. The rain-muted glow from Alan's pub caught Liam's speculative half smile, there and gone in a swipe of the windshield wipers.

FORTY-NINE

NATHAN JERKED HIS HAND out from under a scalding blast of water and turned off the taps. The last he remembered he was lying in bed. Zoe had left to meet up with Liam and Merrit. He'd felt a yawning hole of drowsiness pull him toward sleep in the middle of the afternoon.

Now, flash forward to the kitchen. The bitter smell of burnt coffee tickled his nose. He leaned to the side to switch off the coffeemaker. A dribble of red appeared on the countertop. The moment he noticed the blood, pain registered and a sick feeling began its usual roil in his belly. His middle finger throbbed where a cut bisected the pad of the finger.

He grabbed a paper towel to stanch the blood and jerked open the knife drawer. He picked up each knife in turn. The carving knife. The bread knife. The chef's knife. The paring knife. The all-purpose knife. Five. All accounted for, and none of them appeared dirty or damp as if recently rinsed off. Not that that meant anything.

"Zoe?" he called.

He should have been relieved she wasn't here to witness his latest episode, but he wasn't. Her absence unnerved him as much as her presence would have. He knew knife cuts, how well he did, and he'd cut his finger. Somehow.

The ticking grandfather clock, one of the few antiques he'd kept from his home in England, answered back with a dong for the half hour. But half what?

"I'm grand," he said. "Just grand."

He entered his studio to check the ceramic knives. He pulled open a drawer on the worktable, but they were in the same state of benign disuse as the kitchen knives.

Maybe he didn't want to remember. Maybe these forgetful states of his were protective. He should ask Annie.

The mobile sat where he last remembered seeing it, on the hall stand. He'd started using a password recently, and after thinking about it for a second, he tapped the password and pressed Annie's number. The connection rang three times and stopped. "Annie?" he said.

The silence on the other end of the connection whistled and crackled. Wind, that was wind. And then the sound went dead.

Dead.

His fingers went numb. The mobile landed on the floor. That wasn't Annie. Of course it wasn't. Someone else had her mobile, the someone who had texted him and Merrit. Who must have left the withered bouquet that meant unrequited love. This had to be.

He squeezed his cut finger until the pain drowned out his thoughts.

The front door opened, letting in a squall of wind and rain along with Zoe. She busied herself pulling off her white coat. "I suppose I should buy a proper North Face. I hate to do it, running around in Gortex. Next you know you'll see me in a fleece."

Nathan loosened his grip on his finger. He inhaled to relax his facial muscles. "You must be missing England about now," he said.

She hung her coat on the hall stand, another antique that Susannah had loved and that Nathan had refused to let go. He started toward the bathroom to plaster the cut in privacy, but she hooked his arm. "Oh," she said, "I can fix that right up."

He pulled away. "Not a bother. It's nothing."

"Dad." She let go of his arm. Her sorrowful expression filled Nathan with anxiety. The edges of his vision softened. He backed up the stairs, hoping to reach the bathroom before he lost the plot completely.

"I can help," Zoe tried again.

"I'm fine. Just don't touch me."

"I'll make us tea. How about that?"

"Fine."

He glanced into Zoe's room as he passed it and noticed an open dresser drawer that shouldn't have been open. Zoe never left drawers open. Ever.

He paused and, hearing the sound of the taps in the kitchen, tiptoed into her room to peer at folded stacks of underwear, bras, and rolled socks. His breath caught at the sight of a drop of blood soaked into pristine white cotton. Still damp. His blood. From his finger.

He grabbed the telltale socks, closed the drawer, and tiptoed toward the bathroom. He locked the door. Pain radiated from the base of his skull. Trying and failing to remember prowling through Zoe's belongings. Shuddering at the possibility of something sharp hidden beneath her underthings. Not good, this paranoia. There was no knife. He'd remember a hidden knife.

He stepped into the bathtub and lowered himself to his haunches to wait out the episode, letting his finger bleed into the white sock.

FIFTY

Sunday, 28-Mar

To honor you, dear Annie, I thought I'd continue where you left off writing in this journal. My way of grieving, you might say.

I looked forward to our retreat. I truly did.

I must say, though, fascinating reading, this, your journal. I enjoy the game you played with yourself as you attempted to stick to the facts. You failed most admirably. For all your insight, you didn't comprehend what was right in front of your face.

I comprehend, so I shall keep a wee eye out for my next best opportunity for fun. I might have an idea and it begins with Nathan Tate. I had decidedly mixed feelings about him as I read your words, and then to hear his voice when he rang your mobile yesterday—surprise!

I've decided that I'd like to meet him. He's not my usual type, but then I'm the curious sort, always expanding my horizons.

Do you remember when I said that I saw our sessions as a way to expand my horizons? Utter shite, but you lapped it up. You had approached me from around your desk with your direct gaze and firm handshake. No shying away for you. Back then you wore your hair around your shoulders and kept it dyed a pretty chestnut brown. Your roots showed, and it was those silver bits that hooked me.

You cared to be seen as younger, to connect with men as an attractive and viable woman. It's the caring that brings people down. And this Nathan fella? He oozes care. One way or another, the wanker is in for a fall.

FIFTY-ONE

DANNY SHOOK HANDS WITH DS Sheehy, who was on loan from the neighboring Killaloe District, and his DO, Detective O'Donnell. "Glad to have you. You're up to date?"

"Well enough, anyhow." Sheehy glanced around the cramped Detective Unit office. "No incident room?"

Danny pointed to a table shoved into the corner of the room with a whiteboard hanging over it. "That's it."

Budget constraints. None of them had to say it.

A blank line bisected the whiteboard, with one side labeled *Joseph Macy (EJ)* and the other *Annie Belden*. A mass of paperwork littered the tabletop. Memoranda of interviews, reports, questions, potential leads—all of it in disarray.

"I suppose I'm your 'incident room' coordinator," Sheehy said.

"That would be grand." Danny gestured toward O'Neil and his other DO, Detective Pinkney, who sat at their desks. "We could use the help."

As incident room coordinator, Sheehy would function as the office man, weeding through paperwork, assigning follow-up tasks, and ensuring that no leads fell through the cracks. They had him and O'Donnell in Lisfenora for a week. Danny planned to make full use of them to organize their arses.

"First off." Sheehy handed a folder to Danny. "Just in."

Danny flipped it open, grimaced, and handed it off to O'Neil. Benjy's report on Annie Belden's cause of death. Danny hadn't attended the autopsy because he'd run to the Ennis hospital to ensure that Ellen was settled. The doctors at the Limerick hospital had deemed her well enough to be transferred to the local facility once again. No one had bothered to call him until after she'd arrived in Ennis.

"Eileen Browne, her therapist, predicted an insulin overdose," Danny said, "and she was correct. She also thought suicide, which might have stuck if we'd found her medications in the house."

"Conspicuous in their absence." Sheehy wrote *insulin overdose* on the whiteboard.

"Odd that," O'Neil said. "If you're trying to get away with murder, why pilfer the one item that could lead to a suicide verdict?"

Once again, Danny pondered the nonsensical aspects of the crime scene: Annie's face covered with due respect in sharp contrast with the dead flowers. "What do we know about the bouquet?"

"Nothing yet," Pinkney said.

Sheehy grumbled under his breath, then said, "O'Donnell, you've got flower research."

"Our first priority for the Belden case," Danny said, "is to find a man named Cedric Gibson."

Sheehy raised his chin at O'Neil, and O'Neil nodded. "Yes, sir."

Sheehy wrote the task assignment on the whiteboard. Danny breathed a sigh of relief. They might make progress now that they had enough men for proper division of labor.

"There's another man, Nathan Tate, who'd recently taken up with Annie. I'm circling around him. He needs a light touch because he's none too stable."

Sheehy wrote Danny's name next to Nathan's on the whiteboard. He pointed to the paper piles amassed on the incident room table. "Will I find memoranda from her neighbors in that mess?"

O'Neil spoke up. "Yes, all there. Somewhere." He leaned back in his chair with his hands clasped behind his head. "The last sighting we have of Annie is late Thursday afternoon, when the neighbor across the lane saw her setting out the rubbish for the bin men. Pinkney and I got an earful from her. Annie's security lights are bright enough to read by, according to the neighbor. She nattered on about having to buy black-out curtains for her bedroom, on and on and on, until I got out of her that on the night in question, the lights triggered at 12:30, 1:43—not 1:45, mind, but 1:43—2:18, 2:37, and 5:18. More than usual, according to her."

"The neighbor wrote it down?" Sheehy said.

"Indeed. Quite the long list of offenses she had against Annie Belden."

Sheehy added *Irate neighbors?* to the whiteboard list.

"Cats, badgers, possums, or foxes could account for that," O'Donnell said.

"Any joy tracking the missing mobile?" Sheehy said. "What about family?"

"Joyless thus far," O'Neil said. "Her brother who lives in Spain arrived to see to her affairs. Next of kin scattered for both EJ and Annie, and either alibied or living too far away to be interesting."

Sheehy tapped his marker on EJ's side of the whiteboard. "I found the report about the turf cutter that killed Joseph Macy. When did the tool go missing?"

"There's when it went missing and when Alan Bressard, the owner, noticed that it went missing," Danny said. "He said the pile of antiques sat on the floor for a week. He noticed the *sleán* missing when he went to hang it back up, about three days after EJ's death."

"The *sleán* didn't jig its way out of the pub on its own," Sheehy said.

"Alan's dog lies back there." Danny had thought about this, about how he'd pinch a turf cutter other than by breaking into the place. "It's toward the back of the pub near the corridor that leads to the toilets, kitchen, and back door. Anyone could have stooped to pet Bijou and tucked the cutter into a coat, then strolled out the back door."

"Awkward," Sheehy said.

Danny nodded. Bloody awkward.

Sheehy tilted his head back to peer through his glasses at yet another piece of paper. "Nathan Tate again. The murder weapon was found with his painting supplies at—Fox Cottage, is it? And he warms a stool same as EJ did at the Plough and Trough. I'd say he needs to be brought in for a more formal chat."

"Not yet," Danny said. "Trust me on this one. If we push him too hard, he'll shatter."

"Useless as tits on a nun he'd be then," O'Neil said. "I second that."

Sheehy looked mournful as he gazed at the whiteboard. "In other words, we've got feck all."

"About the size of it," Danny said. "Except for Cedric Gibson."

"We've assumed the cases are unrelated," Sheehy said, "but for the sake of argument, suppose we were to find a connection between Annie and EJ, something that led to both of their deaths—"

"Nathan was friendly with both of them," O'Neil said.

"Just so." In Sheehy's precise printing, Nathan's name straddled the divide between the cases.

Danny sensed Sheehy's wheels chugging toward the obvious answer, the easy answer: Nathan Tate. Not that Nathan didn't intrigue Danny, but there was something to understand about Nathan that still eluded him.

"We need to look into who else knew both Annie and EJ," Danny said. "It could be that Cedric Gibson has a connection to EJ that we don't know about yet."

Sheehy pointed at Pinkney. "Gibson's connection to Joseph Macy, anyone's connection to both Annie and Joseph."

Danny grabbed coffee and settled in for the rest of the afternoon of paperwork and phone calls. His mind kept returning to Nathan. He knew a fact about Nathan that he hadn't reported yet: the horrific scar on his side, a scar that devoted Zoe had surely tried to heal with the cure. Danny ignored the voice that taunted him about his growing interest in Zoe as a wannabe healer.

FIFTY-TWO

THE COFFEEMAKER'S BURBLE SOOTHED Nathan, as it did all day, every day. He cracked open a window and stuck his head out. The breeze tingled against his skin and lessened the pressure inside his head. Since Annie's death, the intermittent buzz he struggled to ignore had turned into a constant background noise, more of a static and crackle. The desperate pitch of it accompanied him everywhere, and exhaustion added its gritty whine to the mix.

His mind was a traitor. He knew this as surely as he heard the soft *can yoouu coo* call from a dove perched on his firing shed.

Can yoouu kill, can yoouu kill

Chilled, he eased the window shut with a soft click. He poured himself a cup of coffee and entered his studio. The static and crackle gained volume as his thoughts wandered to the work tasks for the day. He had thirty pots to trim.

Setting aside his coffee cup, he pulled the bottom drawer all the way out of his toolbox and dug beneath needle-nose pliers, wire strippers, and random nails. He pulled out a rolled length of fishing line left over from his angling days in England. He'd kept it all these years. It was supposed to be more proof, along with his scar.

The static and crackle eased off. He closed his eyes, savoring the internal quietude. He wasn't sure why holding the fishing wire calmed him, only that it did.

Can yoouu kill, can yoouu kill

He didn't remember the time after Susannah's death well. Fleeting images and dark feelings and fear, the blurred terrain of his nightmares. Commonly known as a mental breakdown. Clinically known as a psychotic break.

No way in bloody hell he'd let that happen again. He'd as soon obliterate someone else as let himself go that route. He squeezed the fishing line as his thoughts wandered down what could only be a doomed path. To find the man who had killed Annie, who had played a game with text messages and a sickening bouquet. Maybe Nathan could save himself this time.

He tucked the fishing line into his jeans pocket and pulled out his mobile to peer at an image that he'd snapped before the guards arrived at Annie's house. He was pretty good with flowers. He recognized the yellow carnations and the less obvious purple monkshood. The bouquet maker had gone to some trouble to find the monkshood. That struck Nathan as significant.

An Internet search provided the information Nathan sought. The Victorians had sent yellow carnations to indicate disappointment—as in, *you have disappointed me*—and rejection. Monkshood said *beware, danger is near*. And, as he'd overheard the pathologist say, the withered flowers symbolized unrequited love.

Nathan tapped the mobile screen. If he was correct, the person—probably a man—who took Annie's mobile also had Annie's journal. This person now knew the names of all the players in Annie's life. If she'd disappointed this person in love, it stood to reason that he might come after the rival for Annie's affections. The monkshood said danger was near, which could mean that Annie's killer still lurked in the vicinity.

Can yoouu kill, can yoouu kill

Sighing with what even he recognized as sick gratification, Nathan bent over the mobile again. The purple ribbon could mean royalty, wisdom, and spirituality but also mourning, cruelty, and arrogance. Two sides of the same coin in which Annie represented the side of wisdom and the bouquet maker the side of cruelty.

Nathan knew this was the truth just like he knew that his dreams represented reality.

FIFTY-THREE

MERRIT RANG NATHAN'S DOORBELL. She had waited until Zoe arrived at Liam's house, full of springtime and vigor, to plead errands as an excuse to visit Nathan. She needed to talk to him about Zoe.

She rang again, and after several minutes the door opened. Merrit clamped down on her shock at Nathan's appearance. Don't react, she told herself; not so much as a twitch in response to his sallow skin and sunken eye sockets. Clay-encrusted jeans hung like the low-riders she remembered teenage boys wearing in the States. Only Nathan didn't appear to be wearing boxers beneath them. He led the way into the kitchen, where the smell of burnt coffee overpowered Nathan's gamey odor. He poured what remained in the pot into cups and sat down at the table.

"You need to eat," Merrit said.

"It's hard to eat around Zoe sometimes. She chatters too much when I'd prefer quiet. For the past few days she only talks about the Easter Festival."

"A week from today and counting. There's too much to do, but maybe that's a blessing in disguise. I don't have as much time to dwell on Liam or Annie or Elder Joe." She paused. "I'm sorry about Annie."

Nathan shook his head without looking at her. His gaze wandered over the tabletop, restless, agitated.

"Let me fix you something to eat."

Merrit set about finding eggs and a pan. Five minutes later she placed a mound of scrambled eggs in front of Nathan. While he ate, she threw out their coffees, scrubbed the pot, and started the coffeemaker burbling afresh.

She sat down across from Nathan. He shoveled eggs into his mouth and chewed in a mechanical manner. She tried not to stare at the play of muscles and tendons in his neck when he swallowed.

"To be honest," she said, "I've been curious about Zoe for a while, but I'm especially interested now that she's holding hands with Liam all the time. That's why I'm here. To ask you about that."

"I'm not surprised," Nathan said.

"She didn't mention that she's 'curing' Liam?"

"She wouldn't have. I want nothing to do with it."

Merrit rose and fetched fresh coffee for him. She'd heard something in his clenched tone that she couldn't decipher. She returned to her seat. "Why don't you want anything to do with it?"

Nathan pulled something out of his jeans pocket and fiddled with it on his lap. "I've lived with Zoe and her healing since she was a girl."

"So she's always been—?" Merrit didn't want to say *delusional*, not to a man who wavered on the rocky edge himself, and she didn't want to hint at what could pass down through the family lines either.

Nathan understood her well enough. He smiled, at last. The hollows under his eyes deepened with the effort, a ghastly effect that faded immediately. "Was she always inclined that way? Yes. Around twelve years old, she started up with it." His voice clenched again.

"Healing birds. I don't know where she first got the idea she could heal."

"Is it real?" Merrit said. "I've heard many fantastical things since I moved to Ireland, so I have to ask. I have to know for Liam's sake. He's hopeful. Too hopeful."

Nathan stood and walked into a small bathroom off the kitchen. His retching tore at her. Too much food, eaten too fast. When he returned, he waved away her sorries. He steadied himself against the counter. "Is Liam feeling better?"

"He says so, yes."

"If he's better, you have your answer."

"Jesus, Nathan, are you saying she's for real?" Merrit said.

Nathan slipped into his chair as if he couldn't bear his weight any longer. "I don't want to know. I'm sure Liam knows how to manage Zoe."

True. Liam said he was experimenting, plus Zoe provided a novel distraction. On the other hand, even astute people deluded themselves when faced with their mortality.

Merrit still felt uneasy. Nathan's ambivalence about his daughter didn't do her cause any good. "Nathan," she said to capture his attention. "This is an odd question and none of my business, considering she's your daughter, but why are you letting her stay with you if you don't—"

"Enjoy the company?" He caught Merrit's eye. "I can't give her the boot. All I can do is leave myself, which is probably what will happen."

Merrit gathered herself to leave, but Nathan reanimated with a start and grabbed her arm. "The text messages we received."

She let her arm remain in his grip. It wasn't so much that he held her as that he clung to her. "What about them?"

"I believe the man who killed Annie left the bouquet and texted us."

"Man?"

"Because of the bouquet. Unrequited love."

"That's right." She'd overheard that, too. "I'll play that game with you, but you're assuming she was killed."

"I'm sure of it. I can tell by Danny's interest in me. I suppose I'm a suspect." He unclasped her arm. "I must find the man who killed her. I rang her mobile, forgetting like, that she"—he waved the words away—"and someone answered."

Now Merrit wanted to clasp his arm. "What did he say?"

"Nothing, not a peep out of him before he hung up."

"He'd have to be daft to keep the mobile, wouldn't he?" Merrit mused. "Have you told Danny yet? He should know."

Nathan's gaze clouded over again. He slouched against his chair. "Ay, should do."

She'd lost him again. He returned to fiddling with whatever he held on his lap. She hoped for his sake that he didn't find the keeper of Annie's mobile.

FIFTY-FOUR

NATHAN SAT FOR A while after Merrit left. Outside, budding fuchsias bent double with the force of the wind. He placed the rolled-up fishing line he held on the table next to his coffee cup and let the whistle and howl of the wind bat at the edges of his faulty memory. The sublime scent of river mold that wafted up from his waders. The spray from the garden hose that misted over him as he sluiced river silt off of them.

He'd returned from a fishing trip the day Susannah died. Filleted bass stored in the freezer, and his fishing gear due for a good scrub. He was in fine form, whistling as he went about his business, while Susannah puttered about the kitchen with the ingredients for a new recipe laid out on the counter. She loved nothing better than a Sunday afternoon trip to the outdoor market, followed by sipping Italian red while she considered how to improve a recipe she'd never tried before.

That day, what was it to be? Something ridiculous that you'd only order in an overpriced restaurant. Something to do with quail eggs.

That day, Susannah's favorite aria from *Madame Butterfly* blew around on a slight breeze. Nathan stood near the front door in view of the entryway and the stairs leading up to the bedrooms when she appeared with wineglass in hand. The last words she spoke to him were a joke between them, her detesting the fishy smell of him. "What shall it be for you today? I think the lemon balm soap. Come drink wine with me after your shower."

He admired her in her slim capris as she trotted barefoot up the stairs to set out a fresh bar of soap for him. He turned away then to clean the rods and reels, losing time in a pleasant way. Thirty minutes later, in the garage, he paused in reaction to a muffled sound. A thump? A squeal? Perhaps nothing and memory supplied the details for the moment his life changed forever.

Whatever he sensed propelled him into the house to find Zoe bent over Susannah. Nathan froze at the sight of his wife sprawled, as limp as one of Nathan's dead fish, at the bottom of the stairs with her head at an odd angle.

"I'm healing her." Zoe's intensity stained her cheeks red as she pressed her hands over her mother's heart. "You know I can."

"Stop it." He ran forward and pushed at her. "Haven't you called Emergency yet?"

"I can save her, I can." She spread her hands on Susannah's chest and closed her eyes, infuriating Nathan further. As he reached out to grab her away, Susannah's eyes fluttered open. Her mouth opened and closed, and Nathan recoiled at its similarity to the fish he caught.

"See, Dad?" Zoe said.

Nathan dropped to his knees in time to see Susannah's gaze turn blink-less.

"I did it, though, didn't I?" Zoe scooted closer and repositioned her hands. "For a second, but it worked. Maybe if I keep—"

"Stop."

"—trying. She should be okay—"

"Stop!"

He pushed her, too hard this time, so that she sprawled backward with a stricken expression. Immediately her young skin smoothed out and she crowded in on him with a hug. "I love you, Dad, and I'll take care of you. You adored Mum, I know. She was so dear."

He'd pulled away from her then, repulsed. "You should have called Emergency."

His memory of Susannah's death looked like Zoe bending over her slack form at the bottom of the staircase. It looked like his guilt. His faulty memory didn't lessen the fact that Susannah's death was his fault. Her death opened the doors for the darkness, that he knew. And later, after his keepers deemed him fit for civilization again, he'd settled into his pottery and a semi-itinerant life. What he'd call normal if normal included eluding his daughter.

Can yoouu kill, can yoouu kill

"Not now with that," he muttered.

A noise pulled Nathan back into the kitchen. He tensed. The wind continued howling around the house. *Thump.* He made his way into the studio. The back door whipped out of his grip and banged into the wall. He ran to his firing shed and grabbed one of the aluminum cans. He dropped three bricks into it to prevent the wind from flinging it against the wall again and dashed back to the house. He yanked the back door closed and leaned against it. The wind had blown away the cobwebs. He knew what he needed to do next.

His stomach ached with hunger. Back in the kitchen, he poured himself another cup of coffee and ate a bowl of corn flakes without tasting them. He rinsed the bowl and spoon, set them in the drying rack, and picked up his mobile. He dialed Annie's number.

Can yoouu kill, can yoouu kill

Nathan thought maybe he could.

FIFTY-FIVE

Monday, 29-Mar

Well, well, well, dear Annie, your paramour is a more interesting specimen than I'd imagined. I really must chuck your mobile. I'm flirting with my own ruin by holding on to it. If you were here, you'd tell me that I enjoy the risk. You'd be correct, of course, but we both know that most of the time the guards are sucking their thumbs, hampered by their own ineptitude.

No worries, I've now hidden the mobile off my person but easily accessible. I'll toss it later. I knew keeping it around would prove fun, at the very least to learn who your friends are. You've received a few calls. Hellos from people who don't know that death claimed you. These people can't be that significant, so I deleted the messages.

Nathan Tate, though, he addressed me when he left his message yesterday: "Hello, I hope I'm talking to the man who sent me the text message. You have Annie's journal, don't you? So you know who I am."

No fuddle-headed mistaken call this time. In his way, he's trying to court me. He's doing a bad job of it, but I admire the effort. I look forward to his next call.

FIFTY-SIX

IN ENNIS HOSPITAL, ELLEN'S chest rose and fell on its own now. No more ventilator. Her doctor had tried to talk to Danny about next steps because Ellen's inert body would continue to attract infections and to deteriorate. He'd brushed aside the attempts, still not ready to consider the doctor's opinion about whether or not to continue life-prolonging measures.

Nathan stepped up beside him, full of stink and despair. "Why am I here?"

"Merrit rang me. She's concerned about your health. Since I was on my way to the hospital anyhow, I thought we could get you checked out by a friend of mine. Nothing official. He should be along in a few minutes."

"You lied to me."

"I did, but would you have come otherwise?"

"No."

Danny had detoured by Nathan's house on his way to the hospital, and Nathan acquiesced when Danny said he had more questions for him. Danny arrived in time to see Zoe and a lad squealing off in a beat-up Ford Fiesta. One look at Nathan, and Danny was glad he'd arranged this intervention.

"You're not doing anyone any good with this slow death spiral," Danny said.

"Which is code for, I'm not doing you any good for your investigation."

Danny caught a glimpse of the alert and astute Nathan he'd gotten to know at the Plough. He still existed in there somewhere but submerged.

A brief knock interrupted them. Dr. Singh, whom Danny now called Sanjay, entered. He'd helped Danny a few years back during a prior investigation. Since then, Singh had become Danny's source for all things medical. He wore an off-duty outfit of jeans, anorak, and scarf.

Danny introduced Nathan. Sanjay gazed at Nathan, studying him from head to toe while Nathan edged along the wall toward the door.

"This is a trap," Nathan said.

"No trap, Mr. Tate," Sanjay said. "I'm here as a friend of Danny's who happens to be a doctor, although it doesn't take a doctor to see that you're not well. Danny told me the barest facts. You don't sleep?"

Nathan burst from the wall and elbowed Sanjay in his attempt to flee the room. Danny wrapped an arm around him. It didn't take much brawn to halt the man; he was weak as a newborn bunny. Danny lowered Nathan to a chair.

"I'm not for that place again," Nathan said. "Please."

"I'm concerned about your *physical* health," Danny said. "Can Sanjay look you over?"

"My physical health," Nathan said, "and nothing else?"

"Nothing else."

"Fine," Nathan said.

Sanjay peered into Nathan's mouth and pressed his fingers against Nathan's skin. He pulled a stethoscope out of a satchel he carried and listened to Nathan's heart. He then measured Nathan's blood pressure and pulse. "Too high," he murmured. "Running on fumes. When did you last eat?"

"Yesterday," Nathan said.

"And water?"

"Coffee."

"Bugger all good coffee does you. You're dehydrated. I can talk to someone about admitting you overnight for fluids."

Nathan shook his head. "I'm not for that place."

"Overnight," Danny said. "For fluids and rest. Nothing else. I'm sure they'll give you a sedative to help you sleep."

"I wouldn't mind that," Nathan said after a pause.

Sanjay beckoned Danny to follow him out of the room. "He's in bad shape," he said when they reached the corridor, "but it's nothing water, food, and sleep won't fix. At least for his body. His mind is another issue altogether. He's a suspect, you say?"

"Let's call him a person of interest."

"Hmm. I'm wondering if he was diagnosed with PTSD at some point. His lack of self-care and his instinct to escape—just a thought."

"An interesting thought," Danny said. "Some PTSD sufferers are dangerous if triggered the right way. I want to show you something. It might shed light."

He returned to Nathan with Sanjay close behind. "You're grand," he said as he hoisted Nathan to his feet with an arm over his shoulders. The stench of him was enough to make Danny retch. "Sanjay, if you would, please lift his t-shirt."

Nathan shook his head but otherwise didn't resist.

"Holy Mother." Sanjay dropped to one knee to view the scar at eye level. He manipulated the thick scar tissue with deft fingers. "This isn't just one wound."

"What do you mean?" Danny said.

"This is many wounds in the same place. Is that true, Mr. Tate?"

Nathan's head sagged on his neck. Danny almost roused him with a shake, but thought better of it.

"Self-inflicted?" Danny said.

Sanjay let the t-shirt fall back in place and stood. "Self-harm, cutting—"

"Do men cut themselves?"

"They do, in increasing numbers, in fact. As you might expect, if cutting is their preferred method, men are more likely to make larger, deeper cuts than women are." He placed his hands on either side of Nathan's face and straightened his head. "Mr. Tate? How did you injure yourself?"

He seemed to be searching Nathan, trying to excavate his head. Nathan responded by closing his eyes.

———

Later, after reading to Ellen, Danny visited Nathan on the open men's ward. Unlike Ward 2B, located in a newish wing of the hospital, Nathan's ward consisted of jam-packed beds with frayed blue curtains and a depressing air of the antiquated. A crucifix hung on the wall above the entry.

Bathed and hooked up to a fluid line, Nathan lay with eyes closed, gaunt face in repose. He opened his eyes wide at the sound of Danny's footsteps. Then relaxed again. He offered Danny a smile, weary and dazed, but there all the same. "Hospital vacation. Probably a good thing. Thank you."

"A shower was a step in the right direction anyhow."

"They dosed me with a nice drug. Lessened the noise in my head. I can think straight, and maybe I'll sleep."

Danny pulled up a chair and sat down. "You were correct about one thing—I need you coherent so you can help me with the investigation."

"Self-serving, ay." Nathan closed his eyes again. His head sank deeper into the pillow. "We all are. Even me, with Annie."

"Oh?"

"She was a balm. Being with her took me out of my head."

And his head was a dangerous place, that much was obvious. Danny considered how to proceed with Nathan. Best get straight to the point before lunch rounds and sedatives pulled him away from Danny again. "We're considering a theory that EJ's and Annie's deaths are connected, and thus far you're the only connection between them we have."

Nathan's eyes flew open. His irises expanded rather than contracted. Fear response. Or a sudden realization. Something was going on inside Nathan's head.

"There's no connection," Nathan said. "Or if there is, it's not related to knowing me. It can't be. They both helped people—a connection to health care."

"For EJ, that's a debatable question."

"What would their deaths have to do with me?" Nathan shifted under the sheets. "There's the person who sent me the text."

"I haven't forgotten."

Nathan's confusion appeared authentic, but then so did the fear that lurked beneath the confusion. Danny couldn't get a proper read on him. He changed the topic. "Tell me about your scar."

"Talking about it is part of what sent me to Broadmoor. So I don't. It's unrelated."

"Are you sure about that?"

"Do me the favor of not telling anyone I'm here. I'd rather not talk if I don't have to. I need to think, if I can."

"Zoe?"

"No one."

The lunch cart clanked at the other end of the ward and Nathan's eyes drifted shut. Danny's mobile vibrated. He drew the curtains around Nathan's bed to avoid getting caught using the mobile on the ward.

"Danny here," he whispered.

"This is bloody beautiful," O'Neil said. "I know who Cedric Gibson is, all right, and he's here in Clare."

FIFTY-SEVEN

MERRIT STOOD AT THE door of the men's ward waiting for an orderly or nurse to let her into this area of the hospital. She pressed the entry button again. A moment later, instead of a hospital employee, Danny almost smacked into her as he pushed through the door. His concentrated expression spoke volumes. He was revved up, eager to be gone, but he halted when he saw her. "What are you doing here?"

"It's visiting hours. Remember, I'm the one who called you about Nathan."

"He doesn't want visitors," Danny said.

"Too bad. And Zoe will arrive this evening."

Danny nodded to a row of chairs lining the wall outside the ward and urged her toward them with a hand around her arm. He nudged her down to sit beside him. He lowered his voice. "Have you heard the name Cedric Gibson?"

Some of Danny's perturbed energy rubbed off on Merrit. One look at his spotlighting gaze, the one he'd used on her plenty of times, and she blurted, "He's the one who sent the texts, isn't he?"

"Who told you?" His pursed his lips. "Bloody O'Neil. I warned him about your meddling."

"Oh, stop. Simon hasn't said a word. Your demeanor gave it away."

"No, it didn't."

"Go on, what about Cedric Gibson? Did he leave the bouquet, too?"

"Christ. Slow down."

Merrit smiled and understood in a flash that she missed talking to someone who challenged her. Liam didn't count, being her father.

Danny rubbed at his face. "Your date with O'Neil the other night."

"My date?"

"O'Neil said the two of you met a man named Sid."

"Him? But he's—" In truth, she'd forgotten about him. "He's not a man you'd notice. Brown hair and fair skin like most of the men in the room. He can't have sent the messages. He was standing right there when I received mine."

"Would you have noticed him tapping on a mobile? No, of course not." He smiled, relenting. "Don't get ahead of yourself. We don't know anything yet. Tell me about him."

"He was with Zoe, and he's too boring for her. That's about all I got from him. What did Simon say about him?"

"Nothing that stood out. O'Neil"—was it Merrit's imagination that he emphasized Simon's last name?—"recognized him when he saw the arrest picture for a man named Cedric Gibson. How did he and Zoe get along?"

"I don't think they were on a date—not like that, anyhow. Romantically."

Danny had been scrutinizing her as she spoke, but he looked away now. She squirmed. It was true, she hadn't sensed a spark between Zoe and Sid. She rushed on, past all things "dates." "When did Annie die?"

"About twenty-four hours before you received the text."

"Why wait a day to send it?"

"I wish I knew." Danny glanced at the ward door. "Would you say you have a good rapport with Nathan?"

Merrit thought about it for a second. "I think so. He's helping me fix up Fox Cottage."

"I need to understand Nathan better, but gentle-like. He may or may not be connected to all of this."

"I understand. You need to know one way or another. I can be your unofficial intermediary."

Danny straightened, tension dissipating slightly. "Keep this between you and I."

Merrit clenched her hands, longing to pump her fists in triumph. For eighteen months, she'd wanted him on her side. Or at least accepting of her as part of his immediate circle of friends. *Friends* might be pushing it, but *friendly acquaintances* would do for now.

"You realize you're giving me permission to meddle, right?" she said.

Danny slapped his hands against his thighs and stood. "I might as well accept that I can't stop you, but you aren't a bloody private investigator. I want insights into Nathan, his relationship with Zoe, his mental state. Like that." He'd been rifling through his pockets. Now he stared her down. "Are we square?"

"Cheers," she said by way of answer.

He paused in the midst of straightening his jacket. "You realize that's not a response."

"What should I have said—to be Irish?"

"A simple 'okay' suffices. Or if you want to get fancy, 'not a bother.'"

He hurried down the corridor without saying goodbye, but Merrit didn't mind. She'd passed a test she'd never understood. With one small fist pump, she pressed the button to be allowed into the ward. Nathan in all his turmoil and mysterious complications awaited.

FIFTY-EIGHT

BENEATH THE MEDICATION THAT the doctor had given Nathan, the static and crackle shivered around the edges of his thoughts, waiting to burst through the soft fuzz brought on by the meds. He still heard the refrain that now accompanied him throughout the day.

Can yoouu kill, can yoouu kill

The sound of it gleeful now, having overheard Danny's whispered conversation and the name that Danny had repeated back to his caller, corroborating it: Cedric Gibson, who went by Sid.

Nathan knew that name; of course he did. Zoe had introduced them the night Sid picked her up to go listen to a band. He pictured Zoe inviting the man into his house for the introduction. She'd always been proper about introductions, but Nathan hadn't cared. He'd continued dipping a vase into glaze without looking up.

This man—Sid. He was playing a game. Had to be; why else befriend Zoe? Or maybe Zoe had befriended him.

Footsteps and voices approached his corner of the ward. The curtains around him parted. "He's awake, yes. He needs to eat his lunch."

A nurse bustled in and raised his bed to a sitting position. She arranged him as if he were one of the pillows and swung a tray with his lunch on it over his lap.

"Chicken breast with mash and peas." She adjusted the fluid line as she passed. "You should be feeling better with the fluids."

A murmur and then Merrit peeked her head in. "Nathan?"

He picked up a fork and knife, considered the knife for a moment—not sharp—and hacked into the pallid chicken flesh. He ignored the greyish peas that floated on soupy mashed potatoes.

Merrit squinched her nose up in distaste. "Appetizing. I ran into Danny on my way in. He said you didn't want visitors, but I was already here. Hope that's okay. I won't stay long."

The chicken was nothing but textures on Nathan's tongue. He accepted that he required food if he hoped to hunt down Sid and obliterate him. He'd take on that task to redeem himself of Susannah's death. And Annie's. He suspected he was to blame for her death, too. He didn't know how, but it didn't matter. He latched onto Sid like a life preserver.

"That man, Sid," he said.

"You know about him?"

"Yes, yes, Zoe introduced him to me, plus I overheard Danny's side of a phone conversation." He cut more chicken and placed it inside his mouth. "What did Danny say about him?"

So Merrit told him, and Nathan leaned back into the pillows. Cedric Gibson.

"All I know is that he's someone from Annie's past," Merrit said.

"I'm sure it's him," Nathan said. "It has to be. The man who killed Annie."

"Maybe. That's what the guards are investigating." She adjusted her purse on her shoulder. "But Nathan, they're interested in you, too. You know that, don't you?"

Of course. He was an utter lunatic with a faulty memory, a man who couldn't go a day without losing time or going mental or stumbling to his knees under the weight of his exhaustion.

He knew how it looked.

After Merrit left, Nathan drifted into sleep on the peaceful waves brought on by thoughts of obliterating Sid Gibson.

FIFTY-NINE

DANNY PAUSED OUTSIDE A storefront labeled GENTLEMEN'S GROOM-ING, PETER ENRIGHT, BEARBÓIR. After O'Neil's call that morning about Cedric Gibson, Danny had sped from Nathan's bedside to the station, and from the station to this barbershop.

O'Neil pointed through the window into the shop. "That's Gibson."

A brown-haired man sat on one of the barber's chairs. He wore an ill-fitting sport jacket with jeans and slouched in relaxed fashion with a half smile aimed at his reflection. The beginnings of a double chin bunched up beneath his jaw.

Peter Enright, the barber, glanced at them when they entered. "How are you keeping?"

"Hanging in there, anyhow," O'Neil said.

Cedric Gibson smiled at them through the mirror. Danny hung back, letting O'Neil approach first. "'Allo, Sid, was it?" O'Neil said. "We met over in Doolin."

"Nice to see you again. Simon, yes?"

Merrit's assessment of Sid was spot-on: dull as bricks. Danny wouldn't clock him, if he did at all, as anything but an unassuming bloke who worked an office job, the first generation off the farm, and who enjoyed the little pleasures such as a professional trim and a yearly trip to Dublin.

Sid's smile remained when Danny asked the barber to switch the shop sign to "Closed" and take a break. They didn't have to worry about gossip out of him: he kept his and his clients' confidences to himself.

"I'll be next door at the pub," Peter said. "Fetch me when you're done, sonny."

"Ay, will do." Sid pulled out his wallet and paid Peter. The bell chimed above the door as Peter pulled it shut. Sid glanced at himself in the mirror. "He does a fair job, doesn't he?"

"Your name is Cedric Gibson, is it not?" Danny said.

Sid swiveled his chair to face them. "It is. I go by Sid. How may I help you, officers?"

"Your name has come up in relation to the suspicious death of Annie Belden."

What looked to be genuine sorrow wilted his smile. "I saw the news in the papers. I'm not surprised you were looking for me, but I am surprised you found me so fast. How did you manage that?"

"You come here every day for a shave," O'Neil said. "Plenty of people have seen you about."

"There's nothing like a professional shave." Sid swiveled back and forth a few times. "How did good Annie die?"

O'Neil raised his eyebrows, looking impressed. Gibson may or may not be guilty, but the guilty often forgot to ask this question. Danny considered whether to answer. Cause of death hadn't made the news yet, but it would soon enough. "Insulin overdose."

"Ah, right. She was diabetic. I knew that."

Danny pulled up one of the stools and perched on it. O'Neil remained standing with his notebook in hand. "What brought you to Clare?"

"Annie." His half smile turned apologetic. "You don't need to tell me the timing looks too coincidental. I know."

He knew many things, did Sid Gibson.

"Why visit Annie after all this time?" Danny said. "You had an unorthodox relationship with her that ended her career. So why contact her?"

"To apologize," Sid said. "To close the circle on the past. Annie was a brilliant practitioner of the psychiatric arts, and I like to think that I'm out here functioning in the world thanks to her. I didn't behave well under her care, and I wanted to perform my own version of making amends."

"What were your plans for this reunion?" Danny said.

He shrugged. "I hadn't thought it through. A pint and a laugh?"

"I imagine more along the lines of another cozy writing retreat."

"Bloody hell, that?" Sid rubbed the back of his neck with a wry chuckle. "You get used to being on the inside, you know. I didn't know how to handle my freedom."

The man had all the answers. "Where were you on the night of Thursday, the twenty-fifth of March?"

"My alibi, you mean? I suppose I was in a pub." He pulled a pocket-sized date book out of his jacket pocket and flipped the pages. "Nothing written for that day, but the next night I listened to music in Doolin." He nodded to O'Neil. "You saw me there with that bird, Zoe Tate. I'd met Zoe the night before, which makes her my alibi on Thursday. She can tell you which pub."

"How long were you here for by then?"

"A few weeks."

"Why take your time to make amends to Annie? Why not be done with it and on your way?"

"Good question." Sid puzzled over the answer for a moment. "I suppose I needed to gear myself up for it."

"How did you find out she'd moved to Clare?" Danny asked.

"That was easy enough. I got it from her mum. Clare is the last place I'd expected Annie to land." He nodded more to himself than to Danny. "People are too fascinating for words."

"Her mother gave you Annie's address as simple as that?"

Sid shrugged yet again. The gesture annoyed Danny, which may have been Sid's goal. "She's in a memory-loss home. Annie has a brother, did you know? I used his name to gain access. Annie's mum went right along with it, happy as could be. I could have been the Easter bunny for all she cared. Now you'll ask me how I knew about Annie's mum. The answer is that after I was discharged to a high-support hostel, Annie used to visit to help me run errands, look for a job, and so on—she was very helpful. One day we visited her mother together. She's a nice old bird."

"Odd behavior for a professional."

"True, but I considered us friends by then."

"Meanwhile, she fell in love with you and sabotaged her own career to support your move to freedom."

Sid didn't respond.

"Where did you find Annie's address?"

"In the night table. Her mum had an ancient address book. At some point, Annie had updated her own address and phone number, not that the information does the old girl any good these days. Be lucky if she can read a toothpaste label."

"Do you know Joseph Macy?"

For the first time, Gibson's easy-going composure shifted. His head recoiled, turtle-like, further enhancing his doughy chin. His voice turned haughty. "Like I said, I read the newspapers. Are you looking to solve all your crimes in one go?"

"Do you know him?"

"No." He kicked out his foot, almost landing a blow to Danny's shin. "This is a bore now that you're shooting questions in any direction. Do you have anything meaningful to ask me?"

"We have it from someone close to Annie that you frightened her. You must have known this."

"I'd never hurt her. Not a hair on her head."

"You have killed before. What's to stop you from killing again?"

"I didn't kill the diplomat's daughter." His smile returned. "And I think you know that. It was a tragic accident, but I also don't want you to think I'm hiding anything. You might as well know that I drove past Annie's place a few times. A neighbor might have seen me, and I know that, and now you know that I know that. See, I don't want anyone to assume I'm off my rocker. I'm not. This isn't a repeat performance. The first time I drove past, I wanted to see where she lived. After that, she wasn't home when I dropped in, so I couldn't make amends."

Jesus, the man was making it up as he went. Danny decided to play along. "Did you see anything unusual as you were passing by?"

"It wasn't as if I were stalking her." For the first time, he bared his teeth in a wide smile. "Sorry, I couldn't resist."

"Did you happen to pass by her house the night she died, too?" Danny said.

"I wish I had passed by at the right time. Maybe I could have prevented her death." Sid stood along with Danny and O'Neil. After adjusting a black mourning armband, he buttoned his jacket over his

243

paunch. He stood aside to let Danny and O'Neil exit the barbershop ahead of him. In silence, he followed them out, shut the door, and ambled into the pub next door, just another bland man going about his bland business.

SIXTY

Once again, Merrit surveyed the world from her bedroom window. Watching the weather had become part of her morning routine, similar to reading her horoscope when she was a kid. Today a hulking grey mass of cloud floated north, taking the rain with it. In its wake, sunshine streaked through lighter fluffy clouds and a rainbow grew out of the ground in an iridescent arc. A flock of starlings swirled like an airborne school of fish and settled on a telephone line while lambs bleated for their mamas in the neighbor's field. Spring had truly arrived. She decided to consider this a sign of a good day to come.

This was Merrit's second spring in Ireland, and even in her disenchanted state of mind, spring still came as a revelation after the gloomy winter. No wonder the ancients had celebrated with spring rituals. Beltane. Passover. The festival of Isis. Fertility cults the world over.

And, of course, Easter. This Sunday. Five days from now.

Merrit huffed hard enough that condensation formed on the window. Later the marquee company would arrive to set up the Cool

Chill party space, or whatever it was called, and she had a task list the length of her arm. She tightened the belt on her robe, straightened her shoulders, and opened her bedroom door to the wondrous smell of a full Irish breakfast. She wandered toward the kitchen, telling herself she shouldn't mind Zoe's presence. Merrit was grateful for help in keeping Liam's weight up. Now if only Zoe would do the same for Nathan.

The previous day, she'd left the hospital with an unsettled feeling high in her chest, but she hadn't understood what worried her until six o'clock this morning when the dawn chorus of songbirds woke her up. During their conversation, Nathan had become animated when he turned the conversation toward Sid Gibson. For a moment there he'd closed his eyes and smiled with pleasure, savoring a thought, which would have been fine if his expression hadn't looked like that of a—dare she think it?—madman. One madman recognizing the kindred spirit of another?

She shook off the thought and followed her nose toward the kitchen. "Zoe—" She stopped at the sight before her. "Liam?"

"In the flesh." He set a basket of brown bread on the kitchen island alongside a platter of rashers and white pudding. "What do you say now, oh, ye of little faith?"

Merrit perched on a stool and sprinkled salt on the roasted tomato, fried egg, and fried mushrooms already loading her plate. "I'm glad you're feeling better."

Liam's limp was still in play as he walked around the island and sat down next to her. He labored to pull air into his lungs, and she couldn't tell whether his rosy cheeks were the result of cooking over a hot stove or something else. But he did seem to have more energy. This could be remission, even though she doubted the possibility of spontaneous remission. Or, this could be the calm before the cancer storm.

She spooned up mushrooms. "Zoe's not a healer. There's got to be another explanation."

"Your loss. There's all manner of oddities in this funny world of ours."

"I wasn't raised with superstition and lore as my normal. It's not in me to accept these things the way the Irish seem to—at least as they do around here."

Liam heaped rashers onto her plate and then onto his. He'd made enough food to supply a small army. "That doesn't mean 'these things' aren't there, fleeting and rare in this modern age but still lurking about the sidelines, waiting for a chance to appear."

"Miracles." Merrit heard her scoffing tone. "Sorry, I don't mean to belittle it."

"Oh yes, you do. You want a rational explanation."

"That would be nice. How about a doctor's appointment? We'll hit up a new doctor for a new battery of tests."

"I don't need a bloody doctor to tell me I'm better." He pointed his fork at her. "And let me remind you that you believe in my ability to bring people together, but isn't matchmaking a lowly superstition, too?"

"That's different," Merrit said. "I've seen you in action. You're intuitive. You comprehend people. That's rational."

"Oh yeah?" he said. "You saw Zoe heal Bijou's paw."

Merrit waved her fork in front of Liam's fork. "That was crap and you know it. She cooked up some cockamamie incident to attract your attention. Believe me, she's all about you for some reason. What does she want from you?"

Liam lowered his fork and leaned back with a smile. "Ah. How do you know she wants something from me?"

Now Merrit was confused. "Are you giving me the piss?"

"*Taking* the piss, and no, I'm not taking the piss. It's a serious question. What makes you think Zoe wants something from me?"

Merrit bit into a sausage. "How the hell do I know? I just do. It's obvious."

"Really? It's obvious?"

"I see what you're doing, and I'm not buying that, either."

"Why not?" Liam said. "Your insight just now is no different than the insight I use when I'm matchmaking. If you can't say how or why you know what you know, then aren't we talking about something beyond rationality?"

"You *are* taking the piss." Merrit shoved her breakfast plate aside. "Goddammit, Liam, and you're pissing me off, too."

"Good. The question remains, if I can have this skill, why do you doubt that you have it, too?"

"We were talking about Zoe, not me," Merrit said. "I'm not part of this conversation."

"I'd say you are. I'd say your skepticism about Zoe is about you, not her. One thing you can say about Zoe, she doesn't doubt herself."

"Your expectations for my performance at the Easter Festival are too high," she said.

Liam picked up his laden plate. "Performance? Is that what you think of me?"

With that he excused himself to eat in the living room. Merrit lowered her head into her hands, feeling like a right shit. First Mrs. O'Brien, then Liam. She'd offended him, and in the midst of their argument she'd forgotten the point, which was to persuade Liam to seek a second medical opinion. Everyone had gone nutty—Nathan, Liam, Zoe, even Danny, who had given her permission to meddle. If she were superstitious, she'd blame it on spring fever, but she wasn't, so she wouldn't.

SIXTY-ONE

NATHAN SIPPED HERBAL ICED tea out of his new water bottle while Zoe bustled around the kitchen, arranging smoked salmon on a plate with a bagel, cream cheese, red onion, capers, and tomato. She'd picked him up from the hospital with water bottle in hand and an exclamation about how much better he looked. "A night away from the ball-and-chain daughter does wonders."

He set down the bottle and flexed his hand. The swelling had subsided and the scabs had a dry look to them. His toe no longer throbbed, and the stitches on his forehead were due to come out in a few days. The outside healed itself for all to see. Meanwhile, he couldn't shake the sense that he wasn't truly here. He couldn't feel textures with his hands anymore.

Zoe set the bagel in front of him. The pink salmon flesh gaped at him like an open wound, like a taunt at the parts of him that didn't heal.

"I think a 'thank you' cake for Danny's kids is in order today," Zoe said. "Above the call of duty for him to take you to the hospital."

"No need for that. Danny had his reasons. For the investigation."

Zoe stood with her back to him as she prepared her lunch plate. "I don't like the sound of that. You aren't a suspect."

"You understand why I'm of interest."

"Well—but there's nothing to pin on you. So what if you don't remember where you are most of the time?" She sat down opposite him. Her outstretched hand begged him to meet her halfway. "Dad, please. We're fine, right?"

"Ay." Zoe had collected her hair into loose pigtails. The curls cascaded over her shoulders, partially obscuring a chunky blue stone necklace. Lapus lazuli, he remembered. "That necklace—" he said.

She touched it, smiling. "One of my favorites of Mum's."

"It suits you." He poked his fork into the salmon. The chunky stones didn't suit her, though. They had suited Susannah with her patrician features and statuesque shoulders. She was wearing it the day she died.

Stomach lurching, he forked the salmon over to Zoe's plate. "Upset stomach from the meds."

"More for me." Zoe layered the meat over the salmon she already had and bit. A smear of cream cheese stuck to her lip. Nathan looked away. "I'm excited for the Earrach Festival. Liam asked me to oversee the music, did I tell you? I found a traditional band that also plays popular music."

One by one, Nathan stuck capers onto the cream cheese on his bagel. "The Sons of Erin?"

"Yes. They're brilliant. It should be a ball of a time. Plus, I'm going to let Merrit practice matchmaking on me."

He covered the capers with tomato and onion. "I hope your men friends won't mind."

"Men friends?" She grinned. "You say that with such loaded significance. They're mates, nothing else."

"That fella from last week—?"

"Sid?" She laughed. "He's far too serious for me, but he'll be at the festival. I've invited everyone I know. You'll go, too, right?"

"Yes." He bit into the bagel. His throat tightened, but he forced himself to chew and swallow. Zoe had already demolished her lunch. She stood and placed her plate in the sink. "I'll grab a late shower now. You're fine for the bathroom?"

"I'll shower in the rain if need be."

She clapped her hands. "There's your sense of humor. Fair play."

He returned her smile and bit into the bagel again. She bounced away and trotted up the stairs to the bathroom. Nathan shoved his lunch down the sink and turned on the garbage disposal. He placed his plate on top of Zoe's. The serrated bread knife sat on the counter. Nathan ran a finger along its edge, but not hard enough to draw blood.

Rain tapped the windows like skeleton fingers. He opened the knife drawer. He touched each knife in turn. One finger, one tap, until he reached the carving knife. He tapped it until the trembling in his finger subsided. He slid the drawer shut and exited the kitchen.

One of Zoe's purses hung on the hall stand. Bright yellow with lots of silver buckles and a front pocket. He reached inside it and pulled out her mobile.

A thud startled him. Zoe exclaimed through the noise of the shower. Vexed, by the sound of it, but the water continued to gurgle through the pipes and scented steam continued to leak down the stairs. She must have knocked down the shower caddy again.

Nathan pressed a button on her mobile and groaned. He needed her bloody password. An ache radiated from his tensed shoulders up the back of his head. She wouldn't be too obvious. Not her birthday or any permutation of her name.

The water gurgle stopped. A cupboard door slammed shut.

The password wouldn't be all that obscure either. In fact, she'd joked about using the same password for as many sites as possible, some variation of—

Her childhood nickname. She'd reminded him of the name, and he'd had to pretend to remember.

The hair dryer roared to life.

Her password related to that idyllic time when Zoe loved Susannah and Nathan in equal measure, before the mother-daughter strife began. Shirley Temple ringlets and tap dancing lessons and sing-alongs.

Lollipop.

That was it. On the good ship Lollipop.

The hair dryer shut off.

Nathan tapped in *lolipop*—Jesus, hurry—and poked repeatedly to insert the second *l* into the word.

Another bathroom cupboard slammed shut, and the bathroom door opened. Nathan froze.

"Dad?"

"Ay?"

"I forgot to tell you that Danny—Detective Sergeant Ahern—rang to check that you had arrived from the hospital. He's nice when he's not harassing you."

The bathroom door clicked shut again. Nathan exhaled. Danny would keep at him until Nathan cracked in half and oozed out the foulness inside himself called the truth. Whatever that was. Nathan wasn't sure he knew anymore. Or ever knew, for that matter.

He poked in the *l* finally, holding his breath again—and he was in. Colorful app icons beckoned him. He opened the contacts app and found Sid under "Sid." He repeated the phone number to himself under his breath, shoved the mobile back into Zoe's purse, and ran into the kitchen to write the number down before he forgot.

With the scrap of paper tucked into his pocket, he returned to his seat at the kitchen table and allowed himself a rare moment of satisfaction.

SIXTY-TWO

Wednesday, 31-Mar

Do you remember, dear Annie, our many conversations about living in a world tailored for extroverts? You and I, we're observers. You, of course, put your watchful tendencies to good use as a psychiatric nurse. Highly commendable, though it didn't end up being good for your mental health.

Even off duty, you couldn't help analyzing Nathan. I agree with what you wrote about him in your half of this journal. He's an interesting case. Quite paranoid, as far as I can tell, but not because of the outside world, except maybe for that daughter of his. Zoe. Fly, be free, little girl. But no, all she wants is a redo on her past. Have you noticed that people prefer their cages?

I find myself more attracted to Nathan than to his daughter. While spying on him through his kitchen window—binoculars, as you well remember; that's where my observational skills lead me—I caught him fondling his knives in the most abstracted way.

How tantalizing. I know that look. I'm sure I've been described as abstracted. I wonder if there's a way I can use his fascination with knives. Thoughts are forming—a way through the upcoming complications.

SIXTY-THREE

Danny entered his house through the back door with two pizzas in hand and much-needed kid time in mind. The investigations had reached the tedious stage of burrowing into obscure leads and wrangling paperwork. For Annie's death, Sid Gibson still intrigued him, but nothing concrete had ascended out of the masses of information that DS Sheehy diligently parsed and delegated. Nathan as the common point between the two deaths had led nowhere. In four days, they'd lose Sheehy back to his district.

"Pizza!" Danny called.

"'Allo," returned Marcus from the living room. A moment later the children hustled into the kitchen. Danny stooped to hug them hello, and gave their tabby kittens, Ashe and Fire, back scratches while he was at it.

"Can we eat in the living room?" Mandy said. "We're playing Legos, and I need to keep an eye on things."

From the living room, Danny caught murmuring voices. "Who's with Grandpap?"

"That woman Mum doesn't like." Mandy climbed onto a kitchen chair and opened a pizza box. "Is she allowed in our house?"

Merrit, then. No surprise, since she and Marcus were friends, but he hoped visiting didn't become a habit. "Merrit is Grandpap's friend."

"Why docsn't Mum like her?"

Danny pulled down plates to give himself a second to think. "She annoys Mum, that's all."

"Does she annoy you, too?"

"At times. Doesn't Petey annoy you sometimes?"

"Yes, but that's different."

"Annoyance is annoyance." He tousled her hair. "What are you going to do?"

"Yeah," Petey echoed, "what are you going to do?"

Mandy snorted and retraced her steps into the living room with Petey following on her heels. Tricky kid conversations often left Danny feeling fraudulent in the parenting department. He hadn't realized that Mandy knew how Ellen felt about Merrit. The thought distressed him, though not on Merrit's behalf. Kids should be sheltered from the shite that arrived with adult relationships. In this respect, he and Ellen had failed as parents. He couldn't help but wonder what else they'd failed to shelter Mandy and Petey from. They'd certainly felt more loss than any children should at their ages.

He gathered up the pizzas, plates, and napkins, and entered the living room. Merrit relaxed with Marcus on the couch while the children sat on the ground playing with a Lego space station and a Lego house. Merrit aimed an apologetic grimace at Danny.

Ah, so she had more in mind than visiting with Marcus.

He greeted Merrit in a nonchalant way to prevent Mandy's hackles from rising any further and set the pizzas on the coffee table. "There's plenty for all of us."

Danny wasn't fooled by Mandy's absorption in her Lego house. She'd aimed her ears at them like satellite dishes. With great dignity, she picked up the piece of pepperoni pizza farthest from where Merrit sat, slid it onto a plate, and returned to her spot in front of the blocks.

Marcus bit into a slice of sausage and mushroom. "Merrit was telling me the preparations for Liam's festival have gotten out of hand."

"Do you think people will come?" Merrit said.

Marcus guffawed. "Listen to her. She's after wanting to be let off the hook."

Merrit picked up a slice of pepperoni with a smile at Petey. Mandy scowled as she regarded Merrit from under her bangs.

Danny opened his mouth to admonish Mandy for her bad manners, but Marcus shook his head. "Mandy's been working on her Lego house. It's a mighty beauty, isn't it?"

"It's a hotel for the space station visitors," Mandy said.

Danny lowered himself to the floor beside her. "Smart thinking."

She leaned into him, showing him the tiny yellow chairs and tables while Marcus and Merrit continued their conversation. Danny half listened to them, half listened to his daughter. After a while, he gathered up her plate along with Marcus's.

"Let me help you." Merrit paused with an awkward glance around the room. Her eyes glowed green in the light from the closest lamp.

"Grab the pizza boxes, would you?" Danny said.

"Sorry about that," Merrit said once they were alone. "I wasn't sure what to say with the kids there."

"Next time text me to let me know you need to talk with me."

She was quick to demur. "I wanted to catch up with Marcus, too."

Danny set about wrapping the leftover pizza slices in tinfoil. She rinsed a plate and set it in the dishwasher.

"It's about Nathan," she said. "The other day in the hospital, he expressed interest in Sid Gibson. He'd overheard your side of a phone conversation."

"Bloody hell. He did a good impersonation of being asleep."

"He's convinced that Sid killed Annie." She leaned against the counter with gaze aimed at a drawing of a purple Easter bunny that hung on the refrigerator. "He wanted to know what I knew about the man—what you might have told me."

The doorbell rang, followed by a flurry of children's footsteps. In the other room, Zoe laughed at something Petey said. "Hello," she said, "I'm Zoe. Nice to meet you."

Merrit groaned. "What's she doing here?"

"Peddling her services?"

"Let's hope not." She popped a stray piece of pepperoni into her mouth. "I want to ask you a favor, but it can wait for now."

"Dad!" Mandy yelled. "This lady brought cake. Can we have dessert?"

"Cake," Merrit muttered. "It'll be from scratch, you'll see."

Zoe as Pied Piper entered the kitchen with the children not far behind. She'd wrapped one of her blue scarves over her head like a 1950s Hollywood starlet. "Chocolate cake as a thank-you token for taking my dad to the hospital." She placed the offering, with its swirls of decadent frosting, on the counter and turned her exuberant smile toward Merrit. "What a nice surprise! I was just thinking about you and Liam. I can't wait for the party this weekend."

"Oh yes." Merrit didn't bother to disguise her ambivalence. "That looks delicious. I bet you made it yourself."

"I don't bake often," Zoe said. "I'm more of a meal maker, but I decided to try my hand."

Marcus took charge. "I'll cut our slices and the kidlings can eat while I read them a story."

"I want to stay here," Petey said.

Mandy glared from Zoe to Merrit and back. "The adults probably need to talk."

"Correct," Danny said. "We know a man who is sick, and we're trying to help him."

"Bully for you." She grabbed her slice of cake and marched out of the room ahead of Marcus and Petey.

"What a wee sprite," Zoe said. "She'll be a precocious one, you'll see."

"Like you were?" Merrit said.

"Oh no. I was a homebody as a teenager. I lived with my grandparents, you know. My mom's parents. They didn't live too far from us in Sussex. I was a good girl and kept my precocity to myself."

Danny marveled at Zoe's capacity for sidelining the world of hurt that lurked below the surface story. "You must have missed your dad."

Zoe's cheerful expression dimmed. "I did. I was disappointed. I'd thought we'd be grand, the two of us, after the grief over my mother's death lessened. Silly. What did I know about big emotions?"

Danny sliced off a bite-sized piece of cake and chewed. Merrit did the same. Danny beckoned Zoe to partake also. She smiled her thanks and cut off a chunk for herself.

"What happened the day Nathan was committed?" he said.

"You don't know?"

"It's difficult to get psych records. We're still waiting."

"Ooh." Zoe popped the piece of cake into her mouth. "All this time, I thought you knew." She slipped out of her white coat and unwound the scarf from around her neck. She wore a jumper with a cowled neckline that she proceeded to grab from the bottom.

"Hold on there," Danny said.

Zoe rolled her eyes. "You're not going to see anything a bikini top wouldn't reveal."

In one fluid movement she pulled off the jumper. Her bra surprised Danny. A simple white garment without a speck of lace or frill, girlish in its simplicity. She pivoted so that her back faced them. Between her shoulder blades, two scars marred the smooth expanse of ivory skin. Unlike Nathan's scar, they'd healed into shiny, pale lines.

"He went mental on me. Lost his marbles." She pulled the jumper back on and turned around. She sliced another piece of cake as she spoke. "He's not violent, you know. Not really. His attempt to kill me was pretty feeble."

"You forgave him."

She plopped the chunk into her mouth. "Of course. He's my dad. I understand why he hid himself away from me in Ireland all these years. I wasn't the perfect daughter. I was too insistent about myself, I think. The way I am, you know?" Her smile reappeared. "You can't tell me you haven't noticed that about me."

"Enthusiastic," Merrit said.

"That's my word for it. Some would call me pushy."

Some days Danny's children pushed him to the bleeding edge, and some days he barely contained the urge to tear out his hair or slam his hand down on a tabletop. How pushy would a child need to be to tip a mentally unstable parent over the edge? Answer: not pushy at all. A child being a child could be more than enough.

"How old were you when Nathan first showed signs of instability?"

Zoe picked up the cake knife and set it aside again. "Mum and Dad loved each other. They had a wonderful relationship, the best, and they loved me. I don't remember anything in particular until I hit adolescence, and then Dad distanced himself. I was rebellious in my small ways. What you'd expect, I guess. And I resented Mum's rule more. I was such a pill sometimes!" She laughed, shaking her head. "The big change came around the time Mum died. I wish I could be more helpful."

She wrapped her scarf around her shoulders again. The fringe caught on one of her butterfly earrings. She eased the earring free. "I never blamed my dad for attacking me. In a strange way, I considered it a sign that he cared."

With that she swung her coat over her shoulders and said her goodbyes. After the front door shut behind her, Merrit's comment pretty much said all that Danny was thinking.

"That's one fecked-up relationship those two have."

"Nice use of the word *feck*," he said.

SIXTY-FOUR

THE MOON CUT A swath of pale light across the ceiling above Nathan and, within that pale stream, layers of darkness shifted and merged. He struggled against sweat-dampened sheets, but invisible manacles held him fast to the bed.

An apparition in the form of a dark man wavered at the foot of his bed. A scream began deep inside Nathan but caught in his throat. His chest was about to explode, his heart beating too hard. The shadow oozed toward him along the swath of moonlight. A creature wriggled within its cupped hands.

"No," Nathan moaned and struggled harder to free himself. The dark form spread and merged into the shadows until only its dark hands floated toward him.

"Leave me alone," he said. Or thought he said. "Go away."

The shadow hands floated closer, hands shaped into a cup, a struggling creature trapped inside them. The fingers tightened, snuffing the panicked chirrup of the bird, and then opened to reveal a goldfinch, its bright yellow and red plumage dulled by death.

"Don't," he said. Or thought he said.

The hands closed over the bird and a moment later parted to reveal the goldfinch blinking, fluttering, about to find its wings. The shadow hands crushed down on it again.

And opened. Again. To reveal a dead bird.

Nathan's neck muscles ached as he strained against the invisible shackles. He was doomed to exist here forever, imprisoned with this bird, this dead-then-alive bird, and the shadowy being that repeatedly snuffed out its light and resurrected it.

"Stop," he said. Or thought he said.

The hands turned toward him, the palms empty, the bird gone, replaced by a squirmy worm of a creature. The hands bobbed in front of Nathan's face, now close enough that he recognized himself inside them, and the darkness within those hands descended on him.

He woke to find himself beside the window, gasping within the stream of moonlight. He clenched a kitchen knife so hard his hand ached. He swallowed against rawness in his throat, trying to remember when he had fetched the knife. The carving knife, he now saw.

"Dad!" Zoe pounded on the door. "Let me in."

"I'm fine."

"You've been screaming nonstop for the last five minutes. You're not fine."

He couldn't move, though. His limbs refused to obey orders. Instead, he perched on the windowsill and gave in to tremors that rocked his body. The palsy aftermath of one of his night terrors. The knife dropped with a sharp clack against the floorboards.

Zoe must stop with her knocking and her calling. He needed her to shut up, shut up, shut up—"Shut up!" he yelled.

She did, but he sensed her on the other side of the door, ever-present, even during the years before she'd found him.

"This isn't going to work, Zoe," he said. Or thought he said.

Yes, he did say it aloud. Zoe's sigh told him that much. "It can work. You need me. That much is obvious."

"I can't have you in the house when you're—" Nathan shook his head. He had no words. He wasn't great with words on the best of occasions. "You need to leave people alone. Let them be, especially Liam."

What he wanted to say, of course, was to let *him* be. He didn't want her in the house. Her presence made his scar ache, and the crackle and static paralyzed him at times.

"I'm not leaving." She spoke with firm resolve. "We'll work it out. You'll see."

Or what? Work it out, or what?

Zoe's footsteps retreated toward her bedroom. Her door clicked shut. Nathan breathed again, forcing oxygen into and out of his body. The image of the goldfinch returned. The yellow-tipped wings and scarlet face, delicate scales on its toes, glossy black eyes. More real than reality, that goldfinch. But then, memory, dream, or hallucination … what did it matter anymore?

SIXTY-FIVE

Thursday, 1-Apr

April Fool's Day, dear Annie. It's fitting that this year Good Friday falls on the day after. All the fools with their pranks followed by all the fools with their confessions. Everyone likes to think of themselves as good.

I imagine you alive with head cocked, intrigued and urging me to reveal my internal workings. You'd smell clean. I have a good nose and you always smelled like the outdoors after a spring rain. Sometimes I entertained thoughts of getting intimate with your scent, which wouldn't have worked, of course. That would have been highly inappropriate.

You're not here, alas, but Nathan is. Nathan, Nathan—what shall I do with you, oh foolish man?

Annie, you may not believe this, but he's growing on me.

SIXTY-SIX

GOOD FRIDAY, THE BEGINNING of a holiday weekend with Monday off work for most people. Danny stepped into the Corpus Christi Roman Catholic Church. The sun had decided to come out, and it shone through the stained glass window portraits of various saints that ran the length of the nave. Some smart church designer had positioned them so they caught the morning light from the east and on the other side, as now, the evening light from the west. The reflections spread a warm and inviting glow through the church.

A few parishioners sat in the pews. They were early for the 7:00 p.m. commemoration Mass of the Lord's passion. Mrs. O'Brien looked up as Danny passed her. Her usual proprietary expression blanked out at the sight of him. Danny said hello and continued on. He made his way up the central aisle and cut right when he reached the altar. Jesus in all his malnourished and woebegone suffering hung over them. Danny didn't care for this image of the Savior. Instead of beseeching the high heavens for his Redeemer to save him, he gazed into the church, at them, at Danny himself as he entered a confessional booth that smelled like his childhood. Lemon-scented furniture polish and incense. He kneeled and planted his elbows on the shelf below the grille, through which he recognized Father Dooley's thin, hawkish nose in profile.

Neither man spoke. The priest waited for Danny to begin the usual way: *Bless me, Father, for I have sinned.*

Instead, Danny said, "Hello, Danny Ahern here, come in for a chat."

The grille slid open. Father Dooley bent to peer at him. "Holy Mother of all that's good, have the plagues started? Is it raining locusts out there?" He shut the grille and Danny saw him relax back on the comfortable chair the priest's booth contained.

Danny sniffed the sweet scent of peppermint. "Teatime?"

"Woke up with a hoarse throat, and I've quite the sermon to give today. Now tell me, when was your last confession?"

"Too long ago to matter." Danny shifted. "You need to do something about these kneelers."

"I know it. On the budget for this year." Father Dooley slurped his tea. "What's on your mind, Danny?"

"My concerns are timely," Danny said, "given that it's Easter. In fact, one of my concerns is Easter."

Danny hadn't figured out how to comfort the children when Easter Sunday rolled around without Ellen's resurrection. The problem with religion, and maybe Catholicism most of all, was its adherence to lore and unfounded belief. Belief in the resurrection differed little from belief in the seventh son of a seventh son. Or Zoe, for that matter. But he wasn't about to say this to Father Dooley.

"The children are convinced that Ellen is going to wake up on Easter. They're confused about what the resurrection means. I've tried to explain, but it seems they're convinced God will wave a magic wand from Heaven. I don't know what to say to them anymore. I'm conflicted myself."

"About what?"

"Whether to do the opposite of a resurrection—let Ellen go."

Father Dooley set aside his teacup and hunched forward. "What would Ellen want?"

"To be let go. She would have said her soul would have a nice afterlife."

"A good point."

"No, a bad point. Souls and the afterlife are a matter of faith, and having faith isn't the same as knowing the truth about the nature of death—" He cut himself short. "No disrespect intended."

"You're hopeless, but I have faith"—Father Dooley chortled—"that you'll have a fine talk with the kids. You know that. I think the issue is guilt. You'd be—what? By letting Ellen go, what would you be doing?"

"I did love her," Danny said.

"I know."

"But I couldn't live in the marriage with her anymore." Danny reached into his coat pocket and pulled out a manila envelope folded lengthwise. Months of using it as a placemat at work had left it stained with coffee cup rings and grease smudges. "Open the grille."

Father Dooley obliged. Danny handed through the envelope. Father Dooley slid a pair of reading glasses down from where they perched on the top of his head and peered down his nose as he slid out the sheaf of papers. "Ah, Danny. A legal separation."

"On the road to divorce." By law, they had to live apart for four out of the last five years to apply for a divorce decree. Meanwhile, a legal separation would have signaled his intention to Ellen and begun the process.

"Look at the date," Danny said. "The week before Ellen was attacked. I'd signed them already."

Father Dooley let his hands, with the paperwork, drop to his lap. "I'm beginning to understand how you've tortured yourself all these months."

Nathan and his scar flashed through Danny's mind. It was a world of torture out here, self-inflicted or not.

"Would you like me to absolve you of guilt?" Father Dooley said. "Send you out for the Hail Marys and Holy Fathers and wipe the slate clean of the burden you carry?"

"That would be nice."

Father Dooley passed the papers back through the grille. "I'm talking as Paddy now, who has known you since a lad. Ready?" He paused to flash Danny a grin. "Get your bloody head on straight, man. You're not to blame for that madman who attacked Ellen. You think it happened because you didn't live with her anymore, divine retribution because you wanted a divorce? Think again."

"I'm to blame for abandoning her to her depression."

"Oh, bloody hell," Paddy said, sounding like the boy who couldn't go a week without a walloping from the nuns. "You're putting me in an uncomfortable position, my friend. You know that Ellen offered her confessions almost every week for years."

Danny hesitated before saying, "And?"

"I can't reveal what she said, you know that, but as your friend Paddy, let me assure you that Ellen was her own woman with her own conflicts about the state of your marriage." He crossed himself and bent his head. Danny thought he heard him repeat, "Father forgive me." He raised his head. "I can't say any more."

Danny shifted to ease his aching knees. "She blamed herself for the state of our marriage, didn't she?"

Father Dooley was back. He didn't answer, but his eyelids flickered. "And here you are taking on the blame yourself. Assuming the role that unforeseen circumstances relieved her of. This is a penance you don't deserve. Better to say a few Hail Marys and Holy Fathers than put yourself through hell."

"Pass me your flask, good Paddy," Danny said. "I know you have it on you."

"Such respect for the collar." Father Dooley passed the flask. "Sip. That's good cognac."

Danny sipped and savored the burn—one more bit of self-torture, but it felt wonderful.

SIXTY-SEVEN

On Easter Sunday, Merrit woke to the sound of hail pounding the roof. She climbed out of bed and opened the curtains. A grey pelt of hard rain flattened the celandine and daffodils, and weighed down the top of the marquee. Merrit imagined the tent caving in on itself from the weight of the hail, imagined being let off the hook. She didn't let herself fantasize too far down that track, however, because Liam was looking forward to her debut as matchmaker.

The event felt more like a tryout, and she didn't hold out much hope that she'd put on a great performance. She recognized the itchy tension in the pit of her stomach: stage fright.

Merrit let the curtains swing shut and tried to decipher what she felt beyond stage fright. She came up with nothing but an uneasy question mark, something she'd forgotten to examine what with the festival and Nathan and Liam's health distracting her thoughts.

She pulled on jeans and a sweater and headed toward the kitchen, where the smell of coffee greeted her when she swung through the door. Liam sat at the kitchen island. She sighed with relief. Just the two of them for a change.

"Not a bother," he said. "The weather, I mean. Hail's not enough to keep a good party down."

Through a blur of hard rain, Merrit discerned a mini SUV parked in front of Fox Cottage. Its dingy blue color blended into the atmosphere. "Nathan is here?"

"Inside the cottage since about two this morning," Liam said. "Let himself in with the key you gave him, I imagine."

Merrit pulled on her wellies and slipped out the back door. The hail stung her face and, within a few steps, beaded her sweater. She ran to the cottage and eased open the front door to the smell of fresh paint and fungal griminess. She beelined to the bedroom with the closed door. The wood felt cool against her ear when she leaned against it. From inside the room, she heard mutterings.

She caught her breath, only now aware of how hard her heart pounded, imagining Nathan spread-eagled on the floor like Elder Joe. Thank Christ for the sounds of a bad sleep.

She raised her fist to knock and paused. She wasn't sure what to do. Within the room, the old bed springs squeaked, followed by a groan. Merrit eased open the door. Nathan sat up in bed. He wore the same encrusted jeans as a week ago when she'd visited him at his house. He didn't acknowledge her presence as she stepped into the room. In fact, he appeared to be asleep with his eyes open, peering at a vision only he could see.

Merrit shouldn't wake him up, that much she knew, but could she touch him? He might lash out, might mistake her for a nightmare figment. Yet she refused to leave him like that.

She approached him on tiptoes. Nathan's mouth moved over silent words punctuated by whimpers that reminded her of the dying squeals of a squirrel—short, sharp, and mortally afraid. Merrit lowered herself onto the bed beside him. She placed an arm around his shoulders and leaned him against her. He complied but otherwise didn't respond. His mutterings continued between the whimpers. She wrapped her other arm around him in a hug.

Five minutes turned into fifteen, and after a while his head sagged against her shoulder and his breathing deepened. She shifted him onto his back. He stirred, and from one second to the next, he bolted upright with a strangled yell and shoved Merrit off the bed. He pressed himself against the wall with eyes wide and fists clenched. A few more seconds later, he came to and recognized Merrit as Merrit. He scrambled across the bed to help her stand. "You're not hurt, are you?"

"Startled, that's all."

"I need a warning label. Caution while sleeping."

"Is that normal?"

"Ay, pretty much, when I sleep at all." He curled back onto the bed. He barely dented the mattress, as if someone had sucked out his marrow while he slept. The benefits of his overnight stay in the hospital had dissipated. The skin around his eyes had a crêpey texture, and specks of blood dotted his chapped lips.

"Nathan," she said.

"Mmm?"

"Why are you here?"

He pulled the covers up around his head. "I thought it might be safer."

She clicked the bedroom door closed behind her, wondering, Safer for who?

SIXTY-EIGHT

NATHAN WOKE MID-MORNING MORE groggy than ever. After Merrit had discovered him in the cottage, he'd fallen into a sleep that he would describe as fraught. Goldfinches and knives hounded him through darkness, and now that he was awake he felt more than ever that—

Can yoouu kill, can yoouu kill

—today was the day: the day he resurrected.

He sat up and took stock of himself as he did every morning. No new pains, but the static and crackle throbbed behind his eyes. He shook his head against the fuzziness that wavered around the edge of his vision.

From the direction of Liam's house, a truck approached and idled. Merrit called out a greeting and was met by a man's reply. Nathan had forgotten about the Earrach Festival. He'd let it sink into the forgotten netherworld within his memory banks.

He squeezed his eyes shut against the pain in his head and groped his way to the window that overlooked the neighboring sheep field. Rain had replaced hail. He pushed out the window to allow wind redolent of peat and sogginess to sweep into the room. He held his ground against the chill. In an odd way, he felt calm for the first time in weeks. The static and crackle propelled him in the right direction. He had but to embrace the deeper meaning within the jumble.

Feeling steadier, he closed the window and opened his rucksack. He'd sharpened the carving knife before packing it away. He couldn't recall his state of mind in the middle of last night, only that he'd had to escape his house.

He stared down at the knife that gleamed despite the dull light. He had one escape hatch, the same one he'd used all those years ago. He no longer had the energy to resist. He'd use the knife again as he had on Zoe, who had proved to be indestructible.

His mobile vibrated. He set the knife aside and reached into his jeans pocket. A text message appeared from Zoe.

WHERE ARE YOU?

I'M FINE, he typed. AT FOX COTTAGE.

GOOD. I'M GLAD, BUT WE WERE SUPPOSED TO DRIVE TOGETHER TO LIAM'S HOUSE, TO HELP MERRIT. DON'T YOU REMEMBER?

She always said that to him: *Don't you remember?* No, he didn't. Everything about her weighed so heavy on him that her incessant chattering words sank into a void.

NO WORRIES, she sent. SID WILL PICK ME UP. I'M JUST GLAD YOU'RE SAFE.

Sid. Nathan's pulse quickened, and he tossed the mobile aside to grab his rucksack. He dumped out the contents and rifled through them, shoving a clean t-shirt and water bottle onto the floor in the process. He'd written down Sid's personal number that he'd pilfered from Zoe's mobile. He must still have the number. It wouldn't do to call Annie's mobile again. He wanted to surprise Sid.

Nathan dug around inside the rucksack. Nothing but stray seam threads. His gaze landed on the rain gear he'd dumped by the bedside, having grabbed it up on his way out of the house. He leapt toward it and landed hard on his knees. He pawed through the pockets of his coat until he found his wallet.

There. Tucked into an empty credit card slot.

He sagged against the bed. The static and crackle eased off. He flattened the slip of paper on the floor and picked up his mobile again. Dialing the number felt logical and sure.

After several rings, the line picked up. "'Allo?"

Nathan's voice caught in his throat, but a sound must have registered through the digital airwaves. Sid chuckled. "It's yourself calling, is it? About bloody time."

SIXTY-NINE

Sunday, 4-Apr

Guess who called me out of a beautiful sleep? Nathan can't resist me. I applaud his compulsion. We both flirt with disaster, though I wager I understand his better than he does mine.

Give the poor bastard a week of deep sleep, and he'd become reliable in his thinking. Boot Zoe out of his house, and he might live in a contented fashion. I think you'd agree, dear Annie, that he's his own unreliable narrator. Even more fascinating, he may know the truth but veer away from it because he knows himself to be unreliable. It must be confusing for a man like him.

Which leads me to think about psychotic breaks. After all, I studied up long and hard to convince the doctors and legal system that I was such a victim, too. Education is an amazing source of power. Teaches you the best buttons to push when needed. I'm not going to be the one who ends up in a psych ward again.

Nathan and I have a date to keep today. Happy Easter to me.

SEVENTY

DANNY HELD THE CHILDREN's hands as they trotted through the rain into the party pavilion. Droplets streamed down the glass walls but inside all was warmth and faery lights. Bunting and circular paper globes festooned the ceiling, which rose into circus tent peaks high above their heads. The children were all goggle-eyed wonder. "This is an air castle," Petey said.

Near the entrance, Mrs. O'Brien manned a welcome table. She liked welcome tables; this way she could monitor the arrivals. She waved them toward her and cooed at the children for a moment before addressing Danny.

"Children's activities start in about fifteen minutes. We're expecting more families to arrive from late Mass. There will be an egg hunt and face painting and puppet shows. Plenty for the children to occupy themselves. You'll see the stations around the marquee." With a sour expression, she pointed to a chalk circle drawn on the ground. "And something called a 'cake walk.' That was Merrit's idea from the States to replace our traditional cake dance."

Danny surveyed the space, at the far end of which sat a stage with dance area. Pockets of lounging areas with circular padded benches lined one side of the marquee, while communal dining tables lined the other. The cake walk circle adorned the ground in the center of the marquee and big bunches of balloons marked various stations for children's games.

"Where's the egg hunt going to be?" Mandy said.

"On the other side of the rope. You can't go there yet, or you'll find the eggs too early."

A braided cordon blocked off most of the marquee. The first arrivals blew in with the wet wind and congregated near the entrance. Mrs. O'Brien explained the food. "Picnic to start with a potluck buffet. That was also Merrit's suggestion. Liam was generous enough to provide catering for later. There will be a no-host bar, too." She sniffed. "I don't approve of alcohol on Easter Sunday, but I suppose it can't be helped."

The children jerked on Danny's hands and he released them to join several other kids gathered to wait for the egg hunt. There was something to be said for distraction. The children had been curiously silent about Ellen's great Easter awakening, but he'd caught significant looks aimed in his direction that filled him with sorrow and frustration—frustration with himself that he didn't know how to communicate the ultimate truth to them in a way they would understand. Sudden death would actually have been easier to explain to them.

Father Dooley had gotten it wrong when he'd said Danny would know what to say. Instead of a talk, Danny had plied the children with Easter baskets and their own egg hunt and Marcus's famous Easter pancakes topped with jellybeans. Today was the best Easter Sunday of their lives, lootwise.

Footsteps clicked across the flooring, and he turned to see Merrit approaching with worry and nerves apparent in her clamped jaw and flushed skin. Mrs. O'Brien took one look at her, sniffed again, and abandoned her post to help organize the children.

Merrit caught Danny observing her and shrugged uncomfortably. She wore a fitted black dress that swung just above her knees, hair curled in loose waves and pulled away from her face, and enough makeup to make her unusual hazel-colored eyes glow. She cleaned up well but didn't know how to walk in heels. She wobbled to a stop next to him. "Zoe did me up. I'll be wearing flip-flops by the end of the day, you'll see."

"Where is she?"

Merrit pointed to one of the lounging circles, where Zoe sat talking to several other festival volunteers. "The latest on Nathan is that this morning I found him sleeping in Fox Cottage. He mentioned it being safer."

"For who?"

"That was my first thought, too. None of this feels right, including Liam's sudden good health. The other night at your house I meant to ask you if you could persuade him to see a new doctor for a second opinion."

"I can do that." It would be his pleasure, in fact, because Zoe's healing hobby preyed on him, too. "Now, in fact."

Liam sat at one of the communal tables with a cup of tea in front of him. Danny joined him and watched more children gather for the egg hunt.

"Quite the festivity you hatched," Danny said.

"Ay, but Merrit brought it together. She had help, of course. Mrs. O'Brien is indispensable at such times. They've been working nonstop for the last two days."

"And Zoe?"

"Ah, yes, Zoe." He went silent. The tent shuddered with a wind gust that made the long poles squeal. "Merrit talked to you, I suppose."

"She asked me to ask you to see a doctor. Humor her, would you?"

"There's no accounting for it, but I'm improving. I feel better each day."

"You can't think it's because of Zoe."

More wind gusted. Outside, a solid grey sky promised more rain, and lots of it.

"You might have heard that Zoe claimed that she healed Bijou." Liam sipped his tea. "I know how it sounds. Pure madness. I've been over it and over it, and I can't figure out how Zoe faked it. She had a piece of glass with blood on it, and Bijou has a pink scar on one of her paws that Alan didn't recognize. Explain that to me."

"Perhaps the scar already existed."

"How did Zoe know that?"

"That's the interesting question. She noticed it previously, or even that day. Bijou loves to have her belly rubbed. She'll display the bottoms of her paws to anyone."

Liam looked skeptical. "All I know is that Zoe held Bijou's paw the same way she holds my hand."

Across the way, Zoe laughed with her companions. She'd piled her hair up in a messy 'do on top of her head with dangling curls brushing her shoulders. She was the living antithesis of the gloom trying to batter its way into the party. Like a spring nymph. Or maybe a spring siren.

"And," Liam continued, "why would she stage such an elaborate demonstration for us?"

"Another good question. She could have said, 'Fancy a healing session with me?'"

Liam grunted. "And received the full bolloxing for her efforts. I'm sure she's tried that before."

"With Nathan to begin with, and maybe her mother, too."

"Ay, that may be the crux of her right there. Rejection."

"Daddy issues?" Danny tapped his fingers on the tabletop. "Or mommy issues."

"Issues, anyhow."

"So am I to understand that you don't believe she's healing you?"

"I didn't say that, but I'll relent and see a doctor." He grinned. "If Merrit approached you about it, she must be anxious, indeed."

A kid flurry attracted Liam's attention. The egg hunt was about to start, which signaled the opening of the Earrach Festival. Merrit reappeared, wearing not flip-flops but a pair of low-heeled ankle-strappy numbers on her feet. She clapped her hands and called for the children to line up along the rope. Mandy pulled Petey with her to the edge of the line.

Danny smiled, knowing that his scrappy daughter had figured out they had a better chance of finding eggs if they focused their efforts along the edge of the marquee. He willed himself to enjoy this moment with them. The Ellen topic could wait.

Merrit held up the rope and a pair of gardening shears. Together, she and the children counted down from ten. The children screamed at the tops of their lungs. "Ten!"

"Nine!"

More people entered the marquee. Children tussled to stand in front. The marquee shook under threat from the wind.

"Eight!"

"Seven!"

Out of the corner of his eye, Danny spied Zoe waving at someone while shouting down the numbers with everyone else.

"Six!"

"Five!"

Danny followed her gaze to see Sid with his placid smile contemplating the festivities from the corner of the marquee, unobtrusive and unnoticed. He waved back at Zoe.

"Four!"

"Three!"

Liam nudged Danny with his elbow. Nathan hovered near the entrance. His lips moved in words aimed at no one. In his corner, Sid watched Nathan.

"Two!"

"One!"

Merrit cut the rope with a snap of shears, and in the ensuing chaos of screams and squeals and cheering adults, Danny lost sight of both Sid and Nathan.

SEVENTY-ONE

AFTER THE EGG HUNT and words of welcome from Liam, Merrit parked herself in one of two chairs in her matchmaking station. A red velvet cordon marked it off and dozens of balloons floated overhead. After her kerfuffle with Mrs. O'Brien, Merrit had let her have her way. All the fanfare and tradition she desired. Now Merrit felt like a sideshow freak rather than the main attraction. One of those odd-looking, lonely ones gawkers loved to stare at from afar.

On the bright side, she wasn't nervous anymore. It didn't look as if she would be in demand. The childless adults began gathering mid-afternoon when the bar opened. Mrs. O'Brien had ordered Merrit's station to be positioned within spitting distance of the alcohol, which didn't surprise Merrit.

She was allowed to leave her little prison, of course, but for the moment she preferred to sit here, removed from the chaos. Elder Joe flashed through her mind. His pronouncement about sheep and lambs still bothered her.

Marcus appeared out of the crowd and joined her. "You look thoughtful; a nice look for a matchmaker."

She scooted closer to him. "You caught me pondering something Elder Joe said before he died. I thought it might be a clue to his death, but I can't remember his exact words—something about lambs and sheep. 'You won't be a sheep if you're not a lamb'?"

Marcus slapped his thigh with a burst of laughter. "Bloody beautiful, that. Let me guess, 'hung for a sheep as a lamb'?'"

"That's it. 'Might as well be hung for a sheep as a lamb,' she said. What does that mean?"

"It goes back to the days when stealing a sheep or a lamb was a capital offense. What were you talking about when EJ said it?"

"He'd invited me to have tea with him, but I begged off. He accused me of being 'that way.'"

"Ay, that Elder Joe had his own way of talking. It doesn't make no bother, what he said. Why should it?"

"But it is bothering me."

"Well then." He hesitated. "People can tell you're not invested in your life here. You're aloof. By the lamb business, he meant if you're going to live here, then go all the way in as a sheep, not a lamb."

"That makes no sense." She waved her arms to encompass her matchmaking station. "I'm more here than I sometimes want to be."

"Bingo. You think others don't feel that?" He patted her arm. "No use spitting tacks over it."

"Spitting tacks." Another Irish-ism to store into memory. "Let's change the topic."

"Easy enough. What's the craic with the matchmaking?"

"I don't know whether to be insulted that no one has talked to me or relieved. For some reason, I'd thought this might be the day I'd be reborn in the eyes of the locals."

"It might help if you smiled and called attention to yourself."

In other words, she thought, participate as a sheep, not a lamb, which was the opposite point she'd tried to make to Mrs. O'Brien and then to Liam when she'd offended them: this was not her way. Someone like Zoe would relish putting on a show, but not Merrit.

"Give them time to get used to you," Marcus said.

Merrit let that statement go. Time didn't have the same meaning for the Irish as it did for her. "How about you? Do you want to get married again? I've wondered."

He pursed his lips. "I haven't given it much thought."

Liar, Merrit thought. "You've mentioned Edna Dooley before. Father Dooley's sister, right?"

Marcus smiled, looking nostalgic. "Ay, quite a bit older than he, she being the eldest of the Dooley pack and he the youngest. She's a good soul."

Merrit pretended to remember something. "As a matter of fact, she's one of the volunteers helping Mrs. O'Brien." Without being obvious about it, she observed Marcus as he straightened his posture. "Could you do me a favor?" she said.

"Anything."

"Fetch me a plate of food? No hurry, though. There's a lot going on."

Marcus would know what she was about as soon as he arrived at the food tables and discovered Edna Dooley overseeing the caterers, who had arrived not long ago to augment the potluck with platters of finger foods.

Danny's children ran by with their faces painted like cats. They bumped past Nathan, who grabbed a tent pole for support. Merrit stood and stretched and, catching Nathan's eye, beckoned him to sit with her. He obliged with a blank, faraway expression. Once seated, his gaze prowled over the people passing back and forth in front of them.

"Where's Zoe?" she said. "She promised to be my first client. Not that she needs me. She has no trouble meeting men." She paused but couldn't think of a subtle way to drop Sid into the conversation. "Like her friend Sid."

Nathan stiffened.

"He's here, isn't he?" she said.

Nathan nodded.

"Please don't do anything stupid. Promise me."

Nathan nodded again. He clenched his hands and set his jaw as a wind gust battered the marquee.

"Stay here," Merrit said. "You need food. Promise me you won't move."

Nathan's head jerked in what Merrit took to be yet another nod of assent. She weaved her way toward the food tables, passing Marcus and Edna Dooley. She couldn't hear her own thoughts over the sound of the wind and the rat-a-tat of a fresh bout of hail.

Merrit shoveled meatballs and mashed potatoes onto a paper plate and gathered utensils, all the while scouting the area for Danny.

Mrs. O'Brien stepped up beside her. Avoiding eye contact, she announced that she'd called the marquee company. "Someone needs to secure the marquee against the wind."

"Thanks." Merrit spoke fast before Mrs. O'Brien walked away. "Thanks for everything. Really. Even the matchmaking station."

Merrit beelined to where Danny sat with Mandy and Petey in one of the lounge areas. The children waved and showed her their various prizes and eggs and Easter chocolates, delight overcoming even Mandy's resistance to Merritt. Danny stood.

"Sid and Nathan are here," Merrit said. "That can't be good."

"I know. I'm keeping an eye on him." He indicated Sid standing in the alcohol line. "I've lost Nathan, though."

"He's with me, but I'd better get back to him. He's almighty tense." Wind batted hail pellets against the glass next to them. "The noise is putting him more on edge." Merrit turned and almost bumped into Joe Junior.

"I fancy giving your matchmaking skills a try," he said.

"Later, okay? I promise." She dodged around the drinkers in the bar quadrant. But when she reached her matchmaking station, Nathan was gone.

SEVENTY-TWO

WIND AND HAIL PUMMELED the marquee on all sides. The racket made Nathan want to dig his ears out of his head, anything to make the irritant go away. He veered away from the crowd near the bar and circled toward the stage area, where musicians set up their equipment and Zoe kept up her usual stream of conversation.

He backtracked in the opposite direction. The peck peck peck of hail against the windows ground into his head, almost but not quite drowning out the voice—

Can yoouu kill, can yoouu kill

—that propelled him forward. He'd seen Sid but had decided to wait for the best moment. A rending crash sent up a collective scream that propelled Nathan under the closest table. He hugged himself, rocking, persuading himself that the apocalypse wasn't upon them. Today was Easter Sunday, a day of rebirth. *His* rebirth.

Several pairs of legs rushed past, toward the stage. Nathan peeked out from under the table to see a gaping hole in the marquee and the musicians scuttling around to move their equipment away from the incoming hail. A section of canvas snapped back and forth, and the wind gusted through the hole with an eerie moan.

Now was his chance, while everyone was distracted, before his head split open. He ducked out from under the table. In front of him, Sid leaned against one of the marquee's tent poles, smiling at him, waiting. Nathan's resolve shriveled. Sid had been one step ahead all along.

Nathan dug his hands into the deep pockets of the coat Zoe had bought him. Sid's lips moved, but Nathan lost the words to the wind and hail and yelling voices. He stepped closer, flexing and unflexing his hands in his pockets.

"I'm glad you rang," Sid said.

A mess of lights and paper globes fell onto the stage. Another collective scream sliced into Nathan's head.

"Annie was dear to me," Sid said. "As dear to me as she was to you."

Nathan opened his mouth and clamped it shut again. Don't talk. Let him dig his own grave. Nathan inched forward.

"We've had a misunderstanding," Sid said. "I don't want to be on the wrong foot with you."

Too late for that. Nathan would have liked nothing better than to leave this all behind, but now he couldn't. Because, if he did, the voices and the terrors and the images would eat him alive. He stepped closer.

"The thrust of it is that—"

Sid lowered his voice, and Nathan strained forward to hear him. His vision blurred, and the racketing wind swept into the marquee and pounded itself against the back of his skull. In his pocket, Nathan clamped his fingers around the knife. Sid's words turned into the wind pounding against his skull, into the static and crackle overtaking his mind, into the snap of breaking reality.

And he'd been here before, been here before, been here before.

SEVENTY-THREE

DANNY LET THE CHILDREN run off with the other kids and their mothers to ogle the unfolding drama at the other end of the marquee. He stepped aside for men carrying a ladder and circled toward the communal dining tables. He'd lost Sid in the shifting crowd but caught him again beyond the food spread. Sid stood calm in a sea of chaos, smiling while everyone else wore varying expressions of concern or awe. He spoke into Nathan's ear. Nathan's lips retracted into a grimace and his knees locked as if to pounce. He looked like a rabid dog.

Danny quickened his pace. Mrs. O'Brien stepped in front of him. "Do something," she said. "The festival is ruined."

"I can't now," Danny said. "Excuse me."

Mrs. O'Brien's hectoring voice receded behind him. Danny broke into a sprint, or tried to, but he bumped up against people every other step. Marcus beckoned him, but he shook his head and called for him to mind the children.

Nathan leaned forward from the waist and Sid continued talking. Danny dodged around a table and along the edge of the marquee. Hail bounced off the glass beside him, and the marquee swayed and squealed from the wind assault. A layer of hail had already gathered on the tables.

"Nathan!" Danny called.

Nathan pulled a knife out of his pocket, but instead of lunging at Sid he whipped around, back toward the stage.

"Someone grab Nathan!" Danny yelled. "I'll be talking to you," he said as he passed Sid.

Nathan disappeared into the crowd gathered around the stage. On the ladder, Alan struggled to cover the hole with a large tarp.

"Excuse me, out of the way," Danny repeated.

Someone screamed, and several people scattered, driving Danny backwards a few steps. He shoved his way against the crowd and stumbled forward to see Nathan honing in on Zoe.

"Jesus, stop him!" Danny said. "Grab him." He barreled forward, not caring who he knocked aside in the process.

"Dad?" Zoe said.

She stood her ground as Nathan lunged toward her. Her eyes widened when he raised his arm, knife glinting under the faery lights. Danny arrived shoulder first and shoved Nathan to the ground. Nathan went down easily but didn't want to stay down. He struggled against Danny with wide eyes and mouth forming an O of terror.

Danny stooped with knees on Nathan's chest and worked the knife out of his hand. Nathan's struggles turned desperate. Danny fought to keep Nathan's heaving body from toppling him over. His wretched wails rose toward the ceiling.

"Nathan, stop," Danny said.

The pitiful moan from Nathan's deepest hell spread goosebumps across Danny's arms. He ordered the closest spectators to grab Nathan's limbs, which only made him struggle harder. He arched his back and banged his head against the ground. Merrit arrived and scrambled to sit cross-legged with her legs cushioning his head.

Zoe, meanwhile, stood frozen with hands over her mouth. She stooped next to her father, which incited him to struggle harder.

O'Neil appeared at Danny's side. Danny hadn't seen him previously. He clapped him on the back in relief. "Watch over Nathan. I'll be back."

Danny backtracked toward the communal tables with fury rising with every step. Sid stood where Danny had left him. As ever, he blended into the background, no one paying him any mind. Danny grabbed his arm and swung him around, forcing Sid to walk with him toward the entrance of the marquee.

"What shite did you feed Nathan?" Danny said. "Whatever you said cracked him wide open."

Behind them, Nathan's voice rose into an undone roar.

"I helped him," Sid said. "You'll understand later."

SEVENTY-FOUR

"MR. TATE?" THE QUIET voice roused Nathan from a thoughtless, heavy place where nothing mattered.

"Nathan?" The light hurt. He covered his face with his arm and peered out at the world from beneath it, at his legs under a dull grey blanket and his feet in dingy grey socks at the other end of his long, long body. Strange that his body had grown.

"You're grand," the voice said. "Do you know where you are?"

He rolled away from the voice.

"I'm Brenda, one of the clinical nurse managers for psychiatric care. You're on a hold because you attacked your daughter with a knife. Do you remember this?"

Of course he remembered. They'd been repeating a variation of this question for years. The head nurse had changed and so had the color of the blanket, but of course he remembered where he was: England.

He buried his head under his arms again. Susannah, his lovely Susannah. Grief overwhelmed him as if she'd died yesterday. He sat up and scrabbled at his clothes. "Help," he said. Or thought he said.

"What's wrong? We'll get you bathed and into clean clothes, and then you can sleep."

"Help," he said again. He'd forgotten the head nurse's name. Didn't need to remember it anyhow. They came, they went. He knew this.

He yanked at his crusty jeans, then switched gears and pulled his jumper over his head. He had to see for himself. Maybe none of what he thought of as the truth, was true. Maybe he'd dreamed his way to this reality. Maybe Susannah was alive, maybe he was living a massive delusion, maybe there was no scar. Maybe he hadn't been locked up for years, after all.

Hands arrived to help him tug the jumper off, and an indrawn breath from the head nurse told him what he hoped wasn't true. He looked for himself then dropped back onto the bed, panting in confusion. "How long have I been here?" he said.

The head nurse stepped closer and placed a hand on his forehead. Then she reached for his wrist and held her fingers against his pulse. "How long does it feel?"

"I thought—I hoped—" Nathan's heart thumped hard against the medications swirling through his body. "But I've been imprisoned for half my life, haven't I?" He pointed to the scar that years ago hadn't existed. Instead, there'd been a wound that had festered and oozed, that had radiated pain so fierce he'd blacked out every time he tried to move. "It's better now."

"It is, and you're quite safe here. You know that, don't you?"

"But how long have I been here?"

"Only a few hours."

Cool air circulated throughout the bare room, which, he now saw, had walls covered with foam mattresses. He lay on a low platform with more plasticky foam covering it. His skin pulled away from it with a pop and a pinch of pain when he shifted. "I don't remember this place. This isn't Sussex."

"You're in Ennis, Ireland, and this is the Quiet Room." Brenda helped him pull on his jumper again. "Do you remember how you got injured?"

He rolled away from her again, tucking himself around his scar. "It started with the goldfinch."

SEVENTY-FIVE

SEVERAL HOURS AFTER THE guards hauled Nathan out of the marquee, Merrit used her status as party hostess to slip behind the bar. They'd hired Alan's junior barman to tend to the drinks. He handed her a healthy glass of red wine with the comment that the party "rated as one for the books, anyhow."

That was one way to put it. Merrit allowed the plummy wine to sit in her mouth for a moment before swallowing. The hailstorm had died down to a low groan of wind around the marquee, and the rain slid down the glass walls rather than smacking into them. A man from the marquee company had arrived to fix the tent. Now, with the shelter back up and the Sons of Erin whipping the dancers into a sweat, it was as if nothing had happened. No hailstorm. No crazed assault. No ambulance. Now it was pure booze, music, and faery lights.

Merrit pressed the wineglass against her lower lip, picturing Nathan as the paramedics bound him to a stretcher. His pain wrenched her. He was tragic, tragic as a lamb's last romp before slaughter.

She shook her head against the image, against anything to do with lambs or sheep.

She held out her glass for the barman to top off, please, and wandered back to her matchmaking station. She'd yet to match anyone, unless she counted Marcus and Edna Dooley. Altogether, not an impressive debut showing. Joe Junior had never returned. She decided that inching Marcus and Edna closer together counted.

"Fancy some company?" Simon O'Neil dropped into the seat next to hers and clinked his pint against her wineglass.

"What are you still doing here? Aren't you supposed to be performing Garda tasks?"

"To be continued tomorrow. The boss is long gone." Simon scooted his chair closer to her. "Look at you, matchmaker. What would you say to me?"

"I'd say you were hankering for a shag, not love, and send you on your way."

Simon laughed. "Drop and kick, the lady scores." His skin was flushed from dancing, the hair brushing his forehead damp with sweat. He hooked an arm over the back of his chair and slouched comfortably, considering her. "You're a hard one to read, eh?"

"Aloof, yes, I know. I've heard. And here I thought I was transparent."

"Only when you're panicking."

That got a smile out of her. "Fair play to you, mister. What is it you want to read from me?"

"I fancy another outing, but I can't tell whether you're amenable to the idea."

"Amenable." She leaned back and mimicked his loose posture. "Nice word. For that, I might consider another outing."

"All it takes is good vocabulary? In that case—" He straightened. "We've got company."

Merrit turned to see Zoe with her hair pulled up into a messy knot and makeup smudged below her eyes. Despite the stresses of the evening, she gazed around with a smile. "I'm sorry I left you hanging, Merrit. It looks like the music sorted itself out, though. In fact, all looks right in the world."

"You had other priorities," Merrit said. "How is your father?"

"I drove all the way to the hospital, and they turned me away until tomorrow." She sighed. "I hope he's all right."

"I'm sure you'll be able to see then," Merrit said. "Why don't you fetch yourself a drink? Tell the barman I said it was on me."

"You are too sweet. Thank you." Zoe ducked through the crowd and by the time she landed at the end of the drinks line, she was arm-in-arm with one of her men friends.

"That girl could float through a tsunami," Simon said.

"Seems like it." Merrit swallowed more wine, feeling deflated. "What a day."

Simon scrutinized her with a look that Merrit wasn't sure she wanted to decipher. He cupped her head in a gentle grip and bent closer still. "Enough with you," he whispered, "come here." He grabbed her around the waist and hoisted her over the red velvet cordon. Ten seconds later, he pulled her behind the puppeteer's stage and out of sight of everyone else in the marquee. Before Merrit had a chance to react, he kissed her, long enough to savor but short enough to remain gentleman-like.

"What the hell?" she said when she pulled away.

He grinned. "Hope that helps salvage the day. Now, if you'll excuse me, I must be off to bed. No bank holiday for me tomorrow."

Simon squeezed her hand in goodbye, leaving Merrit to pat her chest against the familiar panicky feeling. Faery lights reflecting off dripping rain created pretty water patterns on the windows that Merrit lost herself in while she got her breathing under control. She could take a lesson from the old proverb, *Physician, heal thyself.* Matchmaker, match thyself.

Yeah, right. She couldn't decide whether Simon was presumptuous or exciting. Arrogant or seductive. Which probably explained his success with the ladies.

After a minute of deep breaths, her lungs calmed. It was just a kiss, nothing long-lasting or permanent. She was free to leave, leading with one of her lamb's feet aimed back toward California. That was her right, especially because her life here came with conditions and expectations that she wasn't sure she could manage—or wanted to manage.

"Shite on a stick," she said, even though that phrase didn't sound correct.

The specter of Liam's impending death loomed large, larger than she'd wanted to admit. One thing to live here while he was alive, but after that?

So here she stood after kissing an attractive man, feeling nothing but lost.

SEVENTY-SIX

THE MORNING AFTER THE party, Danny sat beside Zoe on plastic chairs in the psych ward's waiting area. He was used to the hospital's institutional drabness and chaos, its coating of sickness that stuck to every surface. Sadly, the hospital was his new normal.

Several patients lounged along with the visitors, and veranda doors led to a courtyard where more patients smoked. Beside him, Zoe's usual good cheer struggled for ascendance. "He will be okay, won't he?" she said.

"I don't know."

She opened her purse, pulled out a hairband and gathered her hair back into a loose ponytail. "Poor Merrit. What a party disaster last night."

Danny suspected that the drama had fired up the party atmosphere rather than doused it. In any case, no one was likely to forget Liam's Earrach Festival.

"Liam looked good, don't you think?" Zoe said.

He glanced at her. "I hear you have something to do with that."

"Oh. Liam told you?"

303

"No, Merrit."

"Does everyone know?" she said. "I don't like to talk about it."

Interesting that she brought up the Liam topic then. "Your secret is safe," he said.

"It's awkward at times. I have to be careful."

"I imagine so, or else everyone would be after you to fix them up." She smiled. "You're humoring me. I know it when I hear it."

They waited in silence for a while. Danny couldn't help thinking about Ellen in Ward 2B on the other end of the hospital. She laid there insensate, but who knew what electrical pulses fired within her head. Nathan, on the other hand, felt too much, but likewise, who knew what went on inside his head.

"Zoe Tate?" A harried-looking woman in navy blue trousers and horn-rimmed glasses perched on the tip of her nose introduced herself as Brenda and waved at them to follow her. She led the way to her office without looking back and got to the point after closing the door. "Given your father's history and the assault on you—"

"That doesn't matter," Zoe said. "He shouldn't be punished for that."

"Nevertheless, because of that, he's on a mandatory twenty-four-hour hold. Our initial assessment is that he's a danger to himself and others." She stared Zoe down with a hint of judgment playing across her face. "He's not a well man and hasn't been for a while now."

"I know," Zoe said, "but I thought I could manage it. I thought once we settled into a routine and he got used to me again, we'd be fine. I hadn't seen him in years. I missed him."

"I'm not sure how long we'll have him, but for today, we need to keep him quiet and away from all stressors."

"Me." Zoe's eyes filled with tears. "You mean me."

"Yes." This woman didn't flinch from the hard messages. Danny could take lessons from her when it came to his kids.

"When can I take him home?" Zoe asked.

"We need to monitor him, and then we'll make a decision about how long to keep him."

"You mean, he might be committed for a while—months, even? Years? Forever?"

Brenda treated Zoe to a pitying expression. "Not forever."

On a shaky breath, Zoe pressed fingers against closed eyelids. A moment later, she excused herself to find the toilets. Danny opened his mouth, but the doctor preempted him. "Let her go. It's a lot to process. You're the officer who witnessed Nathan Tate attack her?"

He nodded, about to ask his question, but she waved a hand at him to hold off. "Please describe what you witnessed."

Danny related the events, including Sid's presence.

"Sid," she said. "That's one word that makes sense out of his gibberish anyhow. Do you know anything about a journal?"

"As a matter of fact, I do," Danny said. "A murder victim that both Sid and Nathan knew kept one. It's gone missing."

"Ah. Apparently this Sid character promised to give it to Nathan."

"He did, did he? By the way, you may have heard of Sid. His full name is Cedric Gibson." She flinched; so she did recognize his name. Danny continued, "Yes, him. He goes by Sid. He spoke to Nathan, and whatever he said broke him."

"The proverbial straw, the proverbial camel. It wouldn't have taken much." Brenda retreated behind her desk. "What did you want to ask?"

"Did Nathan know what he was doing when he attacked Zoe?"

"That's easy—no. He wasn't sane, and he may not be sane for a long while to come." She sat down. "That's my gut talking, based on long, hard years of experience."

"And I'll have to wait for the official report. I've heard that before."

She issued a lopsided smile. "Tell the daughter to call before she comes next time. We'll know more tomorrow."

A knock interrupted them, and a man with bushy hair popped his head into the room. "Sorry to interrupt. Someone reported a lass in the toilets crying and screaming. You know anything about that?"

"I expect I do," Brenda sighed. "I'll see to it."

"No, this is on me," Danny said.

Zoe was no longer inside the women's public toilet by the time Danny reached it. He found her out in the courtyard, hunched under a canopy out of the rain. Her ponytail sagged. "I don't know what to do. What am I supposed to do? I need my dad. They're keeping me from him on purpose."

Her woebegone expression surprised Danny. Gone was the self-sufficient, feisty young woman without a care in the world. "You've done well for yourself."

"No, no, no, I'm supposed to have a dad of my own, not be on my own. I'm sick to death of living by myself." She straightened and tightened her ponytail. "I'll be fine. Don't mind me."

Danny considered her, the budding healer with daddy issues. Her smudged makeup made her violet-blue eyes more luminous. Her tantrum in the bathroom may have been a healthy blow-off of excess emotion. Nothing wrong with that, but still, her reaction intrigued him.

He checked his watch. Morning visiting hours ended in an hour. "We should go," he said, "but first I want to stop by my wife's room."

Zoe looked up with a hopeful expression. "I can come, too?"

Bloody hell yes, that was the point, he thought. To continue their conversation—plus, observe how she reacted to Ellen.

He led the way along various corridors and up the stairs toward Ward 2B. Danny directed them left when they arrived at the top of the steps. They arrived at Ellen's room only to be told by a nurse to give her a few minutes to finish Ellen's sponge bath. Zoe craned her neck to see inside the room. The door closed.

"What do you suppose your friend Sid said to your dad to make him turn on you?" Danny said.

"I have no idea what you're talking about." Zoe sat down on one of the chairs that lined the corridor. "What could he have said? He's a nothing. My dad met him once for three minutes."

"Do you know where he's staying?"

"He mentioned Ballyhinch House. That's all I know." Zoe moved on to the next thought, having dismissed Sid as inconsequential. She opened her yellow purse and dug out a hand mirror. She gazed at herself and gasped in mock dismay. "I can't see your wife looking like this. That's not the way to show respect."

"I don't think she'll care." Danny paced restlessly, now questioning why he'd brought Zoe here.

She produced baby wipes out of her bag and dabbed at the skin under her eyes. "I'm sure Ellen is still in her body and that she can hear us. She's stuck and needs help, that's all."

Danny stopped pacing.

"I was sincere before," Zoe said, "when I offered to help your wife."

He watched her reapply her makeup, noting that she chose softer colors than those she'd worn for the party. He could tell himself that he'd brought Zoe here to further the investigation, that this was a ploy to open her up. Yes, he could, but the tension gathering in his chest told him otherwise.

If he were to believe in Liam's miracle recovery from cancer, Danny might still have a chance to tell the children about another resurrection. Didn't he owe it to Ellen to try?

Zoe swiped on some lip gloss and packed her makeup pouch back into her purse. "I'm ready now."

A few minutes later, the door to Ellen's room opened and the nurse left. Danny let Zoe enter first. She pulled up a chair and sat down. "She's so helpless," she said.

Danny stood at the end of the bed, breathing in the scent of antiseptic hospital soap. "It's sad for the kids not having a mother around. You know how that is."

"I do, though I'm a daddy's girl. Isn't your daughter a daddy's girl?"

Danny had never thought of Mandy that way. "Maybe, I don't know, but kids—daughters—need their moms."

Zoe didn't respond.

"They miss their mom as I'm sure you missed yours."

"I'd rather not talk about my mom," she said. "You can't heal the dead."

"But you tried, didn't you?" Nathan had told Danny that Zoe attempted to heal Susannah after her fall down the stairs.

Zoe ignored that comment. "My dad is still alive, though." She placed her hand near Ellen's. "I need him, you see. I've always needed him, and it wasn't fair that they took him away from me. I don't want that to happen again." She brushed her fingers down Ellen's arm. "Can you help me?"

"How do you mean?"

"You can talk to people—that horrible woman in the psych ward, your Garda contacts. Help my dad. Last time they kept him for two years—two years!"

"He needs professional help, and besides, you overestimate my influence."

She stood. "I'm sad for him. And for myself, if I'm honest. Can we go now, please?"

"What about Ellen?" he said.

"Maybe when I'm in a better mood."

Danny let out a slow breath. She was a sham, an utter sham who messed with people's heads for jollies. He lingered a moment while Zoe waited in the corridor. He picked up Ellen's antique silver hairbrush and ran its soft bristles through her hair. "It would be nice to believe in miracles, wouldn't it?"

SEVENTY-SEVEN

BALLYHINCH HOUSE SAT ON ten acres of forested lands. Ivy crawled over its stone façade and moonlight glinted off symmetrical rows of windows that marched across the upper and lower floors. Nothing stirred but a couple of bats flitting after bugs.

"This doesn't look like a hotel or B and B to me," O'Neil grumbled.

His stormy expression probably matched Danny's own. Superintendent Clarkson had returned from his Easter holiday one day early, and, as might have been expected, insisted on a blow-by-blow account of the investigation and expenses related to hauling in DS Sheehy for a week. A wasted day, and none of them got their Monday bank holiday. After visiting the hospital with Zoe, Danny had hoped to spend the afternoon at Lahinch Beach with the children.

Good riddance to that idea. Many hours later they were still on the job as they approached a portico and a cherry red door. Two crumbling stone steps led to the front door, and withered ivy branches sagged away from the walls. Danny felt around under the ivy for the doorbell and pushed it. They waited but the house remained in darkness. He pushed again and this time held the button.

After another minute, a light appeared through the fantail window and brightened as the occupant made his way toward the front door, turning on lights as he went. The porch light popped on and the door opened to reveal Sid blinking at them sleepily.

"'Allo," he said and opened the door wider to admit them. "You found me again, but bloody odd time to be showing up."

They stepped into a two-story foyer with a checkerboard floor and sweeping staircase. Sid tightened his bathrobe as he shuffled them toward a room that turned out to be a family room filled with comfortable old couches and chairs. The house may have been period but the furnishings said late twentieth century. Sid grabbed a blanket off the back of one of the couches and curled under it.

"Drafty old place." Sid yawned. "Sit, sit. Now that you're here you might as well make yourselves comfortable. Once again, I applaud your Garda efficiency. How did you find me?"

"Your friend Zoe."

"Her?" A quizzical frown squinched up his face. "How odd. I must have mentioned Ballyhinch House in passing and assumed it would float out of her spacious head straightaway."

"She's quite intelligent," Danny said.

"I mistook her for a bobblehead when I first met her," Sid said. "My mistake." He laughed. "Oh, ay, big mistake, indeed!"

Danny perched on a side chair while O'Neil wandered around the room examining dusty Waterford figurines and a CD collection. "Whose house is this?" Danny said.

"The family house. Standing empty at the moment." Sid burrowed deeper into the couch, pulling the blanket up to his chin. "A shame, really. But you're not here to talk about that."

The family house. "You're from Clare?"

"A native-born son."

"You never mentioned that," O'Neil said as he picked up a framed photo that sat on a sideboard.

"I haven't lived here in years. It's been a strange homecoming. Can we quicken the pace, officers? I'd like to return to bed."

Sid Gibson would like to return to bed, would he? Benign Sid Gibson, who had starred in Annie Belden's nightmares.

Danny resettled a throw pillow to support his lower back. Only then did he say, "Did Annie Belden know you grew up here?"

"Oh yes. Charmingly perverse of her to move here. I took it as a compliment."

Danny imagined Annie updating her address in her mother's ancient address book, there for anyone to see, and perhaps Sid was one of the anyones she assumed—or hoped?—might see it.

Sid watched Danny, his smile engaged, observant. "She wanted me to find her."

Danny switched gears. He worked to keep distaste from coating his words. "What did you say to persuade Nathan to attack Zoe at the party?"

"He made that fateful decision all on his own. I simply told him I could help him. I reminded him of what *would* help him."

"And what would that be?"

"Lancing the boil. How was I supposed to know how he would interpret that?"

Sid gamed Nathan into attacking Zoe. The question was why.

"There's also Annie's journal. It's missing, and we hear that you promised to give it to Nathan."

"He'll appreciate it."

"You care that much about Nathan." O'Neil moved on to perusing the spines on a collection of leatherbound books. "To give him a gift."

"It gets tiresome not being given the benefit of some feeling," Sid said. "The answer is yes, I feel for the sorry bastard."

Feel what, Danny wondered.

"Believe it or not," Sid continued, "in the end, my intentions toward Nathan are good. And as for the journal, I don't have it."

"You've just admitted that you took the journal from Annie's house, which places you inside her house sometime around her death."

"Am I admitting that? Ay, I suppose that would be the truth of it. I took it because I wanted to hear her voice one last time, even if only in my head."

O'Neil blew dust off a cracked book spine. "You're not worried about how it looks, you pinching the journal—and her mobile, too, while you were at it?"

"Why worry? Her journal and phone had to come up at some point. No use lying to you fine Garda officers. Nathan knows I have them. Or had them."

"Had?" Danny said.

"Annie's mobile is long gone, but Nathan surprised me by calling me on my mobile, not Annie's, which I quite liked. As for the journal, Nathan is obsessed with it. Annie had become his lifeline. Not surprising that her death sent him into free fall." Sid's head sank deeper into the pillow. "Poor bastard. The least I could do was give him the journal as a memento. I've had my closure, and now the journal's with Nathan. I'm sure he'll find comfort in good Annie's words. She wrote about him quite a bit."

"You dropped the journal off at the hospital? When did you manage that?"

"Today. Unfortunately, they refused to let me see him. The woman in charge of the ward should find the journal soon."

Danny thought back to the teeming psych ward with the voluntary patients roaming around and nurses bustling back and forth. Easy enough for Sid to slip into Brenda's office.

"I suppose now you're going to ask me about the bouquet," Sid said.

"I suppose so," Danny said. "What were the meanings of the flowers again?"

"Disappointment, rejection, and beware," O'Neil said without looking up from the book he held.

Sid rolled his eyes up to the ceiling in thought. "Hm, hm, hm—ay, that says it, but you're missing the point."

"Angry, were you?" Danny said.

"You could say so." Sid stretched out on the couch, pushing his socked feet out from under the blanket. "My impulses aren't always sound. That must be obvious. My mental illness troubles me at times, but I'm much better than I was. My goal is continual improvement."

His mental illness. He mentioned it matter-of-factly, like sciatica or a toothache. Playing it like a hand of cards, slapping it down. See? I'm transparent. Here's my hand.

"I suppose the bouquet was your way of having fun," Danny said.

"I'm used to being circumspect, that's all," Sid said. "I got in the habit of it inside Dundrum. When you have people analyzing every word that comes out of your mouth, it changes the way you communicate. Sometimes I had fun with Annie and the others at their expense." He paused to shift the pillow under his head. "I suppose I still find it fun. You make a good point there."

Danny stood and whipped the blanket off Sid. He pulled Sid up by the elbow. "Come along, time for clothes."

"What's this?" Sid said.

"We're taking you into custody. We'll start with obstruction and tampering, and go on from there. There's more to the story."

Sid smiled his forgettable smile that Danny would remember forever. "Pretty quickly here you'll discover you need me. Remember that."

"Holy shite." O'Neil held out the book. "Boss, you have to see this."

SEVENTY-EIGHT

IN THE PSYCHIATRIC WARD, Merrit sat beside Zoe as they waited for news about Nathan. Nothing but faint shadows under Zoe's eyes indicated that anything was amiss. She managed to sparkle inside a psych ward.

Merrit had been drinking coffee when Zoe called, standing by a window as usual and watching the marquee company dismantle the Chill Zone. She'd expected them the day before but had forgotten about the bank holiday. The sight of the men trampling daffodils already battered by the hailstorm depressed her. Everything about the festival had left her unsettled. Even, or maybe especially, Simon's kiss.

She'd jumped at the chance to accompany Zoe to the hospital and satisfy herself that the doctors had stabilized Nathan. After an hour of waiting, Zoe catapulted to her feet when a woman appeared and beckoned them. She introduced herself as Brenda while frowning down at a clipboard she carried.

"We're still adjusting your father's medications," Brenda said to Zoe. "We need to find the correct dose. The antipsychotics can cause drowsiness, tremors, and other side effects, but he's doing well, considering. We're monitoring his delusions. They're quite"—she paused—"entrenched."

She walked away without another word. Zoe ran to catch up with her while Merrit followed. A vague fishy smell wafted out of the commissary as they headed toward a set of doors at the end of the corridor.

"Can I see him now?" Zoe said.

"I'm sorry," Brenda said.

"I don't understand," she said. "It's visiting hours."

"Nathan has indicated that he doesn't want to see you at the moment."

Zoe stepped back as if slapped. She aimed a beseeching gaze at Merrit. "He must be upset with me, but I haven't done anything to him, I swear. I'm trying so hard to be a good daughter. Please, could you talk to him?"

"Can I visit Nathan?" Merrit said to Brenda. "I'm his friend. He may have mentioned me. Merrit Chase."

Brenda perused Merrit over the rims of her eyeglasses. "He has. You've been good with him. Patient, he said. I'll allow you in. A visitor would be good for him."

Zoe grabbed Merrit's arms, imploring her with wide, teary eyes. "It's been two days. I can't bear this. I'll go starkers. Ask him to let me visit."

Brenda pressed buttons on an entry pad beside a set of double doors. "This is the locked ward."

The common room Merrit entered stank of despair and sweat. In one corner several patients gazed at a television airing a sitcom that Merrit recognized from the States. Several more patients lounged on couches that faced the courtyard, and more played card games at four-top card tables or roamed up and down corridors that led to their rooms. Brenda pointed to a man huddled at the far side of the room. Nathan's skin stretched tight around his skull and his mouth hung open. He looked like an old man.

Brenda led the way. A woman hissed at them. Brenda patted the woman's head as she passed, and the woman relaxed. "Nathan does best when he can work with his hands. We gave him Play-Doh."

A spritely mosaic of children's modeling dough festooned Nathan's table. His nimble fingers had fashioned a turtle and a snail and were currently molding a yellow bird. He squinted at his bird with heavy eyelids, and his voice burbled from an underwater place. "I'm a little tired right now."

"Your friend Merrit is here," Brenda said.

Nathan's eyelids twitched. "I need to finish painting Fox Cottage."

"There's no hurry," Merrit said. "I'm not sure why I started the project anyhow."

Merrit hung back, but at Brenda's invitation to make herself comfortable, she sat down next to Nathan. She picked up the red Play-Doh and began shaping a clumsy horse. Nathan still hadn't looked up. She needed to break through his drug haze. She thought about what Liam would do, imagined him during the Matchmaker's Festival when he did that thing he did—she didn't know how to define it—that allowed people to open up to him. She'd been stumbling up against this aspect of Liam's prowess as matchmaker since she'd arrived. Trying to emulate him. Merrit didn't share Liam's talent for opening people up.

She must have sighed or grunted because Nathan finally caught her eye. Merrit's horse resembled a giraffe. She held it up. "Nice llama," he said.

"I was thinking about what Liam would do in this situation. How he would try to reach you. He's good at that."

With slow, trembling fingers Nathan pinched the dough into the shape of a bird wing. He pressed a thumbnail into the clay to create the illusion of a feather.

She tried again. "You're so talented. Do you ever sculpt?"

Nathan cradled the bird for a moment. He closed his hands around it and then opened them up again before continuing with the feathers. "I did. Before. But I stopped. After Susannah died."

"I'm sorry."

Nathan turned the bird around to work on the other wing. "Liam's a showman, but that's not you."

Merrit set her llama on the table.

"You don't need a matchmaker mask," he continued. "You're quieter, so be quiet about it. Like you're being now."

Merrit had to ponder that one. It hadn't occurred to her that she could be herself. She was so worried about her performance that she'd forgotten that her job was to listen and counsel. That was it. The locals preferred fanfare. Fine. Let them produce and manage the festival. Perhaps if she thought about it like that, she wouldn't be saddled with the expectations and frustration caused by the expectations. The lesson also applied to her life in general here in Ireland. Always performing as the resident outsider, even to the point of driving all the way to Elder Joe's house to pick up eggs.

"You might be on to something." She rolled blue polka dots and stuck them to her red llama. "But, Nathan, about Zoe—"

Nathan shook his head and pushed his chair away from the table. With twitching eyelids, he held the yellow bird toward Merrit. "This is for Zoe."

Merrit reached out to scoop the bird out of his hands. Nathan closed his hands over hers, over the bird, and pressed the heels of his hands into hers. His jaw tightened with the effort. Merrit yanked against Nathan's grip. "That hurts," she said, and it did, but she kept her voice low and calm. "Please stop."

Yellow dough oozed from between their fingers, the bird squished to nothing. "Now it will never come back again," Nathan said.

Brenda reappeared with an orderly, who wrapped his arms around Nathan until he was docile again, staring into the middle distance.

"Did he hurt you?" Brenda said.

"I'm fine." Merrit rubbed her hands against each other. Yellow dough dropped to the floor in soft chunks.

"Tell Zoe I can't be fixed," Nathan said. "To not even try. It's too late. The harm's done."

"I don't believe it's too late."

Nathan shook his head so hard his body swayed. Brenda and the orderly steadied him. "Tell her to go away."

The tics and tremors below the surface of Nathan erupted. Brenda and the orderly pressed themselves up against his body to help contain him. Merrit stood frozen as Nathan ruptured all over again. His eyes bugged out of his head and spittle formed in the corners of his mouth. Brenda and the orderly half carried Nathan toward a wall. Their bodies pinned him against the wall in a soft barricade that restricted his movements and protected him from himself. They never raised their voices, but even so, Nathan's agitation incited a locked-ward orchestra of grunts and squeals.

"We'll need to increase his medication," Brenda said to the orderly.

In a moment of insight, Merrit knew what Nathan needed. She didn't know how she knew, but she did. "Let me try something. Please."

"You need to leave," Brenda said.

A nurse stepped up and handed Brenda a syringe and at the same time placed a hand on Merrit's shoulder to ease her away from Nathan, murmuring, "Come with me."

Merrit held her ground.

Brenda raised the syringe.

"Please," Merrit said, "let me try something with him."

Merrit positioned herself behind Brenda in Nathan's direct line of sight. He radiated heat and desperation. The nurse's hand landed on her shoulder again, this time pulling. Merrit ignored her. She grabbed her chance while Brenda positioned the syringe to jab home the sedative.

"Zoe broke you," she said. "She broke you, didn't she? That's what this is all about. You can say it. She broke you."

Nathan's gaze locked on her mouth. His mouth moved over the words, following Merrit's lips.

"You can say it," Merrit said. "At long last, say the words."

His voice struggled over words Merrit couldn't hear. Brenda injected the medication.

"Say it again," Merrit said. "You're allowed."

He sagged against the wall. "She broke me," he whispered.

"Take him to the Quiet Room." Brenda turned to Merrit. "And you, time to leave. Come with me."

Merrit grabbed her feeble llama and placed it in Nathan's hand.

"I smashed them," he said in a dull voice.

"What did you smash?"

"The sculptures I'd made of Susannah. I smashed them all."

"Why?"

"Because I hated them looking at me, blaming me for all that went wrong."

"What did you do wrong?"

The nurse escorted Nathan away. He resisted for a moment, swiveling toward Merrit. His vague gaze sharpened. She recognized him shining out at her from inside his hell. "I shouldn't have told Susannah," he said, and then he disappeared again, back into a medicated stupor.

SEVENTY-NINE

CECIL WALLACE WASN'T KIDDING when he said he'd use up his kids' inheritance to pay for a posh rehabilitative facility. The smell of money permeated the place, from the leather chairs in the waiting areas to the hushed footsteps and low-key classical music to the scent of fresh roses. Danny and O'Neil were shown into the "aquatic centre." Airy, moist, and chlorine-scented warmth greeted them.

"Hopefully we'll get what we need out of the old fella," O'Neil said.

Their escort pointed to the far end of the pool, where a physical therapist stabilized Cecil under his torso and ordered him to kick harder. Cecil looked comfortable enough with his head and arms resting on a flotation pillow. His voice rose over the splashes and murmurs of the other patients in the pool.

"I am kicking, you bloody fascist." He shifted on the float pillow. "Detectives! Coming to arrest my hide for gross indecency?"

Cecil splashed and flailed his way to the side of the pool. The therapist helped him up the steps and wrapped him in a thick bathrobe. Cecil beckoned Danny to a cluster of cushioned loungers.

"Nice digs," Danny said. "Did your kids throw wobblers at the expense like you predicted?"

"Throwing wobblers wasn't the half of it. They about put holes in the roof with their bellows." He cackled. "They're back in Dublin now, and I won't hear from them until the next time I land in a hospital." He crossed himself.

"Your third child—the oldest—did he ever make an appearance?"

"Why would he?"

"Oh, I don't know. You said he was the child who might have cared. Maybe he did care."

Cecil untied the bathrobe cinch, snuggled the robe more tightly around himself, and retied the cinch. O'Neil sat a little apart with notebook in hand. At Danny's behest, he remained in observation mode.

"After we found you," Danny continued, "you said that you heard someone enter Elder Joe's house. You used the term 'sneaky.' By any chance, did this sneaky person provide you with one of the glasses of water we saw by your bedside?"

"Sonny boy, you're off your pills, you are."

"So you haven't seen your eldest son, the one you disowned?"

"What is it you want? Talk plainly, for Christ's sake."

"I know who killed Elder Joe now," he said. "I'm here to update you."

At Ballyhinch House, O'Neil had shown Danny the name inscribed on the nameplate of a copy of James Joyce's *Finnegans Wake*. None other than feisty old Cecil Wallace.

Cecil fiddled with the cinch. "Do tell."

"Cedric Gibson, or Sid as he's known, turns out to be a loyal son, indeed. Granted, most sons wouldn't resort to killing, but he did take care of the problem of Elder Joe's fraudulent and neglectful behavior."

"Elder abuse," Cecil bellowed. "That's what it's called, and Elder Joe deserved what he got."

"Now you scream 'elder abuse'? When we spoke previously, you didn't seem all that peeved by EJ's lackluster caretaking skills or money grubbing. What changed?"

"My state of mind." He huffed and settled back on his chair. "Whoever did him in did the world a favor."

"If you can afford this place, it's a wonder you stayed with EJ at all. You could have found a decent place and still had money left for your kids. Why stay with EJ?"

Cecil grumbled. Danny prompted him to speak up. "I said," Cecil said, "maybe I didn't want to go into a facility. Maybe I thought I'd never get out again. At least at EJ's, I was in a home. I would have left eventually, but—"

But what? Danny thought. But your disturbed son thought you needed saving?

"You still haven't told me what you want," Cecil said. "Get on with you."

"You can place Sid Gibson inside Elder Joe's house. He was the sneaky one."

Cecil's expression settled into feisty-old-man obstinance. "I'm sorry, I can't help you. I don't remember seeing anyone."

So that was the way of it. Danny was pissing in the wind when it came to uncovering concrete evidence against Sid for Elder Joe's death.

"I wouldn't have thought Sid capable of loyalty or familial feeling," Danny said.

"You think wrong," Cecil said. "The thing about Sid is, if he likes you, he likes you—wouldn't raise a finger to shake it at you."

"But do not piss him off, is that it? Sociopaths aren't known for—"

"He's not a sociopath," Cecil interrupted. "He acted one to get himself sent to Dundrum instead of prison."

Danny sipped his orange juice. "What about the north-end kidnapping in Dublin—the diplomat's daughter?"

Cecil set aside his orange juice and frowned down at his hands. "He was younger then, less impulse control. The poor girl's death was an accident."

"But you disowned him for it, didn't you?"

Cecil grumbled a yes.

"So, accidental death in the commission of a crime is not allowed, but killing out of loyalty is dandy?"

Cecil glared at him. "*If* he killed Elder Joe, *Detective*. I taught him his lessons. He understands right and wrong. He knows, and he'll always improve himself."

Danny sat back, amazed. And, yes, that was the word for it because his wonder knew no bounds—wonder at the talent people had for self-deception, for rationalization, for sheer obstinate refusal to accept reality.

He ought to add himself to the list. He understood Father Dooley's question now, when he'd asked what Danny would really be doing if he let Ellen go. What he'd be doing was accepting reality. He loved her, yes, but as the mother of his children. He'd have to accept that he'd fallen out of love with her years ago, that he'd abandoned her—left her lonely—long before he'd moved out of the house. He'd have to accept that he couldn't redeem himself for putting her through so much misery. Better to have cut the cord cleanly, let her move on with her life.

"Fecking hell," he said.

He stood to leave, but Cecil tugged him back down by his belt loop. "Sit your arse down, sonny boy, and quit with the fecking language. This is a genteel sort of place."

"You bloody old turd. I've seen the light of day, and it has nothing to do with your son." Danny gulped down more juice. "When Sid was a lad, how did you talk to him to teach him his lessons?"

Cecil frowned. "I don't know what you mean. I talked like I talk."

"You mean blunt to the point of harsh?"

"Honest, man, honest. You have kids, I take it? Yeah? Right then, when it comes to the tough stuff, talk to them how you'd talk to an adult. Straightforward but soften some of the vocabulary. Tell them what needs to be told and get on with the business of living. And an ice cream cone never hurts either." He cast Danny a furtive glance, gauging him. "Sid was a troubled lad from the beginning. He's my son from my first wife, who abandoned us and ended up dying of a drug overdose. Gibson was her family name. When he was sixteen, he decided he was more Gibson than Wallace. He changed his name and I said good riddance. Still, I fancy my influence shaped him into a better man than he would have been otherwise." He raised a hand. "I know, don't say it, but there's worse out there."

"That's comforting." Danny stood. "Well, you old geezer, you were no help at all."

"The hell I wasn't."

"I'm talking about the case."

Cecil raised an arm and Danny obliged him by helping him to his feet. "One of life's greatest lessons: You can't have everything, so take your comfort where you can."

They left Cecil hobbling on the arm of his physical therapist, subdued and grimacing at the ground.

"We still have enough on Sid to charge him?" O'Neil said.

"Not likely. The DPP will want more, seeing as how he's an expert at playing the system."

At the reception desk, Danny asked to see the visitors' log. He scanned backwards until he found Sid's name. Sid had visited three times. His status had risen to that of favored son.

Maybe they could still nab him for Annie Belden's death.

Back at the station twenty minutes later, Superintendent Clarkson informed Danny that Sid Gibson was off limits. "He's bargaining for his freedom."

"With what chips?" Danny said. "There's enough against him to at least—"

"It's beyond our watering hole," Clarkson growled.

Danny pushed past Clarkson and entered the interview room, where Sid lounged with his usual bland smile, looking relaxed and benign with his ill-fitting sport jacket and tummy pudge. His solicitor shot out of his chair, already bristling. The man sported a fake tan and white teeth. He looked like a bloody American news anchor.

"I told you you'd need me," Sid said.

"Need you for what?"

"We can talk all about it after the legal system sorts me out. Perhaps we can meet for a drink."

Clarkson pulled Danny out of the room and shoved him in the direction of the parking lot. "Fecking hell, Ahern. I said it was out of our watering hole. Find someone who saw Sid Gibson with the *sleán*. That might help us."

But they'd already ventured down that track, and no one had seen the *sleán* go missing. How had Dr. Browne described Sid? A mad genius. Now Danny understood what she meant, even if he hadn't a bloody clue what Sid was playing at. Yet.

"We still have Annie Belden," he said. "I'm getting that journal."

EIGHTY

DANNY WAS STILL STEWING about Sid when he entered the psych ward to see Zoe holding a giant bouquet of purple irises. She paced with lips thinned to lines and a hectic flush staining her cheeks. As soon as she saw Danny she ran to him, almost bumping into him in her agitation.

"My dad won't see me," she said. "Why won't he see me? You have to help me get him released."

"Calm down," Danny said.

"You said you had no power, but I don't believe that. You can do something if you want."

"He shouldn't be let out yet. He needs help."

Zoe shook herself, and her exquisite face smoothed out. She heaved a breath. "Well. If I can't see my dad, I'll bring your wife these flowers. Anything to keep from going about the bend."

She strode away with hair swinging against her shoulders and purpose to her footsteps.

"Detective Sergeant?"

He turned to see Brenda standing with her arm around Merrit. Drying tears streaked Merrit's cheeks. She sniffled and wiped at her nose.

"What did I miss?" Danny said.

"A breakthrough," Brenda said. "A troubling breakthrough." Her warm-fuzzy moment ended. She patted Merrit on the arm and stepped away from her. "What do you need, DS Ahern? Now's not an optimal time."

Danny excused himself and Merrit from Brenda and walked with Merrit toward the exit. "Are you fine to drive?"

"Yes, thanks." She offered him a weak smile. "He admitted that Zoe was the one who broke him."

"Unfortunately, Nathan's hold on reality is suspect."

"I think—" She frowned at the ground. "All I know is that I was certain, and he corroborated it." She slumped. "Maybe I put the thought into his head." She waved goodbye without another word and departed.

Brenda filled the void with her enquiring, harried expression. "How can I help you?"

As soon as he mentioned the journal that Sid had dropped off for Nathan, she about-faced and marched to her office. Danny was a couple of seconds behind her and entered to see her shuffling through the paperwork spilling out of a plastic tray labeled *In*. Her desk was a disaster of paper, and it reminded Danny of the incident room desk at the station that DS Sheehy had done his best to organize before being sent back to Killaloe.

"It's not here," Brenda said.

"Do you mind?"

Brenda raised her arms in an exasperated gesture to go ahead.

Danny opened the top desk drawer. Nothing but Brenda's stash of chocolate biscuits and office supplies. The second drawer stored more of the same, but this time with pretzels. "Stressful job," he said.

"Thank Christ I have the metabolism of a hummingbird. Go on then. Have at it."

The third drawer stored hanging file folders.

"That's the paperwork for the locked-ward patients we're currently evaluating."

Danny found Nathan Tate's folder, pulled it out, and opened it flat on Brenda's desk. A spiral-bound student's notebook sat on top of Nathan's intake form. Shredded paper caught in the binding indicated that someone had ripped pages out. Danny opened the cover and picked up a note that Sid had tucked inside it. He passed it to Brenda.

Hello. If you would be so kind, please give this notebook to Nathan Tate. I promised it to him, and I think it will comfort him. It's written by a mutual friend of ours.

His friend, Sid

Brenda set the note on her desk while Danny flipped to the last written-upon page. Sid must have torn out the missing pages but left a final entry written in his own hand. A fare-thee-well note to Nathan. How sweet.

He scanned Sid's entry, then read it again more slowly. It took a moment for the ramifications of Sid's message to sink into his tired head. "Holy shite on a stick."

"That bad, eh?" Brenda said.

"I have to take this with me for now."

He flipped backwards one page to read Annie's last entry, dated the night of her death. He had to squint to decipher the hasty scrawl.

"Ah, Jesus help me," he said and ran out of the room.

EIGHTY-ONE

IN WARD 2B, ELLEN's IV dripped, the catheter drained, and Zoe hummed to herself. She sat erect in a chair next to the bed. A vase filled with the irises stood nearby, filling the room with their sickly acrid odor.

Zoe picked up the antique silver hand mirror that went with Ellen's hairbrush. "This is a beautiful set. Not my style, but beautiful."

Danny approached and stood at the end of the bed. Zoe's beauty appeared illuminated, as if someone had touched her up with glow-in-the-dark colors. Her appearance distracted him from a vacancy he now caught deep within her gaze.

"I'll prove it to you." She set the mirror aside. "Right now."

"I don't want you to prove anything."

"I know you're skeptical. You don't believe I can heal, but I'll show you." Zoe opened her sunny yellow purse and pulled out a sheath with a rubberized grip. She slid the stainless steel safety sheath off to reveal a filleting knife. Thin, delicate, and razor sharp.

Every molecule in Danny's body went on alert. In the corridor, footsteps strode past and then silence surrounded them except for

Ellen's equipment. The heart monitor beeped at periodic intervals and the fan on the oxygen monitor whirred to life.

Zoe held up the knife. "My dad's, from his fishing days. I kept it all these years." She lifted her shoulders with a puzzled expression. "I'm not sure why. A souvenir, I suppose. A reminder."

Danny gripped the rail at the foot of the bed to steady himself. "A reminder of what?"

She dropped the knife onto the bed, next to Ellen's hand, and burrowed into her purse. The blade glinting within inches of Ellen's skin made Danny's skin crawl. He edged toward Zoe. His hand left a sweaty gleam on the bed rail.

Zoe answered while coating her lips with pale pink gloss. "A reminder of the good times. Sometimes Dad took me along on his fishing trips. Just the two of us. I wasn't bored even though all we did was sit in a boat all day long."

"You carry the knife with you because—?"

"Habit. Self-protection." She stored the lip gloss away and smiled up at him. "I like having a bit of him nearby. It's silly, I know."

"Not so silly."

"I think he found it in my unmentionables drawer, but he didn't say anything. Maybe he doesn't remember."

Danny edged around the end of the bed. Zoe picked up the knife again, considering it and then Danny. "Hear me out." She pointed Danny toward another chair parked in the corner of the room. "And please sit over there."

Danny sat down on the edge of the chair, calculating how quickly he could reach her. An ambulance siren pierced the eerie silence that settled over Danny. His vision shrank to a pinhole aimed at the knife.

"The funny thing is that it's because of those fishing trips that I discovered my ability." Zoe set the knife down near Ellen's hand again. "I don't call myself a 'healer.' That smacks of crystal balls and incense."

She gazed at him with violet eyes made darker by the fluorescent lighting in the room. She was so earnest in her convictions, so sincere. Danny needed to keep her talking. He'd stood here before, in this place, where his job put Ellen in danger. His inability to protect her had landed her here, but she wasn't going to die today. Not like this.

He cleared his throat. "How did you discover your ability?"

"It was those fish, those poor gulping fish. Bass, I think. My dad would hit them hard against the boat to kill them." She crinkled her nose in a dainty grimace. "On one trip, one of the fish slipped under my feet, and I decided to throw it back in before Dad could stop me. Only, his mouth was mangled from the hook. That poor mangled fish mouth. I was a baby about it, cradling the fish, wiping the blood away. Dad told me that it was more humane to put it out of its misery. I held my hand over it—protecting it, I think—and when I looked down, the mouth was no longer ripped." She smiled. "It's the truth, so help me. I tossed the fish back. I was over the moon."

"Did Nathan see what you did?"

"Oh no. I kept it to myself for a while, because I couldn't believe it. I needed to practice before I showed Dad." An expression of disappointment flitted across her face. Danny suspected Nathan hadn't reacted well to the pronouncement when it did arrive. "None of that matters now. The past is the past. I need to make it up to my dad somehow. That's where you come in." She twitched at the knife, sliding it on the bed cover.

It took every ounce of Danny's will not to lunge at her. Her behavior was all about Nathan, he reminded himself. Keep her talking about her father. He forced himself not to look at Ellen, so still, so oblivious, so in need of a healer. Helpless, as Zoe herself had noted the day before. He gripped himself from within, a tightening of control, and set the spiral notebook on the floor. Zoe was too caught up in her drama to notice the notebook.

"I'm not sure what you need to make up to Nathan," Danny said. "You're a good daughter. I can see that."

Zoe brightened. "You think?"

"As you said, the past is the past. You have much to offer."

"I know," she said with a plaintive tone. "I do, I really do, but how can I be a good daughter if he's locked away? You don't understand." She twitched at the filleting knife again. An inch closer to Ellen's hand. "I need your help to be the daughter I want to be. I'll prove to you that I can heal, and then you'll see why you should help me. Because I'll help you with Ellen."

She picked up the knife, cradling it. The knife blade caught the light and winked silver back at Danny, mocking him.

He spoke louder than usual, blurting the first topic that came into his head. "Tell me about Nathan."

Zoe straightened with a look of mild curiosity. "What do you mean?"

"Let's begin with his scar and his PTSD—are they related?"

"PTSD?" She considered the word with furrowed brow. "I thought PTSD came from fighting in war zones."

"Ah, but what is a war zone? A home can be a war zone. Anywhere can be a war zone. How did he get the scar?"

"At home," Zoe said. "But—after all these years—his odd behavior—is it because of that?"

The knife landed in her lap as her grip loosened. Danny braced himself to leap.

"It could be," Danny said. "I have no way of knowing, that's why I asked. Chronic PTSD is a serious condition. I suspect that for Nathan it went unmonitored for too long. Stress and change can trigger episodes, too."

Zoe stuck her legs out, turning her feet around in circles. "You mean me coming here. But this is the point I'm trying to make. I need to make it up to him, be a better daughter."

"Do *you* think there's a connection between your arrival and his worsening symptoms?"

"My feet hurt." She set her feet on the ground. "I wish I could say there was no connection."

"What happened to Nathan at home?"

"You've guessed, haven't you?" She turned toward him, sitting sideways on the chair with one knee drawn up against the seat back. "I tried to help him. In fact, I did help him."

"You mean with your healing talent?"

"It was working. It was." She gazed at him with such appeal, insistent and a little desperate. "Please help me. All I want is my dad. I'll show you, I will."

She sprang out of her chair and onto the bed. Danny knocked over his chair in his frenzy to reach her. Zoe straddled Ellen and held the knife against her neck.

"Stop," he said. "I'll do everything in my power to get Nathan released. I don't need proof that you can heal."

She shook her head. "I see how you look. You don't believe me. I need to prove that I can heal Ellen."

Every nerve in Danny's body exploded, but he couldn't move—he didn't dare move—as Zoe shifted the knife in her right hand. Her index finger rested along the top of the knife. She raised her arm and without looking at Danny sliced two inches of skin on Ellen's neck. Not deep, and not right over the carotid, but close enough. Ellen didn't twitch, not so much as a hitch in her breathing.

Danny's heart broke for her all over again. She truly wasn't there anymore. He gripped the edge of the closest machine as much in anguish as in terror.

"Zoe, stop." Danny heard the begging, pathetic tone in his voice. All his Garda authority had left him. He faced Zoe as himself. "I'll help you. I will."

Zoe rested the knife against her thigh. A thin line of blood dripped down Ellen's neck.

"You have my word," Danny said. "I don't need proof. I'll help you get Nathan released."

One of Ellen's monitors blared with a series of loud beeps. Zoe jerked, startled, and the knife dropped to the floor. Danny dived toward the bed and grabbed her, slinging her off Ellen.

A nurse ran in. "What's going on in here?"

Danny found his voice again. "Garda business. Please check my wife."

The monitor fell silent. The nurse perused one of the machines. "She's breathing fine now. Her oxygen levels are back to normal." She frowned at them and turned back to the door.

The knife sat on the floor on the other side of the bed, and the nurse hadn't noticed the blood on Ellen's neck. Danny grimaced. One of those who only had eyes for the equipment.

As soon as the nurse left, Danny shoved Zoe against the wall, pulled up a chair, and forced her to sit. "Don't move," Danny said.

She nodded, subdued. Danny grabbed the safety sheath off the floor and stored the knife in his pocket.

"I'm sorry," Zoe said. "I wasn't going to hurt her. Let me heal the cut now."

Danny pulled up the second chair and sat facing her. His body tingled with adrenalin. "You already did hurt her. You understand that, don't you?"

"I just want my dad," she said.

"I know you do." Danny picked up her purse off the floor. "Come with me now."

She bit her lip, puzzled, when he cautioned her, telling her that she had a right to silence.

"I didn't hurt Ellen," she said. "I can still heal her cut."

That guileless expression, her perfect young skin and clear eyes. Life hadn't imprinted itself on her face yet. Danny believed her sincerity. She wasn't a Sid Gibson, a studied manipulator. She was like the butterfly pin on her blouse—a beautiful creature, but fleeting. Doomed. Unlike Nathan, she didn't understand how cracked she was.

"Maybe so," he said. "Maybe you can heal the cut—and Ellen— but you didn't heal Annie Belden, did you? More like the opposite."

EIGHTY-TWO

~~Thursday, 25-Mar~~
Friday, 26-Mar 1:15 a.m.

… There went the outdoor lights and now the doorbell's rung. Oh God. My heart. Here it is, the moment I confront my terror. I have a sickness. Why would I move here, of all places, if I didn't in some bizarre way hope to see PatientZ again?

I suppose I have to prove something to myself. I've been waiting for this chance, haven't I? To transform myself into the powerful one in our twisted relationship.

Writing as fast as I can here before I open the door. I don't think he will kill me—he likes me—but just in case, I shall check through the peep hole and write down who I see. Proof, see? Proof. I'll have the last say.

Oh my goodness, it's Zoe. Talk about rolling over with relief. More later—I hope Nathan hasn't self-harmed—

EIGHTY-THREE

BY THE TIME DANNY returned to the station with Zoe in tow, fatigue had laid a soft but implacable grip over him. After handing her off to the Sergeant-in-Charge, he escaped to the closest takeaway and shoveled Kung Pao chicken down his throat, taking a few minutes to gather himself before returning to find O'Neil on a smoke break. They entered the station, no need for words, and proceeded to the custody suite where Zoe waited. They peeked into the room.

"Is she sleeping?" Danny said.

"Out cold."

Zoe rested with head cradled on her arms. Even hunched over a table, she managed to appear graceful. Her lips twitched in a slight smile, and her eyeballs moved under her eyelids.

Danny didn't know whether to be impressed or appalled. "Does she not understand what's about to happen?"

"She must, but you'd never know it."

Just like you'd never know many oddities lurked beneath the surface of her. Danny tapped the window of the suite. Zoe raised her head and her hand in a wave. She looked as sleep-dazed as a child, but not distressed. The Sergeant-in-Charge appeared and shooed them away so he could see to settling Zoe in an interview room.

O'Neil cleared his throat. "Sir."

"*Sir?*" Danny said. "What gives?"

"I need to confirm a final time that you're not bothered by my seeing Merrit."

"We discussed this. What you do is your business."

"Agreed, but that's not the same as it being fine by you."

"Yes, O'Neil, it's not a problem." He scrubbed at his face, realizing that it could become awkward. "Do me a favor and not talk about the ins and outs of it, Merrit being a family friend."

O'Neil raised his eyebrows. "Oh yeah?"

"I'll see her socially because of Marcus. I'm also back on visiting terms with Liam, so there's that."

"Ah." O'Neil nodded. "Right."

Right, indeed. There'd be no avoiding Merrit now, but Danny found he didn't care. He'd take his newfound ambivalence over active avoidance; it used up less of his scarce energy.

They received the go-ahead from the Sergeant-in-Charge with a warning that Superintendent Clarkson would be keeping tabs on them through the video feed. "Of course he will," O'Neil muttered.

Zoe greeted them with an inquisitive smile. "This isn't anything like the interview room in England. I was only a child, of course, but I remember it being stark and scary. This is almost cozy by comparison."

She sat in the middle of the room in front of a fisheye lens that fed into the room next door. Danny and O'Neil parked themselves at small desks facing her, out of camera range. While Danny introduced the interview, Zoe lifted her hair up and brushed it with her fingers. With a couple of twisting movements she piled it up on her head in a perfect messy knot.

She was a confident young woman. Yet Danny had witnessed her childlike and upset in reaction to Nathan's lock-up, and he'd seen her ruthless and unfeeling in her attempt to coerce Danny into helping her release Nathan.

"Do you understand why you're here, Zoe?" he said.

"I do, but I didn't do anything. I like to help people. That's why I'm here, I think."

"'Here,' as in your purpose in life?"

"Yes. My dad knows that. He would have come around. I know we'll be okay in the end. Dad will get better—he's a strong man—and then maybe we can move back to England."

"We're not here to talk about your father," Danny said. "You understand that, correct? We cautioned you regarding the death of Annie Belden."

"Yes, but that was a mistake."

"How so?"

"She didn't understand either, about the healing. I tried to talk to her—"

"About what?"

"About leaving my dad alone. I'd only just found him. Annie acted like she was part of our lives. She had no call to distract him when we were trying to rebuild our relationship to what it was before."

"Before?"

"Before—" She straightened and settled both feet on the floor. "Before my mom's death, before I discovered my healing ability. I sometimes wish I'd never discovered it."

She truly believed her personal folklore about herself. Danny was torn between fascination and dismay. "Tell me about Annie," he said.

"I tried to help her. I wanted to cure her of her diabetes. I knew I could do it."

"How did you know she was diabetic?"

"In the bathroom in the pub. At Elder Joe's wake a few weeks ago. I didn't know her yet, of course. She was testing her sugar levels when I entered."

"Did you administer the insulin that killed Annie Belden?"

She unwound her scarf from her neck and arranged it like a shawl over her shoulders. "It's cold in here."

"When you say you're going to help somebody, what does that mean to you?"

She cocked her head, bemused. "Heal them, of course."

"Let's return to the night that Annie Belden died. Did you offer her a deal?"

"A deal?"

Danny felt his tone tighten as he said, "Like you offered for my wife. Heal her in return for my help. With Annie, I imagine you offered to heal her in exchange for leaving Nathan alone."

"She was unconscious when I arrived," Zoe said. "I didn't get a chance."

At the other desk, O'Neil shifted. "Unconscious?"

"Yes, on the couch. I tried to help her. I promise I did."

O'Neil pulled a piece of paper out of a folder. He handed it across to Danny and Danny handed it to Zoe. She read Annie's last journal entry and let the sheet of paper drop to the floor beside her.

"Annie was awake and well when you arrived at her house," Danny said.

"She collapsed right after I arrived."

"Why visit her in the middle of the night?"

Tears welled up and slipped down her cheeks. "Everything will be okay. I know it will. I want to go back to the way it was before, that's all. We all have goals in life, right? I'll return to nursing school, and Dad can go back to sculpture. His vases are fine, but he could do so much more."

Danny called a halt to the interview and stepped out of the room with O'Neil. Zoe lived within a Nathan loop. Everything cycled back to him, and Danny suspected it would for a long time to come.

"The journal's fantastic as evidence," O'Neil said, "but is it enough to convict her? Zoe's appearance alone will sway a jury to believe her that Annie collapsed after she arrived."

Sid sat somewhere in the building, haggling for his life with the help of his solicitor. Danny knew a few things about Sid's whereabouts the night Annie died. He'd met Zoe at a pub earlier in the evening. Later, he'd stolen Annie's journal and mobile phone.

"This is where Sid comes in, I think."

EIGHTY-FOUR

Monday, 5-April

Dear Nathan,

Since you're reading this page, you've already read Annie's journal entries. Now you comprehend the truth of Annie's last moments on Earth. When I whispered that Zoe was to blame for your heartache, I spoke the truth, no?

After the paramedics carted you off, I realized what a stroke of good fortune it was that you hadn't managed to kill Zoe. For both of us. If you'd succeeded, you'd be locked up permanently and I wouldn't have anything to use in my negotiations with the guards regarding my own wee predicament—it's looming, any day now. By the time you read this, all charges will be dropped.

Life is funny that way, isn't it? Turning shite into fertilizer.

I suppose prison will have to satisfy me when it comes to your daughter. She'll get out some day, and then we'll see.

She should not have harmed my dear Annie. Since she was your dear Annie, too, you comprehend how I feel.

One last thing. You misunderstood the significance of the bouquet. The flowers I chose had nothing to do with Annie. Hardly! The bouquet was a tribute to what I planned for Zoe (through you, as it turned out). I was disappointed in her behavior, I rejected her, I was a danger to her. That's all. Simple, really. It took me a day to find the blooms and let them wither, you see, so I left them the day after Annie died—the evening I texted you and Merrit. I hoped you would understand the message.

I leave you for now, Nathan Tate. It was an odd pleasure, one psych patient to another.

Wishing you a full, Zoe-free recovery—

Your friend, Sid

EIGHTY-FIVE

Two days after arresting Zoe Tate, Danny drove up a gravel lane and into a development of summer cottages. The Atlantic glistened into eternity beyond the Doolin pier. The tourist season had begun in earnest now, as evidenced by the jumbo black Galway tour bus chugging past the pubs. Fluffy clouds scudded by overhead and bright blue gentians dotted the hillsides. Danny scanned the cottages for number 15. These cottages were just some of the many along the west coast that sat empty as a result of the crap economy.

Number 15 looked identical to the others—white-washed walls and quaint chimney stacks. He bumped over a dirt track that should have been a driveway, pulling up in front of a collection of two-by-fours that should have been a porch. The engine's idling grumble echoed against the unadorned walls and weeds and abandoned construction supplies.

This couldn't be right. He must have misread the address on the telephone message the Sergeant-in-Charge had handed him. Gulls floated overhead on the breeze, squawking in agreement as he exited the car and walked over the uneven ground. Danny pushed open the knob-less front door. "'Allo?" he called.

"Come through," came the response. "I'm on the deck."

The deck was the shining accomplishment of the place. It hung over the hillside with a view of the cottages below, Doolin village, and the ocean.

"Brilliant, isn't it?" Sid sat on a folding deck chair with a bottle of beer in hand and a bag of crisps on his lap. He pointed to the second chair with a second beer on the seat. "Thanks for humoring my request."

Perplexed, but willing to be entertained by this stellar example of humanity, Danny lowered himself into the seat. "Your father insisted that if you like a person you wouldn't raise a finger to shake at them, but fair warning, Detective O'Neil knows where I am and is expecting me to call him in an hour."

"Of course," Sid said. "I would expect nothing less."

"You killed Elder Joe. We both know it."

"I did." Sid spoke in a matter-of-fact tone. "Despite what you might think, I'm not proud that I let my emotions take over."

"It was premeditated," Danny said. "You had to sneak the *sleán* out of Alan's pub."

Sid slouched with knees spread and beer held loosely over his crotch. He wore baggy old-man shorts with two jumpers. His spindly white legs stuck out like bleached bones in the sunshine. "My anger smolders, I suppose," he said. "Go on then, have the beer."

Danny popped open the beer and drank. Sid passed him the bag of crisps and picked up a pair of binoculars. He surveyed the sundrenched scene, pausing for a moment on a cottage below them.

"Why am I here?" Danny said. "You got what you wanted. Zoe Tate is likely to be convicted, and you once again worked the system like a pro."

Sid ducked his head in gracious acknowledgment and lowered the binoculars. "You'll see. Thought I'd treat you to some fun. I began my nefarious career in crime as a Peeping Tom. Did the paterfamilias tell you that?"

Danny shook his head. "Cecil said you were trouble from the start, though."

"True enough. I know you scoff, but therapy *has* helped me over the years. Zoe didn't have the benefit of anyone to check her proclivities. Believe me, if you had to make a choice, you're glad she's the one inside the penal system." He shook his head and whistled. "Bloody hell, man, that lassie is more cracked than one of Nathan's ceramic vases. Poor thing."

Danny held his tongue. Sid was no doubt a good arbiter of cracked-ness, being personally experienced on the topic.

Sid checked his watch. "Looks like we're running late today. What shall we talk about until my wee surprise? I know you still have questions, which is the other reason I invited you to visit with me. I knew you couldn't resist."

"And you get to gloat about cheating the system again," Danny said.

"Also true."

"Tell me about the night Annie died. You told me you didn't pass by her house that night, but, of course, you did. Did you pinch her medications along with the journal and mobile?"

"Oh yes. I hoped to confound and delay the investigation for a few days so I could think through my own situation with Elder Joe's death." Grinning, Sid tilted his beer toward Danny. "I know what you're after."

"And what's that?"

"You want to know what I provided your lot in exchange for not pursuing me for that bugger's death—not that you had enough evidence anyhow. But I wanted to be clear of it—unequivocally. First of all, I staged meeting Zoe in the pub that night."

"Right, you met Zoe for the first time the night Annie died. I remember that well enough."

"I'd seen Annie with Nathan and wasn't keen on them as a couple. Thought I could learn something through Zoe. I sniffed out her daddy sickness within five minutes and decided to follow her back to her house to peep for a while, but what happened instead? She drove to Annie's house." Sid peered through the binoculars and lowered them again. "Long story short, I was right there with my binocs and then I closed in to snap photos with my phone."

"Your prowess as a Peeping Tom and stalker," Danny said.

"I would have made a great spy."

"You could have saved Annie's life."

Sid's usual bland smile dipped toward sorrow. "I ran in as soon as Zoe left, but I was too late."

Danny didn't bother to point out that Sid could have stopped Zoe before she injected the insulin. It probably hadn't occurred to Sid, probably never would.

"Here's an easy question," Danny said. "How did you smuggle the *sleán* out of the pub?"

"You may have noticed that I'm the invisible type. It's a quality I cultivate. One night, late, I walked out the back door with it. I liked the looks of it. Made the task of killing Elder Joe more interesting. Stylistically, I mean."

Danny downed the rest of his beer. Sid handed him another one out of a small cooler beside his chair. "I figured it was something like that. The most puzzling aspect to me—"

"Now we're on." Sid trained the binoculars on an SUV passing by on the unpaved road below them. A moment later, he lowered

348

them again. "False alarm. Cross your fingers routines hold up today. You'll like this, I promise."

Danny stretched out his legs. "Which came first, visiting Cecil or revisiting Annie?" he said. "Did you know Annie was going to relocate herself to your childhood stomping ground?"

"Annie, to be sure," Sid said. "Imagine my surprise and delight when I tracked her down here. In our sessions, I'd talked about Clare and my family and Ballyhinch House. My childhood. The typical therapeutic topics. Speaking of which, what did you think about the 'niggle' she wrote about in the journal?"

Danny took a long draw on his beer. "My theory? From the news or local gossip, your father's name rang a bell with her. Cecil Wallace, victim of elder abuse found in the murder victim's—Joseph Macy's—home."

"Brilliant deduction, Detective. That was my thought, too. Imagine, if she'd made the connection back to me one day sooner, I would have gone under investigation and not followed Zoe to Annie's house. Zoe would still be out here infiltrating everyone's lives, and in some future time—weeks, months, or years from now— you'd be arresting Nathan for Zoe's murder. He'd have cracked worse than he's cracked now. At least now he has a chance."

"You helped Nathan," Danny said. "Is that it?"

"Without a doubt." Sid drew his eyebrows together as if pondering the mysteries of the universe. "I started off wanting to grind him into dust, but I discovered he's similar to my father. A man who doesn't deserve harm. A good man. There are few enough of them out there. How could anyone harm Nathan Tate?"

Sid Gibson had to be the most sideways man Danny had ever met. "Yet you sent him on a course to kill his own daughter."

"If successful, he'd have been found not guilty by reason of insanity. No harm done."

"Jesus, man," Danny said, "you love your convenient answers. What did you hope to achieve by helping Nathan?"

"Gratitude is always nice. Another question?"

"Ay, were you harassing Elder Joe in the weeks before his death? Peeping, letting out his chickens?"

Sid smiled and grabbed another beer. "To answer your previous question, I returned to Clare for Annie and checking in on dear old Dad was an added bonus." A slow flush saturated his cheeks. "Imagine my horror."

"If you were so horrified, why didn't you move Cecil out of Elder Joe's right then?"

"And risk him knowing I was about? Might as well sling up my balls and squeeze."

"You left him to die anyhow."

"You take me for a total and utter tit, don't you? I'd have found a way to get my father help. I thought it best to keep my presence hidden from him since I still planned to meet up with Annie."

"You're a brilliant stage manager, even to using Annie's death to your benefit."

"Ah ..." Sid peered through the binoculars again. "Here we go. At last." He continued speaking while following another SUV through the glasses. "Whatever you say about me, I'll make a great witness for the prosecution during Zoe's trial."

"If it gets that far. You bring a lot of baggage with you." Danny sipped his beer, thinking about it. "Nathan will be asked to testify, too. What would it take for a father to bear witness against his child?"

Sid dropped the glasses for a second to glance at him. "Depends on the father, I suppose." He returned to his view through the binoculars. "Blessed be, you are in for a mighty treat now."

Danny rose. Two cars pulled up at the summer cottage below them. The cottage blocked his view of the drivers as they got out of their vehicles and went through the front door.

Sid passed the binoculars to Danny. "Second bedroom on the left."

It took several seconds for Danny to zero in on the correct spot. He adjusted the glasses until a bare room with a dingy mattress on the floor came into focus. "I'm not sure I want to know," he muttered.

"The vision might scar you for life, fair warning."

Through the glasses, shadows darkened the wall inside the room. Joe Junior stepped into the room backwards, holding the hand of a portly woman who remained out of view.

"Joe Junior?" Danny said. "What's your interest in him?"

Sid's voice held a smile. "I was curious about Joe Junior because he looked perfect to go in for Elder Joe's death instead of me. I did what any enterprising man would do and found out as much as I could about him."

Through the glasses, the second shadow on the wall moved into view. Danny dropped the glasses. "For the love of Christ."

Sid guffawed long and hard. "You should see your bloody face! This is beyond priceless."

Danny raised the glasses again, unable to stop himself from confirming the woman Joe Junior pulled toward the mattress.

"You see?" Sid said. "It's addictive."

Danny shoved the glasses at Sid. "That's a sight to scorch the eyeballs."

Sid hadn't stopped chuckling. "These cottages? The O'Briens invested in them."

Danny recalled his trip to Lahinch Golf Course and Mrs. O'Brien's strange reaction when he'd asked if she knew where Joe Junior could be found. Puzzlement turned to understanding. "His secret alibi for the evening of Elder Joe's death. I wondered why he kept repeating that he was alone."

"You've seen it for yourself. Uppity Mrs. O'Brien is shagging the groundskeeper in one of her husband's summer cottages." Sid dropped into his seat. "Life is good, that it is."

He tipped his beer bottle toward Danny, and after a hesitation, Danny sat down and tipped back. They drank, now blessedly out of view of the randy encounter.

"Your hour is up," Sid said. "You'd best check in. You could say you were on the job. Last puzzle piece in place, eh?"

Not quite. Nathan still wavered on the edge of Danny's comprehension, where he would probably remain.

EIGHTY-SIX

A WAVE OF RELIEF swept over Merrit as Dr. Murphy excused himself from the room. "You're cancer-free. I can't believe it."

Liam sat in the second visitor's chair with a smug expression plastered all over his face. "I told you we didn't need a second opinion."

Merrit had insisted they visit a practitioner in private practice rather than return to the oncologist assigned to them by the public health care system. Dr. Murphy had come recommended by Mrs. O'Brien. Merrit had figured that begging for Mrs. O'Brien's superior knowledge on the topic would lessen the ongoing sting of Merrit's blunder about the showiness of the festival. Might be it helped, but Merrit questioned for how long. In any case, Merrit had been correct in her assumption that the O'Brien family used the private sector for their medical care.

"You were sick," she said. "That wasn't nothing."

"I was sick. Now I'm not."

Dr. Murphy stepped back into the room carrying the images from several MRIs. He snapped one of them into a light box alongside an older image of Liam's lungs. In the older image, he pointed to a black smudgy area in Liam's left lung—the cancerous area—and pointed to the same spot in the latest MRI.

Nothing. Wiped clean, as if by a magical eraser.

"I don't understand," Merrit said.

"You don't want to understand," Liam said.

Dr. Murphy, a short man with a full head of silver hair, looked like everyone's favorite uncle, and the indulgent smile he aimed at them solidified him in Merrit's eye. "There's a story here." He snapped a third MRI up on the light box. "This is Liam's left femur. I decided on an image after I examined his leg."

"I have arthritis in my left hip, I know that much," Liam said.

"The arthritis hasn't changed. You'll continue to have problems with your hip." Dr. Murphy sat down. "Has the leg been worse in the last six months?"

"Yes," Merrit interjected. "Definitely. Last fall into winter."

"That makes sense. You never got tested for cancer again, you said."

"Why bother?" Liam pointed to the image of his lung. "The MRI tells the story. That's how the cancer appeared the first time, before they cut out part of my right lung. As soon as I saw a repeat in my left lung, I said no more chemo, no more anything. It looks like I don't need it anyhow."

"You're correct about that." Dr. Murphy swiveled his chair to study the images on the lighted wall again. "It's good you opted out of chemo. My theory is that you never had cancer the second time. Granted, this is only a theory. We'll run more tests—"

"No more tests," Liam said. "I don't need tests."

"What's your theory?" Merrit said.

"Pulmonary embolism."

"What's that?" she said.

"It starts as a blood clot in a limb, such as your leg, called a deep vein thrombosis. When the clot dislodges and settles in the lung, it becomes a pulmonary embolism. Your symptoms do correlate."

"He could have died," Merrit said.

"Yes, PEs are serious."

Liam's gloating smile returned. "So, you'd say it's miraculous that I recovered from it, if an embolism is what I had. We still don't know; it could have been cancer."

Dr. Murphy negated that with a brusque head shake. "Cancer doesn't disappear—not in your case, with your history—which is why we're here, correct? For a second opinion. You now have my opinion."

"But it's a miracle," Liam insisted. "Do these pulmonary embolisms just go away?"

"Yes, they can dissolve after some months, but until that point they can cause pulmonary infarction, cardiac arrest, death. You were lucky, Mr. Donellan, very lucky, indeed. We should put you on a blood thinner to help prevent future clots."

"No medications," Liam said. "I'm fine."

Dr. Murphy looked dubious. Merrit could tell that Liam's attitude confused him. *No, she wanted to say, he's not senile. It's worse than that; he's under the spell of a murderous, self-proclaimed healer.*

"He still coughs," Merrit said.

"He's still healing," Dr. Murphy said. "If Liam experiences the same series of symptoms again—leg pain and tenderness, shortness of breath, fever, back pain—bring him back to me. PEs can recur."

"But it won't," Liam said.

Dr. Murphy raised his eyebrows as if to say, *We'll see. I'm the expert here.* He rose and shook their hands.

Back in her car, Merrit beamed her own gloating smile toward Liam. "Thank goodness, a logical explanation. You can't really think Zoe healed you."

"You're not the one in my body, missy. I can tell the difference between a sudden turnaround and a slow improvement."

Merrit started to argue with him but stopped herself. It was no use. Liam believed what he wanted, like most people did, logic be damned. He must have been feeling better anyhow but didn't realize it until Zoe came along and gave him permission to *be* better.

She started the engine. To the north of them, a grey mass of clouds spat down rain. Between the rain and her car rose yet another Irish rainbow. She laughed at the sheer ridiculousness of life sometimes.

"What now?" Liam said.

"Nothing and everything. Life. We all make-believe our lives in an attempt to achieve happiness."

"Or to remain sane," Liam said.

She sobered up. "That's the same goal."

"Oh, I don't know," Liam said. "If you're fighting for sanity or to keep a grip on what you think is sane, happiness is the least of your concerns."

Merrit thought of Zoe, the happy girl. "About Zoe—what did she want from you in exchange for playing the healer? She wanted something, right?"

"Oh yes. She wanted me to never match Nathan to another woman." Liam's voice grew lighter, trying to distract her, Merrit knew. "Speaking of matchmaking, you're not off the hook because I've received a clean bill of health. I plan to use you. Maybe I'll work half-time at the festival this year."

To Merrit's surprise, she found she didn't mind, after all. She thought about Nathan, gaunt and haunted, and the insight that had glimmered through the drugs and mental disturbance. When it came to matchmaking, all she had to do was be herself. That would have to be enough. No more performing. No more comparing herself to Liam and finding herself wanting.

She needed her own friends, she realized, apart from Liam's inner circle. Liam wouldn't be here forever, and whether or not she stayed in Ireland, she knew that for now, she needed to build a whole life here. A full life here wouldn't stop her from returning to California if that was what her heart mandated. That was a possibility for later, but her moments were now, in Ireland.

"Hung for a sheep as a lamb," she said.

"How's that?"

"Nothing but a new mantra I'm trying on for size." Her mobile dinged and displayed Simon's name. She let the call go to voicemail but looked forward to a quiet moment to return his call.

"You're smiling," Liam said. "You don't fool me."

"I'll call him back later." She leaned her head against the headrest, remembering a question Simon had asked her. "Do you believe in love at first sight?"

"Of course. Don't you?"

"Not really, no. Do you suppose that's why I'm having a hard time with the notion of being matchmaker?"

"Perhaps, but you'll figure it out."

"The other day I had an epiphany—about Nathan. I don't know his whole story, yet I knew what he needed. The words he needed to say out loud. To heal. I had a glimmer of what you must experience all the time. Intuition, yes?"

"Which you've always had."

"Yes, but I *felt* it this time. Not as an educated guess or a theory or an assumption. I knew what I knew."

Liam clapped his hands once, hard. "Halle-bloody-lujah!"

"Very funny."

"By the way," Liam said, "Danny tells me Marcus is taking Edna Dooley out to dinner this weekend. Was that you?"

"Nah, that was them." A wave of quiet contentment made Merrit smile. "But I helped out."

She may not have all the answers about her life, but for the first time in eighteen months she was okay with that. She pulled out of the parking lot in front of Dr. Murphy's office and turned south, away from the rainbow but also away from the storm cloud.

EIGHTY-SEVEN

NATHAN WASN'T SURE HOW long he'd been living in this room in the hospital. Years. No, he reminded himself. A week at most. A different room, a different hospital. Not even in England anymore.

He sat up in bed and wiped the dribble from his mouth. His thoughts were so ponderous he'd forgotten them already. The afternoon sun coated the room in a thick haze that he waded through to reach his jeans lying on the floor. The fabric disturbed every hair on his legs when he pulled them on.

On the bureau sat his goldfinches. A dozen of them in modeling dough. He'd told his therapist here—not Brenda, she was one of the head nurses—about his dreams. The ones that featured hands suffocating and reviving a goldfinch. He'd tried to tell the therapist what it meant to him, these dreams, these goldfinch replicas—the beginning of it all, at least for him. Twelve-year-old Zoe running to him one day, beaming with pride. *See what I can do?*

The sight of her suffocating the poor bird had repulsed him. When she healed it, she'd repulsed him even more. He no longer cared if the staff didn't believe him. Here he was, once again. Yelling down the walls wouldn't make what he had to say sound any less insane.

So, once again, he'd fake it. Tell everyone what they wanted to hear. He collapsed on his bed and curled up, too tired for the common room, after all. His eyes drifted shut, and then drifted open again sometime later. The goldfinches on the bureau fluttered. If he pointed that out, Brenda would up his meds, so he wouldn't mention it.

A knock bolted him out of bed. Groggy and loose, he folded to the floor.

"Nathan," Brenda said. Another knock. "I'm coming in now."

Without a word, she helped Nathan to his feet. "You have a visitor." She hesitated. "Sid Gibson."

Nathan brushed his hands through his hair. "I'll see him. He owes me something. He promised."

He tucked in his shirt over his new tummy bloat and tried to straighten his shoulders, but they refused to hold their positions. One of his feet caught on the other. He stumbled forward. Brenda caught and held him. He shrugged her off and shuffled forward. When he'd settled himself at his table with the colorful dough, Brenda escorted Sid to the chair next to Nathan.

He scooted his chair closer to Sid's, watching Sid's lips form words that floated out of his mouth inside bubbles. He interrupted them to say, "You promised me Annie's journal."

"And you shall have it. Danny confiscated it for the case against Zoe. He promised me he would return it to you."

Case against Zoe. If Sid wasn't here about the journal then—"Why are you here?" he said.

"I would have come sooner, but I ran into difficulties. The lawyers straightened it out, I'm glad to say."

Nathan noticed Sid's teeth behind the word bubbles. Crooked teeth. Sharp little fangs. He blinked and they returned to normal.

"I owe you an apology," Sid said. "I hid the *sleán* in your painting supplies to implicate you. I was jealous of your budding relationship with Annie."

The word bubbles knocked against each other, popping before Nathan could decipher them.

"Elder Joe? Remember him? Killed by a turf cutter?" Sid smiled. "I know it's difficult. The drugs they force into you—it's fiendish. Not a bother if you're not catching my meaning."

His words were coming too fast. Nathan thought maybe, just maybe, there was a fact related to Zoe within all those word bubbles. "Zoe?"

"You landed a rum deal with her as a daughter, didn't you?"

"Rum deal."

"Listen, my friend, I'm after ridding you of Zoe. Hopefully for a long time. In that respect, you can relax. Prison for her, eventually. It will happen."

"For what she did," Nathan said.

"Exactly."

Sid understood Nathan. He was the one person on the planet who did. Maybe Nathan could reveal the truth to him. Maybe Sid would believe him. The one person on the planet. That would be something. Then he wouldn't talk about the past again. Ever.

He bent toward Sid and lowered his voice. A quick glance around the ward told him that no one spied on him, but just in case, he mumbled his words. Sid leaned forward.

"Zoe practiced on me." He pulled up his shirt and lowered his jeans to show Sid his scar, but quickly, before anyone saw. Sid whistled low. "The healing. No one believes her, but she can do it. She practiced on me. Over and over."

Sid looked impressed, maybe even entranced. "You let her torture you?"

Torture. Nathan retreated from the word. He floated above himself, hearing his flickering, unsure voice, sounding like he didn't believe himself.

How it had all begun with the poor goldfinch, and how Susannah refused to believe it even when Nathan corroborated Zoe's claims that she could heal. Susannah had looked at him strangely then, the first time he'd seen wariness aimed at him. Perhaps he'd been losing his marbles already. Perhaps he and Zoe shared a delusion. He'd heard all the theories. He didn't give a shite about the theories. He knew what he knew: he was to blame for Susannah's death.

He retreated from Zoe after that. He let Susannah and Zoe battle it out, mother and daughter. Susannah wanted to send Zoe to a private clinic for treatment. Zoe's fights with Susannah. Her neediness with Nathan. Nathan's love for his wife over his daughter that caused him to side with Susannah despite what he'd seen. The goldfinch. The strife—and Nathan's avoidance of the strife—escalated until the day he found Susannah at the bottom of the stairs.

Nathan paused to catch his breath. Those were the most word bubbles he'd uttered in weeks. Sid urged him to continue. "You have quite a story there, mate."

Nathan remembered the bizarre light in Zoe's eye, a determination when reviving her mother failed, her teariness. "I'm going to practice even more," she'd said. "No more goldfinches. I'll learn how to heal properly so I can save people."

She'd leaned into Nathan, her head under his arm, her arms around his waist. "Now it's us, and we'll be perfect, you'll see." Her hot hands stuck to him through his shirt. His heart squeezed itself off from her with such disgust that she couldn't help but notice. She'd pulled back with her eyebrows drawn together in reproach.

That was the moment his life changed, when doom lowered itself over him. And he'd known then, hadn't he? He'd known his guilt, and his memory began to slip after that. When Sid said "torture," maybe he was correct. Penance and guilt and Zoe always there. Nathan let her cut him. He let her.

He hadn't cut himself. He knew that much. He'd swear by that.

Yet it wasn't torture—not according to Zoe. She practiced on him, improving her healing skills until the moment his mind snapped and he turned her knife back onto her. Sometime later, he came to in a psych ward, safe from her, and now here he was, safe again. Better yet, there would be no Zoe waiting for him or searching for him when he got out.

Nathan's words floated away from him. A vague emptiness surrounded him, comfortable as a cocoon. A foreign feeling of relaxation overcame him. Relief. Gratitude.

"I have a gift for you." Nathan beckoned a nurse and asked her to fetch his personal belongings out of storage. The nurse returned and hovered next to them as Nathan fingered his scant belongings. Wallet. Keys. Mobile. And the last item, which he placed on Sid's palm.

"Fishing wire?" Sid said.

Nathan waited for the nurse to leave before he spoke. "I remember now. The last of it. Everything."

But memory was a mistress, his thoughts said, ever slick and untrustworthy. He shook them off. "Susannah's death wasn't an accident," he said. "She tripped over this wire stretched between the balusters. I don't think Zoe meant to kill her—"

"You said she tried to heal your wife."

"She did, she did. That's what Zoe said." Nathan's word bubbles dissipated again, doubt creeping in. Or maybe that was her strategy. To be seen by Nathan as the good daughter, trying to heal her mother.

Sid's hand landed on his arm. His skin against Nathan's prickled and rubbed, but Nathan forced himself to concentrate on the word bubbles.

"She wanted you all to herself," Sid said. "Then, and now."

Nathan pressed his hands over his face. Convulsive shudders took over his body. His teeth chattered. One of the nurses stooped and placed an arm around him, but Nathan shook his head for her to leave.

When he looked up sometime later, one minute, five minutes, Sid still sat beside him, waiting with his teeth covered, thankfully. He pressed the fishing wire between his hands in a prayerful gesture. "I'll cherish it. Thank you, my friend."

The fog cleared out of Nathan's head for a moment. "Annie," he said.

"Yes, Annie." Sid tucked the bundle of fishing wire into his pocket. "You could say she sacrificed herself for you. If not for her death, you wouldn't at last be safe from your dear daughter."

"You believe me—about Zoe?"

With a slow nod, Sid said, "I find that I do."

Nathan sagged back on his chair. All he'd ever needed was one person—not Zoe—to believe him. Tears streamed down his face, and Sid didn't bat an eye. He watched Nathan in that way of his, like his teeth were about to transform into fangs again.

Nathan waved to Sid, stumbled to his feet, and left the room. He didn't care if he ever saw the man again. In his room, he nestled under the bedcovers and fell into a dreamless sleep.

EIGHTY-EIGHT

DANNY BRUSHED HIS FINGER over the thin scab on Ellen's neck. Two inches long, the cut would heal into a pink line as smooth as the rest of her skin. Ellen used to pick at scabs, rubbing them until they broke open or worrying them around the edges until they snapped off and exposed new skin not ready for its unveiling yet. She didn't care about the scars they left. The dimples on her knees from dozens of falls over a lifetime, the shiny skin on her hand where she'd splashed hot oil on herself, the two divots on her arm from a dog bite. Unlike those, the scar on her neck would eventually fade into nothing. She wouldn't notice it if she woke up.

But she wouldn't wake up. At last Danny understood this beyond theory and medical statistics. He'd felt the truth of it the moment Zoe sliced Ellen's skin. Ellen was destined for a slow and excruciating deterioration—placed on ventilators and poked, prodded, and manhandled every time an infection took residence in her body.

Danny picked up Ellen's hand and rubbed his thumb over the thickened burn scar. He summoned Cecil, the straight talker. He'd have to be blunt. It would be like revealing that magic didn't exist, and the children still believed in magic.

"I don't believe your mom will be resurrected," he said to Mandy and Petey.

The children were subdued for a change. Mandy had brought a book to read to Ellen. *The Wind in the Willows*. She lowered the book. She, along with Petey, turned wide eyes toward Danny.

"I'm not an expert on these things, but I do know that if your mother resurrects, it's not like how you imagine, not like waking up. According to the Bible, even Jesus didn't walk on Earth as a man after he resurrected."

The children glanced at each other. They had a way of communicating without words that exasperated Danny at times.

"You're saying that Mum won't come back to us," Mandy said. "Never again."

"Yes, that's what I'm saying." He rushed forward with more words. "But we can help her resurrect up to Heaven. Like Jesus."

Cecil would have disapproved of that bit of sophistry, but how to talk to his kids in a way they would understand? Ellen had raised them in a devout fashion. If he'd learned anything from the case of Zoe Tate the healer, Liam the healed, and Nathan the survivor of the healing, it was that belief trumped all. Belief became its own truth.

He decided to speak to Mandy and Petey in the language of their belief. "We can help her, and it will be better for her." He pointed to the machinery that kept Ellen dosed with fluids and nutrients. "We turn off the machines. When her soul is ready, her body will"—he paused, still unsure—"her body will die."

"*She'll* die," Mandy said. "She'll go to Heaven. That's what you mean."

"Ah, sweet things," Danny said. "Come here."

The children climbed on his lap. They were too big to fit comfortably, but somehow they made it happen with limbs jumbled together and arms around his neck.

"I'm going to be blunt now, okay?" he said.

They nodded.

"Life sometimes serves us shite." They nodded again like this was self-evident. "And sometimes because of that we have to make tough choices. We mere humans have to decide on the greater kindness. That's the question at the bottom of it all. What's the kindest thing for your mom? Stay like this or—or pass on? I've made up my mind which is kinder, but I'm going to leave the room now and you can talk privately."

They stared at him with identical open-mouthed awe. Yes, he thought, I'm including you in an adult decision process. Please let me not be traumatizing you.

"You can stay," Mandy said.

She grabbed Petey and led him into a whispered conversation in the corner of the room. They darted glances at Danny and cupped their hands around their mouths.

The hum of Ellen's life-support equipment comforted him, Danny realized. When had that happened?

Mandy held Petey's hand as they returned to him. "Dad?" Petey said.

"Ay?"

"You can let her go now."

He hesitated, biting his lip. Mandy nudged her with his elbow. "Say it," she hissed.

"Say what?" Danny said.

"It's like this," Mandy said. "We've been waiting for you to get your head out your bum."

A startled laugh burst from Danny. Father Dooley had said the same thing. He tried to look stern, but it didn't work.

"We always knew what Mum wanted," Mandy said. "She said you knew, too, but you were so sad."

"She talked to you about this?"

In identical moves, they rolled their eyes at him like he'd gone mad. *Of course, you eejit.*

"Dead people," Petey said matter-of-factly. "We talked about it a lot. Mum said going to Heaven is a nice thing and that your work helped the dead people move on."

Danny stood. He paced back and forth. It was either that or laugh again until he crumpled. Ellen had filled their heads with the most lovely nonsense, but here they stood, full of acceptance. No conflicts for them.

"What about resurrecting on Easter?" he said.

"That was a game." Petey grinned at their sleight of hand. "We knew you were listening to us talk in bed. We were trying to trick you for earwigging."

Mandy climbed onto Ellen's bed and tucked the covers around her shoulders. "Mum always said you shouldn't listen in on people. What a lot of nonsense, and you let us go on and on."

"Of course Mum wouldn't come back on Easter like Jesus!" Petey hollered.

"You gave us the best Easter ever, though," Mandy said.

"You played me." Danny collapsed back onto the chair and Petey climbed on top of him again. "I'm an utter eejit, all right. All this time I thought you were waiting for Mum to ascend."

"Daddy? You know you can talk to us," Mandy said. "All you had to do was ask and we would have come clean."

Danny smiled at the phrase *come clean.* "I am duly chastised, and I think ice cream cones might be in order on our way home."

Their identical smiles just about tore out his heart. Jesus, how he loved his urchins.

Petey shifted off of Danny and climbed onto the bed so he lay on one side of Ellen and Mandy on the other. Mandy resumed reading her book aloud while Petey drifted off to sleep. Danny picked up the silver hand mirror and tilted it toward a thin stream of light shining through the window. The reflecting surface caught the light and directed it toward the wall. Danny shifted it until the light illuminated Ellen's face like a light from her Heaven.

THE END